Want Is a Growing Giant

Eliot H. Berg

PublishAmerica
Baltimore

© 2006 by Eliot H. Berg.
All rights reserved. No part of this book may be reproduced, stored in a retrieval system or transmitted in any form or by any means without the prior written permission of the publishers, except by a reviewer who may quote brief passages in a review to be printed in a newspaper, magazine or journal.

First printing

This is a work of fiction. Names, characters, corporations, institutions, organizations, events or locales in this novel are either the product of the author's imagination or, if real, used fictitiously. Any resemblance to actual persons (living or dead) is entirely coincidental.

ISBN: 1-4137-8195-0
PUBLISHED BY PUBLISHAMERICA, LLLP
www.publishamerica.com
Baltimore

Printed in the United States of America

Part I

Want is a growing giant whom the coat of have
was never large enough to cover.

Ralph Waldo Emerson, *The Conduct of Life*, 1860

The want of the plaintiff is a growing giant whom
the coat of malpractice insurance attempts to cover.

Prologue

The year was 1980.
During his deposition, Dr. Frank Farmer sat in the defendant's seat next to his attorney, Sydney Albright. The attorney camouflaged his obesity with an expensive, well-tailored navy blue suit. He rested his folded, soft hands on the table, displaying the pinky diamond.

As Farmer listened, the muscles of his legs and arms tightened, making him ready to spring in attack or defense, but the threat was not the wild panther, it was not physical; it was Dr. Carlos Regario testifying in a heavy Venezuelan accent. Dr. Regario had been a surgical assistant at the operation. Mr. Raymond Rice, attorney for the estate of Mr. Seymour Lieberman, was questioning him. Dr. Regario's thick black curly hair covering his forehead almost to his bushy eyebrows, his dark complexion and deep-set ebony eyes gave the impression of a man always in the shadows.

Dr. Regario, Dr. Farmer and the attorneys were in the offices of Curtwood, Rice and associates, sitting around a long mahogany table. Dr. Farmer was forty-nine years old. This was his first malpractice lawsuit. His dark hair was thinning prematurely, making the worried brow more prominent. His eyes were deep set in the weathered facial skin of a sport fisherman.

He didn't want to attend this session, but Attorney Albright had explained it would prepare Farmer for the real trial. So here he was. To top it off, as a bad omen, on the way to the meeting he had been caught in a very local shower, which followed him from his house to the lawyer's office.

Wearing comfortable slacks, her recording machine between her legs, the court reporter sat to one side at the head of the table. She had the confident air of an efficient, pretty woman.

"And you believe the bleeding was controllable? Please state why that is so," Mr. Rice asked in a quiet tone.

Regario's eyes focused on Dr. Farmer. "Well, the first thing was when he tore a slit in the vena cava and blamed it on me. He was clumsy. I was just holding retractors so he could see what he was doing. Then, as the bleeding continued, he just packed it and said pressure could take care of it. Well, sometimes it does, but not in this case. The bleeding continued and filled the pelvis. We sucked the hell out of it but it didn't help. He made another attempt at suturing the defect shut but he must have had the stitches too loose because there was bleeding from the suture holes. I was relieved at that time by Dr. Miguel Franco. I was glad because I was sure Dr. Farmer was in over his head and there was going to be a bad end."

Dr. Farmer whispered to his attorney, "Regario has no love for me. I was a little hard on him. He fell asleep; he said he had a cramp in his hand, and as he leaned into the operative site he bumped my elbow just as I was dissecting out the vena cava."

Albright, his attorney, said, "I know. Try to look calm. I don't want the plaintiff's attorney to see guilt on your face."

Dr. Farmer looked at the lawyer and then at Regario. In his thoughts, he relived the terrifying events as though he was watching someone else's drama. The characters were unrelated to him. He was observing from above. The Dr. Farmer in deposition was a stranger to him, but he felt empathy toward that Dr. Farmer...

When Dr. Frank Farmer awakened on that Monday, he was thinking about the procedure for the morning. The patient's problems had begun a week earlier:

The patient, Mr. Seymour Lieberman, a retired jeweler, had been in good health until he developed right back pain. He called his family physician, Stanley Reinhart. "It's pretty bad, no, it's killing me!"

"I hear you, Seymour. It sounds urgent. I'm in the office all morning. Why don't you come right over?"

Pain made Seymour's usual resistance to doctors visits all but disappear. He hung up the phone. Ignorance had his fear take flight. What could it be?

Marsha, his wife, plump and frowning, shook her head. "Terrible. Shirley's brother had pain like that and it turned out to be cancer."

"You have to tell me this now?" he screamed as they walked to the car.

But could it be? The thought of cancer made the pain more severe. He thought, *I can feel it extend around to the front of my belly!*

They reached the doctor's office. In the waiting room, he was unable to sit. He paced the room. Once, he tripped over the outstretched feet of another patient. Seymour stumbled, jolting his side, evoking exquisite agony. "Oh, God!"

"Watch your step!" the feet said.

"Goddamn it, watch your feet!" Seymour growled and began pacing in another area of the waiting room.

"Mr. Lieberman?" the receptionist called.

Seymour and Marsha were up immediately.

"Seymour," Dr. Reinhart said, taking Seymour's arm, leading him to the table. "Sudden onset of back pain? Which side?"

"Right. It's been there all day."

"Nausea or vomiting?"

"A little. When I tripped over some jerk's feet out there, I thought I was going to throw up. It's a little better now."

A complete history and physical followed.

Seymour trembled as he obediently answered the questions and responded to the demands of the doctor. He could only think of Marsha's diagnosis. He was now an expert on morbidity. "It's cancer. You can tell me. What's next?"

"It sounds very much like a kidney stone, not cancer. I'm going to send you to Dr. Joel Kenyon. He's a urologist. You'll like him." Turning to the nurse, he said, "See if Kenyon will see him right away." And to Seymour, he said, "I'm going to hold off on pain meds for just until you see Kenyon."

"It's pretty bad."

"I know."

"He's got to suffer like this?" Marsha inquired in a demanding question.

As Seymour stood up, a sharp pain grabbed him. He fell back into the chair. "Oh, oh, God, it's killing me. It's getting worse. I can't stand it."

Perspiration quickly formed. He could feel his shirt dampen. Now he was bending over the chair, tightly gasping the armrest. "Do something! I'm going to die!"

Marsha held his head in her hand, handkerchief to his wet forehead. She yelled, "Do something! Screw the urine guy. Do something now!" and to Seymour, "It's going to be all right. There, there," her voice coming out unusually soft and caring.

"Fifty of Demerol." Reinhart nodded to the nurse. As though anticipating the order she was instantly at Seymour's side, jabbing him with the blissful needle.

"Lie back, it will take a few minutes. The stone is in the ureter. Every time there is a peristaltic wave as the ureter tries to push the stone down the tube, you will get a colicky contraction. Fortunately, the waves only last a few minutes."

"It's getting better. That was the worst pain I've ever had." He gradually was able to stand and, with Marsha's help, began walking toward the door.

"It's just two doors to the left. Kenyon is expecting you. Good luck."

Seymour walked cautiously, holding himself rigid. Marsha supported him.

In Kenyon's office, Seymour was a little more comfortable. The Demerol was working and the contraction had subsided.

After a brief review of the history, the nurse brought Mr. Lieberman to the X-ray unit. A technician guided him through an IVP. "We will be able to visualize the kidneys, the ureters and the bladder."

The right ureter was dilated, suggesting an obstruction, most likely a stone.

As he dismounted the IVP table, he experienced the mother of torture, blinding him, throwing him to the floor, writhing in pain. As quickly as it had started, it was gone. He was pain free. He couldn't believe it. "It's gone!" he called to Marsha.

"Oh, I'm so glad. Poor baby."

"Don't celebrate," Kenyon called from his office. "Those contractions come every ten to fifteen minutes. So enjoy the relief, but brace yourself."

While Dr. Kenyon studied the IVP films, Seymour called to the nurse; he needed to urinate. "Use this metal bedpan, please. We want a sample of the urine."

He retired to the semi-enclosure adjacent to the examining room. Marsha sat just outside the door, ready to leap to his aid if another attack began. The silence, marred only by the faint tinkle of flowing urine, was broken by a single bang, like a stick forcibly striking a steel drum.

"Oh, my God, what was that? Seymour, are you alright?" Marsha cried, pulling open the enclosure door.

"I'm fine. I think I passed the stone."

"Don't empty that pan," the nurse called out. As she spoke, she took the pan and poured the urine through a fine gauze strainer. "There it is."

All three—the nurse, Seymour and Marsha—looked down at the strainer. There in its center was a tiny, dark brown object, smaller than the head of a match. "That's a good one," the nurse said.

"Seymour, you made all that wailing fuss over this? This microscopic thing? And I was so worried. You should try delivering a baby." And with that, Marsha reverted to her usual nagging, criticizing, self-indulgent persona.

Unfortunately, the IVP done to visualize the ureter also identified a seven-centimeter abdominal aortic aneurysm.

When Seymour returned a few days later, Dr. Stanley Reinhart helped him climb onto the examining table and began to explain. "This aneurysm is an expansion of the main blood vessel here." He put his hand on Seymour's belly. "It's like a weakening in an inner tube of a tire; the area stretches out like a balloon. And much like the balloon on the inner tube, if the aneurysm is not cared for, it will rupture. But unlike the blown tire, which leads to a flat, when an aneurysm ruptures the patient dies."

Seymour tried to concentrate on the doctor's words, but his fear cried, *Don't listen.*

"When the aneurysm is over five centimeters, the chance of rupture far outweighs the risk of reconstructive surgery."

Mr. Lieberman did not take the news very well. "What are you talking about? Is this related to the kidney stone? Maybe Dr. Kenyon should be told."

"I had a conference with Dr. Kenyon, your urologist, and the radiologist. It's straightforward. I'll show you." Stanley helped Seymour off the table and walked him to the view box. The brightness of the white-lighted windows sharply contrasted with the darkened room. The shadows on the X-ray film clearly defined the problem.

Mr. Lieberman rubbed his eyes. "It's funny, the benign stone caused so much pain I thought it was going to kill me, and this life-threatening balloon that will kill me has no pain, nothing."

"In many cases, death is the first symptom. In a way you're lucky you had a kidney stone."

"That kind of luck I don't need at the track."

When Seymour was again informed that the mortality after rupture was 90 percent, he felt he had no choice. Now that he knew of its existence, he could feel the monster in his belly. Was it a risk to move? Unconsciously, he put his hand on his abdomen. The pulsations were there. He could feel them—bump, bump, bump, seventy times a minute. Which beat would cause the blowout? Were they getting stronger? Could he feel a pain in his back? Think of something else.

But it was like a finger against your cheek, not strong, but there. Turn to the right, turn to the left and it's still there. You brush your face to free you, but it remains.

To distract himself, he walked across the room, but when he stopped, he could still feel it pounding. A claustrophobic panic swept over him.

Dr. Reinhart asked Seymour to sit down. Putting his hand on Seymour's shoulder, he paused and then said, "Take a slow, deep breath. You are stable. We can fix the problem. Today is Friday. I've arranged an appointment for you with Dr. Frank Farmer on Monday at eleven a.m.. He is a vascular surgeon, very experienced. He did his fellowship in Houston, the home of vascular surgery."

"But is he good?"

"He could operate on me. My nurse will give you an appointment card." He turned to Marsha. "She'll also give you a prescription for a mild relaxant. Have him take one as soon as you get home and then twice a day until you see Dr. Farmer."

Slowly the icy feeling and the difficulty breathing subsided in Seymour. He would bury the fear.

The weekend dragged along, with Seymour trying to protect himself with every step. Marsha returned to the role of a concerned wife, which further aggravated Seymour. Finally, Monday arrived.

When Seymour and Marsha entered Dr. Farmers' waiting room, there were four patients sitting in anxious silence, watching. Marsha wondered who the other patients were. They all seemed to be dressed reasonably well. This comforted her.

She thought their clothes represented a degree of wealth. This made her less concerned about allowing Seymour to go to Dr. Frank Farmer, for she believed that rich folks were more selective, even in choosing their surgeon.

After a thirty-minute wait, they were guided into Frank's examining room. Beth, the nurse, helped Seymour onto the table and offered a chair to Marsha.

The doctor began, "I'm Dr. Farmer. Dr. Reinhart was good enough to send me your medical history and your X-rays." He paused, putting his hand on Seymour's shoulder. "You don't know me except for what Dr. Reinhart has told you. You have a vascular problem. I have been caring for these problems for many years. I am a clinical professor of surgery at the university."

His expression changed from somewhat grim to a soft smile. "This is my commercial. Everyone who comes into this room is frightened, particularly someone with an aneurysm. I imagine you had no idea you had this kind of trouble. The next moment a doctor says you have something life threatening, and you are sent to me." Frank believed to name the patients' fears, to define them, to allow the patient to get his hands around them, helped to decrease the panic.

"Dr. Reinhart said he would let you operate on him." Marsha broke the silence. "So we're here. What happens now?"

Frank completed taking a history and doing a physical exam. During this time, he answered their questions. He was careful not to be overly optimistic.

When he had started in private practice he had said everything would be all right to comfort the patient. Then, when there had been a complication or a bad outcome, the patients and the loved ones would turn to him with disbelief and anger. With time and experience, his emphasis had changed. He would express his hope that all would go well but, at the same time, be sure to outline the risks and possible complications. With good results, his dire comments were forgotten. With bad news, the relatives remembered his concern. At times, this would blur the anger directed toward him.

"To complete your work-up, we will give special attention to the heart and the blood vessels going to the brain. If there is significant damage in either of these areas, we would prefer correcting them before undertaking this elective major surgery. These days, surgery is not a matter of speed as it is of safety."

All the results were acceptable, declaring Mr. Lieberman ready for surgery. Dr. Farmer glanced at Nurse Beth as she read the appointment note to Seymour. "You are scheduled for eight a.m. this coming Monday. The hospital will call you this week to give you all the instructions for admission." Handing the note to Seymour, she added, "Nothing by mouth after midnight."

Dr. Farmer said, "If you have any other questions before Monday, don't hesitate to call me. There are no foolish questions. You might get a foolish answer, however. I'll see you Monday morning before surgery." He worked up a smile as he faced Marsha. "I'll find you right after surgery."

It was one more weekend. Seymour was beginning to cope with the constant threat hanging over him. There were moments when he forgot to think about the pounding in his belly.

For Dr. Farmer, it was a pleasant time; he was not on call and was able to play 18 holes of golf with his wife.

On Monday morning, he came to the hospital in good spirits. He walked from the parking lot directly to the OR suite.

Once changed into his green scrub suit, Dr. Farmer followed the time-honored ritual of waiting.

Normally, the orderly brings the patient from his room to the OR suite about an hour before surgery. During that hour, the patient is prepped, examined by the anesthesiologist, and comforted by the sight of his surgeon.

On the third floor of the hospital, the orderly smiled at the pretty nurse. "I'm here for Lieberman, honey."

"You'll just have to wait. There is some delay. Pt and Ptt hasn't come up yet. That's blood coagulation."

"I know." He leaned toward her. "Smart as well as beautiful. I'm in love."

"Take your bleeding heart and sit over there. Nothing happens 'til I get the labs."

Farmer set the coffee cup on the sideboard and casually studied the calendar of events at the hospital. It listed the usual committees and lunches. It was relaxing.

Without warning the door to the doctors' lounge burst open. "You're needed in room five, STAT!" It was the circulating nurse. "The aneurysm started leaking. Fortunately, the orderly passing the patient's door heard the patient begin to yell in pain. The patient screamed he was having another kidney stone and balked at being rushed to the OR. He changed his mind when the pressure dropped. Now it's barely palpable," she said all this as she rushed Dr. Farmer to the scrub sink.

The adrenalin rush had begun with the word "STAT!" and increased as he moved with her toward the OR door. The familiar symptoms appeared; his fingers rapidly became ice cold, his hands developed a fine tremor. With them came the tightening pain in his mid abdomen and the chilling moisture of perspiration covering his forehead. His calm acknowledgment of the facts as the nurse spoke them belied his tremulous being. All of these negative reactions had become his friends. He had been terrified when they'd first appeared. It had been during his training at the maiden operation he'd observed with the sight of the surgeon's knife creating a thin red line of blood on the white skin of the anesthetized patient's belly. At that stage of his development, he'd had doubts about being strong enough to be a surgeon. He'd stepped away from the table, taken several deep breaths. Slowly, the signs of fear had subsided. He'd become calm and warm. Then, when he'd returned to the operating table, he was fine. Ever since that challenge, he was in control. The adrenalin response came and was instantly banished with two deep breaths.

As the reaction faded, Farmer finished scrubbing and walked into the operating room.

"Once over lightly will have to do," Dr. Michael, the anesthesiologist, called as Farmer entered. "Can't get a pressure. We splashed his belly with a bucket of Betadine and we're ready for the big opening."

As he walked toward the table, the circulating nurse helped him into his gown. Farmer began running over his litany: incision—zyphoid to pubis; intestines into the plastic bag; get control of the aorta just below the renal arteries, if possible. He reached the table. Simultaneously, two surgical assistants appeared, already scrubbed. Quickly, they were gowned and gloved. Roberto had worked with Dr. Farmer on several occasions. The other assistant, Regario, was new.

"Your name is Regario?" The assistant nodded in agreement.

The scrub nurse was the fourth member of the team.

On opening the abdomen, Farmer saw only a red, tense, bulging, pulsating mass, like the bloody half of a basketball. All identifiable landmarks were obliterated. He had been here before. The severity of the challenge calmed him. If he were unsuccessful and the patient died, it would be expected and acceptable. A ten-percent survival rate for ruptured aortic aneurysms was credible. But if the patient made it through the operation, he would be a hero.

"Still no pulse." Dr. Michael's voice was amazingly controlled. "How we doing?"

"Face east and bow to Mecca, Mike," Erik said. "It's a blind shot through this huge clot. I'll try to pinch off the aorta above the rupture."

As he spoke, Farmer reached through the red mass. Once he tore the containing posterior peritoneum, the blood poured out, filled the abdominal cavity and spilled onto the table. Moving the clot aside, he caught a brief glimpse of the vessel and the gaping hole. There was a small segment of the aorta just above the hole. With his right thumb, he compressed the mass above this segment against the backbone. With constant suction, the bleeding was cleared enough for him to see the aorta. Using his left hand, he reached in and successfully applied a vascular clamp. Like turning the faucet handle, the rush of blood was diminished. Now only retrograde, back bleeding came from below. It was relatively easy to identify the portion of the aorta beyond the rupture and place another clamp. Dr. Farmer took a deep breath. Having control of the bleeding he could now precede on a more casual pace.

Time was still of concern, however, for success of major procedures were negatively related to time of surgery.

"I'm getting a pulse," Michael called.

"I can feel it in here," Erik said. "Like a penis getting a hard on. It is getting stronger. Pump that blood. How much did he get?"

"Four units packed cells, six liters holy water and a little manitol."

"Sounds good to me."

The next hour was consumed with the tedious job of preparing for the insertion of a weave-knit graft to replace the blown-out segment of the aorta. As he separated the vena cava from the aorta, he reached a resistant segment. Usually this binding could be parted with blunt dissection. He felt some resistance as he pushed with a bit more force. Dr. Regario, the second assistant, who was retracting the bag containing the intestines, developed a cramp in his hand. He relaxed to ease the pain, letting the bowel move into the wound. At this critical second, it bumped Farmers' instrument. The resulting tear in the vena cava released a flood of venous blood. It was dark, almost black, compared to the bright red of arterial bleeding.

"Goddamn it!"

The operating field was inundated. A second adrenal rush swept over Farmer. As he took deep breaths, he applied pressure to the area. The bleeding was temporarily controlled.

"Now to get that monster closed."

"I'm sorry. I got a cramp in my hand."

"Let me know before you move." Farmer's anger subsided. "You're new, not used to this physical strain." He turned his head toward the scrub nurse. "Have two sponge-on-a-sticks ready. Roberto, when I remove the lap pad, put pressure on with the sponge stick, just before the bifurcation of the vena cava. Regario, are you okay?"

"I'm fine now. It only lasted a minute."

"Good. When I move the lap pad, I want you to suction the back flow from the cava. Understand?"

Regario nodded.

Farmer said to the nurse, "Let's have two double-armed number five-0 vascular sutures. Use two needle holders. Have them both ready." He gently removed the lap pad. "Here we go!"

As he slowly withdrew the pad the defect in the vena cava came into view, pouring blood.

"Pressure, Roberto! Right there. That's got it. Suck, Regario! That's good, I can see for the first time this morning."

To the nurse, he said, "Five-0 suture." He quickly placed a stay suture in the lower corner of the rent in the vena cava. He left the ends long and laid them over Roberto's free hand. "Pull upon this with a little tension."

Looking at the vein, he reached out with his right hand and said to the nurse, "Let's have the other five-0, please."

He caught the other end of the tear with the second suture. With both sutures held taught, the edges of the defect came together, like closing a woman's coin purse. Using a sponge stick, Farmer pushed the sides of the opening together and with his other hand, he placed a running stitch, closing the defect.

"Release your pressure, Roberto." As he did, the vena cava filled up, no leaks.

"Looks good. Thank you all. Scrub nurse, excellent. Roberto, I'm glad you were here." No word to Regario.

A silence of relief fell over the operating room. Dr. Farmer stepped back for a moment. The fatigue of threatened failure evaporated and a new surge of energy filled him. He shrugged his shoulders for muscular relief.

They began preparing the two ends of the aorta for the insertion of the tubular graft.

The material had been pre-clotted. Once the graft was operational, new red cells coming from the flowing stream would fill the interspaces, making the graft blood-tight.

The tension of panic let up. The team was now relaxed. After surviving two catastrophes, one right after the other, their reserve was worn thin, but the rest of the procedure should be routine. The proximal end of the graft was sutured to the stump of the aorta. With an instrument holding the graft closed, the clamp of the aorta was slowly opened to test this first suture line. After the initial, expected leakage, the tube stopped oozing.

The aorta was again clamped. There still was no blood flowing to the lower extremities and would not be until the graft was functioning.

Attention was turned to the distal anastomosis.

As they worked, Farmer noticed that after being dry for twenty-five minutes, blood began to ooze from the area of the repaired vena cava. Suction cleared it up, but it recurred.

It appeared to be on Regario's side. He said, "The torn area is leaking." He suctioned the area to give visualization. The exact site of bleeding was difficult to pinpoint. "I think it's from the top of the repair."

"Let me have five-0." Dr. Farmer could see a small spot where there was blood coming out around the suture line. He oversewed this area and applied pressure with a lap pad. "We'll just give it a few minutes." But it continued.

Regario addressed the team. "Dr Farmer, Dr. Miguel Franco is here to relieve me. Is this a good time?"

"No time is a good time to have to change assistants, but this is as good a time as any. Yea, get out of here."

Regario backed out and was replaced by Miguel. Frank asked, "You don't have a cramp, do you?" spoken in a voice loud enough for Regario to hear.

"Blood is puddling here in the pelvic area," Roberto pointed out. "I don't think it's from the vena cava. It's weeping from the walls."

"Let's pack the area," Farmer ordered. The pack around the vena cava was still in place.

"How we doing?" Michael, the anesthesiologist, called over the ether screen. "His pressure is down a little, not serious."

"I think we are all right here. There's some weeping. It looks like it's mostly venous. Some pressure should control it."

For a period of time, Farmer applied wide pressure. He periodically removed the lap pads to inspect the results and then replaced the pads when he found there still was some bleeding. There did not seem to be any significant vessel, but rather a gentle ooze from the tissues. The portion of the graft that was clamped began to have a red perspiration on its surface, and then began to have drops of blood secreted from the interstice of the graft fiber. This added to the rising pool of blood at the operative site.

"You've lost two more units in the last thirty minutes. Want some fresh whole blood? It may help the clotting."

"Let's do it and fresh frozen plasma as well." Farmer watched the blood slowly fill the pelvic cavity and then cover the lower areas of the open dissection. Suction was barely able to carry the blood from the cavity. The suction bottle had been emptied four times in the last hour. Pressure, inspect, suction, and replace pressure. The dance went on. Farmer was oblivious of time.

Gradually, the smell of blood filled the air over the operating table. It was not the acid-bitter odor of hematemesis or the putrid, heavy, nauseating emanation of melena. This was the pungency of dying flesh, much more subtle and penetrating, filling the nostrils.

The blood thickened, forming a coating on the surgeon's latex gloves, which alternated between sticky and slippery. He had to frequently rinse his gloves in the splash basin behind him.

With a terrible impact, a thought came into Farmer's consciousness. He had seen this disaster once before during his residency—the constant, uncontrollable weeping, no identifiable single source, no response to all attempts at therapy. And finally, death.

"Call Dr. Brisbane in pathology."

"Dr. Farmer, this is Dr. Brisbane; what do you have there? I was just about to call you."

"We are running out of blood for your patient. He's gotten thirty-two units of packed cells, three fresh whole blood and six ampoules of plasma."

Farmer could not speak the name of the demon, which had invaded his patient's body. Once spoken out loud, it was real. There was no pathway to recapturing confidence, no restoring strength. Two blows, one after another, weakened his knees. He thought he had survived. He thought he was on his way out of the dramatic tragedy. As the blood continued to come pushing between his fingers that held the lap pads, he formed a defensive haziness. He became numb.

"Dr. Farmer, what are you thinking?"

"What do you have for DIC?" There it was. He had it out. He thought, *DIC—Disseminated Intravascular Coagulopathy! The rapid onset of a deadly process.*

Following stress and multiple transfusions, the body suddenly begins to form blood clots in the arteries and veins. Soon, all the chemicals the body needs to form clots are gone. Protective clotting, nature's defense against bleeding, is no longer available. Clots, previously formed, begin to dissolve. The blood continues to flow out of now open vessels.

"Is that what you think you have? Good God. You tried fresh whole. How did it respond?"

"Nothing."

"And the plasma?"

"Nothing. Nothing."

"Platelets?"

"No help."

"I'm running fibrinogen levels, pt, ptt, platelets. It may be some other coagulopathy. I'll get back to you."

"I can't get a pressure," Michael called. "We're pumping the fluids. No response."

The last immediately available blood was used.

Dr. Farmer's hands were motionless as they futilely pressed on the lap pads. Nothing more to do unless Brisbane found a miracle. The faint pulsation in the aorta became imperceptible, and then was gone.

Inside his brain, he shouted, *Die! For God's sake, die. End it!* The weeping blood was tearing Farmer apart. He thought, *He's dead. Why doesn't someone say it?* And then, quite suddenly, the operating field was dry. Now he could operate easily, except the field was dry because his patient was dead.

All the frantic gestures made by the CPR crew only heralded the entrance of death.

There was no smooth, painless way to tell the waiting loved ones the patient was gone.

As the first shock subsided, grief took on the form of guilt, blame and anger. The relatives moved from their friends to an outside medical consultant, to their religious guidance and, at last, to their lawyer.

"It's not the money. I only want to see that this cannot happen again." But it was the money.

Dr Farmer returned to the surgeon's lounge and dropped into one of the soft, leather chairs.

At the beginning of this emergency when Viola, the circulating nurse, had made her announcement of "STAT," he had tasted the adrenalin rush.

And the bonding between the OR nurse and the surgeon came alive. It was a dance; he knew his steps and she knew hers. It was sensual and palpable. He was the knight in armor, she the mother of the warrior. At times, this intense passion leaked out of the OR suite and a complicated, short-lived love affair developed. But usually, the empathetic mood ended as they left the field of battle and each returned to a different sphere.

As Viola came from the OR, she saw him sitting alone, staring at his hands. She had no balm for his soul. Only, "Sorry," as she nodded good night.

Too many thoughts simultaneously pushed into his consciousness—guilt, self pity, remorse, regret and fear. Fear of censure, of criticism, and bubbling up, wearing the robe of terror, was fear of a malpractice lawsuit. He knew all this.

The recall ended and Farmer was wide awake, back in the lawyer's office.

The deposition ended. It would be four years before he would actually go to trial, after many other depositions, declarations of information and general inspection of all aspects of his life.

It was at this time, with him spiraling down toward disaster, that he blessed himself for the availability of Amed, his safety net, his medical liability insurance company. It was not always so. Amed had been born five years before this case as a product of a void created when commercial medical liability insurance companies withdrew from the scene.

Chapter 1

The year was 1975.

Dr. Erik Nostrom was in shirtsleeves when he walked into his office. He took the brown Brooks Brothers size 44 jacket off the back of the chair and put it on. He couldn't understand why the manager of the office building kept the thermostat so low.

"It's freezing!" he shouted through the door to Judy Santos, the lady who ran his office. Her prematurely gray hair was pulled back in a bun. Erik was reminded of his thin high school principal. She looked around the corner at her complaining boss. He was fifty-two years old and ruggedly handsome. Standing by his chair he unconsciously brushed his blonde hair, which was beginning to show strands of gray.

"I'll call them again," she said. Erik turned his head and looked in Judy's direction. He thought, *Judy, you did it again.* On rare occasions, her voice and inflections were so much like another woman. It made him think of Frances, his wife. The train of thought brought him to earlier times.

He was remembering why he loved Frances, that laughing face when first he had seen her. She'd been the customer service representative for the medical building being erected. Needing his signature as a potential tenant, she'd caught up with him in the cafeteria. Almost as clearly as a video, he recalled her beauty in motion as she'd approached his table.

"Dr. Nostrom, sign here!" The command had been laced with laughter. She'd brought her face close to his, creating intense sensuality. And in the next instant she'd straightened up, put forth the document, and said, "Please?" He couldn't take his eyes off her mouth as she'd reviewed the paper. There had been no sound.

And then Erik, still viewing Judy, cursed himself for letting the story begin, for once it began, there was no way he could prevent the next scene from crushing him.

It was May 7, 1970. At seven o'clock, he pulled his car into the slot in the doctor's parking lot farthest from the hospital. He got out and began his self-imposed exercise walk. He didn't mind the very light rain falling; in fact the sun was still visible in the east. He looked for the rainbow always present when the sun shone on falling rain. He found it arching across a patch of dark clouds. The air smelled clean. The day was early enough to still be balmy, not hot. All together it was a beautiful day. His step was light as he reached the hospital. He entered the hospital, went to the doctor's dressing room, donned his green scrub shirt and pants and was ready for the morning's surgery.

He was performing a hemicolectomy and just finishing the bowel anastomosis when the phone rang. The circulating nurse picked it up. "Yes, this is room four." And then, "Yes, Dr. Nostrom is here." She listened for moment, her face changing from bright eyes over the face mask to vertical wrinkles of concern. She spoke to Dr. Nostrom. "I'll hold the phone to your ear." She carefully leaned forward, extending the phone toward Dr. Nostrom, automatically being careful not to contaminate the surgeon or the operating field.

Erik tilted his head. "This is Dr. Nostrom."

The voice on the other end spoke carefully so as not to have to repeat the bad news. "Mrs. Nostrom suddenly developed a severe headache and then lost consciousness. They rushed her to the hospital. Are you still there, Dr. Nostrom?"

"Yes."

"They confirmed the diagnosis of a ruptured cerebral Berry aneurysm. It's like a bad stroke."

"I know." Erik slowly put down the needle holder and rested one hand on the operating table. He turned and almost fell onto the stool behind him. His gloved, blood-covered hand came to his forehead as he leaned forward. He sat there in silence, rocking slightly.

The circulating nurse signaled to the other members of the operating team. "Just wait." Erik looked up. In this tragic moment, nature played a joke on him. The blood from the glove had smeared his face, creating a clown-like appearance.

The anesthesiologist, who had not been aware of the drama, looked up for the first time to see this mask. "Hey, it's not Halloween yet, Erik." His laughter stopped in midstream as he saw the eyes of the circulating nurse.

"Call Dr. Stern," Erik said quietly. "Please ask him to join me. I'll continue until he arrives." He had the circulating nurse re-gown and glove him and then he returned to the operating table. He was numb, running on an automatic, basic survival mode for him and for his patient.

The circulating nurse picked up the phone to call his partner. At the same moment she looked questioningly at the anesthesiologist. "Like ice," she said.

With effort, Erik pushed the thoughts of Frances into their compartment and locked the door. It had been five years since his Frances was kidnapped by the stroke, with only "death" on the ransom note.

His thoughts came back to the present time, the present problems.

Chapter 2

He dropped into his chair. As he began to review the print material spread out on his desk, he shook his head. Recently, the mail had delivered more literature on the growing medical liability crisis than on medical subjects. Erik hadn't received his renewal notice, so the premium shock had yet to deliver its blow. He scanned the index of one magazine. The article was on page 53. He folded the magazine and flattened it on his desk. After adjusting his glasses he leaned forward and read, "Over the last two years physicians and hospitals alike have been hit with huge medical liability premium increases."

"Do you want to talk to a Garrett Dobson from the *Medical Chronicle*?" Judy's voice came over the intercom.

"Put him on." Ordinarily, Erik avoided giving an interview to the media. It frequently ended up misquoted or highlighting an accidental remark. Robson was an exception. "Garrett, what can I do for you?"

Dobson made the expected small talk and then said, "I'm doing an article on malpractice. Your thoughts on the subject?"

"My premiums are going up. I haven't gotten this year's bill, but I've been warned it will be something! And I haven't had a suit."

"I'm trying to find the cause of this." Dobson said, "Raymond Rice, a plaintiff's attorney, told me the lawyers stand on the courthouse steps, defending the rights of the negligently damaged patient. They are dedicated, frequently advancing the cost of litigation out of their own pocket, if their gallant efforts are not successful. They recognize there is no price to be placed on the loss of or damage to the patient or a loved one, but these attorneys do their very best to comfort them, to compensate them for their loss." Dobson stopped for a moment. "Dr. Nostrom, I'm sure you agree." He laughed.

"I think I'm going to vomit."

Dobson continued, "He goes on to say, 'All doctors are not bad, but it is the bad doctors who do the mayhem on unsuspecting patients. If the Organized Medical Associations would do their job of weeding out these bad doctors, there would be much less need for suits and the crisis would disappear. But they haven't. There isn't one instance where a bad doctor lost his right to practice somewhere in this country. So it is up to the legal profession to try to weed them out. Fortunately, there are the courts to help.'"

"That's a crock of horse shit!"

Dobson said, "Tsk, tsk, be nice. I talked to a lobbyist for the Medical Associations who will remain unnamed. His pitch ran like this: Doctors are not the cause of this crisis. Doctors are better trained and more able to successfully treat their patients than at any time in history."

"Yes, yes," said Erik.

"Erik, you have to admit there are some pretty poor doctors."

"Yea, but those bad guys are tricky enough to con the patients out of suing. It's the innocent doctor who gets an unsuspected complication, not malpractice, who takes a berating. The attorneys have talked the population—when they serve on a jury—into believing it's a lottery for the patient. They have become a trigger-happy litigious mob."

"That's a good quote?"

"You are one of the few reporters I believe when they say off the record."

"So the doctors and the lawyers are saints; the culprit must be the insurance companies."

"Maybe," said Erik. "My agent called the other day—to soften the blow when he sends me the bill, I think—to tell me he's having trouble getting coverage. He gave me the good news-bad news routine. The good news was he could get a binder for the next six months; the bad news was he didn't know if it would be available at all after that. And by the way, the premiums will go up ten times."

"That's true," Dobson said. "I spoke to the president of All Right Mutual.

He claimed their capacity—the amount of premium they are able to write—decreased when the stock market went down. So they had to divest some of their lines of business. He said because medical malpractice was so labile, they chose to get out of that segment."

Erik's voice became emphatic. "You say that so calmly. So they decided to drop us. Drop us to where?"

"Don't shout, I'm only the messenger. As of now, everyone is blaming everyone else. They all define the problem, but no one has the answer."

"I'm not sure I like you being so objective. Aren't you the *Medical Chronicle*? We are going to need all the help we can get."

"No can do. Give me a call if there's anything new. I'd be interested in any solution that comes onto the horizon." Dobson hung up.

Judy's voice came on the intercom, "Dr. Reed is here."

Erik rose and walked to the door. "Hi, Jack. Come on in. I was just talking to the *Medical Chronicle*'s Garrett Dobson."

"Don't tell me. About malpractice?"

Erik nodded.

"He's called a few physicians. Dr. Sanchez was as angry. He thought Dobson was treating this like a joke."

They took the two seats in front of Erik's desk.

"Are pediatricians affected as badly as surgeons?"

"My premiums may be lower, but so is my income. The crisis has no favorites. In fact, that is why I'm here. Do you have any answers?"

"The only positive forces are those trying to get tort reform. One of these articles," Erik said as he picked up a magazine, "ends with 'Physicians are called upon to talk to their patients and their congressmen to solicit legislative relief.' Apart from that, I haven't heard anything, and the chance of getting meaningful reform is slim to none in this atmosphere."

Dr. Reed shook his head. "I hope someone finds a miracle, for that's what it's going take."

"Did you get your bill for next year's premium?"

"I'm afraid to ask my nurse for the mail."

"Coffee anyone?" Judy came into the office. "It may warm you up, Dr. Nostrom. I know he takes it black, how about you, Dr. Reed?"

"Same. And we could use some heat in here."

With a straight face, Judy said, "I'll call them again."

She returned with the white cups and placed them on coasters. On reflex, the doctors smiled as the aroma of coffee filled the room.

Erik signaled Judy. "Remind me to call Jerry Sims later today."

"Do you need a medical record?"

"No, it's about this storm brewing, this malpractice. All I read is the problem; nobody has the answer."

"Isn't that true," Reed said. "Do you think he can help?"

"Who knows?" Then he saw a headline: that tort reform was the solution to the problem was not uniformly accepted. He handed it to Reed.

He read, "*Legal Review*, November, 1974. By Lawrence Nottingham." He motioned to Erik. "I know this guy. He has a good reputation, good, that is, for a plaintiff's lawyer." Reed then silently scanned the article.

Erik pushed back in his chair, trying to absorb these divergent opinions. Through his window he could see the parking lot in front of the line of tall, full oak trees, the branches and dark green leaves being moved slightly by the breeze and beyond them the bright blue cloudless sky. The tranquil scene contrasted with the bubbling confusion in his brain and gut.

Reed summarized, "So far the doctors are not to be blamed, it may be the lawyers, and it certainly is the insurance companies."

They heard the sound of the intercom. "You have Mr. Simms on the line," Judy called. He glanced at Reed in surprise.

"Hi, Jerry, you must have your ESP radar on. Jack Reed and I were just trying to think who we should call first. We have a problem and are not sure where to place it. It's malpractice insurance. And it's not only a problem for Jack and me. All the physicians in Florida are going to have the same problem. There may be no coverage available. We need to do something."

Chapter 3

"I truly am psychic," Jerry said. "I just finished talking to a physician in Gainesville who was singing the same blues. Only his is even a sadder song. Apparently, this problem was addressed before. A few months ago about five hundred doctors in the middle of the state got together to see if they could come up with a solution. They tried to start their own insurance company. You know how difficult it is to get doctors moving in the same direction. It's like herding cats. I did some background work on this. To start an insurance company covering product and liability, it requires about two million dollars. When the dust of request for money cleared, it appears the doctors pledged about five thousand dollars. Not quite enough."

"You are a real morale buster," Erik said. "My first thought was, could we do it ourselves? But I think you answered that. Do you have any other bright ideas?"

"I'm going to Tallahassee on Monday. There's a legislative aide up there who was talking about this problem with her boss. I'm not sure this will lead to anything, but I think it's worth giving it a try. Do either of you want to come along?"

"Count me out," said Jack. "I'll help from the sidelines but up front is not for me."

In Erik's pause, he could hear Jerry breathing.

"Well?" Jerry said.

"You know, Jerry, I'm not very up on politics or the legislature. I'm just a surgeon. I don't know if I could be of any help. I need help, but I'm not sure I could be of help."

"You lend a certain air of credibility, a doctor and all that. And besides, I think you can describe the trouble first hand."

Jack said, "I think you'd be great."

Erik stared at the phone. A vision of Jerry's face appeared. The qualities of optimism, enthusiasm and "damn the torpedoes and full blast ahead" came through.

"Okay, if you're in, I'm with you. I'll see if I can clear my schedule for Monday. How long do you think it will take?"

"Oh, we fly up in the morning and come back that afternoon. I'll call you with the details." After Jerry signed off, Erik faced Jack with an expression of question and doubt. "Well, what do you think?"

"I feel better now than when I first walked in, but that isn't saying much." Jack stretched his shoulders and then offered his hand. "Good luck. Call me when you get back." He waved goodbye to Judy and exited through the side door.

Soon after Jack left, Judy presented an application to Dr. Nostrom. "You remember we were looking for someone to work in the back?"

"Yes. So?"

"She's here, Mrs. Catherine Collaro, and here is her application. She's married, no children."

Chapter 4

A twenty-four-year-old, attractive Italian girl stood before Erik's desk.

Cathy had left her last workplace seven weeks before this interview. She had recovered from that experience and was ready to face life, love and the excitement of finding herself once again. In that last job, her position had become somewhat complicated when the roles of employer-employee blurred.

Initially, the strength and brightness of her employer had charmed her. He was a 38-year-old successful lawyer. He was tall and slim, with a body that allowed clothing to drape elegantly, the envy of all stocky or fat men. His good looks made him vain and he was relaxed with women.

Very quickly she was able to respond to his business and professional demands. She knew she was a novice in the business world but thought she was doing quite well, thank you. She was happy to awaken each morning and go to work. It pleased her to satisfy her boss, who was also a man.

With time, communications required no sound. He needed a file on Sampson Corporation, and before he asked for it she had pulled it from the file. There was nothing magical about it. Cathy became very familiar with the cases he was handling. Nevertheless, it was very rewarding. With time the conversations became more personal. She thought she was acting as a friend when she listened as he confided in her about his home life, which was wanting. He seemed to be helped by her listening and her occasional comment. She hadn't imagined he was going to see the step from devoted employee, friend and supporter to lover as a merging rather than as a leap. She made it clear that she was a married lady.

This was Cathy's first real job. It was a joy. She couldn't wait to get to work. Telling her girl friend about her job, she said, "I have this great boss, the work is interesting, I can contribute more and more and I get paid for it!"

One night he asked her to stay late. To him it seemed like a most natural progression.

He leaned over her from behind and kissed her neck, turned her around, held her tight and kissed her mouth. He expressed his feelings. "Yes, I'm married, but you know there is little love left at home; yes, it would be clandestine for a while but love will find a way."

She resigned the next day, by phone.

She was now wiser, no longer convinced that she could blithely relate closely to a man and control the situation. And she was without a job.

After hanging up on her boss, she thought of her husband, Rudy. He would probably greet the news with mixed emotions. She thought he didn't like her working, but he liked the increased income.

She played housewife for two months.

Then her eye caught an add: "Wanted: Qualified person for office nurse in a medical office."

Now, she stood before Dr. Erik Nostrom and waited. He was concentrating on the notice he had just received. His agent had informed him he had good news and bad news. The good news was he could find coverage for Erik's professional liability insurance for the next six months. The bad news was it would cost $8,000 as compared to last year's $800 for twelve months. And the agent wasn't sure there would be coverage available at any price in the second half of the year.

She waited.

Earlier, Judy had informed Erik that she and his partner, Dr. Mark Stern, had approved Catherine Collaro for the job as office nurse. All that remained was his approval.

"Ah," Cathy said, clearing her throat. "Good morning, Dr Nostrom. The receptionist said I should see you," Cathy said in her most serious tone.

He looked up to see a face, softly smiling, almost innocent. He wasn't sure why he chose that adjective, but it seemed appropriate.

She was young. It struck him that "young" was relative. He was now fifty-two. Only yesterday fifty had been an old man. Now, as he looked at her, he figured, *What, she's twenty, twenty-one? She's young and I am middle aged.* The appearance of this young thing was poorly timed. The notice before him had created a sense of fatigue. He would now try to figure what to do about this malpractice coverage thing, another headache. He thought, *I miss the blind energy of youth. Shaw was right; it is wasted on the young.*

He nodded at her. "If the rest of the staff says it's okay and it's okay with Dr. Stern, it's okay with me," he said to the young lady before him and turned to the material on his desk. She didn't move.

"Have you looked at me?" she demanded. "Have you looked at my resume? Or don't you give a damn about who's working for you? For if that's the kind of office this is then I'm not sure I want to work here!" Even in anger she was beautiful.

He looked up again, stared at her, and burst out laughing. "Forgive me." He shook his head. "I really was so tied up in this letter I didn't do any of those things, though I did look at you. Please forgive my selfishness. Of course you are right." He leaned forward. "Let me try again. Hello, I'm Dr. Nostrom. Your name is?"

It was probably then when he first became special in her eyes. Before that moment, Cathy had thought her recent experience would protect her, not knowing love was logic's downfall.

He looked shy, almost boy-like, although his image was of a mature, intelligent and considerate man. "I'm Catherine Collaro. I'm applying for the position of secretary-nurse. I was an aide at the New York Hospital before I came to Miami." She ran through her credentials rapidly.

"Stop, no need," he said. "I've got to tell you, I believe what Abraham Lincoln said."

"What's that?" she asked, sounding like a straight man in a comedy routine.

"Well, Secretary of State Seward once asked him to interview a candidate for the job of under secretary of state. Lincoln spent about five minutes interviewing the man and then sent him away. Seward put his head into Abe's office and asked what he thought of the man. Abe said that he would never hire him.

"'Why not?' asked Seward.

"Lincoln answered, 'Because I don't like his face. By the time a man is grown, what he is usually is on his face.'"

She looked at her soon-to-be new boss. "I'm not sure that applies to women. We are born actresses."

"True, but I like the idea and have used it often in the past. I like your face. You have my stamp of approval! Welcome aboard." He gestured "okay?" and turned back to his papers.

Chapter 5

The flight up to Tallahassee was fairly smooth. The new service, running four times a day, allowed easy access to the capital. Of course, once you got there it was all business; no one would want to go to Tallahassee for any other reason. Without politics it was a very small town. Politics may have made it even smaller.

As they were about to board the plane, Erik said, "Go ahead, Jerry, you can have the seat by the window. I'll be along in a minute." Erik waited until just before the door closed to proceed to his seat on the aisle.

"You followed the same routine the last time we flew together," Jerry said. "You want a better view of the stewardess?"

"No, it's a touch of claustrophobia. Funny, when I'm the pilot I'm fine, but as a passenger it's tough until the plane starts to move." As the plane taxied toward the runway he relaxed.

Jerry brought with him a folder containing many articles and reports presenting data on medical liability law and the developing crisis. He pulled out the first paper and pointed to a graph. "You see, the crisis is not about true risk. Look at the reports of the loss ratios of Marshal Insurance. They're about the same as Silver Insurance."

"Hold on. Loss ratio? Remember I'm only a policy holder."

"Sorry. Here's a quick and dirty glossary." Jerry took a deep breath and began the lecture. "Loss ratio is the relationship between what's paid in and what's ultimately paid out. If you give Marshal Insurance a dollar and they pay out one dollar to cover claims against you, we are looking at a 100-percent loss ratio."

"Dollar in, dollar out?" Erik offered.

"Before you think this is a break-even deal for the insurance company, remember the dollar was invested for four years before it had to be paid out. With interest at 6 percent they would receive twenty-four cents for each dollar before it goes out."

"And I always thought insurance was a dull, cut-and-dried business." Erik shifted in his seat, trying to keep his feet from protruding into the aisle.

"More like piracy," Jerry said. "Just kidding."

Erik was distracted as he felt the surge of the plane on take-off, pinning him against his seat. The papers began to slide. He secured them in his lap with his right hand. The view from Jerry's window abruptly changed from whizzing tarpon and grass to the calm, slow passage of a clear blue sky. Gradually, the acceleration and the angle of ascent stabilized.

As the plane tore itself from the ground and rocketed upward, Erik said, "It's hard for me to adjust to the steep climb. In my days of prop engines this angle would cause the plane to stall and fall. Amazing!"

He was aware he didn't understand the complexity of the modern jet. His thoughts leaped to malpractice; did he have any comprehension of this business? He was going to attack and conquer the problem when he had to be taught the basic fundamentals by his lawyer? He laughed at himself. *Thank God I'm a quick study.*

Jerry broke into Erik's meditation. "Getting back to A1A on insurance, there was only one year when there was a loss ratio greater than 100 percent." He pointed to the third number from the top. "In the other years they kept a piece of your dollar as profit; this on top of the twenty-four cents they earned on their investment!"

"So why the crisis?" Erik believed he had followed Jerry's explanation well enough, but now he was confused. If the company was making a profit, why withdraw?

"Hold that thought. I'll be right back." Jerry unhooked his safety belt and climbed over Erik on the way to the restroom. He walked up the aisle, smiling at the stewardess in the pantry. He disappeared into the cramped space that held the toilet and sink. When he finished, he threw some water on his face and returned to his seat.

Once settled down, he said, "It's still vague in my mind, but it has to do with the stock market."

"You're kidding?"

"No."

"It sounds like a great line for a comedy act. You know, the answer having nothing to do with the question."

"It's no laughing matter." Jerry then defined the role of the State Department of Insurance in controlling how much premium a company could write. "They allow a ratio of one dollar of capital and surplus for each two or three dollars of premium written."

Erik held up his hands. "Wait a minute. Let me see, if the company has a dollar, and it writes a dollar in premium, that would be a one-to-one ratio? That is another kind of ratio?"

"Pretty close. A company may write a multiple of the money in capital by as much as three or four times."

"By write you mean sell?" Erik asked.

"Yes," Jerry concurred.

Erik again became aware of all he did not know about the business he dared to try to bring to life. Was he already over his head? Or could he work with generalities and rise above all this?

Erik continued, "The company could sell, say, three dollars of premium?"

"That's right."

As Erik tried to handle all this data, he experienced a sudden, unexpected appearance of the face of the young lady he had interviewed the other day. It was pleasant and distracting. An escape mechanism of the mind brought on by the pressure of all this new information.

But why her? He had seen her one other time after the interview. She had walked into his office to give him a report that had just been delivered. "I'm also the mailman around here" she had said, as though she were completing her job description from the previous day. Her smile was open, friendly but not suggestive or provocative. So why her face? It was gone as quickly as it had appeared.

He returned to Jerry. "How does the stock market get into this mess?"

Jerry took some time to answer. He was trying to simplify his words. "Here is the heart of the matter. Insurance companies invest some of their money in stocks."

Erik turned his head away from Jerry to have a moment of respite. Down the aisle came a pretty blonde stewardess in her crisp, pale blue uniform. She pushed a square metal cart before her.

Having heard her enquiry to the previous passengers, Erik said, "Two black coffees."

"Sugar?" she asked.

Jerry leaned forward, shook his head, then said, in his best Irish, "Just the tip of your finger to make is sweet."

She smiled and handed him a paper cup. Erik gave her a "forgive him, he's male" look and took his cup.

Jerry watched her return to the pantry at the front of the plane. "Enough of pleasure and back to the crash course on insurance. It gets clearer when I complete the cycle. Stocks are valued by the insurance department at the price in the market on the day of evaluation. You can see the value of the company would drop considerably if the price of the stocks in their portfolio went down."

"I don't see the trouble so far."

"There's a saying in the stock market that goes, bears make money and bulls make money, but pigs always lose in the end. This applies here as you will see. In 1973 to '74, the returns on stocks began to skyrocket, yielding two to three times more than the returns on bonds."

"But most of the company's money was in bonds?" Erik asked.

"Usually, yes, but these huge returns on stocks were unique."

"And?"

Jerry stroked his chin. "Most people don't realize that an insurance company is an investment entity. It uses the insurance part as a means to get the money to invest."

Erik figuratively doffed his hat to Jerry. "You slipped in a whole new concept. Yet as I think about it, I can see your point. They collect the premium money and pay the losses and expenses. They make their *vigorish* on the money during the time they hold on to it. Not bad?"

Jerry gave an approving glance toward Erik. "So far so good. With the high returns in stocks, the temptation was too great. The insurance companies began to invest more heavily in stocks. 1973 was great. The returns made the folks in charge of investments look like heroes. 1974 brought on a mini recession. The value of the stocks dropped 30 to 40 percent. Remember, one dollar of value allowed the company to write three dollars of premium, which they did. When that dollar value of the stocks dropped to 60 cents, at the same three-to-one ratio they could only justify writing one dollar and eighty cents of premium. They had to drop some of their lines of business." He took a sip of his coffee. "Cold." He pushed the call button for the stewardess.

She appeared immediately. "You need anything?"

Jerry let the comment hang in the air, smiling innocently, then said, "Some hot coffee please. I'm talking when I should be drinking."

She went to the pantry and returned. "I have no fingertips left," she said with a straight face.

Jerry laughed and said, "Touché." He managed a sip of coffee and continued his conversation with Erik.

"And here is where it gets interesting. The guy who put the company into stocks was really squirming. What to do? He can't say, 'Oops, I made a bad decision.' So, to cover his ass, he declares medical liability coverage to be too volatile. Got to get rid of that book of business. What do you know? If we do that it reduces the amount of premium written to one hundred and eighty cents, well covered by the sixty-cent surplus. No need to throw himself on his sword; all's right with the world. Oh yes, the doctor will have to figure out a way to be insured. We won't touch it. Too volatile."

Erik listened in wonder. This was so dynamic! Up until now he, like almost all physicians, had wanted to only pay their premiums and never hear about malpractice insurance again. The status of his premiums had little to do with the practice of medicine. However, with the crisis, a much larger picture was emerging, a mathematical opportunity.

In his undergraduate period, Erik had found math subjects quite easy. Solutions had come to him quickly while the other students had been struggling. Maybe it was this ease with numbers that had made him seek other avenues of challenge and led him to medicine instead of actuarial studies.

As he pondered what Jerry had just said, the mathematical mind went to work. It did not take a rocket scientist to realize there would be very little risk in this business if you didn't get too greedy. "What happened to that group of physicians in middle Florida who tried to start their own insurance company?"

"They needed two million and were able to raise five thousand. No funds."

"Why are we going to Tallahassee?"

"We are looking for an alternative to the traditional form of insurance."

"Like what?"

"That's what we are going to find out."

The plane rolled to a stop. The two men found their bags and headed for the terminal.

They were silent most of the way to the city. The ride from the airport along Springhill Road was always relaxing to Dr. Nostrom. The road was lined with fields of wild flowers and stands of oak trees. It was a contrast to south Florida flora. Here there were seasonal changes, breaking the monotony of always summer.

The cab left them off at the bottom of the hill at Hunter Street. They began walking the steep incline.

"I could use this kind of exercise in Miami."

"They say you can tell a freshman female student from a senior by the size of their calves," Jerry said.

A very shapely pair of legs walked by. "She must be a senior!" Erik noted.

"Probably."

Chapter 6

They reached the offices of Bob Griffin, an attorney/lobbyist whom Simms had known from law school.

"You'll like this guy; he enjoys what he's doing and is good at it. He was quite an athlete in undergrad, played quarterback, went through school on a football scholarship. The girls loved him! I could hold my own in that department, but Bob had to lock his door to keep the gals out."

"Apparently Bob's attraction has not decreased," Erik said as he noticed the beautiful girl sitting at the reception desk.

"Good morning, may I help you?"

"It's Mr. Simms and Dr. Norstrom to see Mr. Griffin, please," Jerry said. The beautiful secretary repeated the words into the phone. She smiled at Jerry as she waited for a response. "He'll be with you in a moment. May I get you something to drink? Coffee? Soft drink?"

"Coffee's fine."

"Same here." They both watched as she magnificently walked from behind the desk to the small kitchen around the corner. They sat in silence as she returned, placed the coffee on the table before them and glided back to her desk.

"Morning, Jerry!" Bob Griffin said as he appeared from the doorway. He shook hands with Jerry.

"This is Dr. Erik Nostrom, a man with a problem."

"Come on in." Erik and Jerry picked up their coffee cups and followed. After discussions about the trip up, the weather and a general appraisal of the girls in Tallahassee as compared to Miami, they got on to the subject of concern to Nostrom. Jerry quickly brought Bob up to the current thinking about medical liability. The major commercial insurance companies were pulling out, creating a void. "They are turning away millions of dollars in premiums."

"Millions?" asked Griffin.

"Well, let's see, there are approximately fifteen thousand active physicians in Florida needing coverage; the most recently quoted premium was thirty-seven hundred dollars."

Figuring easily, Erik stated, "That's a whopping fifty-five million dollars."

Griffin whistled, then said, "Who else knows this?"

"That's the catch," Jerry said. "This is common knowledge. In spite of this, because the big boys are steering clear, it's suspect. And the funny thing is, as I've mentioned to Erik, they are not staying out of the game because it's risky." Jerry gave a questioning glance toward Griffin.

"Okay. We got the money. You know the rules: To get the legislator to take on your cause you need money and votes. What kind of support do you expect to muster?"

Erik and Jerry looked at each other. Erik said, "Getting doctors to band together on a cause for more that a nanosecond is very difficult." He was shaking his head slowly, and then stopped. "It depends on how much panic is in the streets. My small sample suggests this might be the time."

"Are you sure of that?" Griffin questioned. "I'm Jerry's friend, but I'm not getting involved in something that has little chance of succeeding." His tone cast a pall over the room. The negative force sank Erik deeper into his chair. He realized how fragile the supporting columns of enthusiasm were. He thought, *Forget the whole thing! Am I Christ to carry the burden and die for fifteen thousand?* "I'm pretty sure. Enough for Jerry and me to be committed, but nothing is guaranteed."

"We'll see," Griffin said. "Let's look at the rest of the program."

After three hours of brainstorming from all sides, Griffin declared, "I think we got a plan. I'll play."

"Good!" Erik's relief made the word sound musical.

Once committed, Griffin threw in all the way. "First, contact that group of physicians who had met in central Florida. Don't ask for money; we know that's a no go. But if they could write letters, make phone calls and gather signatures on petitions, this group could be of great help." Enthusiasm gradually increased in his voice. After going over the entire Senate list, he pronounced, "I'm going to contact Senator Rusty Hadley. Rusty has been in the Senate long enough to have paid his dues. You know him, Jerry."

"I met him some time ago. At that time, I wasn't thinking of him as a helping hand. But now that you mention it, he would be fine. Do you think he'll come on board?"

Griffin nodded. "He has been successful often enough to make him a power, and I'd gamble he is young enough to still enjoy a challenge."

"I just remembered seeing him in action on the floor," Jerry said. "He could be a winner."

Griffin nodded. "I could talk to his aide. If Senator Hadley approves, his aide could help us get the problem and possible solutions into the media. One of the forces that catch the eye of the legislators is public interest." He stood up and began pacing. He hit his left palm with his right fist. "Honoring this interest can turn into votes, the thing second closest to their hearts!"

Jerry turned to face Erik and put his hand out with the thumbs-up sign.

Chapter 7

With initial plans made, both Jerry and Erik were feeling a lot better. They had ended the meeting in order to get the afternoon flight back to Miami. As they rushed out of the lobby, Jerry pointed. "We're lucky, there's a cab."

Once on the way they urged the taxicab driver to hurry. Erik added, "We have twenty minutes to reach the airport in time for our flight."

"No problem," the cabbie said. And in the next instant, as he made the turn onto the airport road, always tricky, the cab was hit on the front passenger's side by a farmer's flatbed truck. It was a strange, slow-motion event. Each driver had stopped. Then each thought the other had given him the sign for the right of way, and each proceeded to gently crash into the other. The sounds of an irate Cuban farmer and a redneck cabby registering at full volume filled the air. Jerry and Erik just looked at each other. Thanks to the farmer's lack of auto insurance and the very high deductible coverage of the cab driver, a compromise was reached. Neither side was particularly happy about it. The cab driver returned to his cab. "To the airport?"

Jerry pulled out the plane schedule he always carried. "There are no flights to Miami for the rest of the day."

Erik shrugged his shoulders and said to the driver, "No, take us back to the Madison Hotel." He eyed Jerry. "Might as well get some rooms, call the airline for reservations for an early flight, and chalk this event up to Murphy's Law—whatever can happen will happen, particularly if it's negative."

Chapter 8

After getting the rooms and making new flight reservations they each headed for their room. Erik called home to talk to Frances.

"…and that is a story you wouldn't believe if you saw it on television," he said as he finished relating the day. "But more importantly, how are you?"

Before May, 1970, when the aneurysm made her an invalid, Frances Nostrom had been energetic, optimistic and happy with life and her marriage. The recovery had been slow. Frances struggled to speak simple words. Ambulation was only possible with the support of Miss Lacey, the private duty nurse who had taken on the job of rehabilitating Frances as a commitment.

"She's smiling, Dr. Nostrom. It must have been some story." Frances turned away from the phone, which Lacey held to her ear. She leaned back on the pillow and closed her eyes.

"Any instructions?" Lacey asked.

"We missed our plane and have to stay here overnight. Be home on the morning plane. Call my office and ask Judy to find the time of the flight, rearrange my morning and I'll call her when I get in." Erik got in bed, turned off the TV, and soon was asleep.

Chapter 9

Jerry took his key. He turned to view the night from the lobby. The threatening clouds he had seen on their trip back to the hotel had cleared. Now, the moon's light cast splashes of white along the road. He walked to reassemble his thoughts. Fifteen minutes later he was before the bar he had noticed on the ride from the airport. He walked in and mounted a stool at the bar. "Vodka and tonic with a twist, please."

The glass was cool in his hand.

He began to review. This might turn out to be something. One by one he lined up in his mind the steps to be taken toward a solution of the insurance crisis. Without thinking he began to list them with his pen on the cocktail napkin.

First call the head of that medical group in middle Florida, but before that write out a story to give the other physicians. Stress the need to talk to anyone in the media if they knew them personally. And don't forget to ask them "to do it for me, Al." He smiled as he recalled a fundraiser's advice as to how to motivate folks to give or come on board. He said there were four reasons people give: they will benefit personally when giving; they like to be associated with a winner; they believe in the cause (the least likely reason); and last, and most powerful, ask them to "do it for me."

"Do you always talk to yourself when writing on a napkin?" She had walked into the bar, noticed Jerry sitting near the end, recognized him as the client very recently eyeing her in Bob's office and walked up behind him and sat on the stool next to him. He obviously was alone.

Jerry turned to see white skin, shining blue eyes, soft lips, and a turned-up nose all framed in the softest black hair he could remember. She must have mistaken him for someone else. This vision couldn't be coming on to him. "I'm Jerry Sims," he said clumsily, half wishing it was not her mistake, knowing that she would surely say, "Oh, I'm sorry, I thought you were somebody else."

She smiled; his mouth went dry. "I know. We sort of met this afternoon."

Then he remembered. *Oh my God, I hope what I was thinking then wasn't on my face. It was and she's here to let me know what she thinks of a voyeur.* His shoulders and chest were on fire. He began to sweat. Her perfume added to his dizziness.

"I'm Bob Griffin's receptionist."

"I know, I know. I was just surprised. You know how when you see someone in a different environment you don't recognize him or her? Like when I see a judge without his robes walking down the street."

"Without his robes?"

"I mean in civilian clothes."

"That's happened to me once. I was in a bar and began talking to this good-looking guy, kind of coming on, when I suddenly realized he was the priest from our church."

"What happened?"

"He just said, 'We priests go out some time' and he went right back to flirting with me, smiling all the time. I left right away. Quite confused." She had a soft laugh, making him smile and relax.

They made the usual introduction, with one-liners about their past.

"I'm Linda Grey. Married once, divorced once, now on the prowl." She screwed up her face to look like a demon. "So be careful." She then laughed and touched his shin with her forefinger. He struggled to find the glib, humorous conversation he was noted for, but he was so stirred by this beautiful girl, he was afraid he would stutter.

"Jerry Sims, attorney. I told you that this afternoon."

"I know. I just wanted to see if you remembered me."

Jerry threw up his hands. "You almost ruined the meeting with your boss. I kept thinking of that vision I had just left in the reception room. Couldn't wait until the meeting was over." The skin of his face was hot. "But when we broke up you were gone." He had been sitting facing the bar and turning his head to see Linda. Now he shifted until his knees swung parallel to the bar, touching her leg. "I thought I must have imagined you. There you have it. The confession of your admirer."

She was smiling as she looked into his face. She said, with mock Irish accent, "And as smooth a line as I've heard."

The conversation drifted from one subject to another, mostly seeking humor. Jerry knew there was a protection in humor. He could commit and almost instantly withdraw if the comment was not taken as delivered. "That's why I love you, ha ha." If the listener changed the subject then it was just a funny comment.

"Whoa, it's past 11:30," Linda noted as she struggled to see her watch in the dim light. "The day starts pretty early for me. I've got to run. Can I drop you at your hotel on my way home?"

"Thanks."

As they walked from the bar he gently took her hand. "Boy and girl stuff," he said, smiling. "See, you make me feel like a teenager. I'm looking for a picket fence to walk to show off."

"After those drinks and in this darkness, all I need—nursing a broken leg or worse."

"Maybe you can just imagine it." As they drove to his hotel, the fantasies began to grow more vivid. He would reach over and kiss her, softly at first and then more passionately. Without a spoken word, he would lead her to his room, hold her, and easily unzip her tight, silk dress until it fell from her shoulders. Still no words, and then he would say, "You are magnificent!"

Linda said, "What did you say?"

He was wrenched from his fantasy. "I was day, or night, dreaming there for a moment. My flight doesn't leave until 11:23 a.m. Could I buy breakfast?"

"What time do you get up?"

"Whenever you say."

"I usually have a light meal as I get ready for the day," she said. He had gotten quite excited at the thought of seeing her again and now was disappointed.

She stopped the car. "Here we are. I believe this is your hotel." She kissed him on the cheek as he stepped out of the car. He walked around to the driver's side. She lowered the window. "Why don't you join me for breakfast at my place, say 7:30? My address is on the back of my card."

"I can manage that."

He floated to his room, the fantasy suddenly became alive and well.

Chapter 10

He was awake at six. Reaching for the phone, he called to the front desk. "Call me a cab, please."

"Okay, you're a cab." The clerk laughed, enjoying his little joke. "But if you're serious about that you must be from the big city; cabs up here are not around the corner. I'll have to call Roscoe. If he's wake, he'll be here in an hour or so. You should've told me last night, and then he'd be here for sure."

"How far is this address?" Jerry reached for Linda's card and read the address to the clerk.

"That's about eight miles. There's no answer at Roscoe's."

Jerry hung up. Waves of panic began to sweep over his body. He dressed quickly and all but ran to the lobby. "Is there any kind of transportation around here?"

"My sister has a car. For twenty bucks I think she would drive you to that address."

"Great! Would you call her please? Now."

The clerk nodded and began to dial. "Morning, Glory." To Jerry, he said, "Her name is Glory." He turned his mouth to the phone. "Hey, you awake? Want to make a quick twenty bucks? Yea, some guy has to get to Henderson Street in a hurry. Be here in twenty minutes? Okay, that sounds fine." He hung up. "She'll be here in twenty minutes."

Jerry thought the young man looked quite satisfied with himself. Jerry looked at his watch. It was almost 7:00 a.m. *Where did the time go? But it is going to be alright. Glory will be here by 7:20. It shouldn't take more than 10 minutes to get there. I'll be a few minutes late, but that's okay. I won't look so anxious.*

"We have coffee and some Danish over there. Help yourself." The clerk pointed to the table in the corner.

"No, thanks. I'm on my way to breakfast." Jerry sat in a worn armchair. He began to picture the next hour.

She would meet him at the door in her dressing gown, gesture for him to enter. As he followed into the kitchen just down the hall, he could smell her faint perfume, flowery and yet a touch of musk, mixing with the delicious aroma of frying bacon. He was floating again. It was so natural. He belonged there. They could have been together, married? For years. Easily he reached for her shoulder. She stopped, allowing him to come pressing against her. She turned and was in his arms. The dressing gown fell to the floor, displaying her beautiful body. He stepped back to enjoy this picture. Her neck was longer than he remembered, tapering to her shoulders. Her breasts weren't large, but the nipples were erect, inviting. He bent his knees slightly so his head was at the level of her breasts. It was so natural for his mouth to seek. The breast filled his mouth. Leaning forward, she pressed his head against her. The touch of her hands on his neck sent a chill through him. As he stood and took her in his arms, she could feel him fully erect. Smiling, she took his hand and led him toward the bedroom...

The reality of the morning replaced his dream. It was the clerk's voice. "Glory just called. She had a flat and will be a few minutes late, but she'll be here." The voice was painful.

It was 7:20.

There was no way that he could return to his dream. Impossible to sit still. Bouncing out of the chair he began to walk the length of the lobby.

7:40. "Can you give her a call? Let's see how long it's going to be."

"She doesn't have a phone in the car."

Suddenly an idea popped into Jerry's head. "Do you have a phone book?" Drawing the book from behind the counter, the clerk handed it to Jerry. "Let's see. Grey, Linda." No listing. Wait a minute, the card. He reached into his pocket. "Why didn't I think of that before?" He turned the card over, read the number and almost instantly began to dial.

"This is the office of Robert Griffin. The office hours are from..." He hung up the phone. 8:00 a.m.

Walking slowly into the lobby, Glory smiled. She wore a red checkered shirt and jeans covering her chubby body. "Someone needs a ride?" she called.

"Let's go!" Jerry grabbed her arm and guided her out the door toward the car, a 1960 Ford.

"It'll get you there, don't worry. Just get in." Once seated, she turned the ignition key. Nothing but a grinding sound. Again, turned the key, again only the grinding sound. "We'll have to wait a minute; she's flooded."

"Do something!" His voice began to take on a higher pitch.

She got out of the driver's seat, wobbled around to the hood, lifted it, secured it and looked inside. All this at what he thought was a snail's pace. "I'll just take off the air filter and blow on the carb. Sometimes that works."

He saw the car beginning to be dismantled. Fantasies were gone. It now became a challenge, a fight for life. He must make it to her door. Wait a minute. What am I doing? I only saw her yesterday. Who is she to me, and why should I care? Back home, the boys always said, "Don't date a gal across town. The transportation will always get you." *And here am I, thinking of dating across the state. She may have been just trying to be polite.*

"I think Betsy's ready," Glory said. Off they went. 8:30 a.m.

Linda's car was backing out of the driveway as he approached. "Hi, there. I thought you forgot all about me." She smiled at him as they came side to side in each car. Warmth, almost fire, ran through him and he remembered why he had been so desperate to see her. He would cross the state anytime. She reached out and handed him her card. On the back, she had written her home phone number and address.

"You can call me when you get to Miami. I'm really sorry we missed breakfast." Then she was out of the driveway and gone.

"Back to the hotel?"

"Might as well."

Chapter 11

Erik reached home in the afternoon. Frances and Lacy were on the patio facing the pool. It was a perfect day with a mild breeze gentling the warm sun.

"Hi, ladies. It's good to be home."

Frances was able to smile and weakly wave her hand.

Chapter 12

Jerry Sims had arranged a meeting on Wednesday for six other physicians to be held in his office. The meeting was called for 7:00 p.m.

Jack Reed was the first to arrive.

"This day off?" Jerry greeted him at the doorway. Jerry knew it was a sarcastic comment, though he meant it with sympathy. The uninformed would think that not seeing patients in the office meant he was off playing golf. In truth, these off days are consumed by required hospital, medical associations and specialty meetings, as well as meetings like tonight's. With changes in the way patients financially related to their physicians via managed care, Medicare and Medicaid, it was very necessary to review each contract. With changes in specialty techniques and recent data in specialty, it was obligatory to keep up with the medical literature. Not only for better patient care, it had also acted as a defense against malpractice claims. A good deal of the most recent medical information really came from conferences with the detail men and women, representatives from the pharmaceutical manufacturers.

Jack had caught up on his paperwork and then headed for this meeting. "Nothing like eighteen holes of golf," he quipped.

The only advanced information he had received was a brief statement from Jerry, who said, "There was some light at the end of the tunnel concerning the malpractice mess."

Jack commented, "I hope it isn't a Greyhound bus!"

He entered the attorney's rather palatial office waiting room. He looked around, comparing this setup to his own rather crowded office. "Oh well." He chose a soft leather overstuffed chair.

Close behind Jack, Dr. Richard Goring, neurosurgeon, entered. Within the next fifteen minutes followed Dr. Thomas Frond, the cardiologist; Anthony Sanchez, general surgeon; Dr. Fredrick Cannon, plastic surgeon; and Dr. Stanley Reinhart, general practioner.

After the usual brief recognition of each other, the group settled into a waiting silence. Then, talk of the Dolphins' performance last Sunday, the latest notice from the hospital concerning the new CEO, and then silence. Jerry walked into the room with Erik. "Gentlemen, I hope this isn't a wake. I think we may have something worthwhile. Anyone needs coffee, coke-coco cola, that is. Erik and I just came from Tallahassee where we met with Bob Griffin, an attorney. One of the good ones. We were there all afternoon and it was time well spent." He turned to Erik, who nodded in agreement as he sat down.

"Apparently, our town isn't the only one worried about malpractice. It's all though the state and to some degree throughout the country." Jerry remained standing; he unbuttoned his jacket. "In some states the physicians are trying to start a property and casualty insurance company; in others the medical associations are trying to solve the problem, but aren't sure how. In all states the commercial insurance companies are intentionally pricing themselves out of business."

Erik stepped in. "It's important to know that these companies were not losing money, but they were withdrawing for other reasons. Keep this in mind when, later, we talk about doing it ourselves."

Jerry continued, "Essentially, they are moving out of the malpractice business. There has been enough concern raised in Tallahassee for the legislators to try to find a solution. Erik and I were in Tallahassee a few days ago. As I mentioned. We met with a smart attorney. He in turn is talking to a few congressmen who think kindly toward our crisis. You know, when a congressman does not have a vested interest in a project, he can be brought on your side with the truthful merits of the deal. One of the concepts that was kicked around was this." He walked to the center of the room, turning slowly to reach all t he doctors. "You have to withhold your disbelief until I've finished. They are putting together bills for both the House and the Senate that will allow a doctor's group to begin writing medical liability insurance coverage. The group would be organized as a trust. This trust would not have to demonstrate any capital and surplus."

"It's simple as that?" Goring questioned.

"There probably will be some kind of guarantee. This hasn't been worked out yet. According to Griffin, enough doctors called their reps to get their attention. I think this is a first. Hopefully, there are no laws to prevent it."

Jerry looked around the room. He braced himself. He knew when doctors were not sure of some matter, their attitude was negative. It was this mood reflected on the faces of the group. He saw varying degrees of doubt.

"I don't know about any doctors I know giving guarantees," Goring stated.

"Ordinarily I'd agree," Erik offered, "but even the FMA folks we talked to felt there is enough panic in the streets to have them act to support actions in this direction. Of course, they believe they should be in charge. In other states, the medical associations are trying to find a solution. I'm not sure that I would want to wait for the FMA to act. There are so many factions up there that to find consensus is very difficult if not impossible. If we get this into a shape that could fly, we will need the help of the rest of the state." Erik stood up next to Jerry. "We probably are better off to seek individuals with some local clout. I don't think we will have too much trouble convincing them of the need for this action. Jerry has tentatively approached some folks in Gainesville and Orlando. It's not too likely that we could extend to Jacksonville initially, what with FMA having a grip on that area. Down here, we have a better chance of succeeding by going independent."

"Did you say there would be no need for capital and surplus?" Cannon asked.

Of the group, Stanley Reinhart was the most vocal about his knowledge of business. "I can't see how that would work. You would need some working capital just for stamps. Wait a minute! We could raise that kind of money from just a few docs. If it's going to be a trust, we can't sell shares but we could get it as a loan at some attractive interest. At ten thousand each there could be seventy thousand right here in this room."

"How much all together would we need?" Jack Reed asked.

"If we all work without compensation, at least at the start, it shouldn't be too much," Erik said.

"I'd put it at a hundred thousand to start," Stanley offered. "And if we are planning on having folks from the Gainesville area we'd better plan to have them contribute. If we don't, they will think we city slickers in Miami are trying to put something over on them."

"That's true." Fredrick Cannon spoke up. "One day I was talking to a man from Gainesville about buying a new Cadillac. I said, 'Do you mean to tell me if you could get your car for $10,000 less in Miami you would still buy your car from your friendly Gainesville car salesman?' and he said, 'Yup.' 'Why?' I said. 'Because I don't trust you Yankees down here. The wheels would probably fall off before I got home.' So I agree with you, we surely should let them loan some money."

"I'm in." Anthony Sanchez quietly spoke his vote.

"Me too," Thomas Frond called out. "It will be such a pleasure to tell that agent to shove the contract up his ass!"

Erik looked around the room. "Then we all agree. Ten thousand a man and make room for the mid-state component."

Richard Goring, the neurosurgeon, nodded. "Anything will be better than the note I got from my agent. The number was ten times my last year's premium."

Stanley Reinhart, the family practice doctor, asked, "You mean that this group here is going to try to start an insurance company? What do we know about that? We're doctors."

Erik nodded his head. "Yes, that's true, but there is nobody else. Remember that famous statement 'If not now then when, if not us then who?'"

"I think you all are as scared as I am," Stanley almost whispered, "so I'll go along. Count me in."

In that room, there was the strange combination of exhilaration on being able to see an answer to the frightening problem and wariness on the realization of the amount of work and risk required to bring this plan to fruition.

At the thought of getting 500 physicians to see this was really the only way to handle the problem, Thomas Frond, cardiologist, said laughingly, "Why do I keep thinking of Don Quixote?"

"Really," Jack Reed, pediatrician, echoed.

"It's true that physicians do not usually lend themselves to group ventures where they do not have control," Jerry added. "One of the largest obstacles facing us will be the inability of each physician to surrender to another physician the control of their destiny in any aspect, but particularly regarding medical liability coverage."

Erik interrupted, "We're counting on the blind terror the doctor feels when he thinks of being without coverage. That fear is increasing. What gave this mood validity is the fact that, up until recently, it was unusual for a doctor to be sued for malpractice. In fact, when I started practice, to be sued almost ruined the doctor's reputation. Now, in the last few years, it has become much more frequent. And the doctors are being sued for the patient's untoward result rather than a negligent act on the part of the doctor."

The two-man act was warming up. Jerry said, "The juries are beginning to change from seeing the doctor as a God, who renders life-saving care, to seeing him as a source of compensation for the woes of the patient—but for the grace of God, it could have been them. The growths of malpractice claims have rapidly changed from a very gentle slope to a rocket heading skyward. The avalanche is just beginning."

"The doctors will still be cautious about joining a new group," Dr. Frond stated, "because they think the losses made the commercial companies give up."

"Our job," Jerry answered, "is to demonstrate that at this time the problem isn't really price, but it is availability."

"You said *we* have to convince the doctors, correct?" Dr. Sanchez offered. "Let me see if I understand well enough to be an apostle, and if I can, most of us will be able to go forth." He took a deep breath and then began. "With the commercial companies running out of capacity, thanks to the decreased capital and surplus, they were limited in the total amount of insurance they could write. Medical liability coverage was shelved for the time being."

"Add," called Dr. Reed, "about them having only one year with a loss ratio over one hundred percent, and never having a real loss when you add the investment gain." He smiled and turned up his hands, signifying nothing to it!

The group applauded. "I believe you got it!"

"Okay," Erik called out. "My secretary will collect the checks in the next few days. I guess this group, with whoever we get from the north, will be the founders and initial board of directors. Let's meet next Tuesday."

Chapter 13

Farrell's bar and grill was one of the institutions in Tallahassee. It was down the street from the courthouse, making it a traditional place for lawyers, power brokers and politicians to meet. The room was long and rectangular with a low ceiling. This and the dark polished wood of the bar gave it the impression of a cave. At lunchtime the influential of Tallahassee were shoulder to shoulder at the bar and filled all available tables. Conversations, by necessity, were at least two decibels above usual talk. Lawrence Nottingham, Roscoe Brady and Raymond Rice were sitting at a table in the back of the room. All three were plaintiff trial attorneys.

"Did you get a chance to look over the bill Rusty is putting out?" Lawrence asked. Then without waiting for an answer, he said, "He's looking to allow the formation of a medical liability insurance group in the form of a trust. It's being pushed by the docs. Ordinarily, I would appose anything sponsored by the docs, but in this case it might be worth studying."

Roscoe asked," Are we looking at the formation of a deep pocket? It sounds like the doctors are going to get the money all in one spot so we can just dig in."

Raymond suggested, "We ought to do a 'Brer Rabbit' bit. 'Don't throw me into the briar patch' and act as if we are against it. Maybe they'll give us wrongful death in exchange for us yielding to their trust."

Roscoe said, "From what I hear, the physicians are in panic because the commercial companies are pulling out or are charging prohibitive premiums. They might just go for it."

Lawrence added, "At some point we should broaden the scope of this kind of trust to include lawyers, accountants and architects. A self trust would be cheaper and would give us greater control." Silence fell as their food orders began to fill the table. Roscoe started on his second vodka martini, Raymond had iced tea and Lawrence took Pierre water. Lawrence said, "I'll give Rusty a call later today. I'm curious to know how far they've gotten. Jerry Sims came up from Miami. And he's talking to a few physicians in Gainesville and Orlando."

"I'm thinking," Raymond noticed, "we should encourage this movement. I hear my doc say he's really afraid to practice without insurance. I'd like to keep him around. And besides, we plaintiff attorneys need a new source of clients. Slip and fall is getting old hat. I just about ran out of neck braces." He laughed at the thought.

"You know, Simms stands to do all right if this thing gets off the ground," Roscoe noted. "That guy, like all on the defense side, gets paid by the hour. When the case goes bad, he is sad, but he sends his bill."

"Roscoe, you are preaching to the choir," Lawrence complained. Roscoe ignored him. He was on a role and enjoyed this rare time in the spotlight.

"All the hours in deposition, in negotiations, in trial, on the phone, in research for the case, travel and even copy machine used," he paused, and then continued, "and thinking time on the john are included in his bill. And because his client is an insurance company with deep pockets, his payment is guaranteed." He paused again. "Unless the company goes into receivership."

Lawrence reached over and patted Roscoe's shoulder. "I'll take the client's case on contingency all day long. I'll gladly put out the money for expense to conduct the work-up and trial. They say the average plaintiff attorney wins about fifteen percent of the cases that go to trial. I do better than that. And what they don't say is that most cases are settled rather than tried. Twenty to thirty percent of all that money comes to me."

"Yea, and you won't take a case unless there's a good probability of wining at least 200,000," Raymond added. "Lawrence, I noticed in the *Legal Review* your last case settled for about $2,500,000. That's good advertisement."

"That is true. The day after that statement was released, four general attorneys called asking if I would act as first chair in a liability case. That aphorism has always amused me. They will call themselves second chair, which means doing no work and getting ten percent of the settlement. But why share the wealth? By the way, if a surgeon was caught doing that with his referring general physician, he'd be in jail."

Roscoe questioned, "I wonder if the same list of pro-plaintiff and anti-plaintiff will still apply?"

"What's that?" asked Raymond.

"You know, I think we all have that list. Mine's on the pullout writing board in my desk. My doctors are in three categories. The first category is those where money speaks. I like them—say yes, and he says yes. Then there are those who say yes, but only for the defense; and then there are the worst kind, those righteous sons of bitches. That guy Nostrom is one. I remember when he first came to town. I put his name on the list to send him a patient, sort of a trial balloon. There was a young lady who slipped and fell in the Dade grocery store. I asked her if she had a stiff neck. She said yes. Being a good guy and trying to give this new doc a break—you know how hard it is to start a practice—I sent her to Nostrom. I remember her name, Peggy Walsh. The jerk saw her, called it post traumatic myositis—now that's okay—but then he gave her a couple of aspirins, checked her in a couple of days and told her she was fine and it would clear completely in a week. Before I sent her over, I told him I'd take care of his bill. He sent me a bill for twenty dollars!"

Lawrence, who did not practice at the slip-and-fall level, looked at Raymond with a shrug of his shoulders. "So?"

Roscoe continued, "Well, I figured he didn't know the score. I called him up. 'Doc, I got your bill. That kind of treatment is okay for Jackson, in the charity ward, but this lady is private. Just to reassure her, ease her emotional stress, you should see her at least ten times. And at ten dollars a visit, no, make it thirty-five dollars a visit, that's a much better compensation for your expert service. You pocket $350, she's happy, I'm happy and the insurance company really doesn't give a damn. What do you think of that? That's the way to play the game,' I tell him. He tells me it is really not medically necessary! I could have puked. I hate the wet-behind-the-ears goody attitude. So I gave him line number 42. You know, I said, 'Have you no compassion for your patient? If I go into court with twenty-dollar medical costs, I'd be laughed out of the room. You don't know because you are new around here, but settlements are usually around ten times the medical expenses in these kinds of cases. What do you say? Do I call her up and tell her to make another appointment with you?' He said he didn't think so! The poor lady got nothing.

Can you imagine?"

"Was that a pro bono case?" Lawrence couldn't resist the barb. He was embarrassed by the kind of activities that Roscoe described. His type of altering the facts was on a much higher, wink-and-nod level.

"It turned out that way." Roscoe laughed. The three attorneys left the bar, each one privately considering the potential benefits that could accrue. The practice of law in this town was highly competitive, so there was no reason to share any ideas with the others. Lawrence was already considering adding a new member to the firm, with an expert in this relatively new, potentially lucrative field of medical liability.

Chapter 14

On Thursday four weeks after their trip to Tallahassee, Jerry called Erik. "I just got off the phone with Bob Griffin, our favorite lobbyist. The legislative committee is having hearings on the insurance crisis next Wednesday. I volunteered your services to present the physician's position." Jerry held the receiver away from his ear, anticipating the shout.

"You did what?" Erik leaned over his desk and began turning the pages of the calendar to see what date that would be.

Jerry continued, "Well, it seemed like a good idea at the time. According to Griffin, the committee was going off on a tangent, suggesting there might not be a problem. One of the senators offered, 'After all, it's only a matter of dollars. The docs can afford it. Maybe a few less caddies and yachts.' At that point, Senator Rusty Hadley declared they should hear from someone on the front lines. He told the committee, 'I have been talking with a physician about this problem and I am convinced they need relief. I would like to offer a bill that would help.' Discussion followed and at the end, they agreed it would be reasonable to set a time for the physician to address them. That's you."

Erik listened quietly. "Wednesday? That's six days from now."

"You wanted action. According to Griffin, the senator ended his comments with, 'The action I am considering will require no significant funding.' Immediately, the folks in the room began to thaw. 'No funding necessary? Sure, I will listen,' was the attitude."

"No phone call of reprieve from the capital before you offered me up for sacrifice?" Erik said in jest.

"There's no one better equipped for this than you."

"That's because there is no one else, period. The doctors are bitching, but they are following the old dictum, 'when in danger, when in doubt, run in circles, scream and shout.' I hope they are still behind the idea."

Chapter 15

The following day, Jerry joined the senator's team, working on drafting the bill. In five days, they had to finish a rough draft of the bill. This was the first step. They knew, for the most part, it was the senator's aide who OK'd a bill for reading by the senator. The team began making the rounds, hoping to capture a few minutes with the aides of the senators on the committee.

If the head count were right, Senator Hadley would present the bill the following week.

For the next five days, Jerry, Erik and the senator's staff worked on Erik's presentation.

Jerry stated, "Don't forget there is a good chance the trial lawyers will not appose this."

Erik cautioned, "Can we confirm that? It would be great, but I don't want to make a statement and then fall on my face."

"You got the story of the insurance?" Tony, the senator's aide, asked.

"Yes. It's more a matter of availability than affordability. The change in investing from bonds to stocks, and the decrease in the stock market, decreased the amount of premium the company was allowed to write. Looking around to see which line of business could be sacrificed, they found that medical liability insurance was the most labile, so out it went."

He took a deep breath. "One can see, the problem is not money, but rather the availability of coverage. Forming a self-insured trust would provide this coverage at a reasonable premium." Erik waited for comments.

"I'm trying to figure out at what point I would fall asleep during that presentation if I were a senator." Jerry asserted, "There must be a short, concise and passionate punch. The senator has to wake up first. Then the message has to appeal to money, votes or his moral righteousness. If he is awake and he has no vested interest in the bill, he would probably favor the high ground. And here's the kicker: If he is presented with only two facts, he will make a decision between them—even if there are a hundred other facts that should be considered. So, if we give him a poor choice and our splendid choice, he'll go for us!" Jerry looked at the aide, who was nodding his head in agreement.

Tony, the aide, said, "Remember, the senators are presented with about three thousand bills a year! Most routine bills rarely get past the senator's aide. He usually knows which items are of interest to his senator. These get further processing." He paused. "You can see how fortunate you are to be able to address the senators directly."

Bob Griffin joined in on the efforts to educate the senators, individually, before the hearing. "I needn't tell you all this entails, preferably, a visit to the senator's office, or at least a detailed phone call. The A-one-A in guiding a bill to a successful conclusion is to have the senators informed before the hearing, particularly your splendid choice."

By Tuesday afternoon, all of the senators on the hearing committee except for Senator Pope had been contacted. In answer to an inquiry from the senator, Tony said, "The response wasn't too bad. Most of them had heard something about the medical liability problem, at least in a vague way. They were delighted to be given information that is more definitive. You know, when a topic is introduced on the floor, it is comforting for them to have at least a key word concerning the subject." He smiled and added, "It is even better if another senator's expression reflects ignorance of the matter, and your senator can calmly educate him by dropping that key word."

Chapter 16

"I have some last minute calls to make," Griffin said as he rose to leave the meeting.

Jerry stood up. "I think we are about done for today. Bob, I'll go with you to your office. We can talk on the way." He tried to keep his voice at a casual pitch, but the thought of once again seeing Linda Grey, beautiful Linda, Griffin's secretary, had him terrified and jubilant at the same time, terrified by the thought that she would remember him as only another visitor to the office.

But that was not the case. For when she saw him, she smiled. He didn't hear Bob say, "Good night" and "Linda, will you lock up as you leave?" The memory of her warm, light kisses as they had said goodbye that Saturday morning now burst forth. *Say something clever*, he thought. But he was afraid of disturbing the silent joy of just seeing her.

"How nice to see you again." He heard her voice, sweet laughter behind the formal greeting. He took her hand, offered in greeting. A kiss couldn't have been more thrilling.

"Do we hold hands all evening?" she said.

"Oh, I'm sorry." He let go of her hand, and immediately his hand grew lonely. "I've thought of you often since that morning. It was probably the major frustration of my life. I dreamt of how the moment would be, the joy of anticipation, and then to run out of time. A trip from the heights to the depths."

"I should have reminded you that you need to reserve a taxi before you go to sleep if you want one in the early morning."

"Next time I'll rent a car at the airport."

He saw her frowning as she said, "I appreciated the phone calls and letters," again in a teasing voice as soft as velvet.

Jerry winked. "I reached for the phone many times. But what was I going to say? I'm sorry I'm such a klutz in time management. I started to write, but when I saw the words on paper, they either sounded as though I assumed that you cared at all or so casual as to be meaningless, in trying to be me."

"You're forgiven, if you take me to dinner." She waited a moment. "The aggressive modern woman."

He didn't believe it! All the way to Griffins' office, Jerry had concentrated on how to get Linda to have diner with him. All approaches seemed too daring or so insipid as to be washed away with a negative shake of her head. In one direct, truthful declaration, she swept away all affectations. It might be too soon for love, but almost too rich for only infatuation. Whatever, he was thrilled. He had to touch her again. Reaching forward, he cradled her forearm as he helped her from her chair. It was heaven. Lithely, she moved to her feet, bringing her body so close to his.

"Shall we dance?" Again, her mock serious tone had at once described his exact desires and, with the same stroke, declared them taboo for the moment.

The song of love began with the melody that surrounded Linda, soft and weightless with no discordant note, to be heard only by Jerry. The surprise of being able to hear the song filled his soul with unexplained happiness. The wonder that this pure pleasure-creation was willingly floating near him, then toward him, lifted him to the land of joy. His response called for reckless abandon.

"Well, my aggressive, modern woman, continue the roll. You know this town better than I do. Where should we go?"

Love, for Jerry, up until now had been physical. The quest of the fragrance, the touch, the smile, the sound of laughter, the sensual pleasure of a female body pressed against his, dressed and then naked, the explosive release of orgasm and the peaceful, care-free moment of after play were the rewards of the chase.

This was the driving force during the delicious meal. He listened with interest as she described her childhood and the adolescent years. Her words painted a picture of a sweet, initially innocent, shy girl, who gradually emerged from the cocoon to become a beautiful butterfly, even to a cheerleader.

"Give me an L, give me an I, give me an N, give me a D, give me an A." She was sitting, but from the waist up she went through all the motions. Jerry was thrilled.

Early in his approach to bedding a woman, he had learned the art of listening. "And when you finished cheerleading?"

Then she told the tale of her first true love. He was a visiting assistant professor from France, with all the charm and fascination of a handsome foreigner. She had lost her head and her virginity during her last and his first semester at her school.

They had married for love, but also so that he could become a citizen.

After graduation, Linda had first found work in an accountant's office and then moved on to the office of Mr. Griffin.

The freedom and exposure to the real world that came with her finding employment had begun to punctuate the difference in their values. She enjoyed the broad-based, casual attention of the men at work; he had begun enjoying the intimate visitations of the female students. The birth of their daughter had held them tighter for a while.

"Are you sure you're not wearing a white collar? I'm going on as if I were in the confessional."

"No, I want to know you, everything about you." Jerry was still running his formula: Meet her, listen to her and show genuine interest in her.

Linda was silent. An uneasy feeling told her that she might have revealed more than would allow her to keep, in tact, all the veneers of protection that she had built so carefully. Jerry's kind face made her feel less in danger.

"She is now sixteen, my angel. Was my angel. At thirteen, my golden-haired blessing became a monster, stood in the doorway and zapped me with a death ray. I stole that description from Erma Brombeck, but the effect was the same."

"Is she with you now?" It had not occurred to him that Linda might have a child. Somehow, this planned romantic evening and motherhood seemed to belong in different worlds.

Linda asked, "Are you still with us, dear Jerry? In the past, there have been a few 'don't answer the phone calls' after the young man heard 'children.' I noticed the panic signs: face white, fists clenched as he mentally plays back the conversation to see if he had committed himself in any way to this designing woman." Smiling, she said, "Show me your hands." And as Jerry began to obey, she reached out and prevented him. "No need, my dear man."

Still, it wasn't the first time Jerry had begun his game with a mother. In fact, he could remember, with fondness, a short and happy bonding with a single mother and even a happily married mother. "If you are a designing woman, I throw myself into your hands, angel daughter and all." He took her hand and gently kissed the palm.

For Jerry, the rest of the evening was his usual pathway to heaven. For Linda it was exciting. It had been some time since she had enjoyed an evening with such a compassionate, bright and humorous male who was good looking and so accomplished in bed.

Because they spent the night in his room, Linda was the one who had to rise first. Still naked, she stood for a moment, remembering and smiling, as she admired Jerry's body as he slept. She must return home, shower—although they had shared one late last night—get dressed, and be ready for work at 9:00 a.m. With reluctance, she kissed sleepy Jerry goodbye or good morning. The joyful agony mustered by recalling the exquisite emotion of the initial satisfying sex with a new man could muster, engulfed her as she went through the door, only to have it gradually fade at street level.

Chapter 17

Before the session with the Senate committee, Dr Reinhart called a special meeting of the Steering Committee. They were to join Erik and Jerry in Tallahassee. After the casual, irrelevant comments, Stanley stood. "I am sure that you all are aware of the upcoming hearing before the Senate committee. It is imperative that they approve this bill. I have made contact with an insider at the capital. He assures me that if our board hires the right lawyer as a special consultant, he can guarantee the passage of the bill, not only in the committee, but also in the entire House and Senate. The attorney's fee would be ten thousand dollars." He paused briefly. "By the looks on some of your faces, there is some question about this." He was impatient, after all his work. "The trouble with doctors is that they usually live such a sheltered existence there is no need for business moxie. I was once told that the real world moves on a sea of green, and I believe it." He sat down, allowing the thought to seep in.

After a moment, Erik spoke. "I believe you're right, those in our profession are rather naive about pay-offs. We don't need them to survive, unlike most other industries. Even the mafia has been hesitant to demand protection money from us. A mafia patient told me the reason for this is they were afraid of one day looking up from the emergency room stretcher and seeing a revengeful doctor. In any case, I don't think it's the right direction.

Are you sure there isn't the tout syndrome working here? That is, the consultant has no control of the outcome, but if it goes in the right direction he takes the reward, and if not, we have no recourse." Erik was surprised by his spoken position. In his past, he knew of friends who, after paying the first bribe, had every inspector at their door with his hand out. Erik knew his position was right, but feared he had been too blunt.

Stanley shrugged, looking around the room for support.

Dr. Sanchez began, "I am not naive and I have seen successful, sophisticated pay-offs, but in this case I must agree with Erik. If word got out that we didn't take the high road it could derail the whole project." The nodding heads were noted.

"If that's your decision I will proceed no further," Reinhart stated. "I just thought it would be a good idea to have some insurance," he laughed, "to get our insurance."

The meeting ended. Each member walked into the cool night with his own thoughts. This was not black and white, and, having chosen white, the charms of black still lived on.

Chapter 18

The next day, the fateful Thursday finally came. Jerry, Bob Griffin, and Erik were sitting around the small table in the hotel room, going over the last minute details. The room was too small for the comfort of the five directors on the couch facing the table. Dr. Stanley Reinhart got up and walked to the window. Jerry was reading aloud so everyone could hear over the intermittent elevator noise.

After one hour he said, "I think that completes our review for the umpteenth time. I see you followed Bob's advice and picked a red tie."

"It says 'I'm here to fight, so listen,'" Bob explained to the group on the couch.

They were struggling with mixed emotions. Each one was an A-type and was used to being in command. Today they were standing in the wings, giving the strength of numbers and moral support to Erik Nostrom. They were glad he had developed the idea to this point, but were not sure they couldn't have done the job as well.

This ambivalence had caused a minor revolt a few weeks before when it had come time to choose a chairman. Even though Erik had brought them together, they had hesitated to surrender their individuality and their sovereignty of direction to another physician. For a moment this passion had been strong enough to have them look among their number to find another choice, someone who would be less ahead of them in authority, and someone who would be weaker and would allow the glory to be spread around. The fact had completely escaped them that all splendid creations are, as B. Franklin said, one percent inspiration and ninety-nine percent perspiration.

Dr. Stanley Reinhart, leaning on his self-proclaimed interest and sophistication, had campaigned for the job. Because of the failed consultant episode, he was unsuccessful. Hurriedly, they had nominated Dr. Frond. When Dr. Frond had declined the nomination and added a strong statement in support of Erik, the rebellion was over. For public consumption, this had been followed by a unanimous vote for Erik Nostrom as chairman.

Chapter 19

"Don't forget to empty your bladder before you go in." Dr. Reed spoke up.

"Leave it to a pediatrician to contribute that bit of advice," Dr. Garing called from the end of the couch.

The room was warm when the group had initially gathered, and by now, it was stifling. The air conditioning was barely able to handle the human heat load. The foul smell that was unique to an overheated hotel room added to the stress of the challenge before Erik. He experienced a transient episode of nausea. It passed quickly, leaving him more relaxed.

They all left the hotel room in an informal double file. Comments ranged from the weather, the distance to the capital, who was the presiding senator at the hearing, to the observation, often repeated, that in Tallahassee, one could tell a female freshman from a female senior by the size of her calves. This was in reference to the steep sidewalks in this hilly town. But very little was said about the upcoming contest. This subject was still too fragile. If the meeting did not go well, no one wanted to be accused of interfering with Dr. Nostrom or distracting his train of thought. The acceptance that he was truly their leader was still very tentative.

There were 21 people in the audience. The meeting was open to the public. Representatives of the well-established product and liability insurance companies, legal aides representing their bosses, accountants and brokers made up most of the spectators. The two women in the audience were there for the insurance company.

The committee sat in chairs placed in a shallow curve, with the chairman in the center. He could see all the other members of the committee, but he would have to turn his head a bit.

The procedural business of the committee droned on for a while, and then Senator Hadley's bill was announced and discussion began. The printed form of the bill in its entirety had previously been delivered to the senators, or more correctly, to the senators' aides. Rusty Hadley and Jerry, in the preparatory visits to try to sway the vote their way, courted the aides.

Senator Hadley was given the floor. After a "Thank you for allowing me to comment," he outlined the problem at hand, referring to the written material.

"Dr. Nostrom has taken time out of his practice to be here today to give you gentlemen a front-line view of the crisis."

Erik took the chair facing the committee. "Thank you for giving me this time. It is no hardship for me to be here when I consider the importance of this bill. In order to try to solve this problem, in order to assure that the present and the future availability and quality of the medical care exists, Senator Hadley asks for the adoption of the bill.

"This would allow physicians to lend their emotional and financial support to the solution. It may be hard for those not involved in the heath care business to understand the all-encompassing relationships that exist between a physician and his patient. The motto, 'Treat your patient as you would your mother, wife or child' is at the core of rendering care.

"At times, this optimum care carries with it a risk. In fact, almost every step of omission or commission, every prescription written, has risk. Even aspirin may cause bleeding and stomach ulcers. The physician must feel that he and the patient form a team and are on the same side. Although we cannot, at this time, stop this threat of suit to the doctor, our immediate cause is to assure him of the availability of protection in the case of a suit. The bill before you would create that protection."

He took a sip of water from the glass on the table next to him. He sought visual direction from Jerry, who was subtly drawing his forefinger across his throat and mouthing, "Cut it short!"

Erik dropped the next paragraph, which condemned the tort system and went on with the rehearsed speech.

"…It is important that we recognize that a new non-profit entity would have a fairly wide margin of safety when insuring medical liability losses, even if they offered coverage at last year's rates. The bill that is being presented would authorize the formation of a non-profit trust made up of physicians. No capital and surplus limits would be required, but in order to become a permanent company, the entity would have to sign up 500 physicians. These physicians would pay premiums at last year's level, an average of $3,700, which would generate approximately $1,850,000. To render further protection, the physicians must accept unlimited pro rata assessability in the case of the trust falling into receivership.

"In the written material presented, you will find the details concerning legislative and commissioner control, and most other matters."

The representatives from the insurance companies objected to the picture of them leaving because of poor portfolio management.

A senator from the middle of the state asked how the new formation of the Patient's Compensation Fund would affect this trust.

Fortunately, the three men had done a quick review of the possible shape this new concept could take. Erik raised his hand, signaling that he would answer.

"The plan for secondary medical liability insurance to be provided by a fund guaranteed by the state, funded primarily by contributions from the physicians and the hospital would be an excellent compliment to the trust." He was tempted to go on, but realized that the Patient's Compensation Fund was someone else's battle.

A female attorney, with a voice uncharacteristically soft, quoted Mr. Spence's article in *The Herald*. "Perhaps the doctors ought to be self insured." The plaintiff's bar did not want to appear to be in favor of a bill proposed by its enemy, but they knew it would create another deep pocket. As this lack of objection was delivered to the individual senators, the fate of the bill was secure. It would pass.

Following the Senate's action, Erik was given the opportunity to address the House of Representatives. His performance was stellar, as he knew he was supporting a done-deal bill.

Subsequently, the final version passed by the House was simple. It was a two-page enabling addendum to the Omnibus Bill. The trust could be formed and commence business when it had 500 physicians signed up as policyholders, accepting unlimited liability for losses. It was unclear as to where it actually belonged when it came to regulatory details. No one wanted to redo all the descriptions of aspects of the business, nor did they want to define limitations, or establish a proper penalty for violations. Jerry, Erik, Senator Hadley and Griffin sat around the table. "That was the easiest piece of business I've manipulated in some years," the senator said.

"You manipulated?" Jerry's voice was mock angry. "Please give the credit to the lawyers, to me and, Goddamn it, I can't believe it, the plaintiff's bar."

"Here's to you all." Erik raised his glass. "I'm going to call home, get a Jack Daniel's from the honor bar and go to sleep. It has been an exhausting and marvelous day. We are at first base! But then, I never had a doubt." He ducked as they threw imaginary rocks at him. He rose, gave them a tip of the hat salute and before leaving, asked, "Jerry, let's meet in the restaurant, about 7 o'clock? And we can start itemizing the mountain of work, just to make a list for consideration."

"Sounds good to me."

Chapter 20

In his hotel room, he added the liquor to the ice in his glass and sat on the edge of his bed. He slowly came down from the height of satisfactorily completing this phase of creating a company. As nature does, the descent fell past neutral and left him depressed. He thought of home and then called home.

Lacy answered the phone. "She's resting now," Lacy said. The tone in her voice alarmed Erik. He had worked with Lacy in the care of Frances long enough to recognize trouble. "What is it? Tell me now."

"She had an episode of vomiting this afternoon," Lacy responded carefully. "I called Dr. Garing's partner, the neurosurgeon. He just now hung up. He said for me to watch for any changes. So far she's about as she was before the vomiting."

"OK. Listen, I'm stuck here. There's no flight until tomorrow morning. Call me if there are any changes. I'll call you from the airport."

He emptied his glass and fell back on the bed. Silent tears burnt the skin under his eyes. Unreasoning guilt raged in him. "Sure, I'm here, away from her for my own glory. It's not my fault. I loved her, love her. Love her now? Or has she become an obligation, demanding every minute of my life to hide my wish that she be her old self, or be dead? God, I thought it! It's true. Free me from this constant dread that the bleeding expands, leaving her a vegetable.

"The use of all my time, every hour, every day must override my work, my company and be consumed with doing any gesture that in the smallest way eases her or helps her. No, not help her for that is out of my hands. Without words, her eyes beg my presence to cushion the terror she is living. Once free, happy, capable, and now bound into immobility by the invisible ties of the brain damage."

He roared a primitive sound, lasting forever, leaving him spent and somewhat relieved. The wave of misery passed. He returned to behind the shield that had protected him even from his own destructive thoughts. He was able to sleep.

Chapter 21

In response to Jerry's phone call, Linda shopped for their dinner on the way home. She visualized the meal, checking off the ingredients she had at home and those she would have to pick up. Two twelve-ounce Delmonico steaks. She believed that a man preferred the marbleized texture over the New York strip. There would be about an hour after she got home before she would begin cooking. Even this short time could be used for marinating the meat. She had the triple virgin olive oil, balsamic vinegar salad dressing. Pick up garlic and fresh rosemary and thyme. Thankfully, the package of hickory and apple-wood chips had arrived last week for spectacular grilling. A new steak sauce that she had recently heard of on the cooking show was thrown into her shopping cart, as was a horseradish root. From the same show she had just learned of preparing horseradish sauce using ice cubes, horseradish cubes, salt and white vinegar in the blender. Linda prided herself on having the courage to try new adventures in cooking on her guests. Seeing freshly picked corn, she decided to serve this on the cob. Butter was thrown into the cart. Cole slaw with the meal and her favorite parmesan pasta salad as a starter, and the bottle of Merlot completed her cuisine battle preparations.

"When I was younger, it was a dozen red roses," Jerry called as he came through the door. "But as I don't want our togetherness to be ephemeral, I opted for a more lasting floral statement, thus this plant." The pot held a budding and flowering orchid tree, with its delicate, pale violet-white flowers. With the plant still in his hand, she stepped close, hugged his neck and kissed him. Jerry was pleasantly surprised. "I should have brought the forest!"

"You wouldn't have survived," she whispered into his ear, and then touched it gently with the tip of her tongue.

Sitting on the patio under a clear, star-filled sky, deliciously filled with Linda's gourmet touch, relaxed by the mellow Merlot, with Linda's head on his shoulder, Jerry sighed. "Let me die right now because it's never going to get better than this."

She took his hands and slowly helped him up. "Follow me to the boudoir and we'll see." This done in the best May West tone.

She was right, the love was passionately satisfying the hunger until at last they lay exhausted and smiling. In his sleep and on awakening, all aches and pains were gone. His body was twenty-one again. He refused to move from the bed, knowing that the real world awaited him as his feet touched the carpet. Begrudgingly, he responded to her call to breakfast from the kitchen.

For the first time Jerry did not have the urge to depart quickly after sex. Ordinarily, if in the lady's dwelling, he left in the wee hours of the morning. If in his room, he encouraged her departure with a kiss and cab fare. But now, with the passion subsided, he was puzzled by his eagerness just to see her. It was a very mild itch; he would have to analyze it, but for the present, the sight of her controlled it.

Chapter 22

Erik encountered Stanley Reinhart in the lobby of the hotel as Stanley was hurrying for an early morning flight. Erik knew he shouldn't do it, but his bad angel won over. "It seems that we got through on our own. I hope your friend isn't taking credit. He didn't approach you with that line?"

"Of course not. He was just offering his help. We all want this to succeed. Erik, you know if there is anything I can do just call. And congratulations on the progress so far. When are we going to have the next meeting to begin the work in earnest?"

"Probably next Wednesday. My secretary will clear it with the other members of the board and get back to you."

Stanley walked off. As he departed, Erik thought, *Old Stanley has his dagger sheathed for now, but I must watch him carefully. I'm sure the war is not over. It's a shame, for with all the energy Stanley has, he would be a great addition. The trouble is that having shown himself as an adversary, I must waste so much energy evaluating his every move. Oh well, on to meet Jerry.*

"We have an eleven o'clock flight, so let's not get too deep into the planning. What say to a slow breakfast, some generality talk and off to the airport? Only today let's make it on time," Jerry, already seated in a booth, said as Erik reached him.

"With that kind of talk, all I can say is, how was your night?" Erik replied, a playful leer in his voice. "Did you see Linda?"

"Yes, and I think I'm in trouble."

"She's not pregnant?"

"Oh no. But I kept thinking silly thoughts about her ever since I left her. I have to get over that. Where do we begin organizing this beastie?"

"In response to your first comment, watch out, it doesn't sound like the coat-of-protective-armor Jerry I know."

Jerry was silent.

"Enough of that. I told Stanley we would probably get together on Wednesday, but my secretary would confirm it."

"Speaking of dear Dr. Reinhart, he's devious."

"Tell me," Erik said. "I think the first thing we must do is to confirm the participation of the doctors in Gainesville. You were up there recently. Who looks good to you? Remember, we want prime movers and at the same time, they should be team players. Not yes-men, but not obstructionists either. I know there will be one or more members joining Stanley on their own ego trip."

"I've talked to them in their offices, one at a time. Last week, before this meeting, I joined a group of fourteen in the Derby restaurant. I have to tell you, there was initial panic. Then it was as though a rainbow splashed across the room as I outlined the potential solution. At first, some voiced concern about the unlimited liability, but the majority of the doctors accepted that risk." Jerry dug in his pocket and came up with a paper containing a list of doctors names. "These three are all prominent in the medical community, are enthusiastic about the program and are willing to serve on the board. I outlined the responsibility and the time demands." He handed the list to Erik.

"Jesse Gentile, he's in internal medicine, about 55 years old. Thomas Harmon, ob-gyn. We will need that specialty. He said he was 42. And Kenneth Moning, family practice. I didn't plan it, but he's the same field as Stanley. I don't know if that's good or bad."

"If he's a good man, he might act as a buffer. We'll see," Erik said without lifting his eyes from the paper. "You have the CVs of these doctors? We'll need them for presentation to the present board for approval."

"Right here." Jerry handed Erik a manila envelope. "On paper, they all look pretty good. I understand that the Miami group is going to meet on Wednesday, nominate and hopefully elect these men to the board."

Erik shook his head. "I think it would be better if we just enlarged the original group to include these Gainesville doctors. I'd rather not establish a newcomer complex this early in the game." Erik reviewed the data.

After breakfast, they headed for the airport with planned time to spare.

It was a study in contrasts: Jerry up and happy, with visions of Linda dancing in his head, and Erik somber as he contemplated the conditions at home.

Chapter 23

Catherine Collaro was beginning her fourth week as nurse and assistant in Dr. Nostrom's office. Actually, she was one of four girls. Judy Santos had her own office. The other three each had a semi-cubicle behind a curving counter that ran across most of the office.

Shirley Descart sat next to Cathy. Over the four weeks, Shirley had tried to explain her function. "I've been doing billing for ten years. It used to take me one day a week caring for both Dr. Nostrom and his partner, Dr. Stern." She stretched her arms, something she did frequently. "With the onset of Medicare in 1995 and more recently the growth of managed care, like the HMOs, the paperwork increased tremendously."

Watching Shirley scowl and reach for a stack of papers, Cathy said, "Looks like a never-ending job."

"It's not only the forms I need to fill out to collect the fees, it's the handling of denials. The law says the HMOs must pay an authorized and completed request in thirty days."

"That's pretty quick, isn't it?"

"The catch is to get the authorization I need a phone confirmation. Sometimes I wait fifteen to thirty minutes for a satisfactory response."

"Then the money?"

"I wish. No, once I submit with the correct authorization, the form comes back stamped 'denied.' Then I have to identify the cause for the denial and correct it. Sometimes there really is no error. Then I have to call the company again to get another approval. That's thirty minutes more."

"Now the money?"

"Slowly. When you figure time, the postage and the storage, the handling of one claim could cost ten to twenty dollars."

Cathy whistled.

Shirley added, "With the reduction in fees imposed by Medicare, this expense has to be a significant portion of the fee for an office visit."

At another time, Shirley complained, "These are all new procedures to everyone in the medical field including physicians, hospitals, ancillary services, even the venders and the insurance companies themselves. There were no guidelines. It is all trial and error—mostly error."

Cathy smiled at Shirley. "You've become quite valuable."

"I know," she said as she sat snuggly ensconced among her computer, her typewriter files and telephone.

Sharon Flattery, who sat at the first station nearest the door, handled the scheduling of cases, appointments of patients and others, such as detail persons, male and female. She answered the phone and generally did gofer work. She also transcribed the doctor's dictation of his office visits. Her experience working with the medical vocabulary in the hospital's medical record department prior to coming to work at the office nicely equipped her for this task.

Overall management of the office was the purview of Judy Santos. Among other responsibilities, she handled the accounting, overseeing billing, correspondence with all and sundry persons and organizations. It was Mrs. Santos who had taken Catherine through the orientation of the procedures in the office.

In those four weeks Cathy had found Sharon to be a warm, positive girl; that Shirley enjoyed bitching about everything; and that Judy seemed to be a serious, mature, firm but fair boss. Judy conducted the office and practice operation as though it were her own. And all concerned recognized this as a fact. Overall, it was an interesting, pleasant place to work.

Cathy's contact with patients gave her a new view of medical care. In these four weeks, she had become familiar with most of the equipment and the procedures. The initial hesitancy had evolved into a new confidence. When she had first returned to the workplace she was still somewhat gun shy about going to work in an environment of males. At least here there were two men, which should prevent or delay the development of unwanted intimacy.

From the start, she related to Shirley because she had to let Shirley know of any billable procedure performed in the office operating rooms. Sharon was very helpful in supplying the names of certain diseases and procedures. Judy, the office manager, was somewhat distant to all of the staff. It was her fiefdom and she ran it like a benevolent despot. "Good morning, Catherine, please prepare room one for wound dressing." Or some other directional statement. Judy rarely needed to discipline, but when she did, she followed the rule of "praise in public, criticize in private." The sound of "May I see you for a moment in my office?" spoken softly would strike terror in the heart of the recipient of that request. She appreciated Cathy's energy and brightness and was not hesitant to reward it with a "That's nice" or "Well done."

In the short period, Cathy had measured her two doctors: Dr. Mark Stern was rather quiet spoken. He was deliberate in his decisions, at times over deliberate. It was not unusual for him to ask the opinion of several people about the same problem. He gave equal value to each answer, and then, usually unaffected by the advice, made his decision, which was not dissimilar to his decision prior to the enquiries. This behavior satisfied a compulsion, like touching the slats in a picket fence as you walked by. Most of those questioned were flattered when asked their opinion and felt just a bit superior to Dr. Stern, having mistaken this compulsive act for one of ignorance. In his mild but exhaustive pursuit of the right path, his definitive action was usually correct. His peers did not see him as a leader, but seriously considered his opinion and sought his participation in these medical, social and religious circles. He was intelligent and inquisitive about all things medical. His performance at the operating table reflected his need for the complete information before action.

Unfortunately, it is during serious surgery that at times decisions must be made on the incomplete data at hand. There isn't time to retreat to the library for help. One of the joys of surgery is the feeling of satisfaction that comes when you have met the enemy, the pathology you are fixing, and with your own head and hands emerged victorious, and more so if your educated guess on the way was right. Surgeons who experience this high rarely retire willingly from the practice of surgery. Those surgeons who are constantly troubled by the uncharted course strain to proceed past this decision point and are relieved when the case is completed. The results for the patient are similar with either type of surgeon, but only the first type develops the passion and experiences the joy.

Dr. Erik Nostrom was, in many ways, the complimentary half of the team. Not only in surgery, but in all aspects of his life he was willing to take charge of a situation requiring leadership. The blows of errors in his life had toughened him, enabling him, after a miscalculation, to recognize it, be knocked down by it and to be able to lie and bleed a while and then rise to fight another day. The fear of physical harm had been conquered in his past, where in street fights and boxing in the ring, he had received and survived many a powerful blow. With maturing this freedom from physical fear helped quell all fears, which at his age and station in life were rarely physical. But he began to notice that when faced with a significant decision, he experienced just a transient quiver in his epigastrium, relieved by choosing a course of action. For him, surgery was truly a joy, the more complicated, the more challenging, the better. This had led him first into general surgery and then into vascular surgery with its smaller margin for error. He rarely showed his anger or laid blame for a bad situation in which he was in any way a participant. He had the ego necessary for a good surgeon; if something went wrong in his world he was responsible for not being prepared or for not anticipating the error. And if he were to blame, how could he get angry with someone else? His mother had once told him he was not responsible for the rain.

As Cathy became more comfortable at her job, it was a pleasure, each morning, to awaken to a new day.

Chapter 24

Rudolph Collaro, Catherine's husband, was four years older than Cathy. At the time they met, this age difference, eighteen and twenty-two, was significant. He was strong and an adult while she was still a teenager. She was flattered by the attention of a grown-up man. Having no brothers to guide her, the world of men was a pleasant mystery.

When she had been nine years old, her father was killed in a plane crash. Her mother, Annabelle Ipolleto, did not remarry but had two romantic interludes while Cathy was growing up. The duration of each affair had not been long enough for Cathy to be truly influenced by the men, although each one had taken on the role of a very casual father figure during his stay. Cathy had felt safe with these men. They had flattered her and had been good to her without being scary, all in the attempt to get into the good graces of Annabelle.

From them, Cathy drew a one-facet picture of the adult man. He was kindly, generous and unthreatening. It should be nice to have a serious boyfriend and even a husband. As a girl in her teens, she experienced a nervous, pleasant thrill when she thought of this.

Her only sexual history was an awkward two-and-a-half minute penetration under the boardwalk one summer at twilight. She had not had an orgasm and left the event unimpressed by the wonders of sex. Her girl friends told her fantasies of physical love, but she could not seriously relate her experience to these.

It was not until she met Rudy that she had a relationship long enough and intimate enough for her to willingly participate in sexual activity. Once she felt the quivering build up of tension, the exploding crash of release with climax, and the exhausting contentment of after-play, she became a true enthusiast.

Marriage, pregnancy and motherhood followed in short order. The explosion became a pleasant pop, and life settled down into handling the day-by-day problems of adult-married-parent life.

For two years, she cared for her beautiful son, Cash. He was her passion. Having escaped the neonatal colic, he slept all night and was gurgling and laughing all day. Cash compensated for any fading emotional reward from Rudy. She was in love to a depth only a mother-child bond could plunge. She ignored any signs of competitive posture from Rudy.

Cash learned quickly. His walking, crawling and stumbling were so delightful; Cathy couldn't resist swooping him up in her arms and dancing across the room.

Nasal bleeding was the first sign of acute leukemia. With lightning speed, it ravished him, and he was gone.

She was devastated, unable to function. With time, the pain and the sadness, which produced tears, did retreat to forever lie in the recesses of her mind.

She began functioning, walking, one step at a time, handling one day at a time. Life returned, like a palm tree after a hurricane—richer, stronger, but with scars from the catastrophic event. The need for a refuge outside of the house sent Cathy looking for her first job.

Chapter 25

By her fourth week at work, Cathy was comfortable with the two doctors and the staff.

After helping Mrs. Willard to the counter for assignment of her next appointment, Cathy walked down the corridor to the second examining room. Dr. Nostrom was already there. He had completed his evaluation of Mr. Samson's pulses as Cathy entered.

"That's pretty good," he said to the patient and nodded to Cathy. "I feel bounding pulses on both sides of the legs. You should be able to get back to tennis." He explained to Cathy, "When he was unable to get on the tennis court—he plays singles mostly—he was forced to come see me."

"I'm so glad I did. I'm brand new. In every way." He winked at Dr. Nostrom, finished dressing and headed for the front desk to get the time for his appointment.

"What was that wink all about?" Cathy asked as she removed the old paper covering the leather of the examining table and replaced it with a new sheet from the roller at the head of the table.

"Sometimes there are fringe benefits in this business. You know, we put in a graft from the aorta to both external iliac arteries, bypassing the blocked common iliac arteries?"

"Yes. But I still don't know—"

Erik interrupted her. He hesitated and moved to the sink to wash his hands. "One of the branches of the reconstituted iliac artery is the internal pudendal artery, which gives off the artery to the penis."

He glanced over to see if she was blushing. She had been with him for four weeks, but he didn't know if anatomically correct labeling would upset her. Her face was blank.

He went on, "When the blood flow in that artery is interrupted, as his was before surgery, there is no joy in the joystick—oh, I'm sorry, I meant he was unable to have an erection. At times, when the flow is restored with a bypass, this function returns. Apparently Mr. Samson is one of the fortunate ones."

"Did he expect this gift? I suppose this is a gift. In one of my classes the professor said the Greek Athenians required their judges to be over seventy years old because at that age, they were free of sexual passion and therefore could think clearly."

"I'm sure he thinks of it as a gift, even if he can't be a judge."

"It must be very satisfying to get such good results and to have the patient so grateful."

"I get mixed blessing from the wives. Some come and kiss my hand, others imply that it was good to be out from under him, literally, and now he's back again."

"Is that really so?" She busied herself, smoothing out the table sheet.

"Yes, and that is not the only unexpected outcome. I once had a relatively young man complaining of intermittent claudication—that is, the inability to walk a half a block without pain in the calf requiring him to stop and rest for five minutes before he could cover another half a block. Well, this man—I think he was forty-eight—said he was a swamp inspector requiring extensive walking through the marshes and mud and he could no longer do his job.

"He had a blocked femoral artery, which we corrected with a bypass graft. Two months after the operation he returned for a routine visit. He said everything was fine and he was back doing his job and he was grateful."

"Returned another human to gainful employment. Did you get a gold star?" They finished in the room and went into the hall.

He held up his hand in a stopping motion. "Not quite. Four months later, I had a detective as a patient. We were talking about results and I was bragging a little about this success. He said he'd never heard of a swamp inspector. Being from New York I didn't know. 'What did you say this man's name was?' the detective inquired.

"'Fredrick Walsh, why?'

"'Fredrick Walsh, Fredrick Walsh, I know that name. Let's see. Let me use your phone.' He called headquarters. 'Steve, does the name Fredrick Walsh ring a bell?' He listened, then, 'That's what I thought.' The detective turned to me, laughing. 'Your Fredrick Walsh is a second-story burglar. We caught him last week.'

"I said, 'I only have one question. Did he get caught because he couldn't run away?'

"'Oh, no. It took a patrol car to catch him.'"

"Is that a true story?" Cathy asked.

"Essentially, yes."

As Dr. Nostrom dictated the findings of his last patient, Cathy returned to the front desk to call for the next patient.

Chapter 26

Jerry was sitting in his borrowed office in Tallahassee. He finished his coffee while listening to the phone. "Thanks for calling. I'll get back to you with the details." He hung up. Leaning forward, he put a check mark at the one hundred and seventh call.

He called Erik in Miami. "Get ready for your fifteen minutes of greatness. The news of the enabling act has circulated throughout the state. The first call I got was from a Dr. Rumkin. He said it was just another empty offering that will never materialize. He was pretty poetic: 'It is headed for an apathy-fueled failure, just like the last attempt to organize.'"

"That's the greatness? I can't wait for the bad news."

"The next one hundred and six calls either asked reasonable questions or said basically, 'Thank God Nostrom and his gang are doing something about the crises."

'They have God and Nostrom a little too close together. The last time I had a halo, it dropped eight inches and became a noose."

"You always take positive comments so easily?"

"What else?" Erik walked around his desk and sat down. He realized the rain had started. He became aware of its unique smell through the window.

"It's funny how once a doctor buys into the idea, he goes overboard as though it were a new thought. A Dr. Goodoff went on to inform me that he knows the doctors are concerned because malpractice premiums are beginning to really cut into his total income, though not to the level of sacrifice.

Another doctor let me know it wasn't so much the money as it was the fear and panic of not having coverage and having to fend for themselves in the case of a suit. His brilliant conclusion: that is why the doctors are going to join our company. I thanked him."

"What would we do without them?" Erik asked.

Erik pondered the fate of the doctor who was sued. With coverage, the doctor who received a notice from a plaintiff's attorney initiating a medical liability lawsuit merely forwarded the complaint to his carrier with a brief note summarizing the circumstances. More often than not, that would be the last he would hear about the case, except for a note from the insurance company stating that the case had been resolved, satisfactorily.

"It goes on," Jerry said, relating the phone calls to Erik. "This doctor asked what happens if he doesn't get coverage. I told him if you're not sued, nothing happens. He was silent, and then asked, 'OK, I meant what happens if I'm sued?' I pulled the goblins out of the closet and said, 'The plaintiff's letter will make you weak in the knees and a little nauseated, then terror will begin climbing up your spine, triggering spurts of perspiration as it travels.'"

"You didn't?"

"I did and the doctor is with us."

"You're tough."

"Not really, I didn't tell him about the generic '*mea culpa*' attitude that the uninsured physicians carry around in their back pockets that springs forward in full view as soon as he sees the claim notification. He suddenly remembers the patient and the conversation in which the patient said he was not the suing kind. And to get out from under will testify against his insured brethren."

Erik said, "That's so true." He knew the first thing the uncovered doctor had to do was get an attorney. At this point, the doctor would pay a king's ransom to have had coverage. But like healthy young people who found no reason for health insurance, did not buy it, and regretted not having it when they got sick, the physician had only a nagging concern about coverage and did not leap at the first offer. In the case of this newborn company, almost still in utero, he hesitated, even though this may be the only option open to him.

Jerry did a quick summery and hung up.

Erik walked to the first examining room, smiled at Cathy, and was glad to get the respite from the insurance problem by burying himself in patient care.

Chapter 27

In preparation for the board meeting on Wednesday, Jerry called each of the board members to give them the details of the three physicians from Gainesville, emphasizing the need for having wider geographical representation on the board. "I did the spin," Jerry told Erik. "Now it's your turn. The only one who gave me a hard time was…"

"Don't tell me. Dr. Stanley Reinhart?"

"Right. He was curt. He asked me if I take orders solely from you. He told me you were only one of the members." Jerry changed the tone of his voice, continuing to mock sternly, "You are the chairman just to have someone run the meetings. Business decisions are determined by all of us!" Jerry switched to a normal voice. "He then asked how the other members reacted. I told him that in the end, they all seemed to agree. Just a minute, my other line is buzzing."

Erik took down the phone and massaged his earlobe; he then cradled the phone on his shoulder. Jerry's voice returned. "That was Reinhart. He wants the phone numbers of all the board members I just talked to. This sounds like his first direct confrontational move."

Erik said, "I hope he's not planning on getting to me through you." He pondered his next move. "I'll give all of them a follow-up call. I think I'm in a better position to tell them about your research to find the candidates and to narrow them down to three."

He called each member, saying, "I would ask you to withhold your disbelief and, because of the urgency, consider accepting Jerry's choices. You will have an opportunity to meet them at our next meeting." He went on to say, "I know there are members of our group who feel the Miami physicians were the founders and did the initial work and should be recognized as such. That may be so, but Miami and Gainesville are going to be together for some time. I would like to avoid a newcomer-north vs. original founders-south conflict. So, I think it would be better if the Gainesville group come in as the last three original founders and board members, rather than going through the nominating procedure."

He was able to contact all of the members. He didn't mention Reinhart's position.

Dr. Jack Reed, Dr. Thomas Frond and Dr. Anthony Sanchez listened, and after a few questions, they agreed. Richard Garing gave his consent pending seeing the physicians. If he was greatly dissatisfied, he wanted the right to challenge. Fredrick Canon asked for some details of the financial arrangements, including travel cost and loss-of-time reimbursement.

Erik said, "Like the rest of us, initially there will be no compensation."

Erik would like to have waited one more day before calling Dr. Stanley Reinhart. Unfortunately, he did not have the luxury. As soon as Reinhart hung up from talking with Jerry and getting the list, he called Erik.

Reinhart, talking to Erik, said, "I am calling to let you know that I have talked with Jerry and I agree with your actions. Ordinarily I would have liked to have more discussion by the entire board, but it is urgent and this is a good solution."

Chapter 28

Jerry and Erik sat in the doctor's lounge drinking coffee. "It looks like we are going to get away with bringing in the Gainesville doctors as the last of the founding fathers." Jerry gave the OK sign with his thumb and forefinger.

"Even Reinhart, in his fashion," Erik said. "There is one other aspect to consider, and we have to resolve it before the meeting." Erik had given a time-priority to each aspect of the venture. He approached it much as he would a complicated surgical operation: Do it in the time of emotional neutrality, long before the stresses blur optimum clarity. "One practical and essential step is to get a place to operate, but even more important is getting a CEO."

"Even before we find a place to put him?"

"Yes. I can remember, some time ago, a group of us were trying to form a medical purchasing company. All we had was a board of directors, seven chiefs, no Indians, like we have now. We would meet every Wednesday. 'We aught to do this and we aught to do that,' we would say. But no one was capable or favorably inclined to do any of those detailed things. There was no progress. Eventfully, we hired a CEO. Within a week, we had a hall and a secretary and things began to happen."

"Back to earth, Erik," Jerry said. "I have one who could be a winner. Name's Paul Arpin. 44 years old, at the present working as in-house attorney for Parley's Carpet Co."

"Did he pass the bar?"

"I'll check. He's bright, not overly aggressive, strange for a lawyer."

"Maybe that's why he's not in private practice. Is he aggressive enough for us?"

"He's been with the carpet company for seven years. A few years ago he had a hand in reorganizing the four stores." Jerry had been impressed with Arpin originally, but as Erik probed, he realized his was a rather superficial screening.

"You're comfortable with Arpin?"

"I thought so until you began nitpicking."

"Don't sulk. You know the devil is in the details." Erik got up to refill the coffee cups.

"Ready for Dr. Nostrom in room five." The squawky voice came over the intercom.

Erik quickly filled Jerry's cup. "Gotta go. Call Judy to set up an appointment."

"Will do."

Erik disappeared through the door leading to the operating rooms. Jerry stood up, took a guarded sip of the hot coffee, put the cup down and left for the parking lot. Using his new car telephone, he called Judy. When he finished, he suddenly smiled and on impulse, he dialed Tallahassee.

On Wednesday, Erik came out of his office and into the waiting room. "I'm Dr. Nostrom. Erik," he added. He reached out his hand to a tall, heavy man who seemed comfortable in his open-necked sports shirt under a navy blue jacket.

The man moved easily as he stood to greet Erik. "I'm Paul Arpin." He showed a disarming smile. "Glad to meet you. I think Jerry rates you pretty high."

"Did you have any trouble finding the place?"

"No, Judy's directions were very clear." They walked into his office and sat in the chairs in front of Erik's desk.

Arpin appeared nervous at first, but as he talked, he became animated. "Jerry outlined your operation here. The story sounds exciting."

"Do you know anything about insurance? Oh, before that, did you sit for the bar?"

"You're smiling?"

"I'm sorry, it's an inside joke. I kidded Jerry for not asking."

"Yes, I did. I am a full-fledged lawyer. But applying the law to business is more interesting for me." He sat up in his chair and paused as he began a new subject. "My knowledge of insurance is limited to my review of policies for my carpet business. But I have been taking a crash course on malpractice from a friend who is a lobbyist. He sent me a couple of articles. I didn't realize how much money is involved in an insurance company."

"Pretty industrious."

"But the real bird's-eye view came from my family doctor. I was amazed by the amount of distress the crisis had generated."

"And?" Erik asked.

"I'm interested. But I would be leaving a secure job with good money and future."

Erik threw up his hands. "You've come to the wrong place."

"What do you mean?"

Erik guessed that Jerry had made the job seem easily obtainable, which needed to be corrected if Erik was going to get Arpin at a reasonable price. "Our venture is going to be a rocket ride, with all the sparkles, but it could burn out and crash, and we don't have a complete handle on the controls. So security and future don't rank high on our assets." He could see Arpin's face get a little whiter.

Erik outlined a basic salary with a sparse benefit package.

"It wasn't what I expected."

Erik stood up and offered his hand to Arpin. "Think it over. It's cutting edge, but I know it has its bad edge too."

Arpin hesitated at the door, as though he was to say something, but left without speaking.

Erik smiled, thinking, *I should like to play poker with Arpin.*

On Friday, Arpin called and was hired, pending the usual approvals.

Chapter 29

The board, including those from Gainesville, met in Erik's office on Wednesday.

Dr. Cannon was the last to enter. "I hope getting a new office is high on the priority list. Your reception room accommodated us with little space to spare." He frowned. "You all look like a packed house on opening night."

Jerry made the introductions. "From Gainesville I'd like the present doctors Jesse Gentile, Thomas Harman and Kenneth Moninger." There was applause.

At first, the conversation was rather formal, particularly from the Gainesville trio.

But then, Gentile spoke for the group. "We all recognize the need for the project to become a reality." He turned to the other two, looking for support. "But we are not especially happy with the control resting entirely with the Miami contingent."

Erik held up his hand. "I can say, knowing the folks from Miami, you will not run into any block voting. A good idea is just that, and will be recognized as such, whether it comes from Miami or Tallahassee or anywhere in between."

He realized he was scowling and tried to register a smile. "Dr. Gentile, I'm glad you presented the opportunity for us to clear the air. We truly are all in this boat together." His smile broadened. "I hope we all can swim."

Multiple voices filled the air.

"Good evening," Erik called out over the conversational buzz. "I know you all met for the first time tonight. It might be useful if we each introduce ourselves and give a few words. Dr. Reed, would you like to start and we'll go around clockwise?" The physicians from Gainesville visibly bristled. Here was this Miami Erik Nostrom already acting as the controlling force. They knew it was too late to suggest an alterative leader, but nonetheless they were uncomfortable.

"Sure. I'm Jack Reed, and I'm a pediatrician" Out of habit, he spoke with measured tones as though he were addressing children. "I'm not much into politics, but this business needs all the help it can get."

One by one, each man declared his name, rank and serial number, with predictably solemn comments. Attempts at humor fell flat, tripping over the difference in the culture between the north and the south. This difference in values was destined to reappear in discussion and votes throughout the life of the company.

During this introductory process, Dr. Stanley Reinhart was silent as he studied each of the men from Gainesville, trying to determine which of them could be manipulated to see that Reinhart would be more capable than Erik at running the operation because of his sophistication and his business smarts.

Erik outlined the immediate tasks to be accomplished. Dr. Garing said, "The first on the list is appointing a CEO." They all agreed.

Erik smiled. It was as though Dr. Garing was a straight man in the act.

"Jerry and I have interviewed a candidate who looks pretty good." He excused himself and walked into his office. Coming out he said, "I would like to introduce Mr. Paul Arpin."

The group struggled to make room for him in the middle of the couch.

Dr. Sanchez said, "Mr. Arpin, the first thing we need is a bigger conference room."

"Here, here!"

Erik went to his closet and brought a folding chair. He offered it to Arpin. In his position, Arpin faced the circle of the members of the board.

After an extended discussion, most of the members appeared to be satisfied with Jerry's choice for CEO.

When Reinhart saw a questioning look on the faces of the three Gainesville physicians, he jumped on the opportunity to become their spokesman. "I would like to clarify one point before we hear from Mr. Arpin. Are we now to ratify your selection, Erik, or can we consider Mr. Arpin as one of many candidates?"

Erik pushed, "Let's complete the interview with Mr. Arpin; then we can consider the options. I have an opinion on the matter as I am sure others of you do."

He pointed toward Paul. "Why don't you give the board a rundown and then we can have a question-and-answer session for as long as there are questions?"

"Sounds good to me. I'm Paul Arpin..." He then explained to the board members all that he had discussed with Erik and Jerry, without covering the salary question. He was sure the subject would come up in the conversation after he left.

He then answered questions about his education background—BA and Law at Florida State; his family—wife, Natalie, and two boys; his hobbies—fly fishing; and the kind of car he drove—a Volvo. When there seemed to be an end to the reasonable questions and before the group began stretching their inquiry into his sex life or some other inappropriate subject, Erik stood up. "Paul, did you survive the Spanish Inquisition?"

"It was a pleasure." He turned to include all of the board in his comments. "If you choose me I am sure I am going to enjoy working with you. This business offers a great opportunity." He looked at the faces. "And some challenges. Since talking with Dr. Nostrom I realize there are no traditional landmarks available to determine past experience when the company is using the claims-made method."

Dr. Reed held up his hand. "Do you have a good grasp on this claims-made form of insurance? It is new to most of us." Some of the others nodded in agreement.

Dr. Stanley Reinhart stood up slowly, striking the posture of the professor. "I have taken the time to spend several hours with the insurance department. Paul, correct me if I'm wrong, but this is my understanding:

"There are two major approaches. Occurrence rate covers the loss in the year that it occurred, no matter when it is claimed. In Florida, a patient can report an untoward event for up to four years after the fact and still be within the statutes of limitation." He stood behind Dr. Gentile. "With occurrence, coverage of the claim would be honored. So, the doctor is fully protected against any event arising in the year he is covered. His premium would reflect that." He paused. This was an unexpected opportunity for him to strengthen his eventual bid for leadership. Paul was in agreement with Reinhart's comments so far.

Reinhart continued, "The other form of coverage is 'claims-made.' I understand this is the form we plan to adopt. Here the doctor is covered for any claim arising in the year he is covered. The significant difference is that only approximately 30% of the malpractice events are reported in the year they happen. Companies offering claims-made coverage, in its first year, would only have to reserve for 30% of the risk that would ultimately arise out of that year."

Paul interrupted, "It is similar to jewelry insurance, which only insures against theft for the year you seek coverage, not for the life of the jewel. You can see it would cost much more to insure the jewel against theft for life. Claims-made covers for the year against claims presented in that year, but does not insure for life against any claim arising from that year. I don't know if that helps."

Stanley shook his head and continued, "Theoretically the premium should be considerably less in the first year for claims-made than for occurrence coverage where they accept 100% of the risk arising out of that year." He thought about half the board members followed the explanation. He sat down.

When he saw the interview was over, Arpin bid good night to the group and left. Erik had assured Paul he would call him the next day.

"As I mentioned earlier, I would have liked to have the opportunity to interview other candidates," Stanley Reinhart voiced, "but I must say that I congratulate Jerry for his selection. This man looks like a good choice. In the name of expedience, I would like to make a motion to accept Paul Arpin as our new CEO." Even in defeat, Reinhart managed to grasp a possible victory, not only in his explanation of the insurance forms, but for now it would be recorded that the nomination came from him and he might be able to use it later on in his positioning Arpin onto his side.

The motion was approved unanimously. Erik then presented the details of the compensation package. After inquiry and suggestions, the board accepted the terms. The meeting ended soon thereafter. Jerry and Erik stayed after the remainder of the board left, to go over the schedule of events for the next few weeks.

Erik summarized, "So far so good. Paul will answer the administrative needs, but the real hearts of the matter in insurance operations are credentialing and handling of claims."

Chapter 30

When Jerry, Erik and Paul met the next day, they began working on a critical line of development. Paul said, "I started with those items that would take the longest. In order of things, locating an office, hiring personal including an accountant, a secretary, a receptionist and a marketing man came to mind."

"All this is well and good, but the cold facts of life are screaming; funding comes before all else," Jerry pointed out. "Each of the board members has pledged $10,000. Remember one of the limiting factors in choosing the Gainesville crowd was their willingness to commit to that amount. Paul, your first job is to get the money."

"I worked for the United Way for a few years. This should be a snap. Maybe you and Dr. Nostrom could make an appointment call to remind them that I am coming."

"My pleasure. Paul, please make it Erik, unless we are in the OR," Erik said seriously and then smiled.

"OK, now we have the money. Paul, I think finding an office and the administration staff should be your choice primarily. Jerry will have to pass on the females you hire. You don't know it but feminine charm is his specialty."

Paul was taken aback. Could male supremacy really prevail?

"Paul, I'm kidding. It's an inside joke. I'm sorry."

"You had me going there for a while." Paul then grinned. "I'll have to watch you."

"One way to get expertise in credentialing and in claims management quickly, as we need, is to follow the good old American custom: steal them from another company.

"A CEO who is a good manager in one field can easily become a good manager in another field, like you, Paul; you should make the transfer nicely. It's different for claims and credentialing. A claims man's ability depends largely on his past experience in that line. To a lesser extent, this applies to credentialing. And so, off we go with burglar's mask in place."

The three of them sat in thought. Jerry looked up. "Recently I heard of two claims men who are restless in their present positions. The first is Edward Hartman. He's in California with Physician's Mutual. You know there is a good amount of art in this claim-management business. Well, it appears that his CEO tends to micro-manage all departments, including his, and he is unhappy."

"I met Ed last year at a conference," Erik remembered. "At that time I was attending a medical meeting held in the same hotel as the insurance groups. We shared a breakfast table. Talk about a small world. You know how you tend to tell your troubles to strangers when the need is great? That must have been his condition for he ran off on how his boss does micro-manage. I didn't think much about it at the time, but that was his problem."

"It sounds like it might be worthwhile for you, Erik, to give Edward a call. Who knows?" Paul suggested.

Jerry continued. "The other man who has a great reputation as an insurance executive with some experience in claims-made form is located in Tallahassee. Greg Boykin. He was handed the presidency of a liability company, which almost immediately went into receivership. I don't think he was to blame. He tried every trick in the book to save it. I think that is where he really learned the business."

"I can understand that," Paul ventured.

The group discussed other candidates. Paul had worked with a bright young man who was completing the insurance coverage for his carpet stores. Jerry, who had been involved with other insurance people when he was handling product liability cases, reeled off a few names. They then talked about the attributes they needed in the man they hired. In the end, the plan was for Erik to talk to Mr. Edward Hartman and, if necessary, fly out to California to interview him. Jerry was assigned the task of contacting Mr. Greg Boykin in Tallahassee.

Jerry said, "I'll try to set up a meeting on Friday. I have some other things to do while I'm up there so I'll probably stay and come back on Monday." He tried to present this as a matter-of-fact statement, but his excitement showed.

"Remind me to play poker with you," Erik whispered.

"What do you mean?"

"Written across your forehead is one word. Linda."

"The thought did cross my mind. But business comes first. If I have to sleep with Greg Boykin instead of Linda, so be it." He punched Erik on the shoulder and turned to Paul. "Linda is a secretary I know in Tallahassee, no big deal."

"That so?" quipped Erik.

So Erik was off to Los Angeles, Jerry headed for Tallahassee and Paul remained at home to find an office, staff it and generally start the operation rolling. There would be phone communication at least daily.

Chapter 31

Back in his bachelor's pad, Jerry couldn't wait to get to the phone. Linda's answering service spoke. Jerry left the message for her to call him ASAP.

He had decided to catch the evening flight if possible. He could be in Tallahassee Friday morning, see Greg during the day and have Friday night, all day Saturday and Sunday free to seduce Linda. He thought of their last time together. The visions slowly cleared. Was it truly a recall or was it as he would like to remember? She had taken him by the hand, gently leading him to the bed, undressing him until he had lain supine and naked, facing her as she had stood at the foot of the bed. It was a reversal of the usual scene; Linda was seducing him. In his vision he was free of self-consciousness about his erection; rather he smiled as she admired him. With lover's music, she freed herself of the soft white, silky garment, revealing her exquisite body. The phone rang, the harsh blare of its tone shattering his reverie.

"You called?" Linda asked.
"I'm not too sure that I am glad to hear from you."
"Why?"
"I was having the sexiest daydream."
"About me, I hope."
"Of course."
"Good. The next time we're together, I'll try to remind you."

"Actually, that's why I called. I think I'm going to be in Tallahassee from late Thursday until Monday. I have to do about three hours of work on Friday and then I'm free."

"Beautiful! Oh, I forgot, Cassy called earlier today. She's coming here from her school on Sunday afternoon. That leaves the rest of the time free on my calendar. Maybe I'll meet you at the airport. We will have Thursday night to start."

"Start what?"

"Baby, if you don't know by now you are in deep…trouble."

"I'm willing to learn."

"Classes begin on…when does your flight get in?"

"The airline started a new time schedule; they now have an evening flight from here to Tallahassee. It gets in about 9:30 p.m."

"I'll see you there."

Linda hung up and just sat there, planning the weekend. It was poor timing for Cassy, her daughter, to be coming, but then maybe it could work out. Jerry would have a chance to meet Casey and vice versa. She called Megan McGriff to cancel a luncheon date for Saturday and called Estella Phillips, hairdresser, to get her hair done. Finally, she asked Mr. Griffin, her boss, for Friday off as she had a minor emergency. After he was assured there was nothing he could do to help her, he said OK.

Finishing her calls, Linda ran through her wardrobe, picking out evening sports to meet him and have a midnight snack. No need for sleeping gowns, hopefully. Day wear for Friday? That bra and sweater combination that drove the boys wild. Saturday and Sunday would take care of themselves. For a moment, she could see a night and two days of sex, eating in her room and nakedness. It made her giggle and stroke her body from her cheeks to her breasts to her buttocks. Unconsciously she pulled in her belly.

Walking to the bathroom, she checked the pills. Fortunately, she was in mid-cycle and did not have to worry about end-cycle cramps at an inopportune time.

The phone call just before she left for the airport startled her. Was Jerry delayed, or worse, did he have a change of plans? But no, it was Cassy. Her roommate had left for a long weekend and Cassy would like to come on Saturday instead of Sunday. "You know how much I hate to be alone."

Linda didn't know which was worse, Jerry canceling his plans or Cassy coming for the weekend. Of course, she said yes to Cassy. Now she must break the news to Jerry when they would meet.

WANT IS A GROWING GIANT

The meeting, the trip to the restaurant, the conversation and the unspoken thrill of the hello kiss and casual touching were soft and warm.

Jerry had mixed emotions about Cassy's visit. He was anxious to meet her, but would have rather seen her on Sunday. Linda squeezed Jerry's arm as his words relieved her of her anticipated fear of a daughter-lover conflict.

Reaching her apartment, it began. As though it were guided by an unseen stage director, they floated through the scenes of his recent fantasy, him reaching the part where he was lying on his back, naked, smiling, with her at the foot of the bed. Her nipples were hard and pointing, her hips were tilted forward, showing the soft curve of the Venus monde and the soft curly hair of her vulva.

"You are beautiful."

"Thank you."

"You are beautiful."

"I know." She moved toward him and they were lost in silence, except for the groans of joy.

Chapter 32

Jerry rose early in the morning, having had three hours of sleep. In the shower, he felt the pleasant ache of sex as he thought of last night. As he dressed, he felt light and young and strong, ready for the day's challenge. If they were together, would it always be this way? Would they have this passion? Of course not, but even a part of it would be wonderful.

Once in the cool air of the street the memory dimmed a little, and he began to readjust his thinking. *Back away from the cliff just a little, young man, be careful.*

Greg Boykin was a large man, but he had an excellent tailor so that his bulk was framed perfectly, making him appear imposing rather than fat. "Good morning, Jerry. It's been some time."

They reminisced about Greg's past experiences in the insurance business and about bird hunting. Greg came out a hero in both sequences, by his recollection. Jerry brought Greg up to date as to where they were in the insurance company, particularly about them just beginning to structure the indemnity policies.

Boykin said, "Do I understand you right? You want to go with claims-made format exclusively?"

"That's our plan."

"Good luck!" he snorted. "There are at least a couple of reasons against that, I know. First, it will be hard to sell the concept, particularly when there is an additional fee if the doc wants to leave your company. The new company the doc applies to won't insure him for that. He will have to purchase separate coverage for the tail."

Jerry said, "On the other hand, the first year premium will be much lower, and he has the difference in dollars in his pocket to invest until he leaves. We are thinking of offering free tail coverage if the physician retires after being with us for more than five years." Jerry outlined the justification for the new method of insurance. He reminded Greg that this form was used when the physician's wife insured her jewelry.

Greg wasn't impressed with the argument. "Another reason this would be risky is there is no significant actuarial data available. ISO," Greg reminded Jerry, "the study used most often, is, for the most part, based on occurrence coverage. With claims-made you have no history to lean on. For projecting future risk, you need a good ten years' experience. Here, with claims-made you have practically nothing."

Jerry thought about this for a moment. "This is true, but we may be able to get a buffer by setting the premiums at a conservative level. After all, the physicians will instinctively compare our rates with what they paid last year, as occurrence."

"Who will be handling credentialing?"

"We are still looking."

"Well, this could be crucial. If the credentialing is loose, it could play havoc with claims. I'd like to have a say in who is going to fill that slot," Greg came back, his hands folded across his belly. "I'd also need to report directly to the board. From what you say, your CEO is at the bottom of the learning curve." Greg leaned forward. "Remember, I bring a hell of a lot of experience to the table. I'm not sure I want to risk my reputation serving under a newlywed." He laughed at his putting Paul in the white gown. The rest of the hour was spent going over details, Greg reinforcing the strength of his past ventures.

Jerry left Greg's office and returned to Linda's apartment. "Do you mind if I set up a conference call to Miami and Los Angeles? I'll charge it to my office. That will go on my bill to the insurance company, whenever they are able to pay."

"Don't be silly, my phone is your phone, my home is your home, and so it goes."

"You know why I love you?"

"I'm a cheap phone?"

"That's right." Jerry picked up the phone and arranged the conference call.

"Greg is not our man."

Chapter 33

"That is my last thought about business until Monday." Jerry and Linda then began a delicious marathon of loving, loafing, laughing, listening and talking. Food was tastier; the wine was superb.

"Groan! That's all I have left." Jerry fell on the bed next to Linda and carefully entwined his body with hers. It was 2:00 a.m. on Saturday morning. Their eyes closed at the next moment.

Sleep was deep and refreshing, coming after indulging in the delights of intercourse of many flavors, eating, and drinking to the edge of gluttony. At seven o'clock, the wake-up alarm began quietly tinkling but grew louder with each second. Being unaccustomed to the right side of the bed, Jerry was disoriented, his arm ineffectually flaring out toward the bed stand.

"I got it," Linda called out as she rolled onto her side to quiet the clock.

It was as though they were donning new uniforms, those of sobriety and free of sensuality, as they dressed for the day, preparing to welcome Cassy.

The first greeting between Cassy and Jerry at the airport went smoothly enough. Linda made introductions with what she thought were affectionate and humorous descriptions. Then Jerry made the first error. Cassy's friendly, almost warm manner had fooled him.

"When do you go back?" As soon as the words were out of his mouth and he saw the sneer cross Cassy's face, he knew it was a mistake.

"Can't wait to get rid of me?" She did it as though it was an amusing comeback, but the hard eyes delivered the real purpose. Linda said something about Cassy's sharp sense of humor and the subject of conversation changed to the weather and the scenery.

They ate in Linda's yellow and white kitchen, which was quite spacious for an apartment. Because Jerry and Linda were involved in the new insurance venture, they took turns explaining it to Cassy.

For a short time she listened and then said, "I see that you two have something else in common."

"Other than what?" Jerry mouthed. Linda shuddered.

"Other than sex, of course. One look at you two and I could smell it. It makes me feel like a third wheel. Jerry, I bet you're sorry I came."

"Seeing that we all are going to be frank and open, you did make us change our plans, but you are wrong about us being unhappy you're here."

"Jerry!" said Linda.

"No, I'm glad Cassy named it. Your mother and I are very close as you so delicately suggested, and I want to know her and her life more than just under the covers. You are a big part of her world. Let's start over. I'm Jerry Sims."

"OK., OK., I'm Cassandra Stafford Grey, Linda's daughter, sixteen years old, likes bicycles, men on motorcycles, hiking, dancing and sex. I'm not a virgin, so some of the mystery is gone."

"We may have gotten more information than we need to know." Linda spoke in a puzzled tone. "Is it really so matter of fact these days?"

"Mother, sin and sex, and love and sex have separated when you weren't looking. At school, you sleep with a guy and then try to get to know him to see if you like him. So don't get so uptight over what I said before."

Linda had a questioning expression as she eyed her daughter, and then began to laugh and to gather her daughter into her arms. "I'm going to have to run as fast as I can!" She separated for a moment, then hugged her again and warmly kissed her daughter's forehead.

"Well, Cassy, it is a pleasure to meet you."

For the rest of the evening, each avoided any demanding subject. The conversation was light and humorous, humor being the guardian against exposure of real meaning. Once said, if taken seriously, the funny, biting word could be withdrawn. "Just kidding."

When Cassy went to the bathroom, Linda took advantage of the moment to say, "All this free, modern talk is alright, but I still feel uncomfortable with you and I in the same bed with Cassy here."

"No problem, I'll use the couch. It's just as well, for if we were together the screaming and hollering would drive poor Cassy wild."

"I don't holler."

"Next time we'll make a tape."

The sleeping arrangements put Linda in her bedroom, Cassy in the guest room and Jerry on the couch. As Linda was putting the sheets on the couch, Cassy laughed. "How quaint. You really didn't have to do that."

"I know."

During the night, Cassy left her room and went to the kitchen for a glass of water, wearing only her boyfriend's shirt. Jerry, lying on the couch in the dark, saw her standing motionless for several moments in the doorway of the kitchen, the light outlining her precocious, feminine body. She looked at Jerry, aware of his gaze, smiled and slowly returned to her room.

As he slept, Jerry's dream had her walk toward him as she discarded the shirt.

With the knowledge that he had seen her, Cassy was content during the rest of the weekend. She now had a small edge of his guilt that she could begin to peel away any time she wished.

Cassy return to school on Sunday evening.

Chapter 34

Erik reached Los Angeles at 2:47 a.m. on Friday. The lobby of the hotel where he was staying was quiet but he could hear music coming from the bar down the street. He accepted the key to his room from a sleepy clerk. In response to Erik turning his ear to the music, the clerk said, "They're open 'til five."

Erik had avoided drinking on the plane, an old habit, for many reasons, one of which was he found it eased the jet lag.

Working on the documents during the flight left him tense. He walked the few steps to the sound of the music and entered a dark, long room with a classic bar running down one side and four tables opposite the bar.

"And fuck you, too!" the man yelled over his shoulder as he rushed past Erik, almost knocking him down.

"Go to Hell." The voice came from the girl sitting at the rear table. When the man was gone, she cupped her head in her hands and turned her face down, looking at the tabletop. The music suddenly stopped and her sobs filled the otherwise empty room. Erik took a seat on a stool at the middle of the bar.

"Mind if I sit here?" she asked as she rose from the table and walked toward the bar. Her paper napkin absorbed the last of the tears.

"My pleasure." Erik watched her mount the stool next to him.

"This place is so empty it gives me the creeps," she said. Whatever the life-threatening problem had been a moment ago, it now was gone. "I'm sorry about the language, but just because I wasn't hot to go to his room right now, he storms off. Not even cab fare, damn it."

"Drink's on me." The bar tender offered her a shot glass, which she handled neatly. Erik took Jack Daniel's rocks and ordered a repeat for the lady.

"I should have gone with him. At least I wouldn't be stuck here." She touched Erik's forearm. "Oh, I didn't mean you. You look like a good guy."

Erik really looked at her for the first time. She was young, quite pretty, with large blue eyes and high cheekbones. Her blonde hair hung loosely, but she was young enough for it to look attractive as she tossed it with a turn of her head. Her figure was covered with a black sheath held with shoestring shoulder straps. Her body required no bra and the sheath showed no pantry lines. Only the tone of youth could gracefully support this combination.

"No problem. That was quite a scene. Sounded like the last few minutes of a soap opera."

"I bet it did. I'm Lisa," she offered and Erik accepted her soft, cool hand.

He listened as she related the events that had left her sitting next to him on this early morning. It began in her office. Since she had started as a receptionist, being free, white and twenty-three, she had dated some of the men in the large sales office. Carl, the man she was with tonight, was not one of them. This was a different arrangement. Her rent was due and she was temporarily short.

"I'd do anything for a hundred dollars!" she said to the air, a Groucho Marks comedy line. Who listens?

"Anything?" Carl said.

"Why, you have a hundred bucks?"

"Go out with me."

She knew he was married, but he had been hinting they could have a midnight snack sometime. From his talk around the office, she had heard him describing his wife going to sleep early and him being able to get out and roam around like a vampire.

"Just a date for a hundred bucks?"

"Yea, and then we'll see." He had a washroom laugh.

"You know you're buying nothing else?"

"Yea, we'll see." Again, laughter.

A little more talk and they planned to meet. She paid her rent.

Following the late meal, he drove her toward the hotel, demonstrating octopus dexterity, driving with one hand and unsuccessfully attempting to undress her with the other seven arms. "Let's have a drink. Might warm you up." He pulled into the bar's parking lot around the back. No need to advertise that his car was here.

Lisa picked up the story. "That's about it. He continued to try to undress me or get me to go to the hotel room. I was a little afraid of saying right out that the evening show was over. He had written the dialogue and action a little differently. I bet he's going to yell for his hundred back." She gave Erik the softest smile. "You're a good listener. What do they call you?"

"Edward, Eddy to most people." The question had come suddenly and that was the best he could do.

"Well, Eddy, here's the whole story. I've been with a few fellows in the office, you know, dinner and sometimes yes, sometimes no after that. The word gets around, so I guess he figured if for not only a diner but also a hundred bucks, it certainly would be 'yes.'

"And it might have been, you know, a charity fuck, but with his dirty mouth, he made it a bought package when I had really made no such deal. He pissed me off. He just realized that it was no go, when you came in." She laughed. "And were almost run over by Carl."

The drinks were generous this time in the morning. Erik had two and for Lisa it was at least four. A sailor and his date came in and settled down at the far table.

The conversation between Lisa and Erik drifted to anecdotal times and humorous observations. These seemed funnier with each drink. For Erik she grew brighter, softer, safer and more appealing in the alcoholic transformation.

Her touch lingered as she removed a fragment of the pretzel from the corner of his mouth. She said, "The corners of your lips turn up. It makes you look like a sweet man. Not like Carl. His turn done, even when he tries to smile, as though the action was foreign to him." She giggled at her perfect description. In fact, everything she said in the last hour was brilliant and comical.

Erik agreed and complimented himself on his ability to keep her attentive. He could not remember the last time he had felt this closeness, this warmth toward a female or the last time he had taken more than two drinks. As he thought about it, the warmth that had penetrated his outer shell was in his skin, in his scrotum. Sitting close to him, she ran her hand slowly up his inner thigh until she felt the firm, full erection harboring there.

Erik wakened with his body aching, head throbbing, and his penis sore. The note on the dresser read, "Thanks, you are a sweetie."

It was some time before his mind cleared enough for him to remember he had given her the hundred dollars to clear her with...who? Oh yes, Carl.

Slowly he recalled the last evening's performance. Not since the single days in the navy had he experienced a one-night stand. He wondered why now?

His happy sex life had begun when he and Frances had become lovers and remained fairly high voltage until her brain damage. For both Erik and Frances, following the ruptured Berry aneurysm and her brief partial recovery, the need, the drive and the hunger had faded, and after a few awkward, apologetic attempts at recapturing the remembered joy, their relationship had waned into a platonic compromise. There had been no surrogate thrusting herself upon him. His own sense of loyalty, as well as the very structured and visible day-by-day routine of his life, prevented him from seeking her. He tolerated the unabated restlessness. Often, as he sat at Frances' bedside, he was grateful for the guilt-free conscience, dismissing fear of exposure as a motivating factor. Transient mental lust flamed through his being, but it stayed mental and was forgiven. Her recurrent cerebral bleed had left Frances in a coma, a vegetable, with little chance of recovery, and had put him into a state of suspended animation, tightly focused on the objective segments of his life.

But last night he was in a strange city, free of eyes and accountability until the meeting at 11 o'clock. He had planned only to escape for a moment. He was sure the circumstances would not arise again. It was an interesting interlude, pleasant and unaudited.

He called Lacy. She told him about Frances' brief respiratory distress and assured him that she had taken care of it and that everything was all right. "She's about the same now. You know those periods of pain she had a few weeks ago? Well, they are gone. It's easier on her, but the doctor said it may be the coma is deepened. In a way, I'm glad. It's hard to watch her suffer. If they only would say there is a chance she would recover."

Erik listened silently, then said, "Thanks, Lacy, you're dong a great job. I don't know what I would have done without you."

He sat holding the phone after she hung up. He was questioning whether last night had been pleasant. For him, all sources of pleasure since Frances' stroke were tarnished with guilt and diminished because they did not arise from the "we" of "Erik and Frances" but from the lonely self, for one's self alone. And he could not find the way of pleasing her in return. This returning the joy had made up a strong, significant portion of their relationship and love.

"Fuck it!"

He just looked at the phone, angry at the words of an unwanted world it allowed to come through. Then it passed. He was back. He dialed his office. "All's well back there?"

The voice was younger than he was anticipating, having expected to hear Judy Santos. "You want to talk to Ms. Santos. I'm sorry; she stepped out for the moment. This is Cathy."

"You'll do. So how are things?"

The sound was musical. Strange that he hadn't really taken notice of that before.

Quickly, the picture of her first coming to him for an interview, and the vision of her that had passed briefly, out of content, in the midst of a conference, came to him. She was young and attractive. Desirable? Why desirable? Could it be that the monster released last night would refuse to return to its cage below the surface of consciousness? He thought, *Let's chalk up last night for what it was: a foolish, adolescent break, not to be repeated. And above all, please retain a proper decorum with the office personal.*

Cathy was saying, "So we asked him to call for an appointment. You know he should have returned last week but he had to go to the dentist instead because a filling fell out."

Erik tried to recall the beginning of the report but it escaped him. "That's fine. I should be home tomorrow. See if Judy can set up a conference call among Paul, Jerry and me for 4:00 p.m. I'll check with you from the airport when I arrive." Like an automaton, he prepared for the day.

Chapter 35

After bathing and dressing, Erik gradually returned to the problem on hand involving the trust. This seemed much simpler. He studied the information concerning Physicians Mutual of California and then was ready to meet Edward Hartman in the offices of the insurance company.

Hartman was a tall man who rose easily from behind his desk to greet Erik. The usual identities were made, and he suggested they take the couch rather than him sitting behind the desk. Erik was impressed by this reverse-power move.

"I think California and Florida are leading the country in forming physician medical liability companies."

Hartman nodded. "I believe we're ahead of you; we're working on our first year's premiums."

Erik caught the sense of pride in Hartman's voice. He thought, *It's going to be an obstacle when trying to pry Hartman off the California rocks.* It also made Hartman seem more valuable. "Are you collecting many claims?"

"A bunch more than I would have imagined. And here's a hint for you, Erik. Many of the first applicants had incidences they knew about, but on which there was no legal action. They turn them in day one. Fortunately, we only cover incidences that occurred after the sign-up date—so should your policy."

"What did you do with them?"

"For PR, we offered defense but no liability coverage. They accepted with red faces." Hartman was smiling.

Erik saw it was a mistake to get Hartman reminiscing over the good things about Pacific Mutual. He decided to cut to the heart of the matter. "We are ready for someone to handle a claims division. The Florida insurance commissioner is behind us, and the claims-made form gives us wide latitude in setting the premium rates. This should allow us to support a comfortable reserve and surplus. A cushion like that would give the claims manager some breathing room."

Erik waited. He had heard Pacific Mutual's new CEO was micro-managing the claims. Because the survival of the company was determined by the handling of claims more than any other aspect, Hartman's insecure boss was unable to designate to Hartman the prospective authority over decisions. But resolving claims was an art form where creativity was essential and frequently it was a poker game. The boss' interference was intolerable.

Hartman stared at Erik, then laughed, "No more foreplay?"

The response surprised and tickled Erik. He chuckled. Well, maybe some."

He described, in detail, the events up to date and Hartman outlined the situation in California.

Hartman said, "One event we have advanced more than other states is our push for tort reform, particularly to get a cap on non-economic damages. Once the Allied Industries took up our cause, it has gained great support. This will give some relief to the claims managers. There's nothing nicer than to know the plaintiff's attorney doesn't have 'the sky's the limit' look in his eyes. I'd be sorry to leave this environment."

"I understand there are a few other benefits to Micra; that's what the act is called, isn't it?"

"Medical Injury Compensation Reform Act." Edward said each word carefully. "I brought along a summary of the essentials." He reached over to his desk. "A lot of good stuff." He handed the list to Erik. "Take a minute"

Almost immediately, Erik was hungrily absorbing the information.

He read:

It caps non-economic damages at $250,000. Economic damages (medical expenses, lost earnings, etc.) are not limited.

Edward began to comment on each of the items. "A side effect of a cap is that the necessary reserve is decreased.

It allows a defendant to tell a jury about damages already paid by someone else (collateral source rule).

"If another defendant settled for a million dollars, the jury can now be told this and take it into consideration when determining the amount on our client."

It limits attorney fees. Rather than the usual fee of 40 percent of the whole settlement, attorneys under MICRA can charge 40 percent of the first $50,000, 33 percent of the second $50,000, 25 percent of a settlement between $100,000 and $600,000, and 15 percent of a settlement over $600,000.

"The benefits of this clause are self explanatory. The greedy attorneys are less likely to risk further work-up expense for a measly 15%. Also, there is a built-in deterrent preventing the lawyers from taking a marginal case."

MICRA set the statute of limitations at three years from the injury or one year from the discovery of negligence.

"This one probably will not survive. It's too easy for the plaintiff's attorney to claim the need for more time for discovery. I understand that here in Florida it's two years and four years."

It allows payments for a patient's future expenses to be paid in the future.

"Here, if the patient dies, the medical expenses cease. Before, if you had to pay a lump sum, present-day value of a million dollars for an estimated life expectancy of sixty years, and the patient died in two years, there was little chance of recouping."

It allows patients and their doctors to agree to binding arbitration.

"I don't know about this one."

Hartman watched Erik carefully. "Where are you in this area? I understand the legislature is mostly lawyers."

Erik put the papers aside. "It's funny, most people believe that because of the results coming out of Tallahassee, but it's not true. At the present time only about 30 percent of the congressmen are attorneys. Someone asked, 'So why are the results in their favor?' and the answer was 'The lawyers are smarter than the rest of the congressmen.' This may be true, but I can't help believing those large contributions to the campaign funds rents, if not buys, a legislator or two."

Erik checked to see if Hartman saw this as humor and then said, "We aren't as fortunate as you. In Florida, the allied industries aren't ready to take on the trial lawyers. Without AI's help, all cries against outrageous premiums fall on the deaf ears of both the legislators and the voters. You know that."

Hartman was a smart negotiator. "My present position at Physician's Mutual is firm. You will have to lure me away. How sweet is your Lorelei song?"

Erik waited briefly. "I understand one of the things keeping you here was the freedom you enjoy." Hartman shifted in his chair, a poker player's mistake.

Erik determined Hartman was ready to leave. "My song is in the details of the contract."

In response to Hartman's signal, Martha, his secretary, entered. He said, "I thought we could order lunch from The Place, just down the street. We can continue while we eat, if that's alright with you?"

"Fine."

"A few weeks ago," Hartman said in a light tone, "my visitor was highly incensed that we should be so informal at the midday meal. I believe he was from Stuttgart, Germany."

Martha handed them a menu. "Would you like a moment? I'll be right back."

She returned in a few minutes, heard the selections and called The Place. After a short wait, the food arrived and Martha converted Hartman's desk top into a dining table. The aroma stimulated everyone's appetite.

They continued the discussions during the meal and into the afternoon. Probing questions were answered to the extent possible, as many areas were still too young in the rapidly exploding tort-conscious industry for definitive conclusions. And on some subjects, neither one wanted to commit at this time.

Finally, a rough outline of the terms of the contract lay on the table next to the piled-up dishes. Martha was dying to get into the office and clean up, but didn't want to disturb them.

"What do you think, are you a candidate?" Erik waited quietly, thinking, *Why a candidate? This is the best you are going to get.*

"Candidate? No, I think not." was Hartman's retort. "I'm not running for office, you know. Given an attractive offer I might consider it."

"May I use your phone?" Erik was given privacy of the office as Hartman closed the door. Erik set up a conference call between Paul and Jerry. It was connected in five minutes.

"I don't think we could do better than Hartman at this time. I would like to sign him up, at least tentatively, pending no ghosts in his closet. I believe you all will like him."

"After my adventure with Boykin, I vote for anyone else. Seriously, if you are satisfied I'll go along," Jerry said.

"Your judgment picked me, so that's good enough." Paul voted yes.

Erik hung up and opened the door. "I couldn't act alone, so I called my partners. Forget the candidate. If we can finalize the terms, I'd like you to consider moving to Florida and joining us. The offer is pending ratification by the board, but I don't see any trouble there." Erik realized he blinked first but was not unhappy about it.

Chapter 36

The legislative act, allowing the organizing of a medical liability trust had a proviso: by December 31, 1975, there had to be 500 doctors as policyholders signed up. On that date, the window of opportunity would close.

At 7: 00 p.m. on Monday, July fourteenth, 1975, Jerry Sims, Erik Nostrom, Edward Hartman and Paul Arpin met in Erik's office.

Jerry said, "Happy Bastille Day."

"Are you predicting our future?" Arpin asked.

Cathy had seen the last patient to the door. She was the only member of the medical staff remaining. "Anything you will need before I leave?"

"No. I'm sorry to have kept you this long."

"No problem. Good night."

Erik started, "We have four-and-a-half months left to put this baby to bed. Right now we have ten signed up: the members of the board. We need only 490 more physicians willing to take on the unlimited liability of a company with a board of directors made up of ten physicians who know nothing about insurance—a piece of cake!"

Paul held the applications in his hand. "Seriously, I have arranged meetings at South General Hospital in South Miami, and in Gainesville Regional. I need Jerry for legal and Erik for medical. I'll spin the details of administration."

Jerry said, "Good luck to us. Here are the policies. Edward has gone over them with me. I think they cover most of the bases. We used the standard policy guide for occurrence basis and converted it to claims-made. Edward was a great help, stealing the sample policy from California."

The group reviewed the entire policy. Jerry was comfortable with the legal aspects but didn't quite grasp the medical and emotional forces coloring some of the decisions.

"Why a free tail?" He was referring to the clause, which said that after five years as a policy-holder, if the doctor was over sixty-five years of age and completely retired, the company will insure him, free of charge, for the tail—that is, those claims arising after he retires, but originating during the years he was covered."

Hartman nodded. "It does seem like a give-away, but it's necessary. It acts to convert the claims-made policy to an occurrence policy in that all past sins are covered. This is a must when we try to sell the doctors on the claims-made and are competing with occurrence, the form they are used to.

"We have to make sure the wording of the policy protects us, particularly defining the extent of the liability," Hartman added. "I understand the trial lawyers in some states are already holding seminars on how to find a loop hole in our policies."

Erik shook his head. "It's a paradox. The lawyers were delighted to see the doctors form the trust, but already they are our enemies as they prepare to take our money."

The group again turned to the policy, starting over from page one. It was totally exhausting for them as they crawled through the document, challenging the perimeters of their knowledge and experience. Much of the information they offered was anecdotal, a one case study, frequently interesting but not applicable.

Jerry stopped to make sure the others were still with him. He removed his glasses and rubbed his eyes. "On the offered coverage, I believe the legislature is completing a package to give the doctors some relief. It's the Patient Compensation Fund. We insured the doctor for the first $100,000. The State Fund takes over after that at a very low cost to the doctor."

Hartman was shaking his head, "Let's not plan to have this for long. Enjoy it while you may, but actuarially, this Patient Compensation Fund is doomed. We ran the numbers in California and didn't have the *chutzpah* to suggest it."

Jerry said, "On another subject, pricing. If we begin charging for our claims-made at the same rate as for occurrence, we should have a good buffer against any unsuspected losses."

Paul looked concerned. "Isn't it an overkill to charge that much?"

Hartman said, "No, no. Even if the legislature doesn't explicitly demand a minimum capital, it is necessary for any sound business. This first inflow of capital in the form of premiums will be a good buffer against an assessment. Even though the doctors sign for unlimited assessability, the first time we have to ask for an assessment will be the first day of our demise." He ran his index finger across his throat.

By 1:00 a.m., they finished their review.

Erik suggested, "Let's call it a night and meet again in two nights, on Wednesday, same spot."

"Here are the sample applications for insurance coverage," Paul said as he handed Erik, Jerry and Hartman a copy. "I tried to make it as short as possible, but for the initial input we need to know a good deal. Read them and bring all suggestions to the next meeting. Call me if you have any questions or suggestions before that."

Jerry picked up his copy, "I'm beat but for the first time I have a feeling of accomplishment. I have in my hands the first objective evidence that there truly is an insurance company coming out of the ground."

Chapter 37

They gathered on Wednesday at 6:00 p.m. Time dragged on interminably as they slowly crawled through the application forms.

Erik said, "I must have filled out similar forms a thousand times for other insurance companies. It should be old hat for me, but this time it's my company; it makes a difference."

Both Jerry as a lawyer and Hartman as a claims manager were familiar with these policies. For Paul it was a new experience. He kept demanding explanations for items that were routine items to the others.

"Please don't make us reinvent the wheel, my friend," Jerry finally said to Paul.

"That was my last question. The rest looks OK. It doesn't really, but I'll say that for the sake of progress."

"It has to be 1:00 a.m." Erik put his papers down, rubbed his eyes.

"I believe we've got it." Paul's voice reflected his weariness. "There is enough here, what with the description of the legislative action, the policy and the application for us to go forth and give our pitch for membership." He got visual approval. "We agreed all of us would go to the first meeting."

They acknowledged this. "Good. It will be at the South General Hospital, at their quarterly staff meeting on Monday, the twenty-eighth. We go on at 7:00 p.m. There is an open bar for about 30 minutes, starting at 5:30. Let's take advantage of that time to do some informal one-on-one propaganda."

Chapter 38

It was Wednesday, the twenty-third. In Erik's office, the four adventurers sat in silence, staring at the pile of information. It was the last briefing at the base of Mount Everest before the ascent. They were really going to begin the climb. Only now were they fully aware of the height and the steep incline of their journey.

Paul broke the spell. "While you all were away having fun, I have been plagued by the members of the board. I finally pacified them with a date for the next board meeting. If we have the gathering on this Friday, the twenty-fifth, we would have the two documents ready and it precedes the meeting at South General Hospital."

He put up his hands defensively. "I know, I know. It's squeezing it, but that's the best I could do."

Jerry applauded. "Paul, I think you have the touch of the prince in you. That's Machiavelli. It is perfect timing. I can just hear the howl if we met with the hospital folks before getting the documents ratified by board members."

"Last week I contacted Doctors Gentile, Harmon and Moninger in Gainesville. The enthusiasm is still high, all three agreed to alter their schedules to be here for the meeting. Gentile hesitated for a moment, but then joined in."

"Do they get compensated for their trouble?" Edward asked.

"At this time, no. Not even the airfare or the loss of earnings for those two days."

"I wonder why they do it?" was Paul's statement.

"I've seen the same thing in our group in California," Edward ventured, "but I really do not understand it."

Erik sat, quiet for a while, preparing his sermon. He had resolved this puzzle some time ago. "It has to do with the length of time the doctor spends out of contact with the real world."

"I don't follow that. What real world?"

"For example," Erik said. "Two men graduate from college. One goes to medical school and the other goes to law school. After two years, the law student graduates and begins practicing."

"I'm on my way," chided Jerry.

"For the next two years," Erik continued, "the lawyer accumulates money, and although he may be dedicated to his work, he measures his success by the dollars earned, 2,000 per month to start."

"From your lips to God's ears," Jerry called out.

"I bet you did better than that, you just don't want the IRS to hear," Paul said.

Erik raised his hand. "To continue. For the same two years and for the following two years of his studies, the medical student receives, for his successes, good grades and the praise of his teachers. The imprint of the non-financial reward begins."

"But then he begins to make money, doesn't he?" Edward asked.

"Not yet," Erik answered. "When the medical student graduates, he starts his internship. He will earn $90 a month. Following this, if he is to be a surgeon, he will work in the hospital for the next five years. His compensation will be increase to $120 a month.

"He lives in a small, one-room apartment. In the same building, there is a large four-room suite, expensively furnished with hot and cold running blondes. The suite is occupied by a drug dealer. There is no way that the doctor could consider their comparative worth with dollars as a measure, so he rejects this scale. That drug dealer is a rat. Our hero is a doctor! He must use a non-financial measuring stick: the value of his service and the recognition of his abilities by his professors. He denies money as a criterion, for he has none. In its place are plaques, non-financial awards and degrees."

"Still no money?" Paul asked with a mock-serious voice.

Erik goes on. "He finishes his residency and goes into practice. With time his earnings and net worth become significant."

"At last. Now he starts to make some dough," Paul said.

"Yes." Erik picked up his story. "He meets his fellow college classmate, now a lawyer and they go into an investment together. It is very successful. They sell their interest for a good profit.

"The lawyer goes home, opens a bottle of champagne and, with his wife, toasts the moment. He is completely happy.

"The doctor follows the same routine and, with his wife, toasts the moment, but he is not completely happy. There is no plaque to truly verify triumph; the non-financial reward is missing."

Erik stops briefly. "So, when called upon to render service like serving on our board, the physician responds, unconsciously answering the need for the non-financial reward to balance his acquisition of wealth."

"Non-financial reward?" Paul questioned. "Let me hear that one more time."

"That is the end of my sermon. If you would like to have a copy, please send me fifty cents and a self-addressed envelope."

"You really believe this plays a big role in their behavior?" Jerry quizzed.

Erik nodded affirmatively. "Last month I was at the hospital's annual medical meeting. They were handing out plaques for the ten best physicians on the staff. Incidentally, these awards were highly influenced by the number of admissions credited to the doctor. In the partially darkened room, I could see the faces of the doctors. When one had his name called, his face brightened as though he had won the lottery. As the last name was called, I could see the real disappointment of those who were not called, reflected on their faces and by the momentary slump of their shoulders. Yes, I do believe it plays a big role and I have used it in more than one occasion."

Chapter 39

The board met at six o'clock of Friday. Bitching about the inconvenient timing of the airline schedule, discussing the Florida State loss to Miami at Miami and reviewing the changes in rules about Medicare all preceded the beginning of the work session. All ten were present.

"Tonight we have to review and approve the policy and the application forms so they will be ready for the meeting at South General Hospital on Monday." Erik had already distributed the papers for their perusal.

"Is this the way you are going to present it at the hospital?" Fred Canon enquired as he fingered the paper. "I would have preferred a glossy, heavy stock."

"What I'd expect from the plastic surgeon, where esthetics are paramount," Erik said. "But seriously, we have it in the works. They will be ready by Monday, but I didn't want to delay approval for the meeting with South General. We only have four-and-a-half months to wind up our whole campaign."

Stanley Reinhart complained, "Of even more concern to me is this 'Mom and Pop' attitude toward preparing these documents and distributing them. We should of have had a professional sales and marketing person from the start. Erik, I told you in Tallahassee that I would be glad to help. I could have arranged that. It's well and good for you to get this started, but don't forget, you are only one member of the board. There are nine others. I'm sure I speak for them when I say we are not to just ratify your actions." Most were showing agreement. "We all are taking a risk and giving out time and our reputations. We should be prospective participants." He looked around the room and was gratified to see most of the members nodding.

Anthony Sanchez was not one of them. "I hope this is not going to be a glory train. Let's see how we can get the job done. No matter who does it, we will all be happy if it gets done. I don't think we need unnecessary protocols holding us up." He addressed Reinhart and then turned to Erik for recognition of his support.

Erik nodded appreciation. "Stanley, what you say is true. It is the last thing I have in mind. Actually, Paul and I have been working on the descriptions of the committees necessary to oversee each operation. So far, there are credentials, claims, marketing and sales, investment—I hope we have something to invest—and administration. I think, initially, the board as a whole, rather than an executive committee, should handle the major policy decisions."

Although the board members were asked to accept the documents, they voted on many changes. None of these radically altered the concept, and they did serve to tighten the language.

"I'm glad we haven't gone to glossy just yet." Erik couldn't resist.

The tedious review continued until midnight. Paul rubbed his eyes. "I'm going blind and we still have the last part of the policy to finish. What do you all say we retire for the night and return here, say nine o'clock?"

"You're reading my mind," Thomas Frond answered.

"For Jesse, Tom and Ken, I believe your flight back to Gainesville leaves at 3:46 p.m. We should be finished in plenty of time."

"Your Holiday Inn doesn't have a restaurant, so let's meet for breakfast at Caring Feast, the cafeteria down the street. You can leave your stuff in this room," Paul explained. The group filed out slowly.

Paul thought going over the details of the documents kept the group from seeing the risks they were exposed to. Here they were, going to ask hundreds of physicians to allow them to supply medical liability coverage starting on the first of January. Two terrible thoughts came alive: If they failed to get the required five hundred policyholders by December thirty-first and the company didn't come into existence, there would be a group of angry doctors scrambling for coverage at that last hour. They would look to sue the board and demand return of any prepaid money. The members of the board would be held personally responsible.

He said aloud, "It's going to be close."

Chapter 40

When Jerry reached his apartment, he went straight to the phone, but hesitated for a moment before dialing. He had to steel himself for the call he was about to make. "Good morning."

There was a silence as Linda struggled to recognize the voice at this late hour. "Jerry?"

He quickly related the events of the night, particularly the fact that he would not be on the red eye flight tonight because the meeting was to be continued into Saturday, probably well into the afternoon.

"I can still make the 4:56 p.m. Saturday. We can have a few hours, and I can get the 2:40 a.m. back to Miami and be at work by nine o'clock."

"You're insane, but I love you. It's too much strain."

"It's too much strain not seeing you after I have been holding my breath, planning to be there tonight."

Go, don't go, yes, no, but in the end nothing would do but for Jerry to rush off to Tallahassee. They met in the airport, raced to her apartment, and scattered clothing from the doorway to the bedroom. Love lasted to 1:20 a.m. An exhausted, happy Jerry poured himself onto the 2:40 flight and immediately fell asleep.

Chapter 41

The meeting ended by Saturday afternoon. The policy and the applications were finalized. They had also laid out the presentation for the hospital.

As the meeting ended, Reinhart pulled Erik and Jerry aside. "I know Paul has a candidate for marketing in mind, but I would like to have you all consider Mr. Hugh Brighton. I am sure you will be impressed." Pleased with himself, he smiled and said his goodbyes.

"That son of a bitch!" Erik pointed his middle finger at the closing door. "He knows he's handed me a hot potato. If we don't select his man, Reinhart will play the injured soul, claiming prejudice against him and his suggestions. On the other hand, if Hugh is selected, he might well be a spy for Reinhart, someone to be constantly watched." Still standing, he started to put the papers into his briefcase.

"I know about Reinhart." Jerry offered, "but I'm a little less paranoid. Let's try to be objective. He may turn out to be good." He ducked the sheet of paper crushed into a baseball that Erik threw at him. He sat down in order to retrieve the baseball.

Chapter 42

Lacy was in the kitchen when Erik arrived home. "I'll have a cup," he called as he smelled the fresh-brewed coffee.

"Evening, Dr. Nostrom. Coming right up." She reached a second cup from the cabinet and placed it on the table. The cup was from a carnival he had attended with Frances. "Frances" was written in bold letters across the side. Erik stared at it for a moment.

"How is she?" he asked, hoping it had been an uneventful day.

"No change."

He carried his coffee cup to Frances' bedroom and laid it on the glass-topped table. As he sat beside her, he thought how sleep smoothed the lines in her face, fooling him into seeing her as young and beautiful. In a moment she would awaken, smile with the love light he had all but forgotten, and say, "Hello, my dear Erik."

He held her hand. He thought how different his life would have been if she could have said "Hello."

She was so still. He remembered she preferred fast dancing, which was a paradox, because she usually walked through life with such grace. She could slip effortlessly into the wild jitterbug antics.

Maybe this memory emerged from the buried visions to ease the agony he felt as he accepted her stillness. Her coma wrapped him like a straight jacket, always present, triggering his claustrophobia. They had been good together. He thought of all the discontented marital partners he knew. Would it change if one of the partners had a stroke?

Is our marriage being recalled so romantically because it is seen through these precious, forgiving glasses?

Would it be less painful if he could recall a miserable past? But then would he carry guilt for not being better when he'd had the chance? The truth escaped him. He kissed her forehead and quietly walked from the room.

Chapter 43

A portable bar and table for hot and cold hors d'oeuvres were set up in the hall just outside of the conference room. Erik, Jerry, Paul and Edward were mingling among the physicians. Like the detail men, the four were selling their wares, information about their medical liability insurance company.

Before Erik could end his answer to a question about defense, a doctor called out, "Isn't it true the lawyers your company hires are really concerned about the company instead of being concerned about the doctor?"

"We will have about eighty-four attorneys throughout the state," Erik explained. "They are chosen for their expert knowledge of the local legal climate and the philosophy of the judges. The attorney works for the doctor."

"That's what you say," the questioner muttered.

"Doesn't your company settle cases even if the doctor is not guilty of malpractice?"

Jerry heard the question. "Unfortunately, a doctor doesn't have to be guilty of malpractice to get a verdict against him." He put down his glass to free both hands for gesturing. "We will settle when the non-medical factors show that the doctor will lose."

He looked directly at the questioner. "Particularly if the potential loss is above the doctor's limits. We don't want him to be forced to mortgage his house."

"As if you really care."

And then some kind doctor said, "Let them talk. If you knew so much you would be starting your own insurance company."

Never to be silenced, a voice from the naysayer called, "Doctor Nostrom, isn't it true that you are getting $100,000 a year, even if the company doesn't do well?"

Erik couldn't resist. "My friend, all your questions will probably be answered in our formal talk, but for your last question." He took a brief time to frame his answer. "That $100,000 is what I'm worth, not what I'm getting. At the present time, we are receiving no compensation. We work for the non-financial reward." He couldn't help laughing and was joined by the other three of his team.

The first part of the medical meeting, consisting of reports from the various departments of the hospital, was over. The chief of staff then introduced Erik. "We all are aware of the crisis in malpractice that has been worsening in the last few years. Thanks to the efforts of many doctors, lobbyists and friendly congressmen, we have gotten some relief."

Doctors at the back of the room were cupping their ears. The chief adjusted the microphone. "That better?"

"Yea."

He continued, "They formed the Patients Compensation Fund; they broadened the JUA for those who have trouble qualifying for standard rates; and lastly, they passed legislature that allowed physicians to self insure in the form of a trust. It is my pleasure to introduce Dr. Erik Nostrom. He is a surgeon in town who, with Mr. Jerry Sims, an attorney, and nine other physicians from Miami and Gainesville, has received the OK to start Amed Protective Trust. Erik will give you the details. Let him complete the presentation. Following the talk his team will stay answering questions for as long as you wish. Dr. Erik Nostrom."

"Earlier this year, Mr. Sims introduced me to the concept of self-insurance." Erik then outlined the steps in the formation of the trust. "This company is not for profit. That means any money left over after the bills have been paid and the necessary reserve has been established will be returned to the policyholders in the form of reduced premiums for the following year."

Despite the request to hold questions, there was a voice from the audience. "What If I decide to leave for another company?"

"It could happen, but we must be dedicated to our present members in setting our policies."

He faced the questioner, and then turned to the audience. "We have until December 31st to collect 500 policy holders. If you favor this solution, please get the applications in early. It will be like Maalox to my rapidly forming ulcer."

Jerry ran his index finger across his neck, signifying to Erik that it was time to cut it short.

"Thank you for allowing us to present the Amed story. I believe we have the best solution for controlling medical liability costs. Mr. Jerry Sims, the attorney; Mr. Paul Arpin, the CEO; Mr. Edward Hartman, head of claims; and I will be here to answer any questions. Thank you."

For the rest of the evening they answered questions. Most of them were truly in quest of information. The adversary component had evaporated.

Before the meeting ended, Jerry asked the group to fill out a questionnaire expressing their degree of interest in the project. There were some negative comments such as "I'll wait for the commercial carriers to return" and "I cannot trust a group of doctors to run an insurance company, not with my money."

However, the results showed the majority of the doctors were enthusiastic about it. "So far so good," Paul said. "If this is the general response, we should have no trouble getting the five hundred members we need."

Both Erik and Edward shook their heads.

"Why not?" Paul asked, confused by the reaction.

"You tell him." Erik gestured toward Edward.

"Doctors are notorious for procrastinating until the last minute. They will wait until December twenty-ninth to send in their check and application, even when they know they are going to do it tomorrow."

"Well, that's nice to know," Paul said. "I'll just have to start pushing right away."

When the four men left the meeting, Erik thought, *It's a lot easier for me to sell a plan to a group when they believe I gain no more than they do. I have a good feeling about Amed.*

If I were to guess I would say that Paul is thinking there are so many other items to be resolved by the D-day. Is there time?

Looking at the concerned expression on Edward's face, Erik said to himself, *Edward is wondering if it was smart to leave California, with his secure position, to join this group of amateurs. On the other hand, Jerry's smile says, this is exciting. A good first presentation.* After the analysis, Erik was convinced he had a good team.

Chapter 44

On Friday, August first, Erik and Paul interviewed Reinhart's candidate for marketing and sales. Hugh Brighton was thirty-eight years old and very good looking, with a strong, dry handshake and an athletic stride. His tan, gabardine suit hung well.

Erik thought, *This is as close to a movie star type we are going to get.*

Hugh had handled sale for a property and casualty company in Tallahassee. Stanley Reinhart knew him through their mutual interest in antiques. They had met at a show in South Miami.

The remainder of the interview painted a picture of an ambitious worker with a sense of humor. He was not married.

By the end of the interview, Erik felt more at ease. The chance of Hugh being a disruptive force, surreptitiously reporting to Stanley, became remote. Erik's paranoia, born as a twin with the birth of Amed and delivered full grown, subsided somewhat.

After Jerry evaluated Hugh, all three agreed he was their man. With ratification by Edward, Hugh was welcomed into the inner sanctum of Don Quixote land, the windmill being replaced by the allusive Amed.

Very quickly, Hugh organized the marketing department. The glossy brochures were designed and printed. Arrangements were finalized for advertisements in the local and statewide medical magazines and monthly medical newspapers.

He scheduled conferences in the halls of medical societies and associations. Methods for estimating the number of physicians exposed to Amed's information and for predicting the percent that would sign up were part of the weapons in his armamentarium. He had posted a chart on the office wall showing the number of policyholders. Initially, the response was well below the critical line of development. Below the chart Erik wrote, "Doctors are procrastinators!"

By mid August, the office had received fifty-two applications accompanied by $162,000.00. This, added to the $100,000 borrowed from the board members, was enough to handle the current expenses. Paul leased office space large enough to accommodate the staff of twenty he anticipated the company would need in the near future. For the present, there were many empty areas.

"Helloooo," Jerry called, cupping his hands around his mouth. "Just checking to see if there is an echo in this valley."

"I know. It looks extravagant now, but if we reach our goal of over five hundred, this place will have bodies shoulder to shoulder," Paul said, defending his action.

Erik heard him. "What do you mean, if? If we don't meet our goal we will be in debt this high." He passed his flattened hand over his head. "And we better head for the border."

Paul had hired a secretary and two credential reviewers. There were only the first fifty-two applications to handle, but in the beginning, the process was slow. They gradually developed the guidelines that could be immediately used by a new credentialler. Initially, the three girls answered many calls of inquiry. Paul oversaw the credential department for the time being.

The operation fell into a routine. The lecture series was established. Because there were so many places to go, only one of the team could go to each assignment. Erik, Edward and Hugh made up the core of the traveling team. Jerry, for the most part, answered the legal questions in such a manner that the travelers could mouth them with authority. Almost nightly, either by phone or in person, they would meet and compare notes.

Paul stayed at the home front, pulling together all the aspects of the business. A good portion of his time was spent keeping the board members in touch with events. Because a meeting devoured two days of everyone's working time, he hoped to avoid too many by communicating frequently. At the end of his fourth week, Hugh's efforts began to show results.

On Friday, August 22, Erik walked into Paul's office.

"It was going too smoothly. I gave myself a *keniner horra*," Paul lamented.

"What is it?" Erik watched Paul slump into the chair.

"No sooner than I feel we have a terrific marketing department under Hugh than he leaves."

"What?"

"He is starting his own antique shop in San Francisco with his lover, Arthur. He said he couldn't find satisfaction in his work here. He was going to devote his talents toward creating his dream in a world of love."

"Just like that?"

"No, he will neatly tie things up in two weeks. He said his organization is such that, with a minimal effort, it should run by itself for at least six weeks. And he thought I could handle it for now."

"Goddamn it! I'd like to kick his ass and Reinhart's too. I thought he was through with sabotaging me!" Erik hit Paul's desktop, shaking the papers there. No one in the office had ever seen Erik blow up. Paul was silenced. Erik's rage subsided. He lifted his fist from the desk, opened his hand, palm up. In a quiet voice he said, "So be it." He sat down, facing Paul. "He was good. No chance of changing his mind?"

"I started to try, but the more I insisted, the more he gave me the details of his newfound love in Arthur. I backed off."

"Interesting choice of words." Erik had recovered.

"It's not a laughing matter!"

"I know. So, you are going to fill in until we find a new marketing?"

"Have to. You know he came from Dr. Reinhart, but I don't think we can blame him for this one. It won't be easy telling him."

"I'd like to blame someone. It was tight even when Hugh began to work so well. Now, I don't know." Erik could feel anger raising again, but then, his sense of humor, his salvation, materialized from nowhere. "Do you think Reinhart is still putting long needles into my voodoo doll?"

Chapter 45

Between his practice and the demands of forming Amed, Erik's days flew by. At day's end, he would fall on his bed, exhausted. This pace allowed him to avoid the evaluation of his domestic life.

There was none.

He would check with Lacy and then visit the shadow of Frances lying in a coma. Thanks to the excellent care lovingly rendered by Lacy, Frances' body was spared the ravages of pressure sores and skin deterioration. In fact, the absence of stressful consciousness smoothed the creases of her forehead and softened the wrinkles about her eyes and mouth. The irony brought warm tears to Erik's eyes. How she used to fret about those signs of age, toying with the idea of plastic surgery. Before the stroke, it had been a major decision. God, that she could be here now to worry about such things. Her lips did not respond as he gently kissed her. The pain was too much. He abruptly left the room.

Chapter 46

Jerry was not too unhappy that a trial he was handling demanded he spend three weeks in Tallahassee. He would keep in touch with Erik by phone.

The days dragged by as he worked in his borrowed office, but the joy-filled nights spent with Linda were mercurial. He arrived Friday night, so they were both off until Monday, alone together for three days!

How marvelous to find, after the physical loving, that passion for the total person remained and blossomed. They savored the major and minor cords of love: for him, the comfort of her touch on his shoulder as she walked by, and for her, the aroma of his aftershave lotion lingering in her nostrils though he left the room. The laughter as they both, in off-key fashion, tried to sing along with Cher's "Half Breed," the song coming from the car radio, and the peace that was there for one because of the presence of the other.

"I could die now. I can't imagine how I could be more content. When I leave here, it's all downhill." Jerry put on a sad face, and then smiled. "Erik would tell me, 'You better watch out, you might be falling in love.'"

"And what would you say to Erik? Not a chance?" Linda asked lightly. "Or would Erik remind you of all the other times you thought you were falling in love?"

Jerry answered, "I might say he had found me out. Would that surprise you?"

Jerry was the surprised one. What was he doing? *What the hell—let's see where this is going. She'll say "no chance"; we'll laugh and go on.* However, defenses would rise. *Once that can of worms, or caviar, is opened, the consequences are exposed.* He didn't look at her.

When she answered, she was quite serious. "We're not the same, Jerry. I'm married, a mother of a sixteen-year-old, separated from my husband in France, emotionally just getting by until you crashed into my world. If I upset the delicate balance of my life, I'm in jeopardy. If you throw yourself over the cliff there is the reassuring safety net of 'Goodbye' ready to break your fall."

"You're right." Jerry put his fingers to her lips. "Erik should keep his mouth shut."

The initial good feeling, which prompted the outburst, had led him out on a limb. He scrambled along the branch, back to the safety of the trunk. Silence was the only conversation left to them until time began to cover the raw surfaces of reality.

Linda said, "Don't look so sad, tomorrow will come and I will be lying in your arms. You will know there is nowhere, and in no other arms, I'd rather be. I was burnt once. Can you blame me for wanting to rule out the dark sides before I commit?"

"No."

"Before we get too comfortable again, this is as good a time as any to tell you. Cassy is coming home tomorrow."

"Oh. This isn't the end of the semester, is it?"

"Almost. Thanks to the flexibility of Hillsdale Boarding School, she was able to finish the term early. She has the opportunity to be an exchange student in Surton University of Paris, France, near her father for a year. So, she wanted to spend the next four weeks with me.

"She is staying here?" He thought about it for a moment. "It might give us an extended time to know each other."

"It certainly will be a test of the bond that binds. I would feel much more like there could be a future if this roadblock was resolved."

It was warm in early afternoon on August 25. Linda watched at the doorway of her second floor apartment as Cassy climbed the stairs with boyfriend in tow. "This is Tony. We drove down together in his Beetle. He's staying in town for a few days."

After a moment of shocked silence, Linda said hello to the tall, bronzed, muscular, handsome male standing before her. He had to be eighteen years old! Linda led them from the hallway and on the way to the living room, she adjusted the air conditioning. The afternoon seemed to have gotten warmer.

Tony fell into one of the two overstuffed chairs. Cassy remained standing close to him.

Linda thought, *This is going to be our first battle*. She suspected they were sleeping together. It was one thing to calmly discuss sex in generalities, but quite another to actually see it, hear it and smell it in person.

No matter what Cassy thinks she's doing, Tony is not staying in this apartment.

Cassy laughed. "He's staying with his aunt in Forest Hills. Mother, say something; you look like a statue."

Relieved, Linda said, "Cassy, come sit by me on the couch."

The conversation settled down to exchange of information, a description of their trip to Tallahassee, and plans for dinner until the buzzer sounded.

"Jerry's on his way up." Linda tried to sound casual, but her relief to have support was evident.

"Jerry is her significant other." Cassy winked at Tony. "Like you and me." She moved to sit on the arm of his chair and stroke his hair.

Maybe it was the pack of cigarettes tucked into the left sleeve of his T-shirt that made Jerry immediately dislike Tony; more likely it was his laid-back, "I don't give a damn" attitude, or was it the sight of lovely Cassy, precocious, sixteen years old, bright, blonde and luscious, casually draped over Tony? He thought she was unaware of her vulnerability as she raced through adolescence toward womanhood. Tony was the man who would take advantage of it. *Could it be that I am already developing both the possessiveness and the protectiveness of a parent?*

"I'm Jerry. Glad to meet you."

"All the way down Cassy talked about you. I don't see the two heads." He laughed. "Only kidding."

"You're nothing if you don't have a sense of humor. When are you going to get a hair cut?"

"We just met and you're already sounding like my father," Tony said. He held out his hand. "You're all right."

Linda breathed a sigh of relief for the mini-crisis was over. The young bull and the older bull declared it a draw.

The situation again became awkward when she asked about drinks. Tony said, "I'll take a beer."

"Glass or bottle?"

"Bottle."

Linda said to Jerry, who was standing next to her," Of course."

Cassy sulked as Linda handed her a Coca-Cola, with a "let's have no discussion" look.

For a moment, Linda hesitated, then thought, *What the hell?*, and fixed Jack Daniel's on rocks for Jerry, vodka and tonic for her.

They moved to the kitchen and sat around the table.

"At least you'll get beer in the gravy; I fixed Tipsy pork chops with a bottle of beer added to the beef broth, onions, garlic, spices and caraway seeds."

"That will be a big help." She wrinkled her face at her mother.

They survived the meal and lingered over the coffee.

"I'm going over to Tony's for a while. Be back later."

"Don't be too late!" Jerry said, looking over the rims of his glasses and posing as the concerned parent.

"All right, Dad." She laughed as she snuggled against Tony and led him out the door.

When they were gone, Jerry moved closer to Linda. "We are sure she is on the pill?"

"Ever since I began treating her for acne."

"I didn't know she had acne. You would never guess; her skin is so smooth and clear."

"She didn't have it. The same medication prescribed for acne is used for birth control. All we mothers maintain respectability by declaring our little girl a virgin while treating the 'acne.' If really put to the wall, I'd say it's to prevent pregnancy in case she is raped."

"Enough of them and back to us. Do you have acne?" He couldn't help smiling.

"I've treated it for as long as I can remember. I hope it hasn't been a waste of time."

"It's only fair to test it now and then."

"Only now and then? I think the instructions were twice a day as necessary."

"I'm a firm believer in following doctor's orders."

The rustle of clothing being discarded broke the silence.

Her eyes were shut as he lifted her blouse over her head. There was no need for a bra, for her breasts still were firm. He leaned over and kissed her nipple, which instantly rose hard and pink. His hand felt the copious moisture. She touched him. Their lips responded, changing from pale pink to cherry red. They truly were ready for love.

Before Cassy came home, Jerry had returned to the couch and Linda took sole possession of the big bed. He was dozing off as the door opened. Cassy walked to his couch and kissed him on the mouth. "Good night, Dad," she said lightly.

Chapter 47

Monday, August twenty-fifth, Jerry was in his office early. It was ten thirty before his client left. Sara, who was really the secretary of Mr. Groggin, doing double duty acting as Jerry's temp, came through the door. "There's a Dr. Stanley Reinhart here, but he is not on your appointment list."

"That's alright. I know him. Wait for three minutes then send him in. Whatever bad news he has can wait that long."

Reinhart smiled, shook hands and sat down. "I hope I'm not interfering too badly, but I was in Tallahassee for a few days and thought we might have lunch later on."

Jerry immediately searched for his armor. "Later on? What are we going to do 'til lunch?"

"I am sure you noted the applications are not coming in as swiftly as we predicted." Reinhart presented this as a statement, not a question. "I am concerned. If we fail to meet the five hundred quota, it will be the board, not Erik alone, taking the fall. It could be a real financial fall as well as one of politics." He watched Jerry's face, knowing he had touched a raw nerve. "Have you thought about this?"

"At the meeting where we calculated the rate of enlistment, I thought it was clear; physicians are procrastinators and we expected this dragging in sign-ups."

"I believe those were Erik's words. I have been involved in easily as many events dealing with physicians as has Erik. To the contrary, I found that when the physicians were really interested, they were anxious to be among the first to be part of the action."

"Well, we are stuck with this plan of action. I don't remember you raising a big stink about it at that board meeting."

"You know, folks are beginning to look at me as an obstructionist, or that I want Erik's job. That is not true. I only want to do what gives us the best chance of succeeding. That is why I hesitated to say anything."

Jerry listened with skepticism. He was sure Reinhart would jump at the chance to be chairman. "I know, Stanley. You sound as though this wasn't a *fait accompli?*"

"That is one of the reasons I thought I would like to talk to you this morning. I could wait and we could have lunch, if you are too busy at the moment. I apologize for coming unannounced." He stood up and walked toward Jerry's desk.

Jerry thought Reinhart's tall, thin figure dressed in black give him the appearance of an undertaker. "I appreciate that. I do have a client at ten-thirty. I'm a little late already. Why don't we meet at Farrell's at, say, twelve-thirty?" He said to himself, *What is this scheming monster up to? I can use the time to see if Erik has an idea.*

"I'll see you then. You know, Jerry, I have always respected the way you are able to be objective. You seem to put favoritism aside for the benefit of the cause. I hope we can count on that as we go along." He shook hands and was gone. Jerry began to dial.

Erik balanced the phone on his shoulder as he jotted notes and listened to the story. "What do you think?"

"He may be setting up an 'I told you so' campaign. Although if he's right it will be too late to make much difference; we'll all be screwed. Call me as soon as you know something."

Chapter 48

Farrell's was crowded as usual with the legal and legislative movers and shakers of Tallahassee. Reinhart was talking to four men sitting around a table. When he saw Jerry, he turned and walked toward him. "The gentleman on the right is going to be the next speaker of the House, the red-haired fellow. He is Henry Harrison," he whispered to Jerry. "Not a bad person to have in our corner when it comes to favorable legislation impacting the insurance company, if we get that far."

Now I know Reinhart has something up his sleeve, Jerry thought. They found a booth, ordered— Jack Daniel's for Jerry, Dewar's for Reinhart—and sat for a moment, adjusting their hearing to the high decibel level of the room.

"It's your nickel. Stanley, what gives with the innuendos about the company failing?"

"I believe we are not structured in a position that will best assure the future of the company."

"And?"

"There is an alternative available to us."

"Stanley! The suspense is killing me. What the hell are you talking about?"

"Sitting at the same table I just left, next to Mr. Harrison, the next speaker of the House is Mr. Earl Hagen. I am sure you know him."

"No."

"At present he is a consultant to Gothem Product and Casualty Insurance Co. He has his own management company and is known by everyone in the insurance business, except you, as you say, and is considered a very shrewd guy."

Jerry was puzzled for a moment and then he realized the meaning of Reinhart's alternative. "Are you suggesting we get a management firm?"

"More than suggesting. I have spoken to Earl at length about our company. With his experience it took him only a brief period to identify the weaknesses in our formation."

"I think you are out of line, talking to an outsider without confirming it with Erik."

"As I told the board at our last meeting, Erik is not the only thinking head. The salvation of our company is more important than standing on ceremony," he said sternly. "The ironic thing is that this is just what Erik would do if circumstances were reversed, and in that case you would probably support him. When it is me, you give me this holier-than-thou attitude."

Jerry was stunned by the outbreak, but more by the fact that he had never heard Reinhart speak in more than a properly modulated, soft voice.

"I liked the description you gave of me in my office, you know, objective, above favoritism and all that. It's really me. Seriously, where are we with Mr. Hagen?" Jerry turned his head to get another picture of Mr. Hagen. "You haven't committed to anything, I hope. We aren't going to get a major consulting bill for his conversation with you?"

"We are under no obligation," Reinhart said impatiently. "Besides, Mr. Hagen is not a nickel-and-dime person." He continued, "We will certainly have to give him a bona fide contract before he will go further. I plan to request of Erik to invite Mr. Hagen to our next board meeting. I will call him this afternoon."

The crowd in Farrell's was thinning out so it was easy for Jerry to hear the words. Reinhart smiled, stood up, shook hands and walked in the direction of Hagan's table.

Later that day, in his office, Jerry heard, "Yes, I talked to Reinhart." Erik was responding to Jerry's phone enquiry. "I believe the trust, unlike a reciprocal, may have an in-house staff. The reciprocal must have an attorney-in-fact as the manager. As far as I can tell, that's the structure Reinhart will be favoring."

Jerry signaled to Sara for more coffee. "Even if we wanted to, I don't think there's enough time, particularly if we have to go through an intense evaluation and reorganization."

"Goddamn it," Erik muttered. "If he's going down this path, I wish to hell he would have done it before we started in-house development."

He thought, *This is going to be a headache. Reinhart is a constant annoying pressure, not overwhelming but there all the time.* "We'll do it at the next board meeting, if possible."

Chapter 49

With the start of September, South Florida began to apprehensively look to the southeast. So far, Hurricane Blanche had turned north before reaching Florida and Carolina, staying south, hitting Cuba and Mexico. Erik tracked the course of Doris, the threat since last Tuesday. When he saw that the hurricane headed north almost as soon as she was born, he turned to other things.

In preparation for Wednesday's meeting, he began listing the pros and cons of the in-house structure in one column and those of contracting with an outside managing firm in the other.

He thought, *With outside management, the board is the ultimate authority, but it delegates all prospective control to the company. Underwriting, marketing, claims legal and administration would be in their hands.*

Erik finished an accompanying letter and had Judy send a copy to each board member. She included the minutes of the last meeting along with the date of the next meeting. A basic A1A teaching in political control, Erik knew, was to win over a majority before bringing the matter to a formal vote.

He needed a break from the fatigue of composing the list and letter. After bringing his legs from under his desk, he stretched and stood up. As he walked toward Judy's office he called, "Let me have the phone numbers of the board."

He began dialing. To each one he talked with a prejudice toward maintaining the present system.

When finished, he had a third in favor, a third interested in hearing the new idea and a third confused.

Good enough. He called Reinhart. "Stanley, the next meeting is Wednesday, September third. In my name, would you like to invite your guest, Mr. Hagen?"

Reinhart immediately complained, "That is two weeks away. You are not procrastinating intentionally, knowing delay favors a decision for the status quo?"

"No. I tried to arrange the meeting at the earliest convenience for all concerned."

Erik hung up. He growled into the mouthpiece of the phone and then called Paul. "We are to have a board meeting on the third. I've spoken to all the members. Arrange with Dr. Reinhart for his guest, a Mr. Earl Hagen, to be there. Check to see if he needs any electronics."

"Will be done."

Chapter 50

Erik in Miami gave Jerry, still in Tallahassee, a quick update, hung up the phone, changed his business jacket for his surgeon's lab coat and returned to his patients.

Cathy had escorted three patients to the three examining rooms. Their charts were in plastic pockets on the doors.

Mrs. Gertrude Roth was in the first room. It was her first visit since being hospitalized to have a skin graft put on a very painful ulcer. Cathy was finishing the dressing on her left ankle. "It looks so much better than before she was hospitalized. Then it was an ugly, necrotic, smelly, gouged-out, giant hole. Now the clean, pink skin covering looks so healthy. It is almost pain-free, isn't it Gertrude?"

Gertrude smiled. "Oh, it's so much better."

Erik put his hand on Cathy's shoulder. "It has been some time since I heard anyone enthusiastic about a stasis ulcer, skin grafted or not."

"I suppose so," she said. "But this is my maiden ulcer. I followed it from the first time we saw it to this nice stage. I'm impressed!"

"I hope you never lose that passion."

"Don't tease me," she said.

"I'm not, really. You are like a breath of fresh air to me. I see the cynical ones in the hospital all the time. Ms. Parsons, whom you replaced, was a great nurse but she had seen it all, knew all the possible bad results and constantly reminded me."

Cathy relaxed. "I try to be positive." She turned and pointed to the patient. "Gertrude has just been telling me the strangest story. Tell Dr. Nostrom."

Gertrude's round face blushed. "I don't think the doctor wants to—"

Cathy interrupted Gertrude. "I'm sure he would. Please."

"Well. Alright, if it's OK." She took a deep breath. With her head down, while concentrating on her fingers moving on the examining table, she began.

"There were four beds in my room, each occupied by a woman about my age. I don't know if that was by accident or they do that. Well, you know how quickly you get to know your roommates when everyone is sick and scared." She stopped and looked up to see if the doctor was listening.

"Well, that happened, especially with Sara, Mary and me. The other lady just lay there sleeping, mostly. We three had a high time. Sara was the sickest, but had a funny kind of humor, telling stories about her Romanian childhood. She was Jewish." Then, to make sure she wasn't offensive, she added, "I wasn't judging. She told us so."

Both Erik and Cathy showed approval.

"Mary was Catholic and very Irish. She didn't look so sick, but her doctors were always ordering blood to be taken and checking her heart, lungs and blood pressure. Mary would say, 'The doctors like to see me undress. I still have great tits for an old gal.' She semi-flashed them and laughed." Gertrude started to laugh, remembering the scene.

"Well, then Sara died. It took two days. She reached over and held Mary's hand until the last. After that, there was only Mary and I talking. The other sleeping beauty never awakened for any length of time.

"I was to go home on Monday. For some reason I couldn't get to sleep Sunday night. About eleven o'clock I heard Mary begin to moan. I pulled the cord to get the nurse. She came in about ten minutes later and at first was annoyed with me for disturbing her, but when she saw Mary's white face with sweat running down her cheeks, she called the doctor. He had trouble hearing a blood pressure. The nurse ran off and returned with an IV stand with a bottle of saline and an IV tube. The doctor tried three times but was unable to start an infusion. He was nervous and asked the nurse to call the resident. Apparently, he was only an intern.

"Mary sat straight up in her bed, patted the young man on the hand and said in a clear soft voice, 'Don't bother, my sweet, young doctor, Sara has come to get me,' and she died right then.

"Well, I'll tell you I didn't know to go to the church or the synagogue." Gertrude blessed herself.

Her wound care and her story finished, she limped to the front desk for her next appointment.

"Which religious tabernacle are you going to?" Erik asked Cathy.

"I'm Catholic, well, a casual Catholic. I'm guilty of praying when I need something. 'Oh Lord, let me get the job with Dr. Nostrom,' that sort of thing. After Gertrude's tale, I might just stop by for evening prayer on the way home. Is that awful?"

"*Benedictus Dominus.*" Erik crossed himself and smiled. "Sounds good to me. I'm no one to judge. I'm a Lutheran converted to a reincarnationist myself."

He could see Gertrude's story had deeply affected Cathy. A corner of her vulnerability showed through, leaving her naked for a moment. He wanted to hug her and let her know he was there for her. Something about her freshness, her enthusiasm and her beauty made him want to protect her. He liked the feeling. Cathy left the room. The talk of religion hung over him.

Chapter 51

He thought of Frances. In the days before her stroke, they had enjoyed building their own hereafter world.

"Let's first agree it couldn't be a judging entity. It would be more like a manager of souls as they passed from one stage to another," Erik said.

"A manager with a sense of humor," she added. "How many times do we go around?"

"We can borrow from the Hindus and take nine."

"Like a cat, it has a ring to it."

They were silent for a moment; then Erik said, "For what happens after that, we will have to fall back onto the basis of all religions: too deep to be contemplated by a mere mortal."

"We aught to write it down," she said.

"Maybe we will when we get all the pieces. For now let's see what else we need."

Frances contributed, "There must be different kinds of lives, you know, good life, bad life, rich, poor, good health or bad, and colors."

"That's good. It will explain why there are very good lives and such bad ones here on earth. It will be like a Chinese restaurant menu, with choosing one life from column A and the next from column B and so on until you did all the tours of duty," Erik suggested. "You would be lucky if you chose a bad life and were born a still birth."

"Erik! Stop that." She lovingly slapped his wrist. "One thing. I think we should be able to review our completed life before we move on."

They played with the nature of the alternative lives available and how they were chosen.

"Do you think the soul picks up experience with each life?"

"Let's do that."

"Death would be a conduit from one life to another. It would be something to look forward to."

"Let's not lose our heads." She laughed. "Right now I like it here."

Erik's thoughts returned to the present. The subject had seemed so light in those days. They each had that sense of immortality restricted to only the young. *Does Frances look forward to the next life as she lies in her bed in a coma?* He hadn't thought of eternity for some time. In real life, it was not playful or satisfying. Depression fueled by loneliness immobilized him. He sat waiting for it to pass. Like a beam of light slowly changing direction, his mind wandered and then focused on the departing image of Cathy. She mimicked the essence of Frances when Frances was young and vibrant. He realized for the first time Cathy made him feel happy. Then he was remorseful. He should be mourning, even though Frances was not completely gone. Did Cathy have any idea of her effect on him? As far as he could recall, he had not been overly personal with her. He would have to be careful.

Chapter 52

All the board members were present by 6:30 p.m. The boardroom was much larger than Erik's waiting room, giving each member a good deal of arm space.

"This is more like a real business," Fredrick Cannon called out.

"Leave it to the plastic surgeon to see the esthetics," Thomas Frond noted.

"I believe you all heard from me, and I assume from Stanley," Erik said and nodded toward Stanley, "about the business tonight. Stanley has asked Mr. Earl Hagen to talk to us about converting the management of Amed from the in-house structure we now have to an outsourced management company. Stanley, would you like to introduce your guest?"

"Thank you, Erik. I have known Mr. Hagen for several years. Briefly, he brings with him the experience of working his way up the insurance ladder, of running an insurance company and most recently being president of the Hagen Management Company. You have received his CV, I believe.

"I asked him here tonight to make you aware of an alternative way of managing our company, a way that I feel is more responsible and more likely to succeed than our present course. Please let Mr. Hagen finish his talk and we can have questions to follow. Mr. Hagen, please."

Mr. Hagen was impressive. A well-tailored navy blue suit covered his portly frame. He stood in silence, looking much like a stern preacher surveying his flock. With patience, he brought each face into focus, measuring the degree of skepticism dwelling there and diluting it with a soft smile. He was good.

"Thank you all for allowing me to talk to you. Dr. Reinhart and I have pondered about your endeavors. I believe the timing is right. You have a seller's market when it comes to malpractice insurance. I commend you on going from nothing to a beginning company. You might be able to reach your goal the way you are."

He waited, calculating the relief his words offered. *They must have had some doubt about their ability or they wouldn't have invited me. Now the coup de grace.*

"Unfortunately, my analysis, based on the length of time consumed in the development of similar companies, can be seen on this graph." With one smooth motion he dimmed the lights and turned on the projector. In raw red and white, the lines indicated a "reach-the-target date" at one-and-a-half years. An audible gasp crashed into the silence.

He continued narrating slide after slide, detailing the pitfalls waiting at each turn.

"Gentlemen, there are heroic men and there are old men, but rarely an old, heroic man. My marine sergeant used to tell us that about battle and it still applies to business."

The calm veneers of the board members he had first viewed when he'd begun his talk were replaced by those of controlled fright.

Only Stanley smiled in the darkness. "Goodbye, Erik," he said to himself.

Mr. Hagen was now ready to offer a life preserver to the group. "All of this data is based on start-up situations. This is not the case with my organizztion. You will be contracting with an ongoing, already formed management firm." He turned the cassette to show the next slide.

"I have taken the liberty, at Dr. Reinhart's request, to calculate the time necessary to become approved starting from where you are now." The graph was in baby blue and white. Mr. Hagen had done this before. "As you can see, with our combined efforts we are looking at December fifteenth for approval date, with $2,000,000 revenue. Fears of failure vanish with good management." He turned on the lights. "Any questions?"

"Very impressive," Anthony Sanchez said. "I didn't see the source of your data on the 'ongoing' charts."

"I didn't want to go into too much detail. I was more interested in the concept. I can send the information to you. Paul, I'm sure I can get the mailing information from your secretary. That is Kimberly, is it not?"

Questions about details of his company's operation continued. He answered them easily and satisfactorily. Finally, Dr. Reinhart interrupted, "We are beginning to ask the same questions. I would like to thank Mr. Hagen for coming tonight. I knew you would be interested."

And with final words, Earl Hagen departed. He was in a confident mood. The group fit Reinhart's description: enthusiastic but very naive. He thought, *I think I put just the right amount of hope and fear in my spiel.* A black shade began to cover his sunlight happiness as he recalled the disastrous outcome of the fatal insurance venture in his past. That was some time ago. *It will not be discovered. It will not happen again.*

Paul refilled the coffee cups where needed. "Where do we go from here?"

"Because it was my idea, I think I would like to summarize what we just heard," Dr. Reinhart said. He was relaxed, being assured that what he saw was the replacement of Erik. *They must see Erik's inadequacies. The team of Reinhart and Hagen will prevail.* "We are at the crossroads. There is no doubt in my mind that the course we must follow is with Mr. Hagen."

He turned to his right. "Erik, you did well getting the ball rolling, but even you will admit it sometimes takes a different mind to bring it to completion. Please make it a consensus and accept this change of command." He hadn't meant to say command, but what the hell, plant the seed.

"I don't think I would have been in favor of his form of outsourcing even when we began. We would lose control and not be able to keep the physicians in mind," Jack Reed said.

Fred Cannon added, "He doesn't sound too doctor-friendly to me, either."

Stanley Reinhart interrupted, "He is talking adult insurance. He would leave the handholding to us. Or to you, Jack. This is a business!"

Jesse Gentile and Thomas Harmon, both from Gainesville, said they were not sure the leadership should be in Miami and maybe this was the time to change.

Like waves at sea, the decibels filled the room, then fell to a whisper, then to silence, only to start the waves again.

"I believe all the original thoughts have been expressed. I hear the first argument of the night coming back around. Why don't we count the house?"

"I haven't made a decision yet," Thomas Frond said.

Kenneth Moninger nodded his head. "I'm with you. We need to know a lot more."

"That is fine," Stanley answered. "But we do not have a good deal of time;

today is the third of August. At least let me know if the group wants to proceed investigating in the next few days."

"I believe we must do that," Richard Garing said. They all agreed.

"Could we meet on Saturday?" Jesse asked. "I wouldn't have to miss a day at the office."

"This Saturday?" Paul asked. Much grumbling ensued—too soon, no compensation, no love—but in the end they agreed. It would be Saturday at 10:00 a.m.

Reinhart stepped into Paul's office. "I see that you have things well in hand. Thank you for your help tonight. Mr. Hagen was impressed. I do not believe there is any reason to change your position here when we put in the new system." He reached over the desk to shake Paul's hand.

Chapter 53

The phone call went on for over an hour, Erik doing most of the talking, with Jerry throwing in a question now and then. "That's the heart of the matter. Reinhart has wrapped himself in the flag of glory with righteous selflessness. Follow him and, with Hagen's shield, he will lead us to the promise land of success."

"I'd better run an in-depth search on this puppy. He's not a household word in this part of the country."

"Let's get him. Jerry, you know how I hate to be violent, but be here at our next meeting to keep me from punching his lights outs."

"Let's consider him a necessary evil. Seriously, how did the group react?"

"This guy was impressive. If a vote was taken tonight it would have been a split decision."

"That bad?"

"A few of them are uncomfortable with me as chairman—Gentile and Harmon. It's not personal, but a Miami vs Gainesville thing. Two are all business—Garing and Cannon. If it were a better deal, they would go for it, friends or not. And we know where Stanley sits."

"I'll get on the phone with the Gainesville twins. Catch you later."

Erik fought sleep that night. In the dark, the goblins grew larger. A hand reached into his stomach and squeezed until the juices, hot and bitter, squirted to the back of his throat. Pain said 'no' to any place for his back and shoulders. The best of the worst was curling into a fetal position, rocking slowly. Night made pain more severe and fear overwhelming. He didn't get good vibes from Hagen. When he had ignored the uncomfortable feeling in another time in his life, he had lost the farm.

He thought, *Is it all ego that makes me want to be the chief? Would Reinhart do as well, or better?*

"To be a good surgeon, I must know I am the best surgeon. To be a good chief I must know I am the best chief." He laughed at himself. "It's all ego."

Chapter 54

Dr. Nostrom's office staff layered out quite rapidly. Judy Santos was in charge; below her the three women bonded, at first because of the logistic proximity. When patients entered the office they were greeted and questioned by Sharon. She brought the chart up to date and passed it, the patient and some verbal information on to Cathy. As the patient left, Cathy delivered the billing information to Shirley. Conversations on both ends of the exchange put Cathy pleasantly in the middle.

Circumstances made Cathy more acceptable because the girl she replaced was, at best, not charming. That woman had been in the labor force for too many years and was certain she knew it all. This quality, plus a healthy serving of paranoia, had eliminated her from office worker of the year award.

Gradually, Cathy became a confidant, a messenger exchange bureau and a consensus-maker.

During one lunch period, Sharon followed Cathy into the first examining room. "I don't know what to do."

"You look beat."

"No sleep will do that."

"And?"

"Last night." She tried to see if Cathy would understand.

"And?"

"Last night."

"We're past that. So what, last night?"

Sharon hesitated as silent tears formed and fell. Her voice was wet, like an early flu. "Last night it happened. I was in my room. You know I've been living in the boarding house for three months, ever since I walked out on Billy. That creep was fucking Eileen, in our bed. Anyhow, it was hot. I like to get it all off when it's like that. I'm lying on my bed, trying to decide if I need a cigarette bad enough to get up, get dressed and run to the Seven-Eleven. Of course Mr. Camel won." Talking to Cathy made Sharon feel a little better. "I just threw on a sweater and skirt. It was just around the corner. That's the only good thing about the lousy neighborhood. I got the smokes and was back at my door in a flash." She thought, *I should say something silly and end this story, but I got this far. What the hell.*

She put her hand on Cathy's forearm. Sharon's voice changed; it became tense. "He suddenly was right behind me, his pelvis pushing me through the doorway. He said he had a knife but I never saw it. I closed my eyes and followed instructions." Recalling her emotions at the time, she closed her eyes and continued. "I was so frightened I couldn't think. Now, as I'm telling you this, I can think of a dozen things I could've, should've, said and done. With his sweaty body against my back, my brain refused to function. I think I said, 'Don't kill me,' but I can't remember saying anything, only moaning, like my little mongrel, Softie, when she thought I was going to hit her." Sharon shrugged. "Before this happened, I thought I was cool. That's a laugh." Her giggle sounded off key. "He slowly nudged me to my bed. I tripped over the rug and fell, face down. I was dizzy and my eyes were still closed. I never was so scared. I was weak. My body was so heavy I couldn't lift my head. I stopped breathing and passed out. He pulled off my sweater and skirt. My body was naked and cold. As I came around, I began to shiver. Then the damnedest thing: He took off his jacket, put it over my back and buttocks, and began rubbing me, like a massage." Sharon opened her eyes. "It was crazy. I lay there being rubbed, like a boyfriend would. It seemed to go on for a long time. Then he turned me over and again covered me, my breast down to my upper thighs. I was like jelly. I was afraid to do anything, say anything. I didn't want to change his mood. I was motionless, being rubbed. It was bizarre. His hands were soft, like a musician's. I said, 'You're nice.' I don't know why; maybe he wouldn't hurt me. He said, 'Thank you,' stood up, took his jacket and left, leaving me naked as a jaybird. I lay there, too frightened to move, and then I ran to the door and locked it. I was bare and cold. I grabbed my robe and put it on."

"What did the police say?"

"Nothing."

"Nothing? How come?"

"I didn't call them."

"You didn't call them?"

"What was I going to say? He didn't hurt me and besides I never saw him. I was too scared to open my eyes." She laughed. "I can just see what the cops think. 'She's not sexy enough even for a rapist.' I'm pretty shattered already."

"You have to call them. That guy is going to come back. This time he'll bring his 'Mr. Hyde' side and kill you."

Cathy could not convince her of the danger of silence. In a blurred fantasy, Sharon saw him returning as a lover.

The session ended as the women left the examining room; Cathy talked about Sharon's safety, and Sharon replayed from her memory the pleasure of his touch and the sensuous way her body had responded.

Sharon was grateful Cathy didn't repeat this story to anyone. She had confessed when the experience was fresh. It was one of those times when she had to talk to someone or go mad. Now, in the quiet time, she regretted letting Cathy into her dark world.

With time, both Sharon and Shirley confided more to Cathy. She became the untitled leader, a chief operating officer under Santos. Over the last several months, Santos had become withdrawn. Much of her energy and attention was consumed by concern over her ailing husband. She welcomed Cathy's relief pitching.

Chapter 55

Jerry returned to Miami at seven o'clock in the morning on Saturday, August 6, and headed for Erik's office. "I asked Jake Sampson to Western Union the data to your address. It'll save time. You don't mind?"

"Mi casa is your casa. What does he have?"

"Apparently, Hagen comes with some baggage. Jake said the joy is in the details and we should have them any minute."

Erik usually did not come into his office on Saturday, but today he and Cathy had met at eight a.m. to inventory the equipment and plan the necessary new or replacement purchases. It had been a pleasant moment for both of them. They had been interrupted by Jerry's arrival.

She was in the front office when the delivery arrived, fourteen pages tucked into a special envelope in the hands of a freckle-faced teenager dressed in brown and wearing his special cap. She took the package and handed the boy fifty cents.

"Thank you, Ma'am," he said.

She gathered the material and went to Erik's private office.

On a few occasions in the last two months, in response to her interest and concern, Erik had explained the insurance problem and his hopes of solving the puzzle.

"You can hear this." Erik nodded toward Cathy. He said to Jerry, "She's pretty much up to speed on our situation. It may come in handy."

"Fine with me. Let's see what you brought us." He laid out the papers, based on the time identification, and began reading aloud.

"Jefferson Insurance Co. put in receivership. Mr. Allison, chairman of the board, stated this morning, neither he nor the board were aware of the most recent use of offshore investments. The decreased value of this part of their portfolio was the final event. The company apparently was under capitalized for some time. The rather casual underwriting, the under pricing and unfortunate claims results brought the company under review by the insurance dept. Jefferson's CEO, Mr. Earl Hagen, did not return multiple phone calls for this story." Jerry nodded his head approvingly. "And finally, Jake had added a personal note to the financial statements for the last five years. They should have pulled in their horns some time ago."

Erik studied the data. "I love this. Based on the pumped-up statements, Earl got a $47,000 bonus the same year the house of cards collapsed! This stuff warms the cockles of my heart. I don't know why I worry about Reinhart. To me he's so obvious about wanting to screw up the works."

Jerry said, "You're too close. No one believes good news but everyone takes for granted the truth of bad news, even if they know the teller is a liar. You told me that. Reinhart is a pro as a manipulator, but I think he's out on a limb on this one. How are you going to handle it tonight? You know, if Reinhart gets wind of this, he's just likely to come dripping in righteous indignation, claiming Hagen deceived him."

"My first thought was to send this material to the board members, but you have a point."

Jerry left for his office to prepare for the morning's battle.

Chapter 56

The papers from Jake were scattered over the desk. Cathy gathered them and sat opposite Erik. "This is a hand grenade."

"And right out of the blue. I don't let it be known to many people, but I've always been lucky. So many times in my life, when I was in trouble with no way out, something would happen to save me. Something over which I had no control."

Cathy looked at him. "Like what?"

He hadn't expected the request to document his comment. He thought for a while, then began, "A year after we married, I was still trying to decide whether to stay in private practice or enter the academic world. About that time, I was invited to be the visiting clinical professor at Sutton Medical School in New York for six months."

She started to move as though these few words were the answer to her request for an example of his good fortune.

"No." He laughed at the confusion. "That's not the lucky part."

She sat back, patiently waiting.

"Frances and I packed up and moved to New York. We were living in a boarding house uptown in one of those expensive homes of the past, which at the onset of the depression were converted into multiple small apartments.

"There was a time when we were temporarily broke." He laughed. "Better money management came later." For a moment, he felt uncomfortable about talking of the past and Frances, but Cathy's face showed no displeasure.

"On Friday night we had a quarter and two dimes. We expected money to be available on Monday. We bought a macaroni and cheese package and planned to eat sparingly off that for three days." He remembered the bittersweet sensation of sharing the experience with Frances.

"Hunger began almost as soon as we knew we wouldn't eat. Frances wasn't kidding when she said my calf was looking more and more appetizing every minute. We ate slowly and fantasized about what we were eating—steak, rare; double-cheese pasta, or Caesar salad. The water became wine. At the same time we each shouted '*domino fabixum*' and crossed ourselves."

Erik pushed his chair back, separating him from Cathy. "I didn't realize it then, but there is a big difference between poverty and being broke. We were broke, but we had hope, optimism, youth, and energy. We each had our dream. It was fun." In telling this story, Erik wondered if he was erecting a protective barrier. "Since then I have seen poverty. It frightened, depressed and robbed the wearer of dreams and pride." He remembered this was Frances' observation.

Erik said, "Getting back to my story, it was Saturday morning. We were still in bed. It was 10:30 a.m. when the knock on the door got me out." He made a knocking sound with his knuckles.

"Yes?"

"Is this the residence of Lt. Erik Nostrom?" He was in a pale blue uniform.

"I'm Erik. What is it?"

"I am Mr. Roger Forester, of the elite division of the United States Postal Service."

"Glad to meet you."

"What is it, Erik?" Frances called from the bed.

"Some man for me. I don't know. It's too early in the morning. Mr. Forester of the postal service, what can I do for you? It's a bad time for seeking contributions."

"You misunderstand. I am to do something for you. I have a letter for you."

"On Saturday?"

"It is addressed to Lt. Erik Nostrom, Oakland Naval Air Station, Oakland, California. Special delivery. You were not at that address at the time of delivery and there was do forwarding address. In these cases, when it is a service man, or woman, the letter is turned over to my division. Once in our hands, there is no time limitation. We are like the Royal Mounties; we always find our man." He stood there for a moment, reflecting on the prestige of his position.

"What do you have for me?"

"We started at the naval station in Oakland, California and found your last address. You weren't there, but we knew you were in New York. The navy received a request for your military records from the university. Checking on your application,. there was your present address. It really wasn't very difficult for us." His eyes were bright with the joy of accomplishment.

"Astounding!"

Mr. Forester held out a multi-processed envelope. "Not everyone is happy to see me. It is bad news as often as it is good. When it is bad, the recipient blames me, when it is good I am forgotten as they celebrate their fortune. I'd appreciate it if you would wait until I leave before you open this one." He put the missive on the sideboard, saluted and departed.

Frances bounced out of bed and was the first to reach the letter. "Let me see!" She grabbed the letter, but then handed it to Erik. "It's yours, good or bad." She pouted. "Never mind wandering down memory lane, open the damn letter!"

Erik withdrew two pieces of paper, one folded inside the other. He held up the light blue rectangle.

"Is that a check?"

"Twenty dollars!" Looking at the signature, he read, "Kowalski?"

"Who in the world is he?"

"Kowalski? Chuck Kowalski! We were together on Saipan. It must have been ten years ago. The letter can't be that old. I remember him."

He handed it to Frances and began reading the letter aloud. "Dear Erik, I was going over some old wartime photos and I found this one. I thought you would like it. If you look on the back, you'll see a note to myself: 'Owe Erik $20.00.' I left before I had the chance to repay it. As you know, usually, all debts are cancelled when you move off the island. I couldn't resist; I put in the check and mailed it to your service address. Let me know if you ever get this, with love and remembrance, Chuck." As Erik told the story to Cathy, he could visualize the picture of him and Kowalski in their flight overalls standing next to their plane.

"We went out and spent ten dollars on a dinner. We were rich."

Cathy listened to this story without moving. Being there as he reminisced warmed her, but she felt a nagging pull of envy. She, not Frances, was there, sharing the bravery and joy. She thought, *Why do I want to reach out and touch him? Why this vision, disturbing my life? Last time the boss chased me and here I am, letting the seeds of yearning creep in. Am I going to sneak up on him and kiss him?* The comical clumsiness of that picture caused her to laugh. She thought, *Stay content with Rudy and with the comfortable, professional relations with Dr. Nostrom.*

She picked up the papers. "If there is nothing else, I'll be going. Good luck this morning. You won't need another twenty dollars."

"I didn't mean to bore you with my long story. Got carried away." He stood and opened the door for her. She smiled at him, turned and walked out, leaving a light trace of her perfume.

He was glad she was the listener. She stirred his thoughts of young Frances, Frances before the stroke.

From his memory images came, frame after frame of the happiness of that dinner and afterward of skipping down Broadway toward 42nd Street. They had made love Saturday morning before rising, when they were dollar-poor, and again, later that night, when they were stuffed and rich. It was love with soft screams, groans and laughter, with unbearable, exhilarating tension and release. But it was them together, not twenty dollars, that had made love of life, of today and the promise of perfumed tomorrows, burn brightly for them that day. He rested his head on his folded arms, allowing the silent tears to drop onto the tabletop.

In twenty minutes the grief subsided. He washed his face. The competing facets of his life slipped into their compartments and he was ready for the contest.

Chapter 57

Reinhart and the group from Gainesville were already there. Mr. Hagen had called to say that he would be thirty minutes late for the ten o'clock meeting. Erik read the note Kimberly handed him. He scowled and thought, *I know, this is a set-up to allow Hagen to make a grand entrance after we all have gathered.* As Jerry entered, Erik caught him by the arm. "Let's meet in another room for a moment."

He handed Jerry the note and expressed his suspicions. "We are just going to sit here until he arrives."

"Good plan." He gave the thumbs-up gesture. While waiting, they reviewed Jake's data, deciding the best time to present it.

When they returned to the board room, the gathering was complete, including all of the board members, Paul and Kimberly, his secretary, Edward Hartman in charge of claims and Mr. Hagen. The meeting was called to order and the minutes of Wednesday's meeting read and approved. Dr. Stanley Reinhart was recognized.

"The continued business carried over from last meeting is the matter of management of the company. I believe you all have had the opportunity to consider the question and I make a motion that we engage the firm of Hagen Management Company to handle the day-by-day operations of Amed, answerable to the wishes of the board. The details of the motion are outlined on the presentation before you." Reinhart had placed a copy at each member's seat when he had first arrived. "Let us take a few minutes to refresh ourselves. Then we can open the floor for discussion."

"Thank you, Mr. Chairman," Erik said sarcastically. "I know it's only a formality, but I believe the gavel is still in my hand." He tried to evaluate the reception of his strained attempt at humor: A smile meant the wearer would be with him on the final vote. There were three smiles, three frowns and three faces wearing puzzlement. It wasn't reassuring.

With Erik at the head of the table, Reinhart manipulated to put himself on the right hand and Mr. Hagen on the left. He could respond to any question directed to the chair. This would be his shining hour. As he ran over the presentation and the papers the board members were now reading, he could find no weakness in his position. They certainly must see the strength and the protection afforded by an experienced, up-and-running management team.

Jack Reed was the first to inquire. "Will the board have any say in the day-by-day operations?" He directed this question to Mr. Hagen.

"The board is the ultimate authority, after the policy holders. They give you their money. The board lays out the perimeters within which management functions. After that, you watch us carefully. There is a saying in this business of board vs management—Nose in, hands out—referring to the prospective arena. Retrospectively you can second-guess us until the cows come home. Are we straight on that relationship?"

"So we have no say?"

"I thought he was pretty clear on that," Richard Garing answered for Hagen.

Kenneth Moning interrupted. "Let me understand something. We on the board, at least for the present, receive no compensation, and your company takes, what, 22% of the premiums right off the top?"

"You think it is a license to steal?" Earl Hagen asked patronizingly. "In one of the papers before you, page nine I believe, you will see a projection of the expense factor for the next year for your present operation. Twenty-one percent, pretty close. There is nothing magic in what I do. I run a tight ship, supply reliable administration service out of that 22% and earn a fair return. On the question of your working for nothing, that is ridiculous. Forgive me, but you are not creating a medical miracle to be rewarded by having your names in a landmark publication, you are starting a business, which will financially benefit your docs." He shook his head. "There is no reason to be guilty about being compensated for your labors. I can justify that as 'other operating expense,' if you wish."

There was silence. The appeal to greed was being rationalized in each mind: *Why the hell not? We are busting our humps. I don't see any one else out there. This is Saturday, for Christ's sake. This man could do it for us.*

Erik was frightened by the conversion he saw on their faces. Have they become businessmen so quickly? If they were responding to their greed, there was a good chance they would assign pure self-interest to Erik's stand, dissolving its validity. All the efforts would be for naught.

The weakness of despair was slowly replaced by the strength of anger. Erik thought, *I have brought them from the panic of being without hope of solution to now, when they have a clear direction. So clear, they are willing to discard their leader and rush off on their own, into the arms of a con artist. No wonder doctors are the favorite targets for swindlers. The doctors have the two most desirable attributes: They are intelligent but ignorant of the subject they are buying, and they are too arrogant to recognize the flaw.*

Thomas Frond lifted a folder from his attaché case and opened it before him. "I remember when we first crunched the numbers to see if the company would be viable, the financial margin of safety existed because we were running a not-for-profit program. I'm sure Hagen is not going to be working for no profit, so why are we thinking of going in the direction against what we started with?"

Reinhart raised his hand and said, "May I speak for Mr. Hagen? The savings produced by experienced management will far exceed the price of his services. Isn't that why we are here, really, to keep down the cost of the premiums? Yes, this move would call for a modification of our original method of accomplishing the savings, but not the desirable end result. This would be a change in tactics, not a change in strategy. Let us not get so infatuated with our positions that we are unable to advance." He directed his comments toward Erik.

Anthony Sanchez said, "It seems to me there is more at stake here than just money. Once profit enters the picture, its increase frequently rules over optimum decisions in favor of the physician. It adds another agenda to the equation, which I for one do not think we need. Until now, we have added each member of the administration only after we reviewed at least two candidates and after we had a chance to thoroughly check on them. With Mr. Hagen and company, we have heard only his sales pitch. Stanley, you introduced him; how much background checking did you do?" Sanchez waited.

Reinhart peered at Mr. Hagen. "Before I asked Erik to allow Mr. Hagen to present before us—an appearance he agreed with—I read Earl's brochures and made some calls. Because of the time constraints, I thought it would be a good idea to have the board be acquainted with Earl. If he passed muster we would have some time to inquire formally."

"Then you don't vouch for him?"

"I do not understand what you mean by vouch. I was impressed and thought to bring him here. I really cannot vouch for him completely until we have more data."

"Gentlemen." Hagen stood up. "I came here to offer my help. I told you whom I am. If I am to proceed with you, I will need all the time that is left between now and December. Certainly, I will provide you with an extensive curriculum vitae, but let me officially get started in your name. Dr. Reinhart, I appreciate your defense, though I do not think I needed it."

Kenneth Moning was shaking his head. "We are here to determine what form of administration we want, not for character assassination. Mr. Hagen has been kind enough to come here to talk to us. I like his ideas. He is a business man and we need that."

"I am a physician person," Fredrick Cannon called out. "I wonder how the physicians will take to another commercially run program?"

Erik said, "It is almost lunchtime. Why don't we break for a pit stop and lunch? It's set up next door. Be back at one o'clock. OK?"

Chapter 58

Jerry tapped Reinhart's shoulder. "Could I see you for a moment?"

"Why yes." Reinhart suddenly felt elated. Could this be Jerry's pitch to be friendly, to be on the winning side? *He is telling me I won. Well, it is about time.* They walked down the hall. Jerry said to Paul, "Mind if we use your office?"

"Not at all, I'll be out of here in a minute." He hurried around his desk and was gone. Reinhart walked behind the desk and sat in Paul's chair, leaving Jerry to sit in front of him. It seemed only fitting, to Reinhart, for Jerry to sit before him, seeking his blessing. It was truly a marvelous feeling.

"Well, Jerry, I think it will all work out for the best. I haven't enquired about the legal services available to Mr. Hagen, but I'm sure, at least at first, he will be leaning on you. If there is any confusion, I will be very glad to set him straight. After all, in the beginning you were part of the whole idea."

Jerry put the stack of papers on the desk, "That's very kind of you, to think of me at this crucial time." With that, he began showing Jake's reports to Reinhart, one at a time. He watched Reinhart's shoulders droop and his face go ashen.

The meeting reconvened at one o'clock. The burps and casual conversation subsided; Erik stood up. "Ever since the idea of outsourcing our administration was presented, I have been wrestling with the concept. It will bring strength to our efforts. At the same time, it will bring traditional insurance views and precepts. The ISO tables, used for setting occurrence policies rates, will be leaned upon to determine our rates, for that is traditional. The use of agencies to sell our insurance, with six percent commission coming off the top, will be the way to go, for that is traditional. Experience credentialing will be absolute, for that is traditional.

"If we were in stable times and in a stable line of insurance, no one could fault me for following along. I would be justly criticized for clinging to our newly formed team over the experience of Mr. Hagen.

"We are not in that world. Medical liability claims and cost of handling claims have risen over 300% in the last two years. No existing company has had this experience in the past, and none are prepared for it. In Florida, gigantic companies are folding their tents and silently stealing away. The crisis we face today is partly due to the earthquake-like changes taking place, shaking the industry to its foundation."

He saw agreement and concern on the faces of the board members, including Dr. Reinhart. Mr. Hagen wore a blank expression and Jerry was smiling.

"No, this is not the time to reinvent the path to disaster; rather, it is time to face the storm with unique ideas. Just recently, a method of insurance has been developed called claims-made. The actuaries haven't collected enough data of this animal to say what the rates should be, but we know the first year will be reduced, even with a margin for error. In our truly not-for-profit mode, there is no significant harm done if the premiums are redundant because any money in excess of our costs gets returned to the physicians in discount premiums for the following year. With a management company taking 22 percent off the top and 6 percent to the agent, any safety excess would be gone forever.

"Now is not the time to be traditional. We must be able to adjust to this new threat. Because of the ignorance in the past, I believe decisions drawn from that pool of experience would be a handicap rather than a benefit."

Erik regretted there was no written sing-along for them to follow. He could only hope he had created confusion, and that his concepts penetrated the confusion.

"I thought about being a business man. We gathered to form a trust, meaning we ask the physicians to trust us to protect their interests. Happily, when we struggle to control the cost of malpractice insurance, we have self-interest, for we all are personally seeking coverage. It is true, no one else is doing it, but to steal a phrase from the past, 'If not now, then when, if not us then who?' We have an opportunity to save ourselves, as well as all physicians who care to follow, from exorbitant, uncontrolled premiums at the hands of the commercial carriers. The physicians must give us the money to create our company; they must trust us. If we are to succeed, we must honor that trust. It's true, you will not get a landmark paper out of this, but in these days when cash is becoming king, you will have the satisfaction of answering a call, a non-financial reward."

Sanchez began to slowly applaud and laughingly said, "Get that man off the soap box."

"Too corny?"

"You touched my heart," Jack Reed said.

Stanley Reinhart had not spoken since the group reconvened. In the lull following Erik speech, all eyes began to question Reinhart's silence. Without thinking, he put his hand on the stack of papers Jerry had given him. It was a long moment before he began to speak. "I believe all that must be said has been said. There is a motion of the floor and I would like to call the question."

It was a bombshell. They were stunned and motionless. Only Mr. Hagen responded, "What the hell?"

"I repeat, Mr. Chairman, I request we call the question," Reinhart said in a flat monotone.

"As you wish, I call the question." To Kimberly, he said, "Please read the motion."

"A motion was made and seconded as follows: 'The board engage the firm of Hagen Management Company to handle the day-by-day operations of Amed, answerable to the wishes of the board.'" Seeing no challenge to her reading, she sat down.

Erik held his breath. Jerry had not had the chance to tell him about the scene with Reinhart, so he was as baffled as the rest as to Reinhart's no comment. He questioned the moment of the call for the question, was he reborn or dead? His thoughts raced through all comments made this day. He'd be damned if he could even guess at the outcome.

"All those in favor of the motion say yea." The ball was now rolling toward the row of pins-a strike or a seven-ten split? The whirring of the fan was the only sound in the room.

They were frozen, waiting for Dr. Stanley Reinhart to give them direction. Not everyone would follow his lead but those who would could not act without it. He gave strength to the idea of change. On their own, they would not have dared to move, except as a follower. He sat and waited.

Seeing no yeas, Erik continued, "All those opposed to the motion?"

Four hands went up immediately. With almost visible effort, Reinhart slowly raised his hand. It stood frozen, suspended for all to see. One by one, each of the remaining board members raised his hand. Erik did not know why, but the battle was over. He had won.

Chapter 59

Congratulations and comments mixed in high decibels, and then gradually subsided. Separately and in twos and threes they left the office. Dr. Jesse Gentile stayed behind. He caught Erik by the shoulder and in a soft voice said, "May I talk to you for a few minutes?"

Erik was riding high with surprise and jubilation. He thought, *I didn't expect praise from one of the Gainesville contingent, but what the hell; it's a great night!* "Sure, let's sit in the board room. We won't be bothered there." Erik automatically took a seat at the head of the table. Gentile sat at Erik's left. He ran his hand through his thinning brown hair. While staring at the table Gentile began, "I've hesitated to speak to you, but this seems to be as good a time as any. I'm leaving the board."

"For how long?"

"Permanently."

"Why? You in some difficulty? Can I help?" Erik leaned forward, seeking Gentile's face. It reflected pain and conviction.

"It's personal."

"That's not good enough. Particularly now. I think we have a good chance. I'm enthusiastic."

"That's fine for you. You're the leader. I don't think I'm ready to take that chance. Here it is, September six and we have less than two hundred and fifty members. The average premium is, say, four thousand. We are already on the hook for one million dollars."

"But we are going to make it!"

"But what if we don't? There will be two hundred and fifty angry doctors who will sue Amed and sue us personally."

The decision caught Erik off guard. After the positive vote earlier at the board meeting, he had laid his protective veneer aside to enjoy the moment. This thrust slipped into his unprotected gut. In defense he said, "We all knew there was some risk when we started." Immediately, he sensed it was the wrong approach. He could see his words harden Gentile.

"I don't think we in Gainesville were told that very clearly. Remember it was rushed. That doesn't matter; I don't want to continue. And if my wife ever found out that I was taking such a gamble for my hobby—that's what she calls it—and not getting paid, and even paying my own airfare, she'd divorce me. I made up my mind."

"Nothing we can do to resolve your fears?"

"No. Besides, I haven't been happy about this company being run just by doctors. What do you know about this complicated business? I wanted an experienced outside manager. I only voted the way I did because Reinhart did. I still don't know why he chickened out."

Erik remained silent. The boardroom was cold. He didn't know if he felt the shiver because of the temperature or the fear. Then, he said, "If you're determined, that's what you have to do. Did you mention this to the others?"

"No. I don't plan to. I don't want to give you any more trouble than I have to. I just won't show up at the meetings. Please don't put my name on the minutes of the meetings. Next month I'll send you a letter talking about personal problems and then slowly fade away. Hopefully, I won't cause waves." He shrugged his shoulders. "Sorry." Erik was slow to accept Gentile's hand, but he did it. Gentile walked out.

Erik didn't move. He found the jacket he had placed on the back of his chair at the beginning of the board meeting. As he put it on the jacket felt good on his cold body. He got up and stood behind the chair Gentile had occupied. He made a gesture of strangling Gentile's vision. He realized he was facing a dilemma: to tell the other members of the board and expect a wild stampede away or not to tell and risk the loss of his credibility in their eyes if the deceit was revealed. He smiled mirthlessly, and thought, *To tell or not to tell, that is the question.* He came around the table to reach the window. Looking out, he could see Sanchez in his green Porsche. Erik believed Sanchez was the last one to leave the parking lot. He said aloud, "Not to tell."

Chapter 60

Reinhart pushed the partially opened door that led from Kimberly's secretarial office to the boardroom. He stepped into the room and said, "I didn't mean to overhear that interesting conversation. I came back to retrieve my notes, which Kimberly had colleted and stored on her desk. It was all quite innocent." He was talking to the back of Erik, who was frozen, knowing he was about to realize his worse nightmare. He turned to see a slight smile on Reinhart's face.

"How long have you been there?" Erik asked.

"That is not important. What is important is that I may be able to rescue you from a no-win situation. I believe it would be my duty to inform the others of Dr. Gentile's decision."

"That's your idea of help?" Erik knew he was vulnerable. He waited for Reinhart's blow.

"Gentile's action reflects once again that you are incapable of true leadership. I probably could talk Gentile out of his leaving. I have taken the time, as a real leader, to know each member of the board. Why should I? Not to save you!"

"I know Gentile well enough; he's committed to his wife and safety."

"Possibly. In that case I am committed to speak." Neither man had moved from his standing position in the darkened room. Reinhart finally walked the length of the table and sat at his usual position at the far end. "Unless you are willing to step aside and suggest I take over. Many already see me as the chief. You saw how they waited for me to show them how to vote. No one is solidly against me as they would be against you when they found out you were planning to withhold information in order to stay on top."

Erik sat down in his chairman's seat. He wondered if Reinhart would really tell the board and put the entire project in jeopardy. If he did, would Sanchez bolt? Would Reed or Garing or Frond, or even Harmon and Moninger? "You would act, being aware of the damage it might cause?"

"In my mind, it is less damaging than having you continue as leader."

Even coming from Reinhart, Erik was stunned by the viciousness of the comment. He stood up and walked to the door. "Stanley, I see you for the first time. Before I thought you were understandingly ambitious, but now I know you are dangerous, not only to me but more important, to Amed. Do what you must. The company is strong enough to survive it." As he passed through the door he thought, *It's his hand grenade.* Erik decided to keep the conversations with Gentile and Reinhart to himself, well aware he was taking the biggest gamble of his life. *Will I still be lucky?*

Chapter 61

With the revolt smothered and having no knowledge of the storm over Dr. Gentile, Jerry was free to return to Tallahassee on Monday. Cassy and Linda had the apartment to themselves for the weekend.

"Since you have been away, you have grown so, I feel like you are my sister. It's fun."

"The mother of a girl in school insists her daughter call her by her first name. She says they even double-date as sisters. I don't know if that's true."

"It could get complicated. Who would use the bedroom first?"

"Tony said it could be a kinky foursome."

"I'm proud of you as my daughter and would have it no other way."

They spent the afternoon shopping, mostly for a wardrobe for Cassy, to ready her for Paris.

In the last few years, with Cassy lunging into adolescence with vulnerable independence, Linda had muffled her maternal instincts. However, today, walking arm in arm with this lovely young woman, she enjoyed a rare sense of contentment.

The emotional trauma of parental separation, with Maurice blaming her and pulling on Cassy's heartstrings, had frozen the relations. Linda thought it was natural for a daughter to favor her father, but, until just now, it had been so one-sided. For the first time since Maurice left, Linda was happy with her daughter. She walked with her defenses down, vulnerable to the next phase.

"May I rent a car until I'm ready to leave?"

"Why? I can drive you if you need to go somewhere." Linda knew it was a stupid answer, but Cassy's request was a surprise attack. She could sense the wall re-erecting between them. Was it ever down? Cassy must have known her comment would present a problem. *Why couldn't she allow me to have at least this one day of parental rapture?*

"You go to work. Tony is gone. I'm supposed to sit around all day? For once, why can't you just let me do what I want? I'll be out of your hair soon enough."

Just for once? Linda was about to commit the cardinal sin of reminding the child of Linda's selfless sacrifices, but said nothing. They walked in silence for some time.

"Well?"

"It isn't that simple. You need a learner's permit and insurance. Do you know how to drive?"

"I took Driver's Ed. In school, but of course you wouldn't know that. I wrote to Dad. He thought it was great. Of course I can drive. The question is, may I, dear Mother?"

Linda suddenly was so tired. *There must be some right way for parents to respond to adolescents, but I don't know.* "There is still the matter of insurance."

"I could use yours. The girls in school do it all the time.'"

"It's illegal."

"Mother!"

"I work for an attorney. I know better."

"The other mothers know it too; however they love their daughter."

"Thank you. Forget it." Another silence.

"All right, I'll call Lorna. I talked to her last night. She's off for a few weeks. She'll be glad to drive me; she said she needed the company."

Cassy took Linda's arm and continued walking. She smiled at Linda and said, "Let's talk about curfew, and let's not get hung up on 'in your days' please."

"I'm glad for Lorna, but it is still eleven o'clock."

"Oh, shit!" Coming from Cassy's beautiful mouth, profanity sounded cute.

Chapter 62

As planned, Jerry returned to Tallahassee on Monday. He rented a car at the airport and drove directly to Linda's apartment. She met him at the door as he climbed the stairs.

"Hi."

Kiss.

"Hi."

Kiss.

"That was nice," Linda said as she stepped back to judge his mood. "A Dr. Gentile called here, asking for you." Her voice was questioning.

"Here? How would he call here?"

"He said he called Griffin to see if he knew where you could be reached when you were in Tallahassee. Griffin said he might try my number. So he did."

Jerry hugged her, led her into the apartment and said, "Let's see what that's all about. Use your phone to Gainesville?"

"I thought we settled that."

"Thanks." He pulled his address and phone book out of his briefcase, found Gentile's number and dialed. He smiled at Linda. "One ring, two rings and three rings." He nodded to Linda and said to the female voice on the phone, "Hello, is Dr. Gentile there?"

"Who's calling?"

"Jerry Simms."

Gentile was on the phone immediately. "Thanks for returning my call. I wonder if you would do me a favor. Ask Erik to call me."

"Sure, but why can't you call him yourself?"

"I'm not sure he'd take the call."

Jerry looked at Linda and shrugged. He swung around and sat in the leather chair. To the phone he said, "Whoa, let's go back. I must be missing a part of the story."

"I told Erik I was quitting the board." He paused. "I should have talked to you first. I thought the risk was too great." He went on to relate his discussion with Erik.

"Yes, you should have talked to me. As a director, you are not expected to be an expert in everything. You only have to act as a prudent man would in your place."

"It is now clear to me; I panicked after voting against Hagen on Saturday. By Sunday morning I wasn't as frightened by the uncertainty; it seemed to be manageable. More important, there was a void when I thought of not being a part of this adventure. I hadn't realized that being in Amed, being one of a very small group of decision-makers, made up a big part of my life."

"I don't see any damage. Just call Erik, or I'll ask him to give you a call."

"I'd be grateful." He hung up.

Linda came behind Jerry and began massaging his shoulders. "A tough problem?"

"He thought so, but it was really only a storm in a tea cup."

Jerry knew Erik would be relieved, but not knowing the Reinhart conflict, he had no idea how relieved. Jerry seated the phone and dismissed the subject as not being too important.

Chapter 63

Once settled in, Jerry began a strange routine: breakfast or at least coffee in the morning with Linda and Cassy, in the office during the day, and evenings in constant turmoil. When Cassy stayed in, her performance alternated from looking upon Jerry as a surrogate father to behaving like a precocious femme fatale. Her maturing figure was luscious. At a whim, she would drape herself on the arm of Jerry's chair. At other times, she ignored both of them. Linda was uneasy with this behavior.

On one occasion, Jerry watched as Cassy slowly danced, by herself, to the radio music. She drifted out of the room.

Linda chidingly asked, "Would you like to sleep with her?"

Jerry was caught off guard for a moment, then said, "At the office one man asked the other 'Would you like to fuck a sixteen-year-old?' The man answered, 'Of course, that's why there's a law against it.'"

Jerry moved closer to Linda. "It's not only the law. I'm monogamous by nature, not only in love but also in sex. A cobra's dance is beautiful and fascinating, but I'm not about to press it to my chest. In my workday, I frequently come close to smiling, flirtatious women. You don't know about them, so you can't feel threatened by them. But they and Cassy are on the same shelf: attractive but not my desire." Linda was surprised by Jerry's serious answer. He then completed his argument, designed to ease Linda's consternation.

"There is nothing noble about my attitude. I truly believe you can't accept one-hundred-percent love from one person unless you give one-hundred-percent love. If you have other sources of love, you dilute your primary source. It's not as if they are accumulative, one hundred percent, one hundred and ten percent, and so on. You are my source. I want one hundred percent; I want to be able to accept one hundred percent, thus monogamy." As he talked, he allowed one last fantasy with Cassy. Without Linda's question, his conscience would never have permitted the thought to enter his consciousness.

She shook her head. "You trial lawyers will say anything to win your case, wouldn't you?" Linda leaned over to Jerry and kissed him on the mouth. Cassy came back into the room at that moment, "Hey, knock that off, there are children present."

Jerry had run into the jealousy phase several times in his past romances. The girls accused him of being a flirt, and there was a good deal of truth to it. Then it didn't matter. The sex object accepted him as he was, unsuccessfully tried to change him, or departed. Her leaving bruised his ego, but left his heart intact. "There are many others, and not too far, willing to dry my tears away."

Now, with Linda, he was in virginal territory. He was beginning to define his love. The very concept of Jerry in love was new, consuming and terrifying. He wanted her to think of him when he was not within her touch, free of fear, pain or doubt. He wished he could say, "Yes, I think about women. It's a guy thing, harmless and non-competitive. Let me have it, be happy for me."

He knew it could never be. She would say, or think, "It belittles me. If they knew you were thinking of them, they would be laughing at me. I dream of making a home for you, of dressing attractively for you, of sharing your hopes. And you dream of other women!"

His long-held motto, women for sex only, struggled valiantly against the invasion of Linda. The world of joy she offered him was winning.

He thought, *Perhaps I could give it up. After all, it's not an addiction, or is it? I must be careful not to label Linda the cause of the agony of withdrawal. It is going to take heavy-duty work, but it's worth it. A true labor of love.*

He was standing in the kitchen. His burst of laughter filled the room like an explosion as he thought of the tirade from Erik if he could look into Jerry's brain at this moment. Linda ran in to see what was the matter.

Perhaps for protection, Jerry veered toward the parental role, which Cassy allowed him to play. It fit uncomfortably, coming out more pompously than he would like.

One evening, Jerry, Linda and Cassy stood in the middle of the living room.

"I think I mentioned I'm giving Cassy an allowance until she leaves for Paris. After that, her father takes over for the year she is with him. Now she's broke and wants to go to the show. The trouble with Cassy is that she wants things right now," Linda complained. "I told her if she did her room, at the end of the week I'd advance her the money for the show. Here for ten days. I'd take it out of her allowance over the four weeks she is here, and then we would be even."

"Forget it. I need the money now," Cassy said. "You sound like a bank. I'm your daughter! Don't tell me again about how hard it was for you. You grew up in the last stages of the work ethic." She stamped her foot. "These days that idea sucks. We look at all you 'workers' and all we can see is a wasted life. 'The reward will come tomorrow if we struggle and strain today.' The only trouble is you die before you learn how to enjoy the reward." Cassy threw herself into the leather chair and turned her head into the leather arm.

"Cassy is not alone," Jerry said. "The other day one of my clients was bitching to me. He told his daughter, 'The trouble with you is you want everything instantly.' Her retort was, 'That's not fast enough! I can't wait that long!'"

Jerry walked over to Cassy's chair and sat on the edge of the seat. He smiled as he caught a whiff of her, a combination of perfume and young body odor. He remembered his brother telling him that once while sitting next to a young lady on a floating raft in the lake, he could smell what he thought was woman, was sex, and it was marvelous.

Jerry looked down at Cassy. He thought his efforts at being parental were bearing fruit. How little she knew about the joys and sorrow, the jubilation and pain that lay before her. She was teetering on the brink. How to bridge the gap between the adolescent world she knew and the adult world he knew would replace it?

"It's really a game," he ventured. "And it doesn't have to be a lifetime of struggle. There are three situations I can think of offhand where it calls for work, requires waiting and yields a reward."

"Oh yea, tell me. I suppose I'm going to hear it anyway." Cassy was

WANT IS A GROWING GIANT

sulking but she lifted her head to hear.

"There's this stack of bills waiting to be paid. Let's make it Linda's bills. You have the money in the bank, but it is a pain to sit down, write the checks, go to the post office and mail them. Until you do them, there is an unpleasant nagging feeling. You put in the work needed to take care of them. Once done, however, your reward is a feeling of satisfaction and freedom from that nagging feeling." He bent over to see how this sat with Cassy.

"You must be kidding," she said.

"Never say die. I'll try another," Jerry responded. "Homework. This is more up your alley. It haunts you. You finally attack it. You put in the work. Then you are rewarded with the feeling of accomplishment. The problem is resolved. Not buying it?"

"I'm not even shopping."

"I continue. You are fat. It seems that no matter how thin a woman is she may be convinced she is overweight. You feel fat."

"Not fat. But I guess I'd like to lose a few pounds."

"Fat makes you uncomfortable. You tend to avoid the bikini. You might even blame the fat for losing a boyfriend."

"Was my mother talking about my former boyfriends? Oh, Mother!" Cassy got up and walked to the window, staring out, but staying in easy earshot of Jerry's voice.

"No. That was just an educated guess. It's funny how the same problems come up again and again. My sister went through that. Back to my sermon, you finally decide to follow the diet, which has been pasted on your bedroom mirror for some time. This is the work. You lose fifteen pounds, the reward.

"In all these examples, there was work, there was waiting and there was a reward. If you looked for only an instant solution, you would be frustrated. The trick is to find the pathway to the things you want. If it is instantly obtainable, fine, but if not, apply the WWR formula."

He knew it would be unfair to leave it at that. "Unfortunately, you have to enjoy the momentary joy of the reward, for there is certainly going to be another batch of bills, another assignment and another few pounds to lose."

Casey turned quickly. "There, you said it. Why try?"

"If you're lucky enough to succeed, those small rewards will add up and make you feel better, even good about yourself. And then…" He paused to deliver the winning blow. "You begin to seek out those things you can solve with work and waiting and which yield the reward of that good feeling."

"I want it now," she said, but the conviction in her voice was minimal. She walked out of the room.

Linda stood up, her hands reaching forward, palms up. "And what do you think that did?"

"Who knows, but if you hear my words in her mouth in a few weeks, you will know that we made some inroads."

"You sounded awfully fatherly, Mr. Simms. I wouldn't be surprised if she went to the john to throw up."

"A prophet in his own land…"

Linda threw a pillow at him.

Chapter 64

September eighth. With the fears of outsourcing behind them, the first demand on the board member's energies was the job of reaching the deadline of December 20. Paul had hired two more front desk girls to handle review of applications and to follow up on initial requests for information from physicians. As a result of the first statewide pitch at hospitals and medical association meetings, a hundred more applications arrived immediately. Then there was a dearth of activity. Each morning Paul would bow to the sign on the back of his door, "Doctors are procrastinators."

"I hope you are right!"

He had set up speaking engagements in the remaining locations where his team could carry the word to physicians. After a crash course, he felt the members in Gainesville were ready so he penciled them in for lectures in their vicinity. He kept his fingers crossed, waiting to hear the results of their efforts. In the recent months, they had gradually lowered their guard. The amount of protection they felt they needed from the sneaky New York-Miami crowd had decreased. He wasn't sure they would buy a car from Erik, but they began to accept his leadership.

Kimberly ushered Mr. Garrett Dobson into Paul's office. "Mr. Dobson is here for the interview you set up last Friday. He's from the *Medical Chronicle*."

The greetings passed, Dobson said, "Tell me about your progress. I know you raised the seed money from your own board of directors, the legislature has given you until December thirty-first to get five hundred paying policy holders, and you are doing it all in-house. One of our spies heard about Mr. Hagen. Off the record, you sidestepped a land mine."

Paul brought him up to date. He believed an article in the paper would help. This overrode his usual skepticism. Jerry had once told him he'd never seen the press make a wrong statement unless he knew anything about the subject.

He told Dobson, "I'd appreciate it if you would emphasize the urgency here. You saw the sign on the door?"

"Yes, I have and I will comply." He gave an exaggerated salute.

Dobson left. Paul thought the interview had gone pretty well. The reporter seemed sympathetic and was well aware of the present predicament caused by the delay.

That behind him, he asked Kimberly to have Edward Hartman join him. He thought Hartman had been in claims for many years before coming to Amed. Being more experienced than any other member of the staff, he could recall more incidences of disaster.

The quote "Those jest at scars who never tasted a wound" described Hartman's attitude toward the others, particularly sales. Paul remembered Hartman saying, "It never changes; whoever is in charge of sales wants to give away coverage to any warm body. I searched for proven criteria to rule out increased risky doctors. If there is one, I never heard of it. The only study I know shows a doctor who has had a claim in the past is more likely to have another than a doctor who has none. With the number of claims increasing so rapidly, we can't even apply that as a criterion. One out of eight doctors is being sued each year. In ten years, there would be no one to insure safely."

Paul said, "Jerry was telling me, the sales folks want to sell everyone, and claims want to sell no one—no insured, no losses." He studied Edward. "There must be a balance that allows a reasonably predictable risk."

"There is a great one. The only trouble, it is in retrospect. I can tell you dozens of doctors we shouldn't have insured—after we paid out hundreds of thousands."

Paul said cautiously, "Right now, we are binding physicians with no reported claims. We don't know if they had any incidence where they thought they would be sued, but nothing came of it. The scary thing is, with the climate becoming more litigious, tomorrow those incidences will become true suits."

"What do you do if the doctor reports a past claim or suit?"

"What did your California company do?"

"We prayed a lot. Seriously, they were going through an evolution. A first, the doctors would review the case. If the claim was medically defensible, we would insure them."

"I believe that's the plan here."

"I hope not. We quickly found we lost more than half the cases for other than medical reasons. The frightened doctor would change the records. He didn't know the ink was dated. After he strongly denied the change, the plaintiff's attorney would put on a writing expert who carefully explains to the jury all inks carry code and date, detectable with the proper equipment. Once they catch the doctor in a lie, he screams '*mea culpa*' and the medically defensible case is lost."

"So where did the evolution carry you?"

"After that, we would evaluate the doctor, ask our insured doctors in his community and in a similar specialty, see how strong a witness he would make. It is amazing; if the jury sees a straight, honest-appearing doctor, they will forgive almost anything, but if he is weak, looks shady, they will give to the plaintiff, no matter how defensible his action. In confidence, we would ask, 'Would you want to share the risk of Dr. X?'"

"So, if he looked OK and the previous case was medically defensible, you would insure him?"

"That is pretty much where it was when I left. It is an undependable system at best, but there is no other method available. Even then, unfortunately, we might reject a good doctor because of negative reports from other doctors who were in competition with the applicant."

Paul said, "It is scary. Make the wrong selection and we could lose our shirts. I don't think I truly realized what a gamble we are taking."

"Before you run to the hills, there is a saving grace."

"Tell me, please!"

"The premiums are calculated to cover the losses. If a suit hit one of a thousand doctors, for a million dollar settlement, it would cost each doctor one thousand dollars. Ordinarily, actuaries are able to determine the risk potential. Once we know the total amount of dollars needed, it is politics and prejudice that determine the individual physician's premium, based on location and specialty."

"The actuaries sound like the cavalry coming to the rescue."

Hartman shook his head. "Not so fast. The actuaries need several years of data to calculate the past trend to judge the future. Unfortunately, we are using the new, claims-made method of insuring the doctors and there is little past experience to go by."

"Am I heading for the hills again?"

"Not really, for we are justified in adding a buffer to the needed amount. No one really knows what the premiums should be. As Erik said the other day, we will start with third-year rates. In insurance, timing is everything. If the catastrophe hits in the first year, you are doomed. One of my friends was an insurance agent. For ten years, he passed the hurricane insurance premiums on to the home company. There were no claims. For the company, it was a license to steal. He finally decided to get on the gravy train. He and a group of investors started an insurance company protecting the hotels on the beach. The premiums were huge-found money. Unfortunately, Hurricane Donna hit that year, their first year. They went straight to receivership."

Hartman stood up, stretched and went to the sideboard for coffee. Need a cup?"

"Always."

Hartman said, "For the present, then, we will accept physicians with prior medically defensible cases. We just don't have the time to do more intensive background search and complete five hundred contracts by mid December."

Paul wrote his signature in the air. "Put my initials on those first five hundred. My first guess would be these doctors would have a higher loss ratio than average, but who knows, if that were true it would make credentialing a lot easier."

Chapter 65

The following day, Tuesday, September 9, Paul set up a conference call among Erik, Jerry, Edward and himself. After bringing the group up to date on the progress of the company, he said, "At our last meeting, we talked about losing Hugh in marketing and needing his replacement. I have interviewed three men, and I think I have found a good candidate. Mr. James Eisinger is thirty-eight years old, makes a fine appearance, talks well—did I say he was a salesman? He got his BA degree at University of Miami. He was the assistant director of marketing at K and L, a medical equipment manufacturing company. They moved to Mexico and he decided to stay here."

"I'll marry him!" Jerry called out. "Seriously, you are the one who has to live with him. If he is all right with you, I'm for him."

"I agree," Erik said. "I hope he's tough. You know it's sales versus claims with Edward on the other side of the seesaw."

"You do me an injustice," Hartman said. "I always get along with sales, as long as all applications must go through me. As you know, my real enemy is credentialing. Edward can pull in all the garbage he wants to. It only alarms me when they slip through credentialing."

"It's a good thing you are laughing."

"I'm kidding. I already met Mr. James Eisinger. We talked. I'm sure he'll do fine. I see he's married, with a son, six, and a daughter, four," Hartman said, with a straight face.

"OK, then, assuming negotiations on compensation go satisfactorily, he should be able to start in ten days."

Eisinger was not to start until the following Friday, the nineteenth, but he came into the office the same week.

"We haven't cleaned up your office. I was expecting you next week." Paul greeted James as he came through the door.

"I thought I'd like to begin setting up some sources for my pipeline."

"Pipeline?"

"I take all the potential business; phone calls, inquiries, response to our ads and lectures, and applications from individuals and agents, and stuff them into the back end of the pipe line. This gives me an estimate of the maximum book of business I could expect. They come out of the front end, either a sale or a bust. I then have, an idea of the percentage of raw material that is solid. It also lets me gauge the quality of leads and agents."

Paul sat next to Eisinger. "You mentioned agents twice now. At least for the beginning, we were planning on direct sales; our insured talking us up. I am concerned about agents. First, and most obvious, is the commission, which takes a bite off the top and decreases the financial buffer we are depending upon to keep us solvent. Secondly, I understand the agent really owns the policy. I've heard of agents switching doctors from one company to another for a better commission."

"That can happen. In fact, because he is doing business with the agent, the doctor may not know of the switch, except for a little hidden notice. I think we will do pretty well with word-of-mouth communication. In fact, it is the best. The new doctor is truly ours. We can direct mail advertisement to keep him aware of the great company with which he is associated. In California, we found the doctor let his agent pick his car and home insurance, but insisted selecting his malpractice carrier. We are pretty safe as long as the physician is calling the shots. He will live with a higher premium if he knows he is getting quality. God help us if medicine ever gets organized with managers running the show. Then it would be price '*uber allis.*'" Hartman shrugged his shoulders.

"If time squeezes as we approach December, we might consider agents, temporarily."

He questioned Paul, "I understand we are going to have a universal renewal date as of January 1. That could present a problem. Other companies have staggered dates of renewal, which means doctors will be looking for coverage before our beginning date and will be tempted to seek coverage elsewhere, rather than wait for us. Fortunately, there aren't too many other carriers around."

"That cuts down the market for this year. Can we still make five hundred by December?

"There's still plenty of time left. I'm an optimist, so I'm considering next year. After January, we will give partial-year coverage with renewal on the following January 1st."

Eisinger settled down to reviewing the present efforts at marketing. He smiled as he read their enthusiastic approach. In labeled folders, he organized hospitals, medical associations, individual inquiries and lists of doctors already contacted at least once. He could feel his empire coming together. The last sheet was a column of dates and the predicted number of policyholders up to that date. Next to December 14, he wrote 501.

Chapter 66

Lorna happily introduced Cassy to Troy McCoy, her boyfriend's buddy. Now they were a foursome.

For the first week, Cassy thought the arrangement was perfect. Sleep late, cruise with Lorna in the afternoon and date in the evening. The tingling sensation of the start of an infatuation was upon her, a song in her heart. At the beginning, she was blind to any defect in the source of this pleasure. The dance steps were so predictable, but when the butterfly first spread its delicate wings, all was new and fresh. Too soon, the routine became *déjà vu*. Troy's approach dimmed when compared to the boy-men at her school. She practiced the philosophy most recently expounded to her mother: fuck him first, and then see if you like him. Troy did not fare well after the fucking.

"Am I getting old, or is Troy as juvenile as all that?"

"Cassy, he is just your plaything for the few weeks you're here before you take off into the wild blue yonder," Lorna scolded. "Be happy. He's not to be your life's companion."

"I know. But to tell you the truth, I keep comparing him to Jerry."

"Jerry? Linda's old man? Where did that come from? He's ancient."

"Tell me. I don't know, he looks at me and I know he thinks I'm pretty hot, but he stays so cool. He acts as if he's always in control. The other night, when I was saying good night, I kissed him on the mouth. I could feel he wanted to jump on my bones right there; he was lying on the couch in the darkened living room, but he didn't move. I lost my courage and ran to my room. Even then, I thought he might follow me. I was on fire."

"Did he ever say anything? Did you ever say anything?"

"No and no. In fact, following that night's adventure, he wrapped himself in the 'fill-in father' role. I couldn't even repeat the garbage he was giving out the other night, something about not wanting instant satisfaction."

"Does your mother suspect anything?"

"Of course not. There's nothing to suspect, yet."

"Are you serious, or are you just pulling my leg?"

"Before I leave for Paris, you'll see. That's going to be a nice memory for me to take with me. It's turn-around time. Linda was always flirting with my boyfriends."

Jerry was aware of Cassy, but thought he had resolved the threat she imposed on his relationships. The novel experience of the fully dressed love he shared with Linda, which lasted before, during and after sex, and had its own spiritual joy, was like a precious jewel to him. He could take it out and look at it. It made him noble, made it easy to banish thoughts of Cassy, and of all other women. Still, he could not relax when Cassy was around. He couldn't wait until it was off to Paris for her. Once she was gone and he and Linda had their enchanted cottage back, their idyllic life would return.

Chapter 67

Judy Santos asked Cathy to come into her office. "I want to thank you for filling in for me in the last few months. As you know, my husband has been ill."

"No problem." Cathy gestured.

"I have decided to stay at home with him. He has gotten worse. He can hardly do anything for himself."

"I'm so sorry about your husband."

From the first meeting, Cathy had been impressed by Judy's restraint and her command of her emotions. Here she was, delivering a heart-rending account of her husband's deterioration, but displaying the passion of a weather report. Only her moistened eyes gave her away.

"I am going to recommend for you to step in as office manager. I know you haven't been here that long, but since you arrived, I could see you were leader quality. Both Shirley and Sharon look to you already."

"I'm sorry to hear this. It has been a real pleasure working with you. My last boss was a man. You really helped me."

"I plan to leave in two weeks, if it is all right with the doctors."

Judy's leaving started a new role for Cathy. She was glad she had volunteered to help Judy. In her last two weeks, Judy showed Cathy all the aspects of the business. From the start, Shirley and Sharon accepted her.

Unlike Judy, Cathy was able to mix the roles of disciplinarian and confidant.

One of the first occasions to arise demanding these talents was the follow-up on Sharon's night visitor. She came into Cathy's new office.

"Did you see the papers?" She took out a newspaper clipping and read, "'Attempted rapist shot to death in woman's apartment. Late last evening a black man was shot and killed while attempting to rape a young woman. The woman's boyfriend, an off-duty police officer, entered her room as the rapist rose from the bed. The shot was fatal. The girl, whose name is withheld, said the man had forced her to her bed, stroked her but had not proceeded further. She was sure he would have raped her if the boyfriend had not arrived.'

"It was him! Another ten minutes and he would have been gone. He wasn't going to rape her any more than he would have done me."

"We don't know that."

"Maybe if I had reported him, he would be alive today."

"Sharon, we don't know if it is the same guy."

"Should I go to the cops now, tell them what I know? I think I'd feel better."

Cathy looked at her. Sharon was not only a fellow worker, but now she represented the office. The notoriety could do some damage. Cathy's protective instincts flew to Dr. Nostrom.

"It won't make you feel better. I'm sure it could be worse. It would be hard for them to believe you. More important, you would have that cop as your lifetime enemy. If they accept what you say, they might investigate him for an unnecessary shooting."

"I was thinking of his mother. She'll go to her grave, believing her son was a rapist. It could kill a good Baptist. Oh, I don't know."

For the first time in her life, Cathy was caught on the horns of a dilemma: feel for Sharon or think for the office and her doctor. Rationalization came to her rescue; no statement would best serve both Sharon and the office. She verbalized all aspects of the problem and, at the end, suggested they put the whole affair behind them and go forward. The words brought bile into her mouth. Avoid negative publicity for the office, even if it left Sharon with no closure. Then, what she said was true; the cops and the press would think she was a nut. The guy probably didn't even have a mother. *Why is it, when watching other people make definitive decisions, they seem to do it so easily? You just do what is right. What if there is no right? What if both sides are right, or wrong?* She had read about the agony of executive decision. She didn't expect a real physical pain attached to it. She emerged a wiser and sadder lady, realizing it would take more than changing the title on her identification tag to make her a true manager. Some of the traits making her a loveable person required a reverse metamorphosing, changing from a butterfly to caterpillar, when serving as a manager. Was this growth and maturity, or was it a process of hardening, plunging the white-hot steel into a bucket of oil?

Dr. Nostrom entered Cathy's office as Sharon was leaving. He took the chair in front of her desk. "Employee relations problem?"

"Kind of." She had decided to keep the girl's personal problems to herself. The temptation to violate her own rule was great because she felt she had handled the moment very well, even though it strained her girl-scout naivety, bringing her from girl to woman in one stroke. "I wanted to thank you and Dr. Stern for letting me take Mrs. Santos' place. I'm going to miss her. She was a good boss."

"Mark and I are lucky to have you here. Ordinarily, when a manager who has been around as long as Judy leaves, there is a period of chaos. With you, the change has been transparent, Judy one day and you the next. You were, and are, quite wonderful." He leaned forward and took her hand. It began as a gesture of congratulation, but her hand felt so warm and satisfying, he lingered. He came alive and then was embarrassed. More than appreciation flowed through the fingers. He was afraid he might be intimidating, but when he sought her eyes, she returned his glance with a warm, friendly smile.

"Thank you." She slowly withdrew her hand. She thought, *He said wonderful, but he was wonderful. Could I kiss him? Say, "Oh, thank you, Dr. Nostrom" as a gesture of gratitude? Or could I say, "Thank you, I love you," and really kiss him? I know I will do neither. I'll just sit here, silent and blushing.*

Erik rested his hand on her shoulder as he passed her, and he was gone. His composure slowly returned. What a fulfilling sensation! The last time he had felt this way, he was sixteen. He had borrowed a necklace from his sister. As he'd stood in front of his girlfriend, the magical girl of his dreams, he'd offered the necklace to her. Tongue paralysis had left him frozen. His face had been bright red. He'd watched as she'd swooped up the necklace, kissed him on the cheek and flown away. His comparison was absurd; Cathy couldn't be a girl of his dreams.

Chapter 68

It was Tuesday, October 7. Earl Hagen watched the water flow down the glass of Dewar's on the rocks, forming a ring on the table. Tim Lamar was late. After the conversation earlier this morning, they had agreed to meet at Farrell's.

Lamar had mentioned something about a movement aimed at repealing the medical liability trust bill. Hagan thought there was no gossip circulating, but then, until a committee considered a bill, it was hush-hush. This was September, the legislative session would begin in February, so there were five months for it to grow legs and begin walking through the halls. It wasn't too early for the various committees and sub-committees to begin meeting.

Lamar moved easily from the door to Hagen's table. He was forty, athletic and big enough to be imposing. He sat opposite Hagen. "Sorry I'm late." No explanation. He caught the waiter's eye, ordered Dewar's neat, and turned to Hagen "I heard you had something to do with Amed."

"Very little. I was asked to manage their company, but I turned it down—too disorganized. Why is that of interest to you?"

"You know one of the members of the board?"

"Stanley Reinhart."

Hagen arranged for Lamar to meet with Dr. Stanley Reinhart on Thursday after establishing a 10-percent cut of the fees Lamar would collect.

They met on Friday. After the introductions to Reinhart, Lamar got to the significant part. "Here's the story. One of the commercial insurance companies—I'll tell you which one later—that pulled out of the medical malpractice coverage has been having second thoughts. They had made the decision to walk before the legislature passed the patient compensation fund bill. Like so many big outfits, they move like dinosaurs and couldn't change direction. Now, they see the premiums are going to stay up for a while, but the P.C.F. bill should cut the risk in half. The fellow I've been talking to said, 'Whenever the risk is going down, it always goes down faster than the premiums.' He says, 'The only time the insurance company really makes money is on the down slope of the cycle.'"

"Your friend speaks A1A insurance basics."

"He may, but that's not the point. There is a leak in the office of the lobbyist who will be honchoing this move."

"And?" Reinhart interrupted.

Lamar said, "It seems to me it would be handy for Amed to be on the other end of that leak, to know their attack before it happens."

"As I understand it, a commercial insurance company is backing the efforts to repeal the 'trust' act, they have hired a lobbyist to get this done, and you have a mole in his office. And you are talking to me for what?"

"Stanley, you know I'm just a businessman. Information is always worth something, and this kind of information could be invaluable."

"But you think you would be able to put a price on it?" Reinhart began to run several scenarios through his mind. *What if I keep the information to myself, pay for it at this level? As the crises arise, with this data, I could rescue the day and erode Erik's control; then pushing for rotation of command would make sense. This would really be win-win, helping me, and good for the company. Unlike the Gentile mix-up, I would not have to play hardball. Even though in the end my actions were for the good of Amed.*

Across the table, Reinhart saw a completely amoral face. He thought, *I can work with this man. I would love to see Erik out the door. If they discovered the plan, it could be bad. I'm already considered a loner, though working for the company's good, so how much change would there be, even if uncovered?*

If I introduce the situation to the board and continue to be the sole contact, for security reasons, I could gain about the same recognition and pass the cost of the operation on to Amed. The idea of keeping the wraps on the source for security reasons is slick.

Lamar studied Reinhart. "I probably could set up the whole deal for ten thousand a month."

Chapter 69

On the following day, Reinhart walked into Erik's office. "I believe I am on time for our appointment."

"Come in." He rose from his chair and moved to the front of his desk. "Coffee?"

"No thanks. I am restricted to one cup in the morning." He carefully eased into the chair Erik had indicated. "Word reaches me that there is a legislative scheme designed to repeal the malpractice trust bill." He waited for Erik's reaction. "My informant suggests he could put me in contact with a source of information straight from the office of the lobbyist handling the charge."

As Erik sat down, Reinhart noted the expected questioning gesture. "Earl Hagan said he had heard a vague rumor, but he couldn't confirm it." Reinhart thought Erik was still unbelieving. *I cannot blame him after our last encounter, but this time I am convinced it is a good move.* "Erik, this is very fresh. I don't know if it's true."

"Oily Hagan?"

"I know he is not you favorite, but it's another ear. I thought I'd see what you think. If you say no, I'll let it drop." He watched Erik. *I really put him behind the eight ball; if he says yes, I'll still get the credit if it is successful, but he has the ultimate responsibility if it goes bust. On the other hand, if he says no, and it is true, it will be easy, in retrospect, to point out what we could* have done with the information if only poor Erik had the guts. "Give me the word and I'll collect more details. Knowing the cost and the security would be essential."

"Stanley, I think the first thing we must determine is the validity of the rumor. It's hard to believe, after the bill passed with relative ease."

The meeting ended and Reinhart walked to the parking lot. He was quite content with himself. *I'll get Tim to plant the story in a few ears, have them call me and I'll have legitimate, confirmable reports to give to Erik. Tim said he'd do one better; he'd have someone call the members of the board and have those folks call Dr. Nostrom.*

Why is it, Erik thought, *Reinhart never brings me a simple, uncomplicated idea like momism or apple pie? Instead of having to search for every conniving twist and turn possible in this idea, I should reject it out of hand because it is from Reinhart. But wait. If there is a germ of truth in the offering, and I reject it without cause, I'll be playing right into his hands. As it is now, I feel I rule only until my next mistake. Of the three paths to greatness—born great, achieve greatness or have greatness thrust upon you—I am in the last category, and it can be plucked from me as easily. I must lead because I believe the company will not do as well if someone else is at the head. The risk is to my malpractice insurance coverage as well as that of all the other physicians joining us. Am I too full of myself? I remember my mother saying, "You cannot blame yourself for the falling rain." Am I doing that God-like thing again?*

He recalled Reinhart's words before he left. "I think you are right. The only problem is when attempting to validate the rumor you don't want to bring to life something that doesn't exist. Because of that, I would be very careful running this down. It would be better if I did that, rather than the chairman."

There was some truth in that, Erik thought. *I can't see a great risk. That makes sense to me. If the attack really exists, I'll talk to Jerry, and maybe Bob Griffin, the lobbyist. He should know.*

Chapter 70

On the following Monday, the thirteenth, Dr. Jack Reed was on the phone with Erik. "I just received a strange call from Roscoe Brady, an attorney friend of mine. He said he knew I was on the board of directors of Amed, and wondered if I were aware there was a move on to repeal the trust act. He heard something to that effect from a lobbyist. I thanked him for the information and said I'd look into it. Do you know anything about this?"

"Stanley came to me with a similar story. He was going to run it down. I'm waiting to hear. I'll get back to you."

Erik received a similar call from Dr. Thomas Harmon, the ob-gyn in Gainesville. After delivering the news, Thomas suggested they have an emergency conference call. "If this is true, we would be finished if the appeal is successful."

"That's pretty far down the road. First, we have to find out if it is true. If it is, we then have to see what we can do to defeat it."

Erik thought, *I almost told Harmon about the "leak" Reinhart described, but hesitated. Was I taking as fact the word of Reinhart?*

Now there are three independent sources claiming knowledge of the attempt to sabotage this company. Therefore, it's true! Goddamn it!

Now Reinhart would have to become part of the defense team.

That night, by phone, he told the story to Jerry.

He called back. "I talked to Bob Griffin," Jerry said. "He hasn't heard word one, but he said it wasn't unusual. At the early stages, it's 'need to know.' He added if it were a move against one of my interests, I would be the last to know."

"That makes sense," Erik said. "But it doesn't help."

"I think we have to assume they are on the attack," Jerry answered. "It's typical of a big company: make a mistake and then spend a fortune in legal fees to prevent the consequences from harming them. Then they wait. They know the little guy can't afford a long legal battle."

"Unfortunately, we are in that position," Erik said. "Initially, we were under-capitalized even for normal operations. If they get a restraining order to delay further progress, December 31st will come and go, and us with it."

"Let's think about Stanley's offer. I'm not sure the information leaked from the lobbyist office would do us much good. If we are going down, we don't want to be crucified for not grasping at every straw. In retrospect, they'll question why we didn't do it. Wait a minute! Why am I designing our exit strategy?"

Erik could hear Jerry shift the phone from one ear to the other. "I'm glad you said it. Let's face it, if Amed doesn't survive, no one cares why; just lynch the bastards." Jerry sipped his coffee. "One thing we don't have to worry about is our market push. In fact, the less policies we write the fewer angry doctors we have to face. By the way, they need how many for the hanging?"

"Very funny. Back to Stanley. We go with him?"

"I think so."

Chapter 71

Jerry hung up, leaving Erik thinking about his next move. "Would you set up a conference call, including all members, for five o'clock tomorrow?" he asked Cathy.

"There are ten?"

"Including me, yes."

Over the past month, Erik had been talking to Cathy about the company. At first, it was mostly educational, for her background did not include malpractice. Trying to verbalize his thoughts to a point where they were coherent helped him discover weaknesses in his logic. Initially, he was surprised by the gaps in his line of thinking, gaps that said A to C lacks B. He then had to scramble mentally to get an acceptable B. If it were not possible, he had to go back to build the bridge from one thought to another.

"You are a great help," he said as he realized the beneficial process in their efforts. "Here I thought I was educating you, when actually, I am getting stronger." He saw her face. Earlier today, he had been taking the first steps into depression. Having to work with Reinhart was bad enough, but what if the commercial attack was successful? With Cathy as a listening board, he tried to put a shape to his fears so he could hold them, step away from them, isolate them and mount a counterattack to each part.

He thought, *Friendly legislative forces are still available to put against the commercial company. Goddamn it, I wish Reinhart would stop being so possessive with his leaks. If I knew the name of the company mounting the charge, I'd have a better idea on how to defend.*

We could seek our own restraining order. After all, they would be interfering with the development of Amed.

As he studied her, he thought, *Anyone could have served as a listener as I voice these demons, anyone who is bright, who is not pitted against me, who is honest, trustworthy, sympathetic and empathetic, anyone who would enjoy my success and cry with me in defeat, and anyone who listens and is beautiful and is here.* Like "thunderbolt love," it hit Erik; there was no one but Cathy.

"What?" she said as his stare continued.

"Oh, I'm sorry. I was daydreaming for a moment."

"About this threat? I'd think it would be more of a nightmare, or maybe a daymare." She dissolved the tension with a smile. She went to the kitchen, prepared melted Swiss cheese on toast. Grabbing two sodas, she returned to the office. He thanked her with a nod and began eating. She was the good wife; he was the hardworking, bread-winning husband. It was as if it had always been that way.

"Let's see, where were we?" he said, with the remains of his last bite softening his words. "We must first decide to pay or not to pay for the leaked information. Politically, it seems necessary." He raised his hand. "If the source is true, it can't do us much harm, and it might help." He pointed to a folder behind Cathy. "Would you hand me the latest minutes?"

"These?"

"Yes." He scanned the list of board members. "In any case, I think the board is going to vote for it." Shaking his head he said, "You know the basic rule in leadership? If the mob is going in another direction, get in front of them. If I oppose and they vote yea, Reinhart's points ahead."

Cathy cast a sideways glance. "You know, I'm not very smart, but this whole thing has a smell to it. It reminds me of my grandfather talking about a town in Italy.

"Three horsemen came from the mountains down to the village. Their horses were sweating and snorting, stamping their hooves as they came to a halt. The leader demanded to speak to the village chief. 'I am the point man for the thousand-man army in the hollow behind the hills.' He said if the town wanted to avoid destruction, he could report to his general that there was nothing of value here, just some tired old men almost starving. The army would move on. Because he cared for the village, he would make that report for ten thousand liras.

"The mayor of the town demanded to see the army before he would pay ten thousand liras.

"'Fine,' said the horseman. 'But once they see you, they will send others to judge the town. It will be too late. Until now they will believe my report, for they see no reason for me to lie.'

"The town council met. The fear of invasion filled the room. The mayor was reluctant, but he knew the council was going to pay, so he, being a leader, also voted in favor of payment.

"Taking the money, the mounted warrior cautioned, 'Wait before venturing into the hills. The great general usually leaves someone behind for a few days. If he finds out I was not telling the truth, it would be bad for you, for he would come back in anger, and it would be bad for me.' He passed his forefinger across his neck. The horsemen galloped into the hills.

"The council was greatly relieved as four days went by and no attack came. On the fifth day, they edged toward the hills and finally scouted the land for miles around. There was no evidence of the existence of an army, only footprints of three horses, leading into the town and out again." Cathy brushed the hair from her face and touched her cheeks, now pink from talking.

"That's quite a story, and that is the longest speech I've heard from you since you've been here."

"I'm sorry. It isn't my business."

"Nonsense! You bring an entirely different view to the problem. I agree with you, it could be a con game. Your tale makes me want to do more checking before committing to the demand. I wish I could have you tell the story to the board."

"No chance. It's just my female instincts."

"That has always seemed unfair; we men have to struggle, logically, step by step, from syllogism A plus B equals C to M plus N equals O to reach a conclusion, and women, with instinct, leap over all of that tedious effort to reach the same conclusion."

"It's just our gift."

"You're amazing."

"Why would you say that?"

"Here you sit, looking innocent and beautiful. While all the while, the wheels are spinning in your head, thinking and planning. I'm glad you are on my side."

Here he was again, in the comfort zone of her presence, removed from the raging storm of conflict outside. He needed her. The words, which would leap the barrier between them and would declare their need, stood hesitatingly on his lips. Once spoken, they would be irrevocable. He would be responsible for the disruption of her life. He wouldn't do that without her consent. But how could he ask? His mature logic rendered him tongue-tied. The flaming yearning subsided. His protective, inhibiting veneer reformed. "It's better this way."

She thought, *He talks about instinct, but doesn't he have an ounce of it himself? Can't he feel me reaching for him, wanting to feel him against me? He's wonderful. That's the trouble. If he were more of a cad, we would have gotten it on by now.* She laughed. *What a hussy I've become overnight, or over him. But if he won't, I can't. Let's believe what I have is enough for now. The course to reality could be bumpy. Count my blessings.*

They returned to their respective corners to consider the insurance problem before them.

Chapter 72

The conference call brought everyone up to speed on the problem. The consensus was to agree to pay for the information, at least for the first month. Reinhart insisted on anonymity regarding his source. On October 17, Reinhart informed Erik that he had delivered the money and Lamar promised some surprising information in the near future.

Erik was still depressed. This playing cloak and dagger didn't sit well with him. He had to admit, it would have been much more acceptable if it came from someone other than Reinhart. Erik thought, *Would Reinhart take chances and stretch the truth to strengthen his ongoing bid for leadership?*

This latest event improved Reinhart's credibility and weakened his own. Erik wished he could command, or earn blind loyalty, like Napoleon, so he could do long-range planning without fear of challenges each step along the way. However, he would always have to be right. It was a bummer; he suffered the loneliness of leadership without sovereignty. Erik moved on, as the operation of the company took precedence.

Jerry accepted the recent events and could live with Reinhart's activities. He thought that he, more than Erik, was accustomed to gray area arrangements. He was glad the problem was handled and things were getting back to routine. He had been commuting between Miami and Tallahassee for some time. He would be happy to be able to stay there for a while. His legal activities, unrelated to Amed, justified his presence in the capital.

Chapter 73

Finally, the day of Cassy's departure for Paris arrived. For the last two weeks, Jerry had two diametrically apposed forces crushing him into immobility: He couldn't eliminate the uneasy, delicious feeling filling him when Cassy donned her sexy routine, complete with an innocent "don't be naughty!" smile. At the same time, his quest to solidify his lofty talk of monogamy called to him to seek virtual cold showers. Soon she would be gone. Sanity and a blessed calm routine would return. He thought, with uninterrupted exposure to the good life, he would rise to a mature level. The concepts of one love for life would fit him like a well-tailored, expensive suit. He smiled. *That's where I want to be.*

The farewell celebration included Linda and Jerry, Cassy and Troy, and Lorna and her date, Bruno. Unlike his name, he was soft-spoken, ruggedly handsome and mannerly. Instead of being a disaster, as Linda first feared, he turned out to be an asset, with a sense of humor and an easy laugh. The restaurant gave them a large table. The band could be seen across the dance floor. The music was from the sixties and early seventies, designed for easy dancing. With cocktails—Cassy stealing a sip from Troy's drink—excellent food and wine, Troy again being Cassy's supplier, the evening proceeded from the stiff "Good evening, how are you?" to lively conversation filled with anecdotes and funny stories.

Each couple approached the dance floor differently. First up was Cassy, dragging Troy behind her and doing her "solo with partner" act. Her young, spirited body was made for dancing. Men in the room had to remind themselves that it was against the law to have sex with a sixteen-year-old. Jerry was no exception.

Bruno escorted Lorna to the floor with elaborate courtesy. Finally Jerry stood behind Linda's chair. "Do you want to dance?" This was spoken in rhythm to that old song.

By the second set, they were exchanging partners for brief periods with mixed comments concerning ability and style. Jerry tried to avoid Cassy, but she called to him, "Come on, Daddy, it's your turn." Slowly, he maneuvered Linda toward Cassy, and they changed partners. As her body pressed against Jerry, he became aroused. Cassy could feel him. She smiled sweetly. Fortunately, after just a few more beats, the set was over. They returned to the table. Everyone supplied tales of travel and Paris, either from their experience in Paris or travel in general. Happy voices competed for attention in elevating decibels. It was a successful party.

Chapter 74

On the way home, Linda was wrestling with the thought of asking Jerry to join her in her bedroom. Why have him stay with the routine they had established since Cassy was with them? Forget the couch! The wine, the dance and his nearness to her had made her horny. Then, she thought, *It's only one more day*. She didn't want Cassy to be able to report that kind of intimacy to her separated husband in Paris. Her protective self won out. She helped Jerry make up the couch for sleeping. By two o'clock, they were all settled down for a long night.

Jerry couldn't free himself of the vision of Cassy dancing, of her being near him, looking so grown-up in her party evening dress. An ache made him touch himself. He thought, *By tomorrow night it will be over*. He would have survived the torture. Never again would he get into this kind of predicament.

He thought, it wasn't his fault. If Linda hadn't let Cassy come down, she would never have been in his life. She wouldn't have been thrown against him in such doses. Only a eunuch could come away intact from such a temptation.

Ordinarily, he could avoid the Cassy's of the world, and he certainly would, now that he had a true love. He could begin enjoying a mature life, with a future extending into retirement and beyond. Until recently, he had never really thought about the tomorrows. A recent article he had read declared when a man reaches his forties, for the first time he raises his head and sees a finite number of years remaining in his life. Before, time was limitless; he could start anew if he wished. With the revelation of man's mortality came a wave of depression. It went on to suggest ways of combating the depression: simplify, consolidate and construct a pathway. *Starting next week, I'll do just that. At last, I am strong.*

One second he was awake and the next he was gone. He fit the couch comfortably.

The soft pressure on his cheek set the theme of his dream. A warm breeze flowed over him as he sailed high above the sea, like a gull, free of the gravity pull, free of the need for clothing. It was effortless joy. His body faced the cushions of the couch.

She gently removed the blanket covering him. Turning onto his back, he was looking into her green eyes. Her skin against his side was warm and smooth. A faint trace of the disappearing baby fat remained, giving her the ephemeral softness of the adolescent female body. Once he touched her thigh, he was lost. The recent noble thoughts were blurred and then erased. The need to warm his frozen body by pressing her against him was the only command controlling his actions. Like a starving man who would steal food without compunction, without thought, Jerry reached for her where she sat, naked, on the side of his couch. Their coming together was crushing, explosive, and exhausting. Lying spent, he murmured, "Was this only a dream?"

"If that's what you wish, lover, it was a dream. I'll always remember it." She put his hand on her breast, kissed him lightly on the forehead and effortlessly danced to her room.

His body was wet. He pulled the blanket over him, covering his head. "It was a dream."

Within minutes he was asleep, the perfect escape.

Chapter 75

Linda was up early to prepare the final breakfast. She had mixed feeling about Cassy's leaving. She was aware of Jerry's discomfort since Cassy was staying with her. When that was relieved, she and Jerry could get back to the relaxed and loving world they knew.

On the other hand, she thought she had just begun to know and understand her daughter and would miss her. She smiled as Cassy came into the room. Jerry entered from the family room and sat next to Linda.

Cassy stretched and yawned. "Good morning. I had the craziest dream last night. It must have been the party."

"What was it about?" Linda asked.

"I can't remember. You know how dreams slip away soon after you wake up?" She smiled sweetly, looking at Jerry and then toward Linda.

For Jerry, the day seemed to go on forever before they reached the airport. Every word from Cassy's lips sounded like an innuendo. He held his breath, waiting for a flat statement of joy or resentment concerning last night.

None came.

At last, family kisses all around and Cassy was down the corridor toward the airplane. A brief glimpse of her luscious body flashed through his mind. As she disappeared behind the plane's door, he replaced the thought with his new self-imposed austerity.

That evening Linda was the playful aggressor in bed. Jerry hesitantly responded, but was relieved when he found he could function quite well. He could shed his fears that his guilt would smite him into impotency.

Chapter 76

By the end of September, the staff had processed two hundred and forty-eight application policies written and paid for. One million dollars were collected. The weird phenomenon of having money pour in with only miniscule expense going out became a living thing.

Each of the four principals reacted differently.

"How can we fail?" Jerry called to Paul, impressed as the numbers grew.

Edward, by contrast, was fearful. He knew he would hold his breath until he saw the number of claims springing from the coverage these million dollars represented.

Because Amed was embarking on the relatively new claim-made insurance, there was no multi-year database available to calculate the risk.

Erik could only hope the redundancy built into their rates would be sufficient. Unfortunately, other insurance companies, observing these same high comfortable rates, would think about re-entering the malpractice field. This thought lent credence to Reinhart's information.

Erik called a board meeting for Saturday, October 18. Jerry came down on Friday night and joined him for dinner.

After eating, they went to see Frances. She had experienced a transient episode of respiratory arrest. Lacy handled it, but her doctor transferred Frances to the hospital ICU.

They sat in silence, watching her. She was not aware of them. Her breathing was steady and unhurried. Jerry searched for the words to comfort Erik, but they all seemed either trite or unnecessary. "I'm sorry? Be brave? Stiff upper lip, you know?"

The pressure forced his mind to seek distraction, to ease the vicarious pain he suffered for his friend. His attention fell on the vastly complicated arrangement of devices and equipment in this one ICU room.

The room was 20' by 20', walls painted a light tan, and floors covered with linoleum tile. Even before he began to absorb the orderly visual chaos, his ears were filled with the cacophony of the machine's bells, clicks, and pops; the rhythmic 72-times-a-minute beat recording the pulse; and the soft, swishing whisper followed by a plop as the drop in the IV tubing formed and fell. All these sounds reflected survival efforts for Frances.

She lay motionless in the bed, hardly discernable behind the nasal tube and the oxygen mask.

As Jerry crossed the threshold, his nose was greeted by odors unique to intensive care, and strangely interpreted. Passing flatus, usually scorned, was here celebrated as it signified the returning function of the intestinal tract, which was eagerly awaited by the doctor. This mixed with exhaled breath and escaped oxygen, leaking around the nasal tube, the harsh irritation of the antiseptics always present, the ozone tang emitted from each electronic monitor, body odor, the smell of urine from the catheter bag, and the unidentified fragrances, perfumed or slightly nauseating, combined for the full impact.

His eyes roamed the room. The outer wall had a large window looking onto a rooftop. Vertical blinds covered the glass impregnated with a wire, criss-cross, break-proof design. On the left side, the wall was bare, except for a clock in the center, nine feet above the floor.

The wall opposite the window consisted entirely of multiple-paneled sliding glass doors covered with a light patterned curtain. The only entry into the room was through these sliding doors.

Turning around, he could see, outside of the sliding glass doors, a gigantic nursing station crammed with EKG monitors, nursing chart racks, intensive care paraphernalia and nurses, all there to care for Frances.

By contrast to the bare wall, the opposite wall was covered with all the equipment necessary to care for a critically ill patient.

He was mesmerized by it all. In the corner furthest from the sliding glass doors, there were cabinets, a sink, and the paper towel dispenser above it. Placed next to the cabinets was a large, rectangular steel box containing hidden circuit breakers. Just to the right of the paper dispenser at its lower end was a double row of electric outlets, two large 220 watt, and the rest 110. Coming from the outlets, looking like a medusa head, were eight electric cables. Four went to IV pumps, one to the bed control, one to the suction machines and two to electronic monitor devices on the side of the room.

Jerry could see a long, crane-like arm boasting the patient's TV at its end. When turned off, the black evil eye of the cathode tube, bordered in white, looked down on Frances' bed, like Casper the Ghost. This small box reflected the height of oxymoronic achievement. Frances was too sick to see it, didn't care to see it, and if she did, the placement made it almost impossible for her to see it. In another cubicle, Jerry observed a visitor with poor taste, turning on the TV and watching it, silently declaring his boredom at being forced to visit the sick.

Near the harness was a special outlet designed to receive the end of the cable, which could transmit a call to the nurse from Frances' signaling squeeze bulb.

A green rectangular 4" by 6" stainless steel plaque was next in line in Jerry's vision as he swept the wall. Plugged into its central port were the oxygen valve and a glass jar half filled with bubbling water. This apparatus supplied measured, humidified O2 to Frances through a thin plastic tube holding two nipples, one for each nostril.

In the center of the wall behind the bed, two feet from the ceiling was a long, rectangular structure containing three fluorescent bulbs. Repeated tugs on the cord running from this fixture yielded dim, bright and brightest illumination to Frances. A frosted plastic cover prevented the light from shining directly into her eyes.

When he asked the nurse about the equipment mounted below the fixture, she said, "It's ancient. It's a manual cuff, gauge and stethoscope used to measure blood pressure. Twenty years ago, it was vital. Now it's replaced by electronic monitoring, and it stands ready in those times when both the city electricity and the hospital generator fail, simultaneously, or when I want to check on modern times."

Further along the wall, another arm extended toward the bed, but kept its distance of three feet. A one-foot square brown receiver faced the bed. On top sat the monitor with its black window displaying lines of information. He thought, *The many wires leaving Frances and crisscrossing over her body on the way to the receiver make her look like a victim of a Lilliputian attack.* The wires came from four pasted-on EKG leads and from the modern, automatically intermittent-inflating blood pressure cuff. Also, there was one from the oximiter on her left fourth finger. This recently invented small, clothespin-like device with its photosensitive cell read the red color of the blood flowing through the nail bed. A computer converted the data into O2 saturation levels. 100 percent was desirable.

The last line brought information about her rate of respiration.

The nurse returned. By now, Jerry knew her name was Karen.

A small red sign in the middle of the wall warned, "Staff use only—Uso para empleados solamente."

To the left of the florescent light was a large, round, clock-like device with only second and minute hands. Karen explained, "This is used during a code to tell the crew how long the patient has been unresponsive, and when to say goodbye."

Jerry recovered from his reverie as Erik stood, kissed Frances as she slept, and motioned toward the door. "Dr. Garing said he would have to wait before he can say if Frances suffered any further brain damage during the arrest."

Jerry acknowledged this with a nod. "Are you alright?"

"I don't know."

He looked at Erik. "Never mind." Jerry observed the wet, red eyes as Erik turned away from him.

"I'm numb. It seems she has been sick and away from me forever. Now, I don't know her. I remember her so well. Loving me, filling my life. Work was a joy; the world she gave me was a joy. Did I dare have a complaint in those days?"

"You were pretty happy, as I remember."

"I can't bring those memories to the body lying in that room. God forgive me, but she's a stranger."

"I know. It's a terrible strain. You're the doctor, but from what I hear, my psychiatrist would say this is a defensive mechanism to protect you from emotional damage. The last thing you need is to feel guilty about those thoughts." He paused. "Or any other actions you must take to survive, emotionally. You have done all you could do. Give yourself a break."

They walked to the parking lot in silence.

Chapter 77

The board gathered at ten o'clock on Saturday the 18th. "Gentlemen, I believe our contact has really earned his fee this time." Dr. Stanley Reinhart couldn't hide the satisfaction he felt as he told the board of the latest information. "I have a rough draft of the bill they plan to present in the next session." He handed out copies of the draft, savoring the nods of approval from each of the board members.

What a coup, he thought. *I couldn't have it better if I had written the script.* He was remembering the disbelief at first, and then the elation he had felt when he had received the document. *Now, do not overplay this hand. If I wait, one of the directors will suggest I assume a larger role in steering the company. Maybe even voice the need for changing the chair.*

The draft clearly spelled out the reasons for repeal and the deficiencies in having a trust. The trust would not participate in FICA, which required all other insurance companies to contribute to make up the losses when one company would go into receivership. If the trust didn't share the load, each other company had to pay more. This was not a competitive level playing field, giving the trusts an unfair advantage. Another point: it was unfair to the uninformed doctors to offer insurance when the trust had only the ability to assess its members to assure protection, while the legitimate companies had to maintain adequate capital and surplus for this backup. Further, there was little safeguard regarding the qualifications of the principals in control of the trusts. At present, the trust was run by physicians only!

As the group realized the impact of this draft, they were moved to slow panic and silence. Dr. Anthony Sanchez was the first to speak. "I'm glad we have a source for this information, but I wish I didn't have it. This scares the hell out of me."

The ebbing of confidence of the group was almost palpable. Those who sweat were sweating and those ulcer-prone were in exquisite pain.

Erik turned over his copy of the draft. "OK, this presents a problem. But when you consider each of the items, they all were sited during the original hearings. There is nothing new here. Jerry and I will go over all the original arguments. I can remember most of the defenses against these charges."

"I hope you are right," Dr. Jack Reed said. "I'm with you."

The three words bolstered Erik. He feared that, in their panic, they might turn to Reinhart, figuring anything was better than what they had. His fears were unfounded. Dr. Gentile, now a true convert, strongly backed Reed's words. The group agreed to stay with Erik for a while. Once again, he yearned for blind loyalty, but knew he would have to be successful this time and every time.

Catharses consumed the remainder of the meeting, each man seeking a stable platform to help him cushion the frightening news. In the end, they scheduled a conference call in three weeks and voted to continue paying the monthly ten thousand dollars to Reinhart's contact.

The following Monday, Tim Lamar called the two lobbyists who were in contact with the board members. He informed them of the draft and had them call the board members. The validity of the draft's existence was established. The members called Erik to give him the bad news and to ask if he had some positive answers.

Erik did not. He could only tell them he and Jerry were going over the original proceedings, results to follow. Until this conformation of its existence, Erik was denying that the draft was legitimate. As solid as the mounting evidence was, he clung to his doubts, supported only by the fact that the idea came from Reinhart. *Forget it! You don't like the man, so what? Put aside your poor bruised ego and begin to work at finding a way to salvage what you can.*

Chapter 78

Later that day, he met with Paul and Jerry to bring them up to date. "So, that's where we are. We have a real dilemma. Should we continue to push to get as many policyholders as possible before the end of December?" Erik turned his left hand palm upward.

"If the legislature repeals the act, or even if we are restrained, we will have a bigger mountain of debt to repay, and more angry doctors ready to lynch us or, far worse, to sue us." He turned his right hand palm upward. "On the other hand, if we don't continue marketing, we are doomed, and we might as well close shop now and repair the damage already done. At least we couldn't be blamed for persisting when we had information telling us it was risky. That would be a difficult position to defend. Talking about 'no good deed should go unpunished,' here we are, working for no compensation, struggling to get the doctors reasonable protection, and if we fail we will be persecuted."

"Do you remember why I left the tranquil life of the carpet business?" Paul gave a weak laugh. "I really don't think you have a choice. We have spent too much money to come away undamaged. I read the draft of the repeal bill. If the original position brought the trust into existence, I can't see this new bill surviving. I had a similar situation in my past life. We had obtained the right to open a store in the region after presentation to the county commission. Soon thereafter, our competitor served us with a restraining order. It was declared null and void by a judge, who happened to be a friend of our chairman."

"Interesting."

"How well do we know the judge?"

"If it comes to that, we're screwed. Most judges in this area lean toward the plaintiff's bar and, by reflex, against malpractice companies."

Paul shrugged. "Just trying to be helpful. In any case, I agree with you. We have to continue pushing for business if for no other reason than to have a more defensible exit strategy."

Chapter 79

"Surveying the office," Jerry stated as he looked down the row of desks, "you wouldn't know there was a hand grenade with its pin pulled resting in its midst." The girls were busy with calls, documenting information, handling the mail and answering inquiries. The cacophony of fax chatter, typewriter clicking and the strange sounds of the new IBM computer added to the appearance of busy, busy, busy. Jerry smiled at the attractive operator. "I guess Paul agrees with us about staying full throttle toward glory."

She answered, "It's the twenty-second of October; we only have fifty-three working days to deadline." She frowned and returned to her phone. Jerry advanced to Paul's office to clarify certain legal points.

Meanwhile, in Erik's office, "It's Garrett Dobson," Cathy called from the outer room. "He said he is from the *Medical Chronicle*." She waited.

"I'll see him, Cathy." Erik reached for a memo pad and drew his pen from his shirt pocket. "Hello. What's the *Chronicle* doing I should know about?"

Dobson entered. He hadn't changed. Erik remembered him as a thin, short, nervous man about forty with wit and a sharp sense of humor.

"It's what you are doing," Dobson said. "I understand you are the head honcho for a new malpractice trust, correct? The paper receives lists of all new enterprises having to do with medicine. The company's name is Amed and you are organizing under the new trust legislation."

"Sounds like the article is already written."

"Just a few details. There are ten members on the board of directors? Why are you all doing it? It's a non-profit undertaking, so you aren't there for the money."

"Damned if I know. 'Because it's there,' like the mountain climber said, explaining why he climbs. The litigiousness of the times created the vacuum and I was the one nearest the door. Before this crisis, I thought insurance business was dry as dust—dull, dull, dull. Now I find it exciting, demanding, risk-taking, and combining all the aspects of law, medicine and negotiation. Being of a surgical mind helps."

"How come?"

"In both environments I have to make definitive decisions on imperfect information."

"You and your board are voluntary, no salary or fees?"

"Right now, all the seed money and premium money is going to pay for the staff and administration. Once we get stable, with reserve funds, there may be an opportunity to be compensated for expenses, but right now, it isn't part of the plan."

Erik answered questions concerning operations, how the company had actually begun, and where the seed money had come from.

Finally, Garrett left with no mention of the repeal. It was just an ordinary new-business interview. Erik was relieved. He thought, *I hope my omission doesn't destroy my credibility.*

On October 27, the article appeared in the Monday edition. It was a good commercial for Amed, producing an increase in inquiries from doctors. The board members were nervous. They were afraid the positive story would make the rebound more severe in case of failure.

It was morning the following day when Dobson called again. "Good morning, Erik, or should I say master of omissions? While you were talking, so naively, about the joys of forming an insurance trust, you failed to tell me about the repeal action. Instead, I write boringly when I could have had a scoop. What gives?"

"You're right, I should have, but I was waiting until I was absolutely certain. You see, once the word is out my company is history."

Dobson said, "When I heard a whisper about the appeal, I did some checking. Strange thing, only two of the thirty lobbyists I had conversations with had heard anything about it. You know, in this town, rumors spread like wildfire. It's hard to keep a secret. Where do you stand at this moment?"

"Off the record, for now?"

"OK"

"I am caught on the horns of a dilemma. All my information comes through Dr. Stanley Reinhart. Someone contacted him, claiming to have a mole in the office of the lobbyist managing the repeal. Reinhart refuses to reveal the name of the mole or the lobbyist. But through this source, he was able to get a draft of the proposed bill." Erik outlined his decision to go forward trying to get the five hundred policyholders. "Every new policy written is a nail in my coffin if we are unable to make this repeal go away. And if you print the story, there won't be five hundred to worry about. I know reporters hate to carry a hot item, but I would really appreciate it if you could hold off for one week."

"You have a good reason I should?"

"My nurse thinks it's a scam."

Dobson laughed. "Good enough for me."

"Seriously, in a few days I will know if we are able to get a restraining order. If we do, we may have a chance. Jerry has gone over the arguments presented originally and believes ultimately, the court will find in our favor. Unfortunately, time is not on my side."

"I'll wait one week, providing it's mine alone, first, when it breaks."

"Done."

Chapter 80

Erik was pleased with the extension of time but didn't have much time to relax. It wasn't two hours before Cathy announced Reinhart was on the phone.

"Good morning, Erik. Are you holding up? I empathize with you. The strain of making the decision to go ahead must be like carrying the weight of the world on your shoulders. I play a small part and I ache all across my back."

"I appreciate your help in supporting me on continuing to seek doctors." Erik's voice sounded tired.

"I know you think I'm competitive, but realistically, that was the only way to go. I called to give you some news. I am trying to decide if it is good or bad. Lamar said he was about to obtain from his mole the names of the legislators sponsoring the repeal bill."

"That's great!" Erik meant it, but it also further confirmed the existence of the bill. If he was holding onto some hope of this being a scam, Cathy's version, he now must say goodbye. "We can begin lobbying them toward our side. It puts a face on the masked man."

Reinhart nodded toward the phone. He thought, *You do not know how competitive I am.* "I will call you as soon as I have the list. Get Jerry on board."

"James Eisinger from marketing is on the phone," Cathy said. Erik found himself smiling as her voice reminded him of his reference to her theory. If it were true.

"Morning, boss. There's something strange going on. We are up to three hundred doctors, but there have been none in the last two days. They are calling, asking about the stability of the trust and about a plan for repeal of the trust act. Four inquired how they could cancel their applications and get their money back. What's happening?"

Erik was silent. He knew Dobson would keep his word and not print the story, but maybe his inquiry among the lobbyist had given it life.

"We have a problem." He then gave the latest details to Eisinger including those concerning the list of sponsors.

"Deny it for the time being," Erik advised Eisinger. "Paul is working up a press release to acknowledge the existence of the rumor, but denying any conformation, and to state business as usual. He is going to hold onto it for a few days or as long as possible."

Chapter 81

Cathy walked into the office. The sight of Erik's face, reflecting fatigue and frustration, stirred her. For the first time, the prudent forces restraining her from acting out her emotions gave way. She surrendered to her need to comfort him, to love him. She walked around the desk to stand behind him. Her hands rested on his shoulders, softly massaging his tight muscles. She could feel him let go. The fragile contact through her fingertips began to warm him. The fear-stimulated, sympathetic contraction, chilling his skin, loosened its grip. He stood and turned to hold her. They were bound together, in silence, for a long time. Their single silhouette faded into a black outline as the evening filled the unlit room. Slowly they parted.

"I'm sorry," he said. "I don't understand. But for that moment, I needed you." He was stronger. He was himself again. The bliss of her body against him became a blurred sensation.

"I know," she said. "It was the stress. I won't let it beat you! Tomorrow will be for our team. I'll see you then." She was confused, but her mature self knew they would never go back to yesterday. His veneer had yielded momentarily and she was swept inside. She left, warm and fulfilled.

Chapter 82

On Tuesday, November 11, Jake returned to his office. On Jerry's orders, he had been following Reinhart all day, hoping to identify his mysterious contact. He sat on the bed and began untying his shoelaces. The brown hiking boots fell to the floor, spilling street dirt on the carpet. After taking off the stocking, he rubbed his aching left foot. He put his feet on the wooden chair in front of him and leaned back. He thought, *My sixty-four years are beginning to show after a day like this. What did he know?*

Last Friday he had observed a meeting between Dr. Reinhart and a man Jake identified as Tim Lamar. There had been other contacts—a handsome man half Reinhart's age, two business suits and the salesman in the pro-golf shop—but Lamar seemed to be the live one. He and the doctor had met briefly again this afternoon and then Lamar had headed for the tavern.

Jake chose diamond-checked brown socks and soft leather loafers. *Perhaps Lamar will meet his lobbyist tonight.* As tired as he was, duty lifted Jake from the bed and out the door.

There were twenty customers in the tavern at the bar and around tables in the corner. Almost as a requirement, the room was dim and smelled of beer.

He saw Lamar ordering at the end of the bar. "Jack Daniel's on the rocks, Billy, please." The bartender acknowledged, delivering the glass filled with ice and clear brown liquid; water of condensation was running down the outer walls of the glass, puddling on the bar. Tim reached for the glass with his right hand and the bowl of peanuts with his left.

"I'll have the same." Jake signaled with his raised hand as he took one of the empty stools next to Lamar.

"You drink my drink. Might as well say hello. I'm Tim Lamar."

They shook hands. Jake said he worked for a research firm. He usually didn't tell the truth to suspects. Their conversation used up the weather, sports and the difficulty with public transportation.

Lamar was full of his greatness as he reviewed the course his scheme had taken; there was the latest check for ten thousand dollars in his breast pocket.

He could no longer keep this success to himself. Even before he had entered the tavern, he'd known he had to tell some other human being, preferably a stranger. It would be best if it were someone he would never see again, but it had to be someone who would listen and marvel at his brilliance. He needed an audience for the monologue that was racing through his head.

"I just received ten thousand dollars for doing nothing," Lamar said after the fourth Jack Daniel's. They had been drinking for two hours. Jake couldn't remember why he stayed except he was too tired to move on. There would be no contact with Lamar's source tonight. His expectation for the evening was a headache at best. When he heard ten thousand dollars, the amount hit him between the eyes. *That's our ten!*

"Very interesting. That's the only way to go. How come?" Jake arranged his face to show casual interest.

Lamar evaluated his listener. *Is this the one ready for my story? Hell yes.* "One day, I was playing with myself—no, not that way." Lamar laughed. He thought it was funny. "You know. 'What if' kind of playing. What if I were to spread a rumor that something was going to happen, and then get the potential victim of this terrible event to believe it and to pay me to stop it from happening? You see the fucking balls of it; I'd be getting paid for stopping something that was never going to happen. If this could work one time, it could be a life's project."

Jake could see the enthusiasm in Lamar's face. The idea was crazy, but what if it worked? *Is he going to tell me it worked?*

"It worked! If I do say so myself, it was fucking genius." Lamar looked around to make sure there was only one listener.

"I hear about this new malpractice trust being formed. A bunch of amateurs running it. A truly naive mark. They needed to get five hundred doctors to sign up by December 31, this year. Therefore, the pressure was on.

I say to myself, 'What if—see, there's the game again—what if someone tried to do away with the law that let them do this business in the first place? I hear there are some folks who are not too fucking happy about the new players."

Suddenly, Jake was cold sober. *Don't let Lamar see I'm so interested.* He stifled a fake yawn.

"I'm not boring you?" Lamar was incensed.

"No, no. But it's a wild story." Jake reached out and patted Lamar on the shoulder. "Did this really happen?"

"Goddamn right. See." He reached into his jacket. Being a little drunk, he first tried the right inside pocket. Panic grabbed him—no envelope! He searched with such force that he tore the lip of the left pocket. The envelope popped out and fell onto his lap. He opened it and displayed the ten thousand dollar check. He covered the names. "That looks real to you?"

"Sure does. So how did you pull it off?"

The bartender came down to their end of the counter. "Another round?"

"On my tab," Lamar said and waved the bartender off.

"Like the perfect sting. An insurance man I know introduced me to a member of board of directors of this company. Luck was with me, for I find out this doctor was no friend of the chairman. I spin the yarn to him about this group planning to appeal the law that brought the insurance company into existence, playing taps all the while. I was so good, it even sounded plausible to me. He wanted all the details. I said, 'I can't give that away.' You could see he was disappointed. His tongue was hanging out. I've been in cons before, but this guy was ripe. I said, 'But I have a leak in the office of the lobbyist running the show.' Now he's almost coming in his pants, so I put it to him. 'For a fee of ten thousand dollars a month, I could give you information."

Lamar took a swallow of his Jack Daniel's, put the glass down and put both hands to cover his eyes. "Would you believe it was that easy?" His voice was slightly slurred. He put his hand on Jake's forearm.

"So the mark presented the idea to his board. I understand his performance was even better than mine, except he believed it. While they were thinking about the deal for a week, with their thumbs up their asses, I cinched the fix. I paid one lobbyist to call Dr. Frond and another one to phone Dr. Cannon, two members of the board of directors. They repeated the rumor I had written out for them. It cost two Gs, but it was worth it. It brought the rumor to life. Can't you just see the fucking panic at the board meeting? These two directors independently reporting the threat, now making it a fact."

Lamar stopped talking, downed some Jack Daniel's. He thought, *Now someone knows how great I am. He surveyed the room. Maybe I should have grabbed a larger audience?*

Jake tried to look in awe. "So there never was any action to repeal the legislation creating the trust act?"

"Were you listening? Of course, there was no fucking action. That's the beauty of the whole tamale."

"And they continued to pay your monthly fee?"

"You saw the check." He looked at Jake. "You still don't believe?" He slapped his forehead with his open palm. "But I'm not the kind of a guy who sits back and plays with myself. No, sir. I got busy and drew up a rough draft of the motion to restrain the company from proceeding. I slipped that to my contact. He acted as if he was glad to get this bad news. Funny thing, he insisted from the first day that only he should get the information and that the deal was off if I spoke to other members of the board, especially the chairman. Go figure."

"I am impressed!"

"And I'm not finished. Here's a real touch. Last week I told my contact I would have the names of the fifteen legislators sponsoring the bill! Won't that be a bombshell?"

"Let me buy the next drink. That was really something." Jake said. He didn't have to fake his admiration.

Tim leaned back, sipping his drink, nodding in agreement. "It really was."

Chapter 83

On the next day, Jerry said as he walked into Erik's office, "Jake said he wanted to talk with both of us."

"I didn't know he was working for us at the moment."

"I asked him to help us verify the rumor. He was trailing Reinhart, hoping to find the contact."

Jake walked in. "Gentlemen, please sit down for what I have to tell you." He looked serious, then abruptly went from tragic to comic mask and unwound the tale.

The news was like warm sunshine melting the frost of panic, fear and uncertainty. "So there wasn't even the rumor? This guy did it all by himself? Unbelievable!" Erik was laughing. The relief was overwhelming. Jerry caught Cathy's arm and did a small jig around her as she entered the room. "We're free, oh Lord, we're free, and we're free at last!"

She hadn't heard Jake's report. "Have we all gone crazy? I could hear you in the waiting room."

Erik caught her shoulders in both of his hands. "Jake brought us some very good news. The whole Lamar thing was a scam, just like your Italian friend! You were right! I love you! I'll tell you later."

The three men burst into spontaneous laughter. It looked and sounded like a drunken New Year's Eve party.

Sharon came in from the reception desk. "I just came in to get these prescriptions signed." She placed them onto the desk in front of Erik. He signed them and she left, wondering what in the world could have happened.

Jerry called his office to instruct them to hold off on further inquiries regarding the rumors. Erik called Paul. "Wait in your office and get James, Jerry and I will be right over. Please have Edward join us. Yes, something has come up." Erik withheld the news. He wanted for a moment to savor the feast, in this room, among the three of them. He was cautious. He thought, *How quickly we forget bad circumstances with the arrival of good, salvation-like news*. He wanted to enjoy the ascendance from the immobilizing, tortuous depths of defeat to the jubilation of triumphing over an unseen foe. The bitter taste changed to honey. He wasn't a religious man, but he gave thanks to the powers that be for sending this revelation, over which he had no control, to rescue him. His breathing was easy; the stomach pain was gone. The relief was tranquilizing. As the laughter subsided, they sat exhausted, watching each other for continued conformation that it was real.

His last call was to Garrett. "I want to thank you for withholding the story of the rumor. You deserve a reward. No, I can't tell you over the phone. This is too special. It will have you, as a journalist, ecstatic. Please join us at Paul's office."

The Greek gods, looking down at the success of their creations in their victory over evil, had to be celebrating.

Paul, Jerry, Erik, Eisinger, Edward and Dobsons stared at the report Jake had developed.

"This is unbelievable! Tell me one more time," Dobson said. "I want to have Velma come over. She has been assigned the coverage of the emergence of new companies. She will be thrilled. When I gave her this subject, she was bitching it was so boring! Wait until she sees this!"

Velma was still rushing as she entered Paul's office. A brief summery of the day's report and she was ready to write the story. "I love it! The white hats uncover the black hats. It isn't often that it is so neat."

Chapter 84

It took some convincing and the hint of a mysterious revelation to have all members of the board agree to attend, on such short notice, the meeting on November 15, Saturday morning.

The greetings and initial conversations were casual. Then, Erik said, "Please find your seats. I would like to introduce Mr. Jake Sampson." Jake had been sitting in a chair behind the board table. He stood up and walked until he was between Erik and Sanchez. The directors looked at Jake. "Who's he?"

Erik continued, "Jake is a consultant, acting as Amed's general investigator. He has worked with Jerry in the past, and I have employed him as part of the planned due diligence in this matter."

He wanted to be the one responsible for the relief they would experience when they heard the news. He would be their savior, and maybe—he laughed at his thought—for one brief moment, he would have their confidence.

Reinhart believed he was in a strong position. The only new information he was aware of was the list of the names of the sponsors of the repeal bill. He had received these last night, somewhat embellished by Lamar with touches of reality. Reinhart had not informed Erik; better keep it for today.

If Jerry, armed with this list as inside information, was able to contact the legislators, one on one, and deflect them, save the day, the board would have to see that only Dr. Stanley Reinhart was fit to continue leading the company. He smiled, awaiting the announcement. He didn't know the list was part of Jake's report.

Erik began, "Gentlemen, you have been hit with a bombshell when you first heard of the action to do away with the trust. I am humbled by the strength you all have mustered in facing this crisis. To vote to go forward, despite the potential danger, was admirable. I am proud of you." He savored the questioning looks on the faces of the board members.

"Jake will hand out his report. The several pages are summarized on the cover sheet." Erik began to read:

"'In my research into the veracity of a plot to eliminate the trust, I found that the plot did indeed exist.'" He paused, surveyed the deepening depression on their faces. *Am I truly a devil to enjoy this moment so much?*

He continued. "'But the plot was entirely in the mind of one Tim Lamar. He invented the whole concept of creating a fantasy movement to repeal the law. He found Dr. Stanley Reinhart receptive to his scam. He dreamt up the rough draft, and most recently, the list of legislative sponsors. There never was any repeal effort. There never was a lobbyist or a leak. The only reality was the ten thousand dollar checks. This burned such a hole in his pocket, he had to brag to someone, and unfortunately, he spoke to me.'

"The details of each transaction are contained in the complete report."

There was silence. They couldn't believe the cavalry had come to their rescue. They were afraid to question for fear that what they had just heard was incorrect; they couldn't have heard correctly. It lasted several moments, a frozen tapestry. Dr. Sanchez was the first to find his voice. "OK, let's see. There was no threat. It was all make believe, and we are home free, minus twenty thousand dollars? Then, we are safe? We are in business?"

"Yes!"

After the first sound, the dams broke. Questions, statements, and "Goddamn him" poured out, tumbling over each other. They swept their brows and tossed clenched fists into the air in triumph.

Someone shouted, "I knew we could do it!" Jack Reed read a few lines, put down the report and hugged Thomas Frond, standing next to him. They stood up, danced in place, laughed raucously. One by one, they became emotionally exhausted and sat down. Reinhart had not moved. His mind refused to accept what he had heard. He could not find a pathway to reality. He muttered, "What about the list?" No one heard his soft comment. All eyes turned to Erik. The applause began with Fredrick Cannon, crescendoing to a deafening boom. They stood, some with tears of relief flowing unashamedly.

Jerry whispered into Erik's ear, "Churchill, this is your finest hour!"

Chapter 85

After the irrational hoopla while each member of the staff and board congratulated themselves and each other, the atmosphere quieted down. In a pendulum swing the other way, a somber mood fell upon them, then gradually returning to a normal ambiance.

"It's five hundred or bust for Amed trust!" Paul shouted in an unlikely departure from his usually controlled demeanor.

When the article appeared in the *Medical Chronicle* describing the events, it put Amed on solid footing. The applications and phone calls began to come into the office.

Tim Lamar was indicted for racketeering. The frightening episode slowly faded into the past. Only Reinhart emerged somewhat damaged. He wrote to Erik.

>Dear Dr. Erik Nostrom, Chairman of Amed,
>   I am embarrassed by my role in this matter. You must know, at all times, I had only the welfare of Amed prominently in mind. The thought there was a threat to our company's existence was devastating. I was willing to grasp at any straw to save us. When Tim Lamar approached me, I truly believed I was on to a solution. I confess, the role of savior was not unpleasant. I am trying to be as

honest with you and myself as possible. In any case, we are here and in good condition. As a member of the board of directors, I am committed to our future and to you, as chairman.
Sincerely,
Stanley Reinhart, M.D.

"He wants us to think he is squeaky clean to the end," was Jerry's comment on hearing the letter. "We are safe for the time being. Oh, by the way, I'll be in Tallahassee for a few weeks. You can reach me at Griffin's office or at Linda's."

When Jerry was alone with Linda, he could, for a moment, capture the peace he had once known. Then she would look directly at him.
"What?" he asked, tensing.
"Nothing. You look tired. Amed's troubles are really stressing you. Come here." She patted the cushion next to her. So believing.
How much time would it take for him to again accept her love? The pain of the one foolish act was on his shoulders. It pinched his lower back. It was always there when they were together. His protection against it weighed on him like a knight's armor, producing clumsy movements. Because it was eased when he was not with her, he had to fight the temptation to avoid the encounter. *What kind of hell is this?* he thought. He would bear the torture, wait it out, and survive. There must be an end to his sentence. He had risked his first real love, the first time he could imagine a long life with one person, the first time he had felt contentment, and the first time he had understood his woman. He had fucked it up by the uncontrolled urges of his past. *If we live through this, it will be forever*, he prayed, although he did not know who would be listening.

His training as a trial attorney made it possible for him to play the role needed to please Linda. It went on like that for some time.

Chapter 86

For Erik, the continued clash of guilt against desire had rounded off the edges. They no longer tore him from one emotional base to another.

He had a wife. His memory of their life together remained fresh and vibrant. The lingering remains of her body lay in the hospital. Not totally gone, which would allow closure, but rather, responsive enough in occasional, tiny, barely perceptible movements of a finger, to say, "I'm still here, you bastard!"

The physical contribution from Frances, the happy, funny, loving girl he knew had been missing for years, ever since the kidnapping Berry aneurysm had stolen her. The ransom note demanded life without parole as the only condition that could bring them together. He was not willing or able to concede to that.

Honor her, as he would to her grave, and respect the bands of marriage, for her and for the public, as long as a thread of life remained.

The compromise was clumsy, but it allowed him to assuage the guilt as he responded to someone who filled his need for love.

Had he a love? Cathy was in his day-by-day life in so many ways. There was her morning greeting with a smiling face, accepting him without being judgmental, and her serious countenance as she studied a patient's chart, a bill or an appointment, the many facets of her total being, each appropriate for the moment's situation, each adorable in its own way. He was alive when she was there.

He blocked out her other life. He could not explain, even to himself, how he could overcome such obstacles of jealousy and envy. She had a husband. She slept next to her husband. She fucked her husband. She had family and friends in that other life, all supplying her with solace and support. One of her first statements when they had begun to talk about their personal lives was, "I am a married lady."

He convinced himself there was a huge void in that other existence, and one she allowed him to fill. She seemed to resolve her guilt easily. When his masochism forced him to press for details of the other life, particularly sex with her husband, she merely said, "Please, let's not go there" and magically, it seemed to be enough. The Cathy he knew only lived in the hours she was with him or in his thoughts. The rest was like a blank cartoon square the artist forgot to draw.

As if unspoken, they both knew a meeting, outside the office perimeters, would trigger an emotional explosion. They feared the pieces would never fit again. For now, the desire and the fear were poured together like a supersaturated solution of sugar, waiting for that one, inevitable crystal to fall in, turning the liquid into rock. It stayed that way for some time.

Chapter 87

December 10, Wednesday, four hundred and ten policies were done. They stood in five piles, the last one waiting for ninety processed applications.

The tension acted like a magnet, drawing in Erik, Jerry, Paul, James and Edward. They did busy work around Paul's office, the activity helping to dilute the adrenalin building in each of them.

In reality, the show belonged to Eisinger, head of marketing. He had developed a call and recall system for the girls to use. At this late date, all the advertising and the mail-outs were history. He figured they had contacted every doctor in Florida at least once. The only remaining source of customers—he still was commercial enough to think of the doctors as customers—was the special meeting he had arranged for Monday, December 15, at Central Miami General Hospital. Its location made it ideal, being accessible from most corners of Miami.

The whole group decided to attend this one, there being little else to do.

The meeting began at the hospital. Eisinger stood by the door, counting the house. There were one hundred and fifty doctors, as close as he could see, as they gathered around the open bar. He was counting on alcohol to pry the last application out of this bunch.

After an hour of lubrication, Paul motioned for the team to start ushering the doctors into the meeting room.

As the seats filled, Paul called Kimberly at the office. "It's about that time; bring whatever finished applications you have. No, don't tell me."

After several pleas, the crowd quieted; Paul addressed the assembly. Each of Amed's players was introduced with a short description of their contribution. He then welcomed Erik to the podium.

"Good evening. As the farmer walked toward the large pond on his property where some young women were swimming naked, an older woman scolded him for being a peeping Tom. 'Ma'am,' he said, 'I'm not a peeping Tom. I'm only here to feed the alligators.'

"Well, I'm not here to paint pretty pictures. As you know, Amed has accepted the challenge to form a doctor-managed, not-for-profit medical liability insurance company owned by the doctors, the policyholders." He ran through the basic information.

"The legislature has given us the opportunity to do this if we can show them there are at least five hundred doctors who believe it should be done, who recognize there is no viable alterative and who are willing to put their money where their mouths are.

"We had 410 on Wednesday, 428 on Friday. We need 73 more, and have fifteen days to do it.

"Mr. James Eisinger, head of marketing, has his team set up at tables across the back of the room. For all of you who waited, this is your opportunity. The team will hand-guide you through the application and we will issue binders, pending formal enquiry. You will leave here insured as of January 1, 1976.

"Are there any questions about any of this?"

"My present insurance goes until March. What should I do if I want to switch?"

"Two ways. You can cancel your present policy as of now. There is a small penalty charge. Or you can wait until March. Even though we are going to have a single university date, January 1, we will write you for the remainder of the year in March."

Kimberly entered the hall and carried a sheath of papers to Paul. "May I tell you now?"

"Yes."

"Forty one!"

Erik overheard the number. To the audience, he said loudly, "Four hundred and sixty-nine as of right now."

"With this one that I add to the thirty collected tonight," Eisinger called from the back of the room as he laid an application on top of a pile, "I make it thirty-one, a total of 500!" He threw up his hands and shouted, "I believe we made it, with two weeks to spare!"

First the team and then all in the room began cheering and shouting. Someone found a champagne bottle behind the bar. He began spraying it, racecar-victory style.

It took two hours for the crowd to quiet down and depart, leaving only Kimberly and the team. They walked to the parking lot, happy and exhausted; they made plans for tomorrow and then each left. In the end, they were silent, using the last of their energy to wave good night.

Chapter 88

By Friday, December 19, Paul's office concentrated on completing the details in all applications. The work was blissfully tedious, free of the panic of only a week ago. They had received an additional thirty-four applications, providing a safety buffer.

"What's that about not counting your chickens before they are hatched?" Eisinger asked as he entered Paul's office.

"You better be smiling. I'm done hearing bad news! I'm closing the book."

"Not quite yet. The Henderson doctor group, all 130, the group we went out of our way to work a deductible…"

"No!"

"Yes, they just called and cancelled. They are going to form their own company. Apparently, some risk retention company from California is going to supply the necessary capital and surplus under their umbrella. And this may be only the beginning."

"130? Today is Friday, the nineteenth. Have you called Erik?"

"No, let him be happy for a few more hours. What can he do? What can any of us do?"

Stress galvanized Paul. "There is a solution!" He had to travel faster than the terror trying to overrun him. "James, get your girls back on the phones.

You get on the phones." He called, "Kimberly, bring in the attendance list for the other night." When she appeared, he said, "Take half of those who did not sign. Give James the rest. Thank God James asked for the phone numbers the other night."

"It's a carry-over from my former life," Eisinger said, but he didn't know what Paul was looking for.

"When they answer, just ask them if they plan to sign on, yes or no. If yes, tell them we will get right back to them. Give their data to James' team, and go on to the next number."

Soon, all phones were working. When someone got a positive, they would call it out and vocally add it to the total.

"Got one. 406!" Everyone was busy.

"Got one. 412!"

At the end of the day, it was, "Got one. 442." By then, Erik had absorbed the news, was immobilized for a moment, and then returned to the office to man a phone.

The next day was Saturday, December 20. The doctor's offices were closed. Eisinger had asked the team to report to the office. They came, drank their coffee, and ate their Danish in relative silence.

"What miracle is Mr. Eisinger planning today?" one reviewer asked.

The others gestured, "I don't know."

Eisinger brought out the lists of all physicians contacted but not signed in the past. "If they were not marked 'definitely not interested,' let's separate them by counties."

He then found the list of doctors who were already policyholders. "Separate this group in the same way." He spread the lists over the conference desk.

"Tomorrow is Sunday. Get a good day's rest, call on your Gods, formal or informal—there are no atheists in the fox holes—go fishing, but come in early Monday, ready for bear."

On Monday, December 22, the Christmas decorations that had been draped on Wednesday and Thursday marking the brief days of victory now seemed incongruous. The men and women gathered in the front of the office. They waited for instructions from Eisinger.

He began his instructions.

"Take a county; get the list of wavering doctors in that county and the list of those already with us. Ask the member to call the candidate. You remember, in their contract they agreed to help us one time a year. If there is going to be a need, this is the time."

The crusade was on. It was slow going. Everyone had heard the pitch. They were going elsewhere. They were going bare.

This group was the most belligerent. They weren't sure of their decision and resented someone pulling their head out of the sand, where, ostrich-like, they were hiding.

Some of the present members were resentful when asked to make a call. Others were flattered and jumped in enthusiastically. They were most productive. Once having made the decision to go with Amed, they emphasized the positives in their own minds and came across to the potential member as objective and believable.

The resiliency of the members of this informal sales force was weakening. They had survived the yoyo ride from peaks to the depths: the decision not to go with a professional manage—were they right?— and the attack of the scam. They had reached their goal of five hundred, only to have it cut out from under them with a threat, which could snowball.

It was like winning the sixth game in the World Series, which kept you in the series, and now being three to three in the eleventh inning on a two-out, two-strikes home run, and then have the ball called "foul."

After the night's jubilation, the following morning's fatigue made it hard for the players to climb to the top of the mountain one more time.

The phone receiver felt just a little heavier, the gastric juices were just a little more biting and unresponsive to antacids.

The secretary was frazzled. "No, I'm not lining the pockets of my boss!" and the phone hit its cradle with a boom. "Screw it! This guy wasn't going to contribute to a game designed to line the pockets of my boss. Doesn't he know we are on the same side? The enemy is a malpractice suit, not the insurance company."

"You're preaching to the choir, Sylvia."

"Got one! 500!" Kimberly shouted.

It was 2:13 p.m. on December 24, 1975.

"Kimberly, did you say 500?"

"Yes, I said 500!"

"And a Merry Christmas to all!"

In the office and in the cubicles, everyone stood and applauded. They were cheering for Kimberley, the winner of the lottery, and for themselves.

Part II

Chapter 1

The years 1980 to 1987.

The pathway had been rough for Dr. Farmer. Starting in 1980 with the acceptance of the death of his patient, his guilt sprang up, full-grown. For the next four years, he continued working as a surgeon but he suffered waves of terror. His fingers looked swollen and clumsy, though they weren't. How dare he expose an innocent human being to these mitts?

The first operation after the death of Seymour Lieberman was a mirage. As he moved toward the table, the cold, wet garment of fear smothered him. His stream of thought pinned him. He could not move. He thought, *It is only a vein stripping, no open cavities, no anticipated significant blood loss, no long case; even you can master it. Is someone watching me, checking up on me?* Then his hands appeared normal, the hands he had known before the death. "Hell, use them. No one will know what is inside the gloves. I fooled them."

The next moment the darkness was gone. His breathing became smooth and quiet. He now was the same physician whose morbidity and mortality rates for the thousands of procedures he had preformed were very acceptable.

Review all my charts! I'm better than Dr. Sanchez is, better than most. I've had deaths before. Why is this so different? This is the first time you were sued!

He could not escape so easily. The plaintiff's attorney had reviewed many of his cases. Dr. Farmer was amazed when the attorney identified case after case of his in which he had made an omission, though minor, or in which he had said, "Oops!" He had dug up cases with acceptable or unacceptable complications.

Dr. Framer found out that in the hospital, there was a network of clerks, orderlies, nurses and medical librarians all on watch. For five dollars, a phone call related the physician's awkward moment to the attorney's office. They thought, no harm done, and it's easy money.

Those bits of information may have had no value at the time. They were stored away under the physician's name to resurface and be used in an unrelated case. The main purpose of this information was to develop a "*mea culpa*" panic in the defendant doctor.

"Doctor, what is cystitis?"

"An infection of the bladder."

'How do you determine if it is present?"

"With urinalysis. If you find many white cells in the urine."

"How many?"

"Oh, I don't have a number. Many."

"Fifteen?"

"That's probably at the low end."

"Twenty?"

"Getting closer."

"Should it be treated?"

"Of course. Try to find the appropriate antibiotic."

"Would you say it was below the acceptable standard of medical practice not to treat cystitis?"

"I would think so."

"Then, Doctor, why didn't you treat the cystitis in Mrs. Southerland?"

"Who?"

"One of your patients who had twenty white cells in her urine on initial exam."

"What has that got to do with this case?"

"Please answer the question."

He looked at the report. "That was not a clean catch. If you look further, you'll see, when we repeated it, she was fine!"

"Oh, that's right," the attorney innocently said for the plaintiff. "I see it here. Let us go on."

This whole exercise was to have the poor doctor feel uneasy or guilty. He would be thankful he escaped this time, but how many other peripheral items would the attorney have up his sleeve? How many other actions or omissions sprung from the doctor's memory to make him cry out, "I'm guilty!"?

Dr. Farmer realized he was very naïve in this, his first malpractice case. Conversely, the plaintiff's attorney reflected the sophistication gained by handling thousands of trails. Dr. Farmer felt he was fighting uphill and blindfolded. His attorney casually twisted his pinky diamond ring as he maintained a casual, unflappable posture, which did nothing to reassure Dr. Farmer.

Anger combined with guilt, exhausted him. He had devoted his entire life to shaping himself into a good doctor, prepared to do his best for the patient. There was monetary compensation, but money was not the dominant motivation in his life.

Hell, he was very smart, magma cum laude. He could have made a good living in many other fields if it were only money. After his bachelor's degree, he wouldn't have had to spend an additional nine years of his life in training, at slave's wages, before he was equipped for private practice as a surgeon. In other fields, he would not become consumed by his vocation.

With all this devotion, this dedication, he found himself in the middle of a minefield; one wrong step and disaster. Must that misstep be a gross, negligent floundering? No! It is merely a deviation from perfection. One wrong answer in this test of patient care and he could lose everything: his money, his practice, his confidence and pride.

He did very well in academic pursuits, but he could remember getting 70 percent on one test. Then he'd had the paper returned to him to do better. In his surgical practice, for imperfection, the paper he got back was notification of a lawsuit.

Was it too late to start over in a less threatening occupation? Unfortunately for him, as for the majority of physicians, he was terminally addicted to the God-like position he enjoyed in his world. The joy of having total strangers put their lives into his hands could not be matched in any other endeavor.

Chapter 2

On Februarys 15, 1984, Dr. Frank Farmer watched his attorney, Sydney Albright, close the folder and hand it to Doris, his secretary.

As Albright shook his hand, Farmer asked, "Is that the end of them?"

"No more depositions, interrogatories, curriculum vitae or other enquiries until the trial. You have been through the first fire." He walked to the door leading to the waiting room. He motioned for the man sitting there to come forward. The man wore an old brown suit. A pipe stem protruded from the handkerchief pocket. There were small tobacco burns on the left sleeve. With a shuffled gait, he entered the room.

Albright brought the man toward Dr. Farmer. "I want you to meet Percy Jones. He is going to help us pick a jury and give us a feeling on how the jury is reacting to our defense." Albright surveyed Jones approvingly. "It's almost a lost art. We are glad to have him." Jerry Simms, attorney for Amed, who had joined the group in Sydney's office, nodded to Percy.

He was a small, thin man, gray hair, beard, and sixty-two years old. Having retired from active claims work three years ago, he came back, at times, to follow a case. This allowed him to vicariously enjoy the adrenalin rush. Dr. Farmer liked him. He said, "You are another thing I didn't know existed: someone to case the jury."

"We keep it a secret," Jerry said.

They walked to the courthouse.

Six potential jurors sat in the jury box. Mr. Raymond Rice, attorney for Seymour Lieberman's estate, and Sydney Albright for Dr. Farmer took turns questioning them.

Percy was bringing Jerry up to date. "Sydney has already excused two of the potential jurors, one at a time. They both had previous injuries. You could see them ready to award Seymour any amount. Now, he has a problem. Five have been chosen so far, and five have been excused. The next candidate is not the best for us and has already been accepted by the plaintiff. If Albright turns her down, juror number twelve will be chosen in her place, and he is as anti-doctor as we have ever seen. I suggested we take this one."

"It's a predicament."

"There's your answer, Albright's nodding 'yes.' He has accepted her. We are all set. All in all, this isn't a bad jury, three women and three men. I'm only worried about number four. He sounds like a perfectionist and may expect his doctor to be one, too."

Chapter 3

That night, Mr. Albright met with Dr. Farmer. "There are some basic things that help our side. Jurors hate bow ties and sports jackets. When we go to court wear a dark blue suit."

"Pinstriped all right?"

"It will do. Use a conservative, straight tie. Fold your hands in front of you; it will keep you from fidgeting or covering your face or picking your nose. Let them see your wedding ring; they don't know you're divorced. Hold your head up, look straight at the jurors, not arrogant, but friendly."

Dr. Farmer was leaning forward, looking like a poor math student being lectured on algebra.

"And relax." Albright's face formed a small, understanding smile.

He continued, "When their attorney asks a question, do not rush to answer. Hesitate, look at me, and give me time to object, but don't look frightened or pathetic. You might count one, two before answering."

Dr. Farmer wrinkled his face. "What for?"

"You would be surprised how often I can get you out from under a tough question by objecting. Sometimes, I will be objecting just to get it on the record, to prepare for an appeal. So, pause, even if you are sure of the answer."

"I should have gone to acting classes."

"That wouldn't be a bad idea. However, you will be good. We once had a client who was so scared, we actually filmed him in a mock trial and used the pictures to coach him. He still fell apart on the stand. He couldn't wait to confess. When you are asked a question, what are you going to do?"

"Wait."

"That is right. What is your name?"

"Dr. Frank Farmer! Oh, I'm sorry, too fast. Ask again."

"What is your name?"

Silence.

"That's much better. After you pause, what do you do?"

"Look at you."

"Correct. Now, when you think of your answer, remember, only answer the question he asked you."

"What else would I do?"

"That seems quite obvious, but we have a problem: doctors tend to be professors and take off, teaching the jury. Every word you speak is a trap. It may start a whole new line of questioning. Tell me about brain surgery."

"It is a subspecialty of surgery, which concerns itself with correcting pathology of the brain where that is possible, like resecting tumors, etc."

"That is exactly what I was talking about. 'It is not my specialty,' your answer is 'It is not my specialty.' If you had waited, I would have objected on the basis that it was not your specialty, and you would have been saved the trouble of answering at all. Remember: listen to the question, understand the question. If you do not, ask him to repeat it. Pause. Look at me. Answer slowly, clearly and to the jury. They are your audience."

"When do we go over the case?" Dr. Framer asked. "Enough of the performance instructions."

"We are in trouble if you don't realize that we have been talking about the case all evening. The more aspects of the trial we review tonight, the fewer times you will be blindsided. Want some coffee?"

"Black." Dr. Farmer passed his hand over his forehead. It was wet. He hadn't realized he was sweating.

Sydney poured two cups, handed one to Dr. Farmer. "The more embarrassed you are tonight, the calmer you will be tomorrow and all the days of your testimony. So, we are not going to be educators; only answer the specific questions asked. Now, there is one more patch of quicksand: your ego—no, not you specifically, but all doctors, all intelligent people. It is hard not to be right, not to know something. It's as though ignorance of anything was unacceptable. That is fine in all other aspects of your life, but as a defendant, it can be a killer. Remember, you are a defendant, not an expert witness. You do not have to convince the jury you are smart. They already know that; you are a doctor! They resent it. It is a strike against you. You are superior to them and they are going to knock you down. You shouldn't appear guilty, but you can't come across overconfident. If your demeanor stirs a little sympathy, we are ahead."

Dr. Farmer thought, *It's no use; I screwed up the operation, I'll screw this up. It's been too long.*

The session ended and he returned to his room.

Chapter 4

Dr. Farmer found it hard to sleep. He didn't take his usual Dewar's nightcap, for he wanted to be clearheaded in the morning. When he dozed off for a moment, he was in the grip of a vice, with the plaintiff's attorney turning the screw tighter and tighter. He sprung awake, body wet and guts burning. As he walked to the kitchen, he was cold and shaking. He poured a glass of milk, added a few ice cubes. After the first swallow, he put it aside and poured two ounces of scotch. He drank them neat. "The hell with it! Four years of torture is enough. I've sweated too much time already. I should have asked them to settle day one. Sydney said if the verdict was over my limit of coverage, I would be responsible, and it could go as much as two million or more. What was I supposed to do? I must have been stronger, then. Could it really go for millions? Didn't I hear the insurance company picked up the difference because of bad faith? Then, I should have asked them to settle right away. I served four years, and I have about a week to go before the jury decides." The scotch activated his calm. He walked into the family room. The picture of his wife, taken five years ago, one year BS—before the suit—was still on the mantle. She had left him two years ago. She said it wasn't the suit; it had been coming on for several years. She said something about him not being able to see the real Doris.

Hell, before the suit, he had been as he always was. True, he was away sometimes and worked late, but that was par for the course. The irony of it all was he broke it off with Camille, his girlfriend, shortly after he had received the suit papers. He remembered his sense of guilt and the feeling the suit was judgment calling. Doris, at times, hinted at knowing he was having an affair, but that was usually as a second front in a primary argument. He didn't think she ever really believed it. Anyhow, she was gone. He had no wife and no mistress. He was too nervous to find someone new. Beside, he hoped, in some crazy logic, if he stayed celibate, the punishment would be enough. The gods would take that into account and find him not guilty when the verdict came in. He reached up and smashed her picture. He didn't know why, but it made him feel better. He returned to bed and was able to sleep.

Chapter 5

On returning home, after spending the day as an observer at Dr. Farmer's trial, Dr. Stanley Reinhart viewed his living room. The warmth of his antique motif furniture was comforting. He ran his hand over the smooth back of the Louis XIV chair. He remembered when he had bought it. He had gone to Connecticut in the spring. He had been happy then; in fact, it had been before this whole medical liability business. Until then, his life was orderly and predictable. He had recovered from the tragedy of his wife's fatal accident three years before. His practice had been stable and still interesting, although the first signs of federal interference with his way of caring for his patients had him concerned. It was not too serious. As chairman of the family practice society of Florida, he had enough recognition. In actuality, he had little to do with the running of the society. By custom, the permanent secretary managed things.

So why had he agreed to participate in the Amed endeavor when Mr. Jerry Sims had asked him?

At first, it had been flattering. Like many other circumstances, he would have his name associated with a significant movement. With his experience and knowledge in finance and business, he did believe he could contribute something worthwhile. He had thought, *I would not be surprised to have the directors formally appoint me head of the finance department. Think about it, why would I not become chairman of the entire endeavor? It probably would only be a matter of time. Dr. Erik Nostrom seems to be organizing the efforts, but who is he? I do not believe he has any background in insurance, or in leadership of any kind, as far as I know. Yes, I could contribute and lead.*

When he was in college he had published and sold a financial and investment report for campus use. He continued following business activities with considerable interest.

He thought, *I will be quiet at first, not to appear arrogant. In a short time, however, the other directors will recognize my talent. When they insist, I will reluctantly accept the chair, a well-earned mark of my value. It will be sweet.*

None of these things happened. He had truly tried to bring support to the trust. Even now he felt an experienced, outside manager would have been more appropriate in the long run. In the last year, he could see that the policy of a doctor-motivated company, with little reserve development and big dividends in the form of reduce premiums, was unwise. No seasoned insurance man would allow that to happen.

The business of the imaginary threat to repeal the trust bill, it could have been real. What if it had been and he had ignored it? What chaos!

He believed that to take a chance on incomplete data was the sign of a leader. Of course, if one gambled, at times he was going to be wrong.

In the end, it worked out all right. The trust had even recaptured the twenty thousand dollars.

So why didn't the trust accept him? Why Erik? He sat at his desk and wrote:

> At the present time, Dr. Nostrom is in command. I can see changes beginning. Competition for the malpractice insurance business is returning to Florida. The plaintiff's bar is becoming more aggressive in their attempt to protect their awards. The frequency and severity of these awards are increasing. The Patient Compensation Fund is failing, and the need for increasing our limits is here, even if Erik doesn't recognize it. I believe the honeymoon is over. The time has come for hard decisions and tough policies. We must begin to act like a business in survival mode. I question if Erik is up to this. I know I have the abilities necessary.
>
> At all times, I am only motivated by searching out the best for our company.

He dated it November 1, 1980, and slipped it into an envelope. "Soon, very soon."

Chapter 6

Dr. Farmer put aside the pills he had ordered for depression. It would do no good. The days since the first notice of a suit had grown increasingly narrow. He could not lift himself from the pressure of his fears. They were free floating. At times, he thought he almost corralled them, enabling him to put them into a compartment, which would allow him to go on with his life, find other sources of confidence. Then, the haunt slipped out from under, forming a dark, foul-smelling, threatening cloud. It tasted bitter and made it hard for him to breathe.

When the trial itself began, anxiety partnered with the depression. From the plaintiff's attorney and from the plaintiff's witnesses, Dr. Farmer was told how careless he was, how the cocktail, two days before the operation, was irresponsible.

He should have recognized the DIC much sooner, and of course, he should have known instantly what to do. Hadn't he read the article in the *New Medical Journal*? It was incomprehensible that any doctor in his right mind would take a patient, who had a potential for uncontrollable bleeding, to major surgery. Dr. Farmer heard, "This man stood, frozen, while he watched Seymour Lieberman die, ill equipped to care for him!"

He listened as this liar, this twister of truth, this devil who could present innuendo as fact, pleaded to the jury. The attorney was even able to produce tears as he demanded a dollar amount, as an example, so high that no other doctor would dare go to the operating room so ill prepared and with such disregard for his patient's life.

Mr. Sydney Albright said comforting words, but Dr. Farmer knew they were wasted. Albright couldn't cry. Dr. Farmer watched the jury shake their heads—no.

He refilled his glass. His laugh was empty as he thought of the fuss about a drink two days before the surgery. Now, he could get plastered and no one would care. No one cared, period. He pictured his life after the conviction as a burden. It was a backpack full of rocks, with more being added until he was flattened, crawling on his belly. Then, as he thought of not being at all, the weight fell away. He became lighthearted. Fuck them all, he just wouldn't be here. There would be no disgrace, no fat judge calling him guilty, and no stares of satisfaction from the relatives who had said they would never sue him. No waiting forever for his confident self to return.

He leaned forward so that the end of the barrel of the shotgun rested under his chin. For a nanosecond after he pulled the trigger, he heard a roaring sound, and then he heard nothing as bits of his brain painted the ceiling above him.

That afternoon, the jury returned. The foreman stood and said, "Innocent of all charges."

Chapter 7

On February 15, 1981, Paul Arpin studied the fourth-quarter reports for 1980.

There were 5,213 policyholders. He remembered the race to get the first five hundred. Since then, the company had matured. He smiled as he recalled their first suit. It had come only sixteen days after opening for business.

It was on Friday, January, 23, 1976, when Mr. Johan Chekoff, originally from Czechoslovakia, filed. He had undergone repair of a right inguinal hernia on January 2, 1976, and claimed that since the operation, his right testicle hung too low, causing him to sit on it on occasion, with considerable discomfort. He was strong, but this was more than he could bear.

What was strange about the case was that the patient was bringing his grievance in small claims court. This was the only time a malpractice case was handled in this manner, as far as Paul could determine. Mr. Chekoff's case had been rejected previously by three lawyers.

So, there they were. On one side was Dr. Bryant Snyder, surgeon; Mr. Russ Slovak, defense attorney for the trust; and Paul, who insisted on coming because of the bizarre nature of the case. Across the table was Mr. Chekoff.

He spoke with an accent, though he had been in this country for thirty-two years. The David vs Goliath drama was apparent to the judge. He leaned forward. "Do you have legal council, Mr. Chekoff?"

"No, your honor. I am sixty-four years old. I was born the same year Czechoslovakia was created, 1918. I lived through Hitler, escaped and came here in 1944. I am hardworking and law abiding. I have an accent, but I think well. I do not need a lawyer, Your Honor."

"Very well. But since there may be some technical questions, I will act as your advisor."

The accent of the judge sounded familiar—a faint trace of Czechoslovakian!

The surgeon tapped his attorney. "Are we in trouble?"

"We'll see."

"And you are also the judge?" Mr. Chekoff could see the benefit of this as he recognized the comforting inflection of speech.

"In small claims court I am able to play both roles."

Mr. Chekoff was silent for a moment. "Your honor, I request a jury trial. I am here to get satisfaction in front of a panel of my peers. They laughed when I tried to have this injustice heard in a regular court. Therefore, I am here. I must have a jury. I must have my story recorded, officially."

"I could not act as your advisor if you have a jury."

"I regret that, but my mind is fixed."

"And there is the matter of finances. To have a jury could be very expensive if they found against you. The loser pays court costs, which could be hundreds of dollars."

Everyone's attention was directed toward Chekoff. The conflict within his brain was showing by his growling facial expressions. Finally, "If I can not have a trial by jury, it is of no meaning. I am leaving!"

"And the claim?"

"I have had my day in court." He shook hands with everyone and left.

"Case dismissed!"

Paul laughed softly.

Chapter 8

"What's so funny?" Janis asked.

"I was reminiscing about the first case we had. Mr. Chekoff. You weren't with us yet." He gave her a summery of the case.

"I cannot believe it!" She was still smiling as she left his office.

Paul appreciated her ability to see humor in life. He was sure she felt sorry for poor Mr. Chekoff, but her reaction to the story was Freudian. He understood the "funny" feeling comes when hearing a tale of tragedy from the unrealistic punch line.

He watched her leave. He felt lucky to have found her. She had adjusted to the office routine so well.

In May of 1977, Kimberley, his previous secretary, had to leave to follow her husband to Alaska, where he was starting his orthopedic practice. Paul had been lost without her until Janis came on board. Almost immediately, she had taken charge. He had thought Kimberley was good, but this Janis was spectacular. Her files were concise, easily retrieved; her easy management of the personnel shielded him from many petty complaints and gripes. He appreciated it when she gradually erected a wall between him and the staff. Now, most requests for his time were filtered through Janis. He didn't comprehend, or perhaps ignored, the fine resentment building toward Janis. On the contrary, he was growing more dependent on her, at first for her efficiency, but more recently, on her companionship and affection.

Chapter 9

On Paul's application for this job as CEO of Amed, he had listed his marital status as divorced.

His ex-wife was named Sherrie McDonald. She was beautiful, English-Swedish, and desirable. In high school senior year, she had been going with Spider Black, a good-looking baseball player, almost twenty years old.

"You're taking me to the prom, aren't you?" Sherrie asked Spider. They were standing beneath the stairwell, against the wall.

"You bet, baby. Who else but the prettiest, sexiest lover?" He pressed against her back and passed his hand around her and under her sweater. She shivered as he cupped her breast and put his mouth on her ear.

"Oh, lover," she whispered.

When they parted, she walked down the hall to join Rebecca, who asked, "Well?"

"Spider, of course."

"You're so lucky."

"Luck has nothing to do with it." She thrust her pelvis forward and laughed.

Paul hadn't committed to choosing one of two eligible girls. For two years, he had admired Sherrie, but the group of girls she went with seemed too sophisticated. He thought, *They know sex. I don't.* He was at the stage of kissing, hugging, upper-body feeling, masturbating and daydreaming about intercourse with Sherrie if he dared.

He froze whenever he was near her. Usually, he had no trouble talking to, and flirting with, other girls, but Sherrie was too much. She smelled elegant in real life and in his fantasies.

"Are you taking anyone to the prom?" Sherrie was close to him and spoke, facing his profile. He knew the voice, the perfume, but couldn't believe the words. As he turned his head, she was full face before him. This was the first time he looked into her eyes at close range. She was intoxicating. He had to sit.

"I didn't mean to frighten you," Sherrie said.

"It's alright. No, I was thinking of someone, but I haven't done anything yet."

"Take me?"

This wasn't what she wanted. She had pictured her walking into the ballroom on the arm of Spider. What a splendid couple they would have made. That rat had never mentioned he had just received an offer to play semi-pro baseball in New Orleans. Even when he had been deep inside of her, telling her he loved her, he had been thinking about packing for the following morning's departure.

With only three weeks before the prom, she was in a panic. No escort! Her father had offered to take her. What a downer. Then, she had overheard Florence talking to Lois.

"Paul hasn't actually asked me, but I know he will in the next few days," Florence said to Lois. "Who you going with?"

"Oh, you know, Buddy Wilson. I think he's going to rent a limo."

"I'll hint to Paul when he asks me."

Innocent Florence was throwing a lifeline to Sherrie. It took only thirty-five minutes for her to locate Paul, to rope and hog-tie him for her date to the prom.

He almost asked, "Why me?" It was beyond his wildest daydreams for him to go to the prom with Sherrie. He didn't give a thought to Florence.

The senior semester ended. Sherrie no longer bathed in the very satisfying glances of the admiring male senior students. Nothing would do but for her to get married and enter the next rung of social life. Her father liked Paul, so she chose him. It was a compromise. In exchange, her father would set them up in style and be a continued source of financial and emotional support.

Paul was so in love and naïve, it wasn't difficult for her to maintain friendly contact with her male friends. From the beginning, she had looked upon Paul as a stepping-stone to better accommodations.

She took advantage of his absence while he was in Michigan University, her father's alma mater, to send her "Dear John" letter.

> I care for you, but it's not in my nature to be alone and lonely. No one's to blame, not you or I, but I met Charlie. We fell in love. I am certain it wouldn't have happened if you had been home. I wrote to you about how really lonely I was. I'm sure you understand and wish the best for me, so I'm sending the divorce papers next week. Please sign them and mail them back to me. I will not be looking for alimony.
> Thanking you in advance,
> With love,
> Sherrie

Paul had heard of this kind of letter, received by servicemen and occasionally a student in the university, but this came as a live, unpinned hand grenade. A headache moved into his skull, just behind his eyes. Thinking became muddled. He wandered through the divorce proceedings in a catatonic state, saying "yes" and "no" at the appropriate times. He dropped out of classes, but for one of the rare times he followed the advice of his roommate and claimed an "incomplete," preventing the "failed" notation.

Over the next two years, he followed the classic drunk period, followed by the ulcer period, the denial, the hate, the "why me," the recognition and finally, the resignation and acceptance period.

He emerged a wiser and sadder man, and reentered the junior year at Michigan. He thought he never again would be drawn to a self-centered, heartless, desirable woman. The taste was buried, not abandoned.

Chapter 10

By January, 1982, the notifications of unfortunate medical results in the form of incidences or suits were now coming in at a steady pace, about one hundred a month. After quickly reviewing them, Edward Hartman, head of claims, would separate them into three categories: those that required only further observation for the present; those that needed more information to determine if it were an incident, calling for no immediate action or if it were a legitimate claim; or a true claim.

The first two columns were distributed to a regional officer; those in the third column Edward continued to study.

In cases in which the indemnity was less than $50,000, the regional adjuster decided to settle or proceed toward trial. In most of these cases the claims were dropped by the plaintiff's attorney after the initial letter. The chances of winning were not great, and the contingent costs to try the case, which he would have to front, were too high.

The other cases were settled at a mutually accepted dollar amount. After six years of experience, the adjusters were quite comfortable making the call.

When the liability potential was over $50,000, Hartman helped the adjuster in evaluating the case. Most frequently, a defense attorney was assigned.

With the increase in severity, Hartman considered extending the adjuster's authority to $100,000.

On his desk was a claim that the surgeon had operated on the wrong side when repairing an inguinal hernia.

"It reminds me of our first case, remember the Czechoslovakian?" said Kerry Staple, one of the early adjusters. Hartman smiled and nodded his head. "In this case, it was really sad. Apparently, Dr. Stafford was a Columbia Hospital trained and anal-retentive. He demanded all things be done his way. When he was dissatisfied with the way the nurses did the drapes covering the patient, he began doing them himself, much to the great annoyance of the circulating nurse. On this day, he went about arrogantly laying out the drapes until only the right lower quadrant of the abdomen and groin area could be seen."

"Don't tell me, wrong side?" Hartman shook his head.

"Yep." Staple said, "The nurses stood around, thinking, 'Mister, you must know what you're doing. You told us enough times.'"

"Did he continue with the operation?"

"Through the skin and down to the fascia. It was only when he freed the cord and found no hernia sac that he realized he was in deep shit. He didn't say anything, nor did the scrub nurse. Now you have to give him credit for *chutzpah*. He asked the anesthetist, 'There is a consent for bilateral hernia repair, isn't there?'

"'Don't see it.'

"'Well, add it. I'm sure I discussed it with the patient. Whoever filled out that sheet must have gotten it wrong.'

"'O.K. If you say so.'

"Dr. Stafford then cut a hole in the paper drapes in the region of the left groin, and proceeded to perform an excellent repair on the correct side."

"Is he being charged with mayhem?"

"Among other things. He would have gotten away with it, but for the fact that he was so scrupulous in documenting his physical findings that he dutifully noted 'no hernia found on the right.' Now, we have an operative report describing the findings of bilateral hernias, with the proper procedures to repair both, written in fine language by Dr. Stafford. The surgical assistant, supplied by the hospital, speaks very little English, but says *'Si'* in the right places to agree with the surgeon, and incidentally protects the hospital, which are the ones with the most liability and the deepest pockets."

"Where are we now?"

"The nurses only recall him doing both sides. They are vague about the consent and can't recall if there was a sac on the right. The patient made an excellent recovery with no complications or disability. I can buy it for $15,000."

"Off you go."

Chapter 11

The double role Cathy was forced to play since 1975 could not remain in its state of dynamic equilibrium. Moving from the compartment containing Erik, with its charm and warmth, to the life with Rudy left Cathy with traces of regret.

"Goddamn it, between your fatigue and the fucking period, there's no time for fucking!" Rudy jumped out of bed, pulled on his pants and stormed out of the bedroom. The anticipation of rejection made Rudy hesitate to pursue further.

Despite her basic needs, Cathy's sense of betraying Erik each time she attempted an orgasm with Rudy blocked her.

As though fates were conspiring to drive a wedge between them, Cathy had developed a facial rash since she began using birth control pills. Changing brands didn't help. With the choice of an IUD or diaphragm, she chose the latter. Placing this contraption did not heighten the joys of foreplay.

Gradually, Cathy and Rudy reached a silent agreement: abstinence except for special occasions, to be determined at a later date.

In this arrangement, they moved through the bedroom, the living room and the kitchen with equal reserve. As the negative connotation of sexual satisfaction increased, Rudy felt less obliged to react to her emotional demands.

"Yes, dear," he said without looking up and without comprehending her statement, and, he realized, without caring.

He thought, *This was not the way I wanted my world to be. I am the man! In the beginning, I thought I was the ruler, because she loved me. When she decided to quit her first job, I supported her decision even though I didn't know why she did it. In the days she stayed at home, life was sweet, despite the decrease in income.*

He had hinted at her returning to work, but that was for both of them; cash had been running a little low.

When she went to work for that doctor, was that when the situation had changed? She complained about little things, but, all in all, she seemed to enjoy working. Recently, she was happier on weekdays than weekends. *I haven't done anything to bring about that change. Why should she become distant to me? In the beginning, she moved so well during sex. Now no sex. How long has it been? Almost five weeks! Christ!*

It was Sunday morning. Cathy and Rudy were lying in their bed, reading the newspaper. She had the regional section, concentrating on an article detailing the recent rise in product liability insurance, including medical.

She put the newspaper aside and walked to the bathroom. The sound of splashing water against the tile carried into the bedroom. He put aside the sports section to look at her as she reentered the bedroom. She was stunning, having grown from a pretty girl into a beautiful woman.

When she fell on the bed, the warm, moist aroma of her body reached him and excited him. This, and the abstinence, tripped the tightly wound spring of sexual desire.

He thought, *By God, I'm going to make this a special occasion!*

She found the article she had been reading, oblivious of the rising storm developing beside her. He rolled toward her, gently removed the paper. Resting on one elbow, he moved his free hand from her belly over her venous mound and into her pubic hair.

"Like holding a trembling bird," he whispered. The phrase was clichéd by his inevitable usage in his foreplay routine. It no longer stirred her.

"Please, Rudy." His fingers had begun to move slowly, stroking her clitoris. She carefully removed his hand. Trying to appear nonchalant, she returned to the paper.

"Come on, you can read this later." He was smiling, talking softly. "Feel this." He guided her hand to his erection. "Isn't this a special occasion?"

"Why do you say that? What's come over you?" She wasn't alarmed. He was being playful, but she wasn't ready; in any case, she would have to go to the bathroom, insert the diaphragm and come back.

"For a moment, we were newlyweds. You were breathless, thrilled and thrilling. Do you remember?" He opened her robe so that he could press his chest against her breasts.

She put her arm around his shoulder and lightly kissed him on the forehead. "Easy, boy." She pushed on his arm. In other times, this degree of rejection was enough to turned things off. He would find his cave and sulk. Today he wasn't moving. The picture flashed in her mind: adolescence, under the boardwalk, the boy couldn't be pushed away. She had resisted at first, but then had given in and lived through her first, very unsatisfactory sexual experience. She remembered the mixture of fear and desire that had been present.

He shrugged off her hand and moved his head so that he could kiss her breast. Despite her misgivings, she could feel herself becoming moist. She moved her hips to get out from under him, but he believed it to be a gesture of consent. He could hear nothing else.

"Rudy, OK, but I must get the diaphragm."

"Please, let me in for a moment. I'm dying!"

"No, the diaphragm..." She relaxed, struggling to find a way to voice the next line of defense and objection, and he was inside her.

It had never happened like this before, with him. It was crazy. *What has gotten into him?*

"Only for a minute," he said, but he began to move.

Her mind separated from her vagina. "What the hell." She pulled him to her. There was an explosion!

When it was over, she did not experience the joy and contentment or any of the after-play emotions. She was raging angry with Rudy, and more at herself.

"What the hell was that? Suddenly you're a gorilla?"

"I'm sorry, but it's been so long, and you looked so sexy this morning."

"I thought we agreed on mutual consent. This stupidity is not mutual consent. I don't think I want to live here if that's the way you are going to behave. Just grab whenever it pleases you! I don't think so!"

"I'm sorry. That's all I can say." He lifted his head, smiled, and said, "As I recall, you did some moving down there."

"That's it! I'll sleep in the guestroom for now on."

"No, I'll do it. It was my fault and I'm sorry."

Their daily routine, since then, was to have the evening meal, say goodnight, and retire to their separate bedrooms.

Chapter 12

"Viewed from this year, 1985, the course of medical liability insurance companies has taken a strange turn over the last ten years." Paul was having an interview at lunch with Garrett Dobson, editor of the *Medical Chronicle*. "In fact, in that time, you have become editor."

Dobson nodded recognition. "It doesn't seem that long ago when I first heard the name of your company. It was early in 1975 when they were still searching for a no-fault solution. At that time, 99 percent of claims and settlements arose from the commission of surgical events. Medical omissions weren't considered significant enough to be factored in."

"We are now in 1985. Yesterday, I found, in the latest statistics, omissions such as missed pulmonary pathology in chest X-rays and misdiagnoses made up over fifty percent of the claims."

"Why is that? What has happened?"

Paul said, "A good part of the change is due to attorneys. The plaintiffs' attorneys are getting better at convincing the jury that an acceptable complication is medical malpractice rather than just an unfortunate result."

Dobson was writing on the yellow-lined paper in his notebook. He lifted his head. "Aren't the defense lawyers also getting smarter, or at least able to counter the changes?"

"It's catch-up." Paul had been standing. He stepped around the desk and sat down next to Dobson. "The duel between the plaintiff's bar and the defense lawyers fascinates me. As an example: In New Mexico, a plaintiff's lawyer claimed the three steps in one operation could be considered as separate entities. Therefore, a policy, which has $250,000 coverage for each claim and a $750,000 aggregate coverage for all claims, could be responsible for all the money in this one case. Because the defining language was vague, the judge found in favor of the patient and awarded all $750,000. Immediately, two things happened: the plaintiff's bar began giving lectures around the country on how to do this trick. The defense attorneys began giving courses on how to tighten the policy language to eliminate this loophole. Within the year, the issue was put to bed."

Dobson shook his head. "When I started covering malpractice, I thought it would be pretty dull stuff, but now I see it as piracy on the high seas. Plaintiffs are trying to steal the insurer's money with false or exaggerated claims, and the defense is trying to sweep everything under the expected complication rug."

Paul reached for his pack of cigarettes and offered one to Dobson.

"No thanks. I'm trying to quit. Some of the recent reports are scary."

"Maybe I'll quit tomorrow," Paul said as he raised his hands in a sign of hopelessness. "Getting back to malpractice, ironically, better medicine is costing us. In surgery, the patients get well or die. In internal medicine, the doctors, with the better medicine, can keep the patients with complications alive forever. The dollars assigned to that continued care in a claim settlement grows accordingly."

"That is a pretty harsh view of the success of modern medicine," Dobson said, shaking his head.

"You think? This is not for print, but it is better for us if the patient dies. The continued care is less; the claim for the cost of disability is less; and the financial compensation for the loss of the joys of life is not considered." Paul was building up a head of steam.

"Please, if I can't print it, do not tempt me with such juicy tidbits."

"One area you are free to handle is the appearance of competitive companies in Florida. In 1976, we really didn't need a market department. We were the only game in town. For complicated reasons, like decreased capacity, the commercial insurance carriers dropped medical liability. Now, as they have adjusted their capacity and see the profit margin, they are returning, and more threateningly, they are low-balling. Their premiums are 10 percent to 20 percent below ours, and below actuarially sound numbers."

"I can see this must give you reason for concern."

"In any other line of work this would be true, but doctors are a breed unto themselves. Paying for malpractice insurance, even thinking about it, is painful. As long as the total cost is less than ten percent of their income, they face the one day of reckoning, pay the bill and then bury their head in the sand, ostrich-like, until next year. Because of this, and probably loyalty to a physician-owned company, we will gamble that over ninety percent will renew, buying the known product rather than the cheaper, suspect item."

Dobson put his notebook into his inside pocket. "Sounds like you have it made."

Paul smiled but shook his head. "Nothing is that sure. As long as the physician, himself, makes the decision, what I said holds. Unfortunately for us, there is a growing trend for physicians to form groups. They, in turn, will hire an office manager."

"Your ESP is working," Dobson interrupted. "I've all ready started on an article. 'Managers of Doctors.' I can't mention his name, but I interviewed someone who took over a forty-two man partnership."

Paul was surprised.

Dobson continued, "He said the first thing he did was to survey his expenses. The first thing he saw was the cost of malpractice insurance. He thought all companies were the same and went straight for price. He said that reduction would look good on his first annual financial statement. So I know that problem."

Paul picked a bit of tobacco from his lower lip. "The game goes on," he said. "The twist, back in our favor, is that if any one of the physicians had gone through the agony of a claim with us, he would insist on staying with us, no matter what the cost."

"Is this ping-pong or what?" Dobson said. He sat back and resumed the interviewer's pose. "In your experience, how does justice compare with the ultimate outcome of claims?"

"Talk about a loaded question."

"No, really, you've seen enough to have an impression."

Paul paused. He weighed the risk versus the benefit in talking openly to a reporter, even a friendly one. He stuffed out his cigarette, pocketed the pack. "I might stop today." Then he said, "As long as the physician is held to a standard of perfection, the answer is, justice is bruised." Paul saw the surprised expression of Dobson's face. He waited a moment and then said, "Not being a doctor, I see the practice of medicine as demanding and, at times, frustrating. The physician works under stress and fatigue."

"Yes, but that's why he gets the big bucks," Dobson said.

"Those bucks are getting smaller and smaller what with Medicare and HMOs cutting the fees. The paradox is the patient population applauds the decrease in the doctor's fees, at the same time, because of the flat cost of their premium; increase the demand on the physician."

Dobson had heard this argument before and nodded sympathetically. "One physician said, 'The patient no longer puts his wallet in my hands, his life yes, but not his wallet.' It truly is a changing relationship."

Paul made a gesture of agreement. "In any case, he doesn't know when the stress is going to take its toll. He may forget an order, may overlook a differential diagnosis."

"Each one could lead to a malpractice suit?" Dobson asked.

"They could. If my doctor had only one patient a week, like Dr. Welby on the television show, he could reach perfection. He has 20 to 30 or more patients per day, and emergencies in any one of the twenty-four hours in that day. And each one demanding and expecting a week's worth of time." Paul reached into his pocket for a cigarette, but thought better of it with Dobson looking on. "In a fair world, the patient would only ask that the physician be sober, keep himself healthy, stay up to date in his field of expertise, and do his best without ego or monetary considerations. They would forgive him and accept his results. In that case, I would say there is justice in the outcome. Only unfortunate outcomes resulting from violation of this trust would be compensated. But that is not today; more and more, the patient sues on results rather than culpability." He realized his voice had risen to oratory pitch. "Am I preaching to the choir?" he asked Dobson.

"Shouldn't the defense attorney be able to educate the jury of the difference, as you described?"

"The individual juror puts himself in the place of the patient, with a lottery state of mind. If he were damaged, he would like his jury to give him millions of dollars, no matter who's to blame. As a juror, he acts accordingly, never to be dissuaded by facts."

"You sound bitter."

"These are my favorable thoughts." Paul laughed.

"There must be some times when the plaintiff does not get exaggerated rewards."

"Sometimes, there is a component of the case, unrelated to its merit, which turns it in our favor."

"Like what?"

"This case, for instance: Milton vs Larson."

Dobson began to read the file. "I am a speed reader. I'd like to scan it now, if it is all right with you."

"Be my guest." Paul walked to his outer office, leaving Dobson deep in concentration.

Chapter 13

Dobson read.

Mr. Steve Spencer, attorney for defense, sat quietly, watching and listening to the witness, a policeman in full uniform. The performance of Mr. Raymond Rice, attorney for the plaintiff, was good. Questioning softly and with compassion, he spoke for the estate of Mrs. Sarah Milton, deceased.
"So how has your father acted since the death of your mother?"
"It has been four years now. After the shock of the sudden loss of his wife, my mother, he seemed to withdraw into his own sad world. Little by little, he stopped joining the fellows at the weekly poker game. He dropped out of the team in the bowling league. In spite of this, he was able to go to work at the post office.
"Some time ago, Charlotte, who works next to him, called me and asked if there was something she could do for my father because he didn't seem to be getting back to his old self. I told her I wished I knew.
"I said, 'Do you think it would be good if you took him out for a drink? It's been a year now. Maybe it'll take him out of his blues.' I don't know if she ever did. He never mentioned it to me. He would come home, eat his dinner. There was little conversation. Then he would sit in the gloomy living room, looking out the window. He had a glass of Jack Daniel's on the floor next to

him. In the darkness, all I could see was the occasional glow of his cigarette as he inhaled, and then the smoke rising across his face. It broke my heart. He doesn't deserve this. Someone should pay!"

"Objection, your honor, inflammatory."

"Disregard the last remark."

The trial could go either way. Mrs. Sarah Milton had been a forty-three-year-old female, married with one child, the policeman. She had worked as a secretary, making thirty-two thousand dollars a year. The longevity experts set her life expectancy at seventy-two years. So, lost earnings would be $928,000 before reduction for present-day value. Add on loss of wifely services, the son's loss of maternal services, and general pain and suffering, the estate was willing to accept five million dollars to ease their grief.

She was in good health until she entered the hospital for removal of her gallbladder. The procedure went smoothly. After sixty-five minutes in the operating room, she was wheeled into recovery. Her husband was allowed to see her.

He kissed her. "Welcome back." He joked, "I told you there was nothing to it. Right now you look beautiful."

"Yea, with no make-up? At least they had the decency to put my teeth back in my mouth before you could see me."

"I saw you without your teeth before."

It was routine. Immediately after surgery, Dr. Charles Larson, Steve's client, visited Sarah, checked her incision and shook hands with Mr. Milton. "She looks good. We are just going to wait until she voids, and then she can go to her room. I left orders for something for pain and antibiotics."

"You off to the golf links, Doctor?" Mr. Milton laughed, not knowing how irritating the clichéd comment was to the surgeon.

"I don't play golf."

Actually, he was about to leave the hospital to go to Marvin airport. It had been three weeks since he had practiced touch-and-go landings with his Cessna 172.

Sitting at the controls of his plane offered him one of the special moments of his day. In that time, he was free of the constant litany of professional demands. The vibration and hum of the single engine shook off the claustrophobic squeezing of maturity. Again, he was a young man, in love with flight, enjoying the sensual pleasure as the wheels broke contact with the earth. He was free!

The sky was cloudless blue, wrapping him in contentment. For security, he watched the instruments with a side-to-side motion. Usually, the indicating needles were in the up position when all was well, so a general impression was all that was needed to keep control. Only on take-off did he ask the engine to generate maximum power. Once in level flight, he maneuvered the controls to create a beautiful hum. He knew his ceiling limit for this gravity feed carburetor was ten thousand feet. At that level, he put the plane on automatic pilot and relaxed. It was at these times his atheistic defenses collapsed and he could feel God as his co-pilot. It was a reverie.

"Tower calling Cessna 172. I repeat, tower calling Cessna 172."

"Tower, this is Cessna 172. You ruined my moment."

"Cessna 172, please return to the airport. You have an emergency call from the hospital."

Dobson turned to the next page and continued reading. The autopsy placed cause of death as intraabdominal bleeding.

The defense position stated, "Bleeding from the arteries leading to the gallbladder and the liver in this type of surgery is an unfortunate but recognized complication and does not represent actions below the acceptable standard of practice. The possible occurrence of this complication was explained to the patient by the surgeon as he obtained her informed consent."

In this case, the patient had presented an anomalistic pattern with the hepatic artery, the largest vessel in the area, hidden along the pathway usually occupied by the cystic artery. This vessel had been partially torn. Because the fascia covering had been acting as a temporary tamponade, it went unnoticed. Later, after the patient was in her room, the artery had freed itself and poured blood into the abdominal cavity. The nurse's notes were vague about the time between when the patient had reached the room and when she had been found unresponsive, finally expiring.

The plaintiff insisted that there was lack of surgical skill, that the surgeon should have examined the blood vessels more carefully, that it was necessary to identify the hepatic artery and the cystic artery before cutting either, and that only in this way could the unusual variations be safely handled. If even the minimal degree of expertise had been demonstrated, poor Mrs. Sarah Milton would be alive today. Her husband would not be terminally depressed, her son would still have a mother and they would be able to enjoy the way of life to which they had become accustomed with her salary contribution.

As testimony piled up, some for and some against Dr. Larson, the jury listened intently, nodding with pro and con responses.

The plaintiff's attorney, while questioning Mr. Milton, was just completing his picture of the pathetic, destroyed husband when the research secretary for the insurance company burst through the door of the trial room and ran down the aisle to Mr. Spencer, Dr. Larson's lawyer. She handed him a file she had obtained from the city's statistical department. It was policy in the company to run down the background of all significant players in a medical liability case. When Mr. Rice completed his questioning, Spencer slowly rose and walked directly in front of Mr. Milton, the husband.

"It has been four long years since the tragedy, is that correct, Mr. Milton?"

With his head down, he said, "Yes, and I miss her every day."

Spencer held up the shaft of papers. "Do you recognize this document?"

"I'm sorry, my tears blur my vision."

"I'll read for you. 'As of this date, 9-27-1977, certificate of marriage between Randolph Milton and Gloria Labelle. Is that you?"

Mr. Milton twisted in his chair, looked for his attorney, and remained silent.

"I can understand your problem. Apparently you failed to mention, in your grief, that you went and got married a year after her death."

Mr. Rice jumped up and literally ran to the witness box. Grabbing the document, he stared at it. Because he was presbyoptic, he had to read with outstretched arms. As soon as he comprehended the writing, his hand began to shake quite violently. "This is of no consequence!" he said, but with fading conviction.

"Please let me continue." Spencer spoke up. "I imagine your grief made you a poor husband. Do you recall this other document?" Spencer presented a second official sheet. "I'll read for you again. 'Certificate of final dissolution of the marriage between Randolph Milton and Gloria Labelle, 8-18-1978.' Less than a year. Your grief made you forget this episode also?"

When Spencer asked to recall the policeman-son to the stand to establish perjury, Mr. Rice signaled for a recess. Both sides knew that once credibility was damaged so badly, the jury would find against Jesus. The merits of the case were such that either side could have won, and in pre-trial, the odds were in favor of Mrs. Milton's estate. If Mr. Rice were able to get an appeal and retry the case, all of the grief tactics could be buried, attribute it to emotion. Presenting an objective case still put the plaintiff as the winner of two to four million. Even if the company won on appeal, the cost of another trial could reach $100,000.

Agreeing on $50,000, Mr. Rice announced to the judge that the sides had reached a settlement, and the case was dropped.

Dobson closed the file. Paul saw he was finished and reentered the room. Dobson said, "Now, you have made it difficult for me to cling to an editor's neutrality, but I will continue to try." He handed Paul the file and departed.

Chapter 14

Jerry watched as she entered the lobby of his office. Gracefully, she moved to the secretary's desk and looked in the general direction of his office. He could see she was a young lady with aplomb, like the women he passed in Lord and Taylor's, for whom he stepped aside to inhale the fragrant perfume and have another view as she went by.

With light sensuality, she moved toward his office. Opening the door, she said, "Jessica, your secretary, said I should go right in. Is that all right?"

Her voice was soft. He wanted to hear more. "Oh, yes, come in." The boredom of his caseload was replaced by the excitement of the nearness of a beautiful woman. He rose, walked around his desk and offered her a seat. As she accepted the chair, he pulled over another and sat near to her.

Recognition overwhelmed him with joy, guilt, sorrow and fear—it was Cassy! He moved his chair away a bit, leaned back to view her from her small feet in high heels barely covered with Italian leather, to her golden hair, down to her shoulders. "Hello. I thought I would have to go to Paris to ever see you again. And then, I don't know if I'd look you up when I landed there."

"I know. I'm sorry I ruined it for you and Linda, but I felt alone, and you were mature, attractive, and you were Linda's, the biggest attraction of all."

He could not listen logically. The flashback to that night, with her, mixed sensuous joy with dread. Thoughts of what followed flipped by like flash cards.

He could never again accept Linda's love. The pain of guilt had increased when he was with her, so the frequency, duration and intensity of their meetings diminished. She had never mentioned Cassy's name without causing fear to spring into his mind. *Will the next words scream, "Cassy told me about your affair?" Will I survive it?* And then, Linda continued with the news that Cassy, her loving daughter, had completed her year with honors, or that she was doing well in French class, and so on. And a casual, "Say hello to Jerry."

Passion had slowly seeped out of their relationship. Linda accepted it as the anticipated end of an affair, nothing more; men were men and fidelity was fleeting. Jerry could not forgive himself. He had the one great love of his life and he had made it impossible to continue. The worst of it was, Jerry now knew what love could be. Before, his blissful ignorance had allowed him to pursue his strictly male-chauvinist goals. Now, the fun of that way of life was gone, as was the desire to seek another Linda.

With Cassy as the only source of true affection for her, Linda had eventually joined her husband in Paris, where they had decided to try to re-establish a family core for Cassy's sake.

With Maurice and Linda wiser and sadder in their life's pursuits, the arrangements worked out pretty well. They accepted companionship as a reasonable compromise.

"I hope you haven't carried all the blame." Jerry said, "At that time, after the dance, with you rubbing that beautiful body against me, mix in the booze and the wine, and I was a melted puddle of desire, abandoning all my rules. I was the lusting pastor in *Rain*. If you hadn't come out, I might have gone into your bed."

"You're kind." She touched his arm.

He felt warmth that frightened him. "And maybe I would not have. It happened. I'm a big boy. Perhaps all the high and mighty convictions I had so recently accepted as my way of life for the rest of my life were written on water, only to vanish on the first wave of sensual promise."

"That is a mouthful. The priest at my French Catholic school would suggest five Hail Mary's and an act of contrition. My psych professor, also French, would declare you had two choices: to fuck or not to fuck. Each had fifty reasons arguing in their favor. You fucked, and were left with fifty reasons why you shouldn't have. No wonder you are wallowing in guilt." She laughed and wagged her finger at him. "Why don't we have a true confessional over dinner?"

She put his exact thoughts into words before he could find a way to say them. It was a *déjà vu* of Linda's words on their first meeting in Griffin's office. When he looked up into Cassy's smiling face, goose pimples burst out on his skin. "That's a plan, but what made you think of it?"

"I don't know, food and a little wine always make things more consensual." Jerry said, " I'm staying at the Windsor. They have a recognized restaurant. Want to meet me there, say at seven o'clock?"

"Make it seven-thirty and it's a date. I'm tied up until then."

"The thought of a date with you, and you being all tied up sounds exceptional. I'll see you then." She was laughing as they parted.

Chapter 15

Meeting, following the maître d' to their table and ordering drinks proceeded, relaxed and natural. She asked for a Cosmopolitan; he ordered Dewar's scotch. "It's easy being with you, Jerry. You are a lot like my father, looking so confident."

"If he's as I am, it's a mask. Inside, I'm frequently on guard and fearful."

"It doesn't show."

"I've had a good deal of practice."

They shared fried calamari with their drinks. "This is the season and the place for stone crab claws, if you're not allergic to seafood."

"That is just what I'm talking about," Cassy said. "I would never order stone crabs, with the bib and stained fingers and all, with anyone else. With you I'm free."

"I don't know if it's free. The last time we met, it was quite expensive."

"That was yesterday. When I reached Paris, I was really shaken. I had put on such a show for you, so cool, but I wasn't. For several months, I only went to school, wandered along the banks of the river, watching the boats. A boy from class began walking with me. We dated after a while. He considered himself a young man, and sexually tried to prove it. He was a boy, with his bravado and his ignorance. Despite that night, I wished he would be you. With time, though, I adjusted to my contemporaries. The memory of you faded, until now. I've been modeling in Paris for some time, and now they want me in New York. I couldn't come back without seeing you. Maybe for closure."

"I was surprised to see you. How is Linda? I imagine she's bitter toward me."

"Not really. She's tough. She said men are like that and she should have known better. And, in a way, she is grateful to you. With a more tolerant view, she and Maurice have bonded once again. In a way, I could take part of the credit for that." She put up her hands to shield her from Jerry's imaginary blow.

"Of all the *chutzpah*. However, you may be right. I'm glad you told me; you eased some of my guilt. Maybe I may live again."

"I'm truly a lady of rescue; you are welcome."

Relief was present in the silence between them.

As he observed Cassy, who was smiling, Jerry began to experience the warm, exciting sensation of being near a beautiful woman. She had matured to a desirable lady. In the old days, she would have been a ten on Jerry's rating system. Perhaps here was where he should begin his return to the he-she world. How appropriate it would be to have sex with the same girl who had sent him into the tailspin. Where behind this bait was the hidden, steel-toothed trap ready to spring? The paranoia of a bruised ego.

"Tell me about Paris, your school, your life." He began the well-used seduction routine of listening and showing interest.

"The traffic is crazy. I was in a taxi coming from the airport when we were approaching the circle. My heart was in my mouth as the driver kept going at forty miles an hour. I shut my eyes, waiting for the crash. Nothing happened. We slipped into the circling mass with ease. Later on, I found that, unlike here, in Paris the incoming traffic had the right of way." She was energetically gesturing the almost-miss with her hands. Her fingers were thin and graceful. She went on about the streets, the tiny perfume shops, the size of her classes, and the attractive professors. "Strange, I am so comfortable talking with you."

"The sexual tension is gone," Jerry said, judging her response. "Once a couple has had sex, they are co-conspirators; the question of will-she-or-won't-she is answered. The fear of rejection is diminished."

"Do men seriously worry about that? They all seem so brazen."

"At every new encounter. See, the man has to take the risk. Once he sticks his neck out with the request, he is vulnerable. The girl can shoot him down at any time along the way with a polite or outraged rebuff. If she initiates the seduction, she is rarely denied."

"I know." She instantly changed from earnest listening to outright laughter. "I remember very well." She was quiet for a moment. "Is that true tonight?"

"Are you doing it again, saying what I am trying to find the words to say?"

"I don't know who the cat is and who the mouse is, but yes."

"The lady said yes."

With the uncertainty gone, they leisurely finished the food and the wine. In the elevator, they experimented with holding hands, laughing when it seemed awkward. The routine of undressing, mutual admiration of bodies, followed by main-attraction sex, ended with two smiling, sleepy people wondering, what next?

They had breakfast in the room. "To complete a perfect moment, I'm going to eat, and the hell with the camera. I'll regret it tomorrow."

"Any other regrets?"

"Only that I have to be in New York tonight." She was thoughtful. She gazed out the window at the blue, cloudless sky, and then at Jerry. "Should I put it off for a while?"

A gorgeous, twenty-year-old, model-status female, a bright, ambitious, energetic and loving woman, was poised, waiting for his decision. Solomon could not have been asked a more difficult question. Grab her, run with her, and enjoy another day. Another week? Take an unaudited time in heaven, and then a lifetime of living with the 50-percent argument against it. He had been there once before and regretted it. "I'll take you to the airport."

"Smart move."

Chapter 16

By 1985, the concept of claims-made coverage of medical liability insurance became acceptable. Even the excess carriers, usually slow in responding to change, had adopted it.

One executive was heard to say at a conference, "It is only our suicidal tendency that makes us cling to occurrence policies." He then announced that his company was adding claims-made policies.

The physician-run companies were beginning to stabilize, having been in existence for nine years. Although this was a short time when developing trend lines to predict losses and needed reserve, the numbers were starting to have meaning. Even the actuaries, the most conservative of all creatures, were using them.

In general, the companies had a few ways of protecting themselves: put aside an estimated amount of money for each claim to cover anticipated loss and limit the amount of coverage. Dr. Jones would take $1,000,000/3,000,000 coverage. (When Amed began, the need for this amount of coverage had just been emerging.) This meant the company would pay up to $1,000,000 for the first loss. They would then have $2,000,000 left to cover all other losses reported in that year. If poor Dr. Jones had a loss beyond that, he would be liable. The policy read this way, but in Florida, there was a wrinkle that helped the physician: bad faith. If the physician asked the company to settle within his limits, and the company did not, the company became responsible for the amount of an excess verdict.

Most of the physician-run companies were not big enough to sustain several $1,000,000 hits, so they went to excess carriers, affectionately called Re-insurers. These folks would take the liability for losses over the amount the company wanted to retain. In the case of Dr. Jones, the company retained the first $250,000. With a $1,000,000 loss, the excess carrier paid $750,000. For taking that risk, they received a portion of the premium.

When Amed had first started in business, there had been no need for excess coverage because a legislative act had just enabled the Patient's Compensation Fund. Under this law, a state agency was responsible for physician losses over $100,000. The premium for the physician was only $1,000/year for the excess coverage. The accuracies felt it was an expedient measure, poorly thought out, and financially inexcusable. For Amed, it was attractive. They only had to reserve for the first $100,000 loss.

A significant portion of the earnings could be returned to the physicians in the form of reduced premiums the following year, an incentive for physicians to stay with the company. If the funds set aside as reserve grew too large, money was returned to the present policyholders. This was not altogether an altruistic gesture. Since reserved amounts of cash were tax-deferred, the government kept a close eye on them. If the reserves grew too high, the auditors demanded the company either return the money to the physicians as an expense to the company or convert them into surplus, which was after-tax money. In retrospect, this direction would have been preferable.

This difference arose in 1980 at a board meeting in March of that year.

"Mister Chairman, I know that I have presented a difference of opinion in the past, and we have managed, somehow, to find a consensus. I hope we are able to do the same on this issue. From the start, I was arguing for a build-up in surplus." Dr. Stanley Reinhart rested for a moment, judging the impact of his words on the other members of the board.

Dr. Anthony Sanchez called from his seat, "At that time, I believe we were more interested in demonstrating to the signed-up physicians that a physician-run company could do well for them."

Dr. Thomas Frond was nodding affirmatively. "Yes, and we thought the patient compensation fund was going to be permanent."

"Not all of us. If you remember," interrupted Dr. Reinhart, "I offered to set up a program, including investment strategies."

"And, as I remember," Dr. Fredrick Cannon answered, "you were also interested in managing the investments. To be honest, I was hesitant about having the responsibility of a large surplus in the hands of any of us."

"It was just that paranoia that put us in this spot," Reinhart said with uncharacteristic bluntness. "And it was Erik's backing that made us procrastinate. I have said before, and I mean no disrespect to Erik, but at times, it takes one mindset to start a company and a different one to run it once it is stable. It is in matters like these, the formation of a surplus, that we need a new guide. Erik is still concerned with pleasing the doctors. Well, I am more concerned about saving the company. After all, we cannot help the physicians if we do not have a company. As for the investments, my investment company has handled many physician accounts. But it is not germane to the subject. We should have begun increasing our surplus day one. I said it, but Erik blocked it."

"Why the urgency now?" Dr. Jack Reed asked.

"Stanley is right," Erik said. "There is a good chance that the Patient's Compensation Fund will shut down. We now may have to go to the excess carriers to cover us over $250,000. We would be in a better bargaining position if we had a larger surplus."

"That sounds like complicated financial maneuvering. Maybe Stanley should be in charge," Dr. Kenneth Moninger said. "Erik, I don't believe you have any experience in that area."

Dr. Thomas Harmon, from Gainesville, said," We are coming onto the annual elections for board members and subsequently, chairman. Perhaps we could resolve the whole question at that time. I'm sure Dr. Reinhart would make himself available." He smiled at Reinhart.

With the withdrawal of Patient's Compensation Fund from the active insurance role, Amed was forced to seek excess coverage. As a result of the annual election by policyholders, the third of the members of the board up for re-election were retained. The only other candidates were two write-ins for Popeye and one for Superman. One profane vote was disallowed.

At the meeting following these elections, the board had to choose a chairman and the heads of the standing committees. The question of them handling the surplus had many members reconsidering Dr. Reinhart as the new chairman. Before the meeting, many evening calls were placed, and many convincing arguments presented.

Jerry and Erik were in Erik's office, counting the probable yes, no and maybe votes. The maybes were the swing votes.

Cathy brought the coffee. "I try not to say anything, but this is so unfair. Dr. Nostrom has worked so hard for these doctors; you would think they would show some loyalty. And for them to consider Dr. Reinhart, it's outrageous!" She pounded her small fist on the table.

Jerry smiled at her. "Well, Erik, you have at least one supporter. Give them hell, girl."

"I always knew if I made a mistake, I had a good chance of being replaced. I was never able to generate blindly loyal followers. A partner would want a special favor, let his buddy be insured, settle a case, which should be tried, to avoid embarrassment, and so on. Every time I declined—and it was the right thing to do—I accumulated another enemy. On the other hand, when I managed to get a regulation passed, which enabled the board members to get compensated, they considered it the result of their efforts, and they thought anyone could have achieved that."

Jerry patted Erik on the shoulder. "I think it's even worse. Your real fault is your inability to blow your own horn. You need a publicity agent. I tried it, but we are too close. I don't cast an objective shadow."

"You aught to resign and let them see how well they would get along," Cathy offered.

"Trouble is, they would blame me for any failure for having left them."

Jerry threw up his hands. "Why are we so hard on the board? I bet when they think about it, they will realize that you are the only choice."

Chapter 17

The board meeting began at 6:30 p.m. on Friday.

Erik was standing at his place. He raised his coffee cup. "I give a toast of congratulations to Dr. Garing, Dr. Frond and Dr. Sanchez on their re-election to the three-year term."

Everyone stood up and applauded. They talked to each other, reached over and shook the hands of the newly elected.

Dr. Reed said, "I heard it was a close election. I believe there were two votes for Superman."

Dr. Frond said, "99.6 percent in my favor isn't bad. Just like Ivory soap."

There seemed to be a procrastination in sitting down to the real business on hand, that of electing the chairman. As far as Erik and Jerry could predict, they put three for Erik (himself, Reed and Sanchez), three for Reinhart (himself, Gentile and Harmon). Cannon, Garing, Frond and Moninger were hard to place on either side. They had commented pro and con on both candidates, or said nothing. Dr. Reinhart was smiling. Jerry thought, *Either he knows something I don't, or this is his poker face.*

The CEO, Paul Arpin; Janis, his secretary; and Jerry were the only ones present, other than the board members. Paul was in a delicate position. He couldn't afford to show favoritisms toward either potential candidate, for the winner would be his future boss. The thought of working with Reinhart was disquieting. The relations would be entirely different from those when serving with Nostrom.

Before Erik could start the meeting, Jerry pulled him into the side office. "Your inexperience in finance, particularly in finding excess coverage, is going to kill you. I overheard mutterings to that effect. Except for that, I believe you are a shoe-in."

"Any suggestions?"

"You know the old adage, 'You don't have to know everything, you just have to know where to find someone who does.'"

"Brilliant, as usual. I got it." They returned to the boardroom.

"Gentlemen, shall we begin the meeting?" All agreed. The discomfort was palpable. The demands of considering change were fatiguing. Almost any solution was preferable to the uncertainty.

Erik was the only one to remain standing. "As the first order of business, I would like to discuss my plan for offering a contract to an insurance intermediary. There are three highly recommended companies. I plan to have them present to the board at the next meeting. These people are specialists in guiding companies like ours through the task of finding and placing excess insurance coverage. They know the domestic market, and the European scene, including the chiefs of the London syndicates. They find the strongest group and the best percentage to us for placing the re-insurance. This addition will take care of the responsibility of selection. Of course, the board will have the oversight position." Jerry gave him the index-finger-to-thumb, three-other-fingers-stretched-straight sign of approval.

Erik continued. "The second item to be discussed is the selection of an investment company. As we noted in the last meeting, the reserve and surplus funds now represent a significant sum. It is large enough for us to have professional investment management. For fifteen or twenty basis points, it is a sound move. I believe these two steps will answer our fiduciary obligations to the policyholders."

He tried to present the data in his most matter-of-fact demeanor, though his hands were wet and frozen, his mouth was dry and his pulse was racing.

He sat down and took some water. For a few moments, he feigned concentrating on the papers before him, trying to collect his composure. Then, "Any questions about these two items?" There was the usual off-the-top-of-the-head questions and comments expected from a group of intelligent people who are ignorant of a subject.

Erik easily parried them. "I'll send you all the data on both items. We should be able to start the selection process by next meeting. I believe there is some urgency."

Jerry squelched a laugh as he studied the face of Dr. Reinhart. Before anyone else, Reinhart had realized the impact Erik's words would have on his election chances. He sat, white faced, slumped in his chair, like a prizefighter after a hard thirteenth round.

"The next item on the agenda is the election of officers." Erik watched, trying to gauge the effect of his speech.

Dr. Reinhart rose. "In the spirit of continuity, I would like to treat the election of the position of all officers in one action. I make a motion to re-elect those presently serving, for the coming year." He sat down.

There was an extended silence; then, Dr.Sanchez raised his hand. "I second the motion!"

"Discussion?" Silence.

"All in favor of the motion?"

"Please record the motion was carried unanimously."

Once again, Erik had survived the vote. He thought, *Must it be every year?* This year was an exception. He had made a mistake and he could have easily died politically. Were recognition and forgiveness alive and about?"

He worried unnecessarily, for it would be some time before his role as leader would be challenged.

Chapter 18

The following evening. Erik was seeing his last patient, Ms. Rosemary Loran. "And even my slice has improved." She laughed as she did a miniature golf swing. She was four months post-op, a femoral-popliteal bypass. "I must thank you. When I first found I couldn't walk, and more importantly, I couldn't play golf, I knew my life was over. Now I break a hundred."

"I'm glad I could do it. It wasn't always possible. When I started in surgery, there were no bypass techniques, no materials available. The ischemic patients suffered until amputation was preferable to the pain. And now, we are able to fix many of them." He took her arm. "Let me see you in four months."

She kissed him on the cheek and walked to the appointment desk. He stood by the examining table.

"Feel pretty good?" Cathy asked as Ms. Loran left.

Last night, until the final resolution, Erik had been tight and cold. So strained, holding himself on guard. Even after victory, he had been cautious. They might strike again at any time. Only by dawn could he carefully let go.

This morning, the positive rebound set in; he was joyous, lighthearted, as though he had swallowed a spring day. "Yes. For one brief Camelot moment, I feel fine. The results of surgery can be so rewarding. It's a love affair with success sweet but fleeting. God is in her heaven." He bowed to Cathy. "And all's right with the world."

They were alone in the examining room. He kissed her, a glancing touch. "Once again, I thank you."

"For what?" She watched, his face brimming with hope and enthusiasm. For as long as she had known him, he bounced from the top of the world to the depths. She rode the roller coaster with him.

"For being you, for bearing with me, not only for now, but for all the time I have wasted."

Cathy had struggled to find reason in her life with Ruby since the episode of forced intercourse. With some reluctance, he had accepted her imposed abstinence. But that in itself had aggravated the situation. Her physical need for sexual release had been in conflict with her repugnance toward him ever since that night. He had tried to talk it away. He had sworn it would not happen again. He was sorry. He had fought a losing battle, for behind her anger toward him stood the impenetrable wall of her love for Erik. Once her mind had relieved her of marital obligations, she was free to consciously think of Erik as her only lover.

After four months of conflict, the strain had become unbearable. She had demanded a separation. As a last noble gesture, Rudy had volunteered to move out. Divorce proceedings began immediately and concluded quickly.

With the obstacle of Ruby behind her, Cathy was free to openly love Erik. Her physical needs were answered through nocturnal fantasies of the two of them together with vibratory assistance.

During the day, like jealous demons, Erik's social conscientious and sense of obligation would not allow him to accept the gift of love she now openly offered. They both knew the status was too volatile; the smallest push would topple the massive dynamic equilibrium and bring them crashing down into open acceptance. His brief kiss was the push.

Erik was standing close to her. "Today, please don't say, 'Let's not go there.' I must go there."

In times before when she had sensed he was near to shedding the burden of social pressure, she had let him know she wasn't ready with that phrase. She feared if they stepped off into a free fall, and he had second thoughts, they would be doomed. In response to the phrase, he would take a tangential course, still loving, but not leading to a forced advance.

Today, his stars had to be in ascendance. Like a stiff shot of Jack Daniel's, he was fortified by his recent success. He could no longer tolerate the role of a yearning spectator.

She said, "OK." As simple as that. Then, "I do." Two simple words, changing a lifetime.

He had kissed before, but now it was excitingly clear; they did not have to stop, did not have to suppress the rising anticipation.

"Don't move." She quickly moved to the outer waiting room, locked the door, and returned. In that instant, as she left, Erik felt she was rejecting him. As she returned, humming, "Down and Down I Go," he knew they were ready.

The metallic click had the force of a cannon shot from the empty, silent waiting room. They stopped and stared. It was the outer door, which Cathy had just locked. The free fall was from exquisite joy down to the molten cauldron of bubbling guilt and fear. They were immobilized for a lifetime. And then they wrenched themselves back to reality, straightening their clothing, he rushing a hand through his hair, she searching for the wall mirror to check her makeup.

The front door swung open.

"Good evening, Dr. Nostrom," the cleaning lady said. "Working late?" She pushed the canvas-covered cart carrying a broom and waste bags ahead of her. She stepped aside to let the doctor and his nurse go by. Her face was expressionless. They could imagine what she was thinking.

Once in the hall outside the door, they began to laugh, the response to almost being caught, and being saved by the fates, rather than by intent.

They became quiet, each storing the revealing but traumatizing events of the evening in a separate compartment. The forces of wanting to go forward in the new, exciting, satisfying relationship against going back to safety drained them.

They had been soul mates for some time, but now it was screaming for completion. They went to their separate homes, but they knew they would have to be together. The addition of sexual acceptance, though unsatisfied, as powerful as it could be, would not increase their bond that had been perfected long before tonight.

Chapter 19

"All you see in the papers these days are the high settlements or jury awards, and it's all our fault." Attorney Roscoe Brady sat at the round table. Laurence Nottingham and Raymond Rice had joined him. "We are not the ones making the jury members litigious."

"And you can say that with a straight face?" Nottingham said, "You know, we have become more sophisticated in the last ten years. Before that, the doctor had to be drunk, caught with the knife in his hand or defecating on the courthouse steps, and it still was hard to sell to the jury that their God-like physician had done something wrong. Even then, they were willing to forgive him with a small slap on the wrist. I think Medicare made people aware of how much money their doctor was making. Now the jurors believe the doctor should sell his yacht; that's why he's paid the big bucks, and besides, he's insured. It's not his money."

Attorney Rice added, "I agree with them. Doctors are just in it for the buck. It is a license to steal. Just think you have a business where you sell the product and are able to tell the customer how much to pay and how often he should buy your product."

Nottingham laughed. "Add the best line—we protect the public and weed out the bad doctors, who are responsible for all malpractice—and you will have completed the campaign to preserve unlimited pain and suffering awards, and unrestricted attorney's fees."

Attorney Rice held up his hand, traffic-cop style. "Don't knock it, they have worked. And pretty soon, we are going to need them again. The docs are trying to get an amendment passed, which would limit non-economic damages to $250,000. They may get it passed."

"You may be right." Nottingham said, "Their media campaign is having some impact. The trend was for the juries to look upon the defense as a deep pocket, a lottery, what would I want if I were the plaintiffs. The poor defense attorney had to move the jury from being in favor of the patient to neutral. Recently, I am beginning to sense a bias toward the doctor, and now, I have to move the jury to neutral. I still win, do not get me wrong, but it is getting harder."

Roscoe Brady shook his head. "Even if, by some fluke, they get that amendment passed, we can get it declared unconstitutional by the Supreme Court. We've paid enough for those judges."

Rice asked, "You don't believe the rumor? We have the best Supreme Court money can buy, or at least rent."

"We'll see."

"On another subject," Nottingham said, "did any of you see the article in the economic review? The number of bedpan malpractice companies being put in receivership is increasing. It suggests that there may be some consolidation of those little ones, and eventually, there will only be three players."

Roscoe Brady asked, "Why are they going bankrupt?"

"It's a humorous paradox," Nottingham said. He turned to face Brady. "In the late seventies, the bedpans began to make money. They were charging occurrence rates and rendering claims-made service. Eventually, that would even out, but in the first years, there was money to burn. Like all good things, this goldmine attracted competition. There were over thirty insurers starting in Florida alone. Soon there was a shark-like feeding frenzy; they began eating each other by lowering premiums and insuring poorer risks. With the total loss ratio rising above income, and with no significant reserve, the weaker companies went bust."

"Oh, too bad," Brady said, crying crocodile tears.

"Don't be too happy too soon." Rice stepped in. "Remember when the companies first formed in seventy-five, we saw them as a new deep pocket. And they were. If they go out of business, leaving the commercial companies or the consolidated groups, there will be more resources for defense in the remaining few. It could get harder." There was silence.

"Roscoe, I want to congratulate you. I see you have entered the million-dollar club," Nottingham added. Roscoe was the last one at that table to settle a case for more than one million dollars.

Conversation covered many of the recent cases and legal decisions. The men departed, each content with their grasp on the changing medical liability arena.

Chapter 20

Before she had begun to work with Paul, Janis Walters's day work had been boring and fatiguing. Once home, she would take a brief nap and arise for the evening activities. She came alive with the anticipation of the game. She applied the bait with loving strokes over her body, under her breasts, behind her ears, over the shaved pubic hair. She viewed herself in the full-length mirror.

"Not bad," she said to her reflection. "I bitched about it then, but those exercises drilled into me during my fashion model days really kept me tight." With effort, her abdomen flattened. Her silhouette still had men longing to jump her bones.

This was the first time she had returned to the club since working with Paul. Sitting at the bar, she nursed her cosmopolitan.

In the ten years of existence, the club had honed a reputation for attracting adventurous men, twenty-five and older, and women eighteen to, at most, forty. Many were coupled: first date, each reaching beneath the formal veneer of the other who started out as a stranger; those returning, cocktails being prelude to the decision to ascend to the bedroom above; veteran pairs, smoothly moving from door to bar to bed with a casual, knowing rhythm. More roamed as singles, pocketing the wedding ring, and available to play the game for the night. The room was dimly lit with combinations of fluorescent tubes yielding a pale violet hue. The odor of perfume, men's cologne and moist mahogany wood of the bar was noted and then faded as the players adjusted.

She had been here before.

"Janis!" He was tall, tennis-tanned with a toothpaste commercial smile. "I have always been lucky. This is the first time I've come to the club in two months, and whom do I see but the love of my life. Do you remember?"

"It would be hard to forget you."

"You're just saying that."

"No, really."

"I said I was lucky. Should we pick up from our last goodbye?" He put his hand on her shoulder and leaned toward her. "It was a kiss like this, as I remember."

She gently touched his cheek, preventing his advance. "Not tonight. I'm only watching and thinking tonight."

"Both are very dangerous pursuits for a beautiful woman."

"I know. It's unlike me. I'm on a new tack." Her facial expression hung between smiling and thoughtful.

His hand on her arm didn't receive the soft, yielding acceptance he had known in the past. "OK, I'll go to the nearest phone booth and change from lover to buddy. Tell me." The background music was invasive. She held her hands to her ears.

"I think a booth is indicated. It's more like a confessional, which seems appropriate." He helped her off the stool and to the back of the room.

"I came here tonight to say goodbye, goodbye to the club, to this life. I was free, independent, knowing that tomorrow I could find a new love, a new job, a new club; I was woman." She partly sang, partly hummed the tune. "It is from another, younger time. The lonely nights, the hangovers." She shook her head, her face suddenly showing sadness. "The search for something to do on Christmas, the question of accumulating memories for future recall, these all began to seep in and register on my consciousness."

"And *quo vadis?*"

"Recently, the Hollywood version of life, with the housewife being cared for by a loving, devoted and faithful husband, seems more appealing. The merchandise is still prime." She outlined her face, breasts and hips with her hands. "He would be getting a fair deal."

"If my last marriage hadn't left me broke, I'd propose to you as we sit."

"You're sweet."

"You have a target, the knight in shining armor, the man to be father of your kids?"

"As I said when you first came over, I'm watching and thinking. If and when, you'll get an invitation."

"Seriously, he'll be one lucky guy; you are tops. Good luck."

He held her hand for a moment and then wandered back to the bar. After a while, she left for home.

Chapter 21

Janis undressed and lay naked, stretched out on her king-sized bed. About twelve years ago, she had moved into her apartment. The décor had subtly gone from a softly feminine presentation to neutral, with glass, aluminum and wood replacing cushioned frills. It struck her that her room and her passion had hardened. The yo-yo ride of new love, flaming love and flamed-out love had decreased in length of cycle, becoming pleasant on the upswing and merely uncomfortable on the down. With this reverse metamorphosis, she grew stronger, more self-reliant and lonelier.

Paul was a change from her club companions. He had told her of his stepping-off-the-cliff-in-love disaster with Sherrie. Like breaking in a skittish colt, Janis would have to proceed with caution. With time, she would make herself indispensable and sensually satisfying. She knew she had the tools and techniques to get under his skin. Once this was accomplished, a gentle withdrawal should frighten him into making it permanent.

She thought, *I have become truly a scheming bitch. But it isn't all bad; I'm attractive, great in bed, better than Sherrie, I bet. I would be good for him. I could appreciate a calm, dependable life, and so would he. Before we settle down, I will supply him with that big romance he wanted from Sherrie. As that cools down, we'll move into long-range planning. Children? Maybe too old at thirty-seven, though it's possible. Would a little Paul running around the house be an added attraction? But how many couples can I think of who grew distant as the kid grew closer?* She got off the bed and walked toward the window. She stroked her flat stomach, picturing it swelling. Her mind continued, *Some men enjoy the pregnancy, at least until the last month, and maybe not the first-month vomiting. But after the delivery, they're in competition with the kid, a competition they always lose.* Janis became angry. *Sex shrivels up and I lose that weapon!* She hugged herself. *And the sex as well.*

She walked to the make-up table, sat down, and raised the index finger of her right hand as though she were lecturing. *There is a plus side, I know; kid fills the house and gives my man bragging rights. People are suspicious of men without children.* She put her hand to her forehead. *I'm getting a fever over this!* Her skin was cool. *Some childless couples I know get so selfish, like compensating for not contributing.* Again, she looked into the mirror, turning her head, straining to see her profile. *I wonder about my maternal instincts. I'm OK if "good aunt" counts. If I could only wipe out the picture of when I'm just about to come, the brat screams from the crib, or later on, he bursts into the room. Goodbye fucking! We could always hire a babysitter and go to a hotel. I'm wandering; let's get back to the plan. He's a good catch. I become all things to him and reluctantly say "yes" and we marry. That's fine. Let's get off the Hollywood-burning-passion bit. I'm all right with the premeditation taint. In the end, it is for a good cause for both of us. I can live with that.*

She spread the cleansing lotion over her face, carefully massaging away the lines under her eyes. When she was seventeen, running through the fields, the warm sunlight of youth had washed her wrinkle-free cheeks. Because only the happy parts of those times remained, she was saddened at no longer being seventeen.

Chapter 22

Paul Arpin was preparing the third-quarter statistics for 1982. There was a direct written premium of $45,242,624. He smiled, recalling the struggle to get the first million. How easily he could say million and now say forty-five million. He thought, *More important is the 85 percent of doctors who are still insured by us from last year, despite the raise in premiums.* The doctors had stayed—all 4,162 of them.

He walked over to the office of Ed Hartman in claims. There was another man in the room sitting in a chair in front of Hartman's desk.

"Third-quarter results?" Hartman asked.

Arpin noticed the man, but answered the question.

"The numbers are good. The trick is to increase premiums next year and yet to compete by discounting groups. Ever since the doctors went from individual purchases to being represented by a group manager, price has become all important."

Hartman frowned. "At the same time the cost of defense continues to increase. Look here, the cost per case, both in indemnity and expense, has gone up."

Hartman introduced Joseph Conti. He was shorter than Hartman. A thin strip of white hair framed his bald head. "Joseph has been with us since 1977 in the claims department. He's constantly fighting with marketing and credentialing."

Conti acknowledged the reputation. Laughingly, he said, "Just making my job easier; if we don't sell any premiums, we won't have any losses."

"He forgets the old axiom, 'you need a good fire once in a while to sell fire insurance,'" Hartman said.

As the conversations ended, Arpin could see Conti as a valuable member of the team, with a depth of experience.

Chapter 23

On the following Monday, Joseph Conti dropped the folder on Hartman's desk. "I don't know how to handle this case." He passed his hand over his scalp. "The doctor is screaming '*mea culpa*' all over the place and I can't believe his story. He said the girl and her mother were right when they claimed Lamarella contracted vaginal herpes from him when he examined the girl without gloves."

Hartman shrugged his shoulders. "Why?"

"He didn't want to panic the girl." Conti looked at Hartman hopelessly. "Here's his sad story." Conti picked up the folder and read Dr. Rafael Gomez's written statement.

"I knew that she had a bad experience when, as a small child, she was hurt by a man wearing plastic gloves. Ever since then, she would freeze at the sight of anyone approaching her with latex gloves. The girl wanted to be fit for a diaphragm, a simple procedure. Unfortunately, I didn't realize I had a herpetic lesion on my hand. I did the job with well-washed but bare hands. Some time after the fitting, she developed vaginal herpes. I'm sorry. I realize my actions were below the standard of medical practice. My attorney strongly suggests we settle within my limits of $1,000,000."

Conti delivered the doctor's story in a stage voice. Back to normal tones, he said, "We're out to dry. It's one thing to have a doctor who makes a poor witness, you know, nervous or stupid, but for him to throw his ass on the plaintiff's spear is insanity. I'll try to get out of this with my balls intact, but I don't know."

Hartman looked at the folder and then at Conti. The room air conditioning had been off for a while. It made Conti sweat a little. His bald head was moist. Hartman felt fine. It was quiet. He let Conti hang a little longer, and then he said, "Sometimes it is better to be lucky than smart."

Conti braced himself. He thought, *My God, I hope Hartman's not going to try to find something good out of something bad. I don't need the Pollyanna cheer-up right now.*

"Look what I have for you." Hartman knew his friend was in agony, and he was about to ease his pain. He held up a pink carbon copy of an application. The questions were printed and the answers were written in long hand.

"This came in two days ago," Hartman said as he handed the report to Conti. "A friendly desk clerk at the courthouse saw this original complaint come across her desk. Before she could act on it, an attorney rushed in and withdrew the complaint sheet.

"The clerk said, 'Fortunately for you and unfortunately for him, I kept a copy and thought you might be interested.'

"I told her to expect the usual appreciation."

Conti carefully unfolded the report. His street-fighter instincts said it was going to be good. In the box marked "A brief description of the complaint," he read:

"I charge Dr. Rafael Gomez with statutory rape of my fifteen-year-old daughter, Lamarella Bustos. On the night of September 14, 1982, and other nights before that, he had sexual relations with my under-aged daughter and gave her a venereal disease: herpes!"

Conti sat down at Hartman's desk. The air conditioning came on with a loud clang and then a buzz. He re-read the complaint and then read it aloud. His voice became louder until it was a shout, almost obliterated by the raucous laughter. "I'm free. Oh, Lord, I'm free at last!"

Two days later in Hartman's office, Conti was interviewing a very nervous Dr. Gomez. "That was an interesting story last week," Conti said. "I didn't know what we could do."

Dr. Gomez wore an expensive, Italian-cut gray suit, and a pale blue silk tie. His skin was smoother than expected in a fifty-one-year-old man. Hartman thought Gomez was about the same age as Erik, the chairman of Amed. The doctor's cologne was heavier than Conti could forgive.

"I must tell you, we know about the original reaction of Mrs. Bustos. We have a copy of the police report."

Dr. Gomez couldn't comprehend the pink sheet he was staring at. "I never saw this paper!" When he had agreed to meet Conti, Gomez had been sure it was simply to reinforce his story. He felt a little sorry for Conti but he had a good chance of getting out of this mess without too much damage.

"I'm sure of that," Conti said. "It's a primary complaint accusing you of rape involving a minor."

The words were a hard belly punch. Gomez leaned forward in his chair as though he were hit. Mrs. Busto's lawyer had seemed so sure Gomez's story was foolproof.

"What happened to turn this criminal case into malpractice?" Conti asked.

Dr. Gomez was going to protest, and then he turned his palms up in a surrendering gesture and smiled. He was an amoral man. Like his ancient forefathers in Sparta, he did not regret the action; the crime was getting caught.

"Oh hell, I'm screwed no matter what." He began to tell the story

"Silvia, Mrs. Bustos, finds out from their gynecologist that the eruption in her daughter, Lamarella, is vaginal herpes, a sexually transmitted disease. Right off, Mrs. Bustos is suspicious, for she has herpes and she got it from me. It didn't take her long to reduce Lamarella to a wailing, slobbering dishrag, confessing she was fucking me.

"I first knew I had a problem when Mr. Friends, Bustos' attorney, called to set up a meeting. Mrs. Bustos had called him to tell him about her filing a complaint and to find out what the penalty was for statutory rape. Friends had a fit. He said he would rush to the station and withdraw the complaint. He told her he would arrange a conference. I thought if the lawyer were at the meeting, Mrs. Bustos wouldn't attack me. I know her; she was capable of murder if she got mad enough.

"We met at her house. It was a scene, all right. Little Lamarella sitting on the couch, red eyed from crying. One cheek was swollen where I suppose Silvia had hit her when she'd found out her daughter was screwing me. I was doing Silvia at the same time. By the way, for a while, that set-up was every man's dream." He smiled briefly. Conti wasn't usually judgmental, but as he listened, he felt contempt for Dr. Gomez.

"We were in the kitchen, sitting around an oblong table. Attorney Friends held a copy of the complaint in his hand. He said to Silvia, 'I know that you're upset with this scumbag, but what good does it do to put him in jail?' Silva nodded vigorously; it was what she wanted. 'I know you're pissed off, want to hurt him, but there may be a better way, a way that will punish the doctor and at the same time compensate you a little for your suffering.' I was sitting on the edge of my seat, waiting for this salvation, and so was Silvia. 'I'm sure the good doctor has no desire to spend the next twenty years in jail, do you, Doc?' I had no argument if this could get me out alive and get Silvia off my back

"By this time, the hole I was in began to smother me. My breathing was wheezing and I was sweating. I would have agreed to anything.

"'Here's the story.' At that point, Friends outlined the tale about the ungloved vaginal examination by an old family physician. I would reluctantly say it was malpractice; the insurance company would have to settle. He said that I probably would be put through the wringer, but in the end, the worst would be a suspension, the way the medical board is scared of being too tough. So what can I say? It was a way out. It's not your money, after all. It was all Friend's fault. He made me think it was legal. He's the lawyer. I could testify to that, if it would help."

As the doctor talked, the perspiration was clearly visible on his face. Conti thought this son of a bitch had once been a shiny-eyed young man hoping to become a doctor, believing, *If only I'm able to be a doctor, I'll be the luckiest, happiest man in the world. Lord, I won't ask you for anything else.* So he had become a doctor and look at him now. What a waste! Conti ground his teeth. *If I ever had the chance to be a doctor, I would protect it with my life.* Conti shook his head.

His own attempt at medical school had fizzled when his wife became pregnant and finances ran out. He had all but buried the pain and regret, but it hit him in the back of his heart as he looked at Doctor Gomez. Only anger could drown his feelings, and this grew rapidly. With effort he brought himself under control, resisted the temptation to personally punish this man.

The phone rang. "This is Freddy Friends. I want to speak to Mr. Conti."

"This is Conti."

"I'm the attorney for Lamarella Bustos. I believe you are handling the suit by my client against Dr. Gomez?"

"Yes, I am. Have you talked to Dr. Gomez lately?"

"I wouldn't do that without arranging for your attorney being there. It wouldn't be ethical."

"Ethical, my eye!" Conti muttered to himself. He said, "Then I suggest that you come to my office to talk settlement. It's a pretty clear-cut case. Is tomorrow at ten good for you?"

"Fine. This is the first time I've had the pleasure of dealing with your company, Amed. They said you all were efficient and now I agree with them. I assume we are looking at the limits of his coverage, one mil? We can take care of the details tomorrow. Good talking with you, Conti. See you tomorrow."

Conti smiled, hung up the phone, and showed Dr. Gomez to the door after getting his assurance to return tomorrow and not to talk to Mr. Friends.

He was still smiling as he finished the report to the legal bar concerning the conduct of Mr. Friends, and the report to the board of medicine concerning Dr. Gomez.

"So I'm not a doctor. I'm not bad at what I do."

He wrote across the Dr. Gomez file, "Closed without indemnity. Expense reimbursed by plaintiff's representative."

Chapter 24

Erik woke up at 5:30 a.m. The shower was hot enough to raise goose pimples, the water easing the ache across his shoulders, the steam clearing his sinuses. In that moment, his muscles were free of tension and he felt sensual stirrings in his groin. As he left the warm cocoon, the cold air outside the shower stall reminded him of life's realities. The reflection he saw while shaving said: beginning to get craggy, but still handsome. He lifted his head to erase the slight double chin. He thought, *They say Jack Kennedy did that when he was photographed, for the same reason.* He dressed, climbed into his Jaguar and headed to the hospital. The ritual of his daily life began.

At breakfast in the hospital, the conversation of the cafeteria committee, made up of any doctor present, followed their usual pattern of solving the world's problems with sparse information.

"He'll never replace Johnny Carson. Did you see the show last night?"

"I missed it."

"Talking about Johnny, did you see the papers this morning? I tell you, once you retire, you get into all sorts of trouble."

Erik, as an inwardly laughing spectator, thought, *It's true. Physicians, being recognized experts in their field, assume expertise in all aspects of life and are capable of the strangest and most absurd statements.* At times, he was a guilty participant, but this morning, the role of observer pleased him.

He consumed his coffee, orange juice, scrambled eggs, turkey sausage and toast and walked to the OR. The first case was Mr. Smith for a carotid endarterectomy.

The patient was anesthetized and prepped from hairline to the mid chest on the left. A rolled towel was placed under the neck to elevate the operative area. Erik and his OR team were relaxed as the case began. A thin line on the betadine-stained skin turned red as the scalpel cut from behind the ear to the mid clavicle.

Everyone knew where the hand grenades lay. Erik approached the first one. After exposing the carotid artery, he prepared to insert a plastic tube into the clamped blood vessel. "Once I get the fat end of this tube in, open the clamp and I'll thread it toward the heart, then you apply the special carotid clamp to hold it in place."

"I know," Franco, the first assistant, said wearily. He had done this procedure many times.

"Just singing the routine. I still remember when Dr. Blanding's assistant didn't get the clamp on in time. The catheter was blown out of the artery, with blood spurting to the ceiling. So forgive me."

The placement went well. Blood from the heart ran into the tube. The opposite end had been inserted and clamped into the distal part of the artery. Now oxygenated blood was running through this bypass to the brain, extending the length of time the artery could be clamped. The part of the artery stenosed by atherosclerotic plaque was now visible through the incision in the vessel, in a dry field, smiling up at Erik. The faint odor of exposed flesh and dried blood on the gloves sneaked past his mask and into his nostrils. It wasn't pleasant, but it was a familiar part of the procedure.

When the operation began, the room was cold, but now, with the body heat, the gowns and the tension, a very thin film of perspiration formed on Erik's forehead.

He peeled out the yellow-white, partially calcified, crusted, cheesy material, leaving a thin but smooth artery wall, achieving the purpose of the operation.

The next hand grenade involved clamping the artery, removing the catheter and closing the incision in the artery with a vein patch that had been previously harvested from the saphenous vein in the groin.

"I'm ready for the patch," Erik said.

The nurse prepared two needle holders, each with a 6-0 monofilament suture with two needles. "Two 6-0 ready."

"I'm about to clamp the carotid."

From the first moment after the clamp was applied, the brain complained of the lack of oxygen bearing blood. If the deprivation lasted for more than a few minutes, the brain would make plans to shut down and the patient would suffer a stroke.

"All set?" Erik asked. Franco and the scrub nurse nodded. "Here we go. Start the timing."

Efficiently, but without rushing, Erik removed the bypass. He clamped the vessel, irrigated with saline and sutured the vein patch in place with the hair-fine monofilament thread. Before completing the suture line, Erik briefly released the clamps, flushed the proximal and distal segments of the vessel to wash out any clot. The escaping blood spurting through remaining opening was caught in a gauze pad. The clamps were re-applied. With two passes of the needle bearing the thread, through the arterial wall and the vein patch, the incision was closed.

"Looks good so far," Erik said.

The nurse then hung the bloody gauzes separately on a rack to make the sponge count easier.

"Opening the clamp." Erik called to the anesthesiologist, "Time?"

"Seventy-two seconds. Patient looks good."

As the blood rushed through the vessel, some oozed from the needle holes for a few seconds and then stopped as the red cells plugged the minute defects.

A small drain was brought out a separate stab wound and the incision was closed.

Erik sat in the doctor's lounge. He was drinking black coffee, looking at CNN on the television, and not really seeing the program. It was time to go to the recovery room. He stood, without moving. *You have to go*, he thought.

"How is he?" Franco asked.

"I haven't checked yet."

"Want me to?"

"No, I'll go." It was cool in the room. He began to shiver. He took a white lab coat from a hook and put it on. He walked to the recovery room and stopped at the foot of the bed.

Nurse Sharon stepped back, allowing him to reach the bedside. It was time for the moment of truth.

"Mr. Smith, squeeze my hand." He waited. No response. Erik felt weak. No response screamed in his head: stroke! He recalled the agony of watching another poor patient struggle futilely to move his legs and arms, eyes pleading for relief, salvation; eyes sad and accusing, every post-op visit a testimony to his failure; the family growing more bitter; the terrifying formal letter from the attorney converting a rare but expected complication into a malpractice claim.

"Squeeze my hand." Louder. No response.

"The chart says he's hard of hearing." Sharon offered the chart to Erik.

"Mr. Smith, squeeze my hand!" Mr. Smith turned his head toward Erik. "OK, Mr. Smith, don't break the fingers." Erik laughed too loudly. With his other hand, he gave the thumbs up sign to Nurse Sharon.

Strength surged from the squeezed hand into Erik's body. Relief was heralded with a sigh and he was stable again.

Today, all systems were go; Erik felt great. The second case, a left inguinal hernia, was routine. Finishing his morning of surgery, he dictated his operative reports. The malpractice part of his brain reminded him of the importance of this document in the case or complications and suit.

He returned to the cafeteria for lunch and another session with the cafeteria committee. The topic of discussion this time was the seven deaths caused by cyanide that was found in the Tylenol capsules.

"I predict Tylenol will disappear from the shelves. Who would buy it?" one doctor asked.

After lunch, Erik went to the hospital library to review the treatment of thyroid crisis. He had scheduled a thyroidectomy for next Thursday. He carefully memorized the signs and the treatment of a thyroid crisis. He had experienced one such attack while he was a resident. At that time he had almost lost the patient. He wanted to be ready if it should happen again.

He made it to the office by 2:00 p.m., said "Hi" to the girls and felt warm as he stood close to Cathy. Slowly he reviewed the list of patients waiting to be seen. They filed in and out of the examining rooms all afternoon, told their problems, reported their progress, showed their incisions, or their lumps. Most inquiries and responses were standard, but, for Erik, it never got boring or dull. Each patient was unique; no patient's cholecystitis was the same as the next; no effect of loss of circulation mimicked the one before. Cathy, working with him, shared each adventure. They would be at their best professional behavior while at work, but he enjoyed a private thrill each time she said, "Doctor Nostrom," and she, when he asked, "Cathy, would you please…"

Many evenings, Erik had to attend medical meetings, or board or staff meetings of Amed. On those evenings, he would eat at the meetings, or much later at his home.

On the days he finished before the sun went down, he would drive to the Sliver Nursing Home.

Frances had not improved after the last episode of respiratory arrest.

She remained in a deep coma. A tracheotomy tube was inserted to insure adequate air exchange. Erik had planned to set up a hospital room in their home so she could be in familiar surroundings, but the level of care her condition and her breathing required made the ventilation center a necessity. Since he had moved her from the hospital, he felt a chronic panic.

It was easier to believe she would recover and leave the hospital, for didn't people usually leave the hospital? But from the nursing home, especially a ventilation center? There they usually died. The wish that she should die and end her misery, and his, dripped guilt over him. More than ever, she was a failing stranger for whom he could wish a blessed death. He refused to equate this fading creature to the memories of Frances. That exercise would blur the clear, happy vision of his remembering.

It wasn't that he wanted to go to the nursing home, it was that he couldn't *not* go. It was a painful habit as strong as the pleasant nightly Jack Daniel's. Once at the home, he checked the ventilator. At times, the oxygen tank was empty, or the humidifier was dry. He called to have the nurse fix it. While she was there, he asked her to turn the body on her side to allow him to inspect for bedsores, one of the more common indirect causes of death in these immobilized patients. These were acts of futility, prolonging life for what? But he did them, and paradoxically, feeling good about it. There was no comfortable place for his mind, wishing her dead and knowing that when she died it would be the young Frances dying, with the mountain of memories of the before-the-aneurysm days crushing down on him, squeezing out torrents of tears and tossing him onto the ground, quivering and useless. He could only hold himself rigid and wait. Motivated by the other part of him, he reached out and held her hand. He thought, *Live for another day; I don't know why.*

As he walked to the parking lot, away from the nursing home, he shed these thoughts. He forced them into their compartment and closed the lid. Now the other world, the world of satisfying accomplishment at work and the world containing Cathy began to shine forth. It illuminated all the dark corners, rendering them bright and warm. For him, it was a balance of necessary obligation against efforts to eke out a significant reason for living. From his car, he called her home. "Just leaving the nursing home. I needed to hear you say hello."

"Hello. You were just on my mind; the Nurse's Association magazine had an article on the qualities of a vascular surgeon. If I had known, I would have treated you with a greater respect."

"Oh, really."

"You know I don't need it in print to tell me. Will I see you tomorrow?"

"Remember, I have to be at the hospital at seven."

"That's right. One thing nice about working together—there is a built-in alibi checker. I'll miss you and see you in the office."

Since the night in his office, they had moved to a different togetherness; they were relaxed and open with each other in their need and yearning to be together, in soul and in body. However, he hesitated to receive her in his home, with Frances filling every corner. Cathy was concerned about having him seen leaving her house in the early morning hours. After that first experience, the risk of an office romance was apparent to both of them. They were grateful the one encounter had not ended in disasters.

Chapter 25

By 1985, Amed reached a plateau; the revenue and the number of written policies slowly but steadily increased. It had accumulated an acceptable surplus. However, clouds were forming, threatening the future. The increasing frequency and severity of settled claims caused the loss ratio to climb well above the combined earning and interest income. The surplus was diminishing. This experience was felt throughout the industry. Jerry was sent to the annual convention in Scottsdale to get a feel of the degree of concern in the other companies.

Paul and Erik met Jerry in Paul's office. "I just got back. The lawyer made a big deal about not talking about consolidation. He said the group would be in violation of the conspiracy laws. And, of course, all anyone talked about was consolidating." Jerry laid the pamphlets on the table.

"I was talking to Jeff Ruffle, of Trick-True Risk Insurance Company," Paul said.

"That's cute," Erik said.

Paul continued, "He said his company was looking at other lines of product liability insurance. He also said we might be seeing him in Florida because the other form of diversification is to extend into other states."

"That was some conversation. Did he stop to take a breath?" Erik asked.

Paul reached into his desk and pulled out two magazines. "Over the last two years, the lament of being one state, one line bedpan company has become very popular. Two companies in California, one being Trick, by the way, have set up risk retention groups in other states."

"I had a chance to talk to the folks in Nevada, a neighboring state to California," Jerry said. "They believe the invasion won't last."

"How come?"

"The doctors in California are absorbing the start-up costs of creating the risk retention in Nevada without getting any benefit. Already, there is a backlash, conservative challenge. They don't agree with the need for expansion in any form and are pushing to change the board," Jerry said. "One of the actuary analysts predicted that in ten years, there will only be three or four medical liability companies, and they will probably handle other lines of insurance."

"And probably only the commercial carriers." Paul added, "The pros believe the doctor owned and run companies are a transient species. We filled a need when they pulled out in 1975, and there was no other source of coverage. Now, with this competitive environment, we will not survive."

"I don't know if our enabling act would allow us to go to other states or to go into other lines," Erik said.

Jerry said, "It might be better if we were a corporation. Many of the trusts and mutuals are considering changing."

The conversation went on. All three knew the pressure was building. As the doctor moved from a sole practitioner toward forming in groups, he no longer had complete control of choosing his malpractice company. The group usually hired a manager who selected a carrier on the basis of price alone, mistakenly believing that all carriers were the same.

As more insurance companies enter the state to do business, the price of premiums go down, many reaching loss-leader status. Most of these newcomers either went out of business in three of four years, or were forced to raise the premium, making them higher than Amed, and thus, non-competitive. The problem was to hold on and stay in business in those years. Fortunately, Amed had developed enough capital to survive for several years ironically, thanks to Dr. Reinhart.

The phone rang. "It's for you, Jerry," Paul said.

"Thanks." After listening to the caller, Jerry said, "I have a client. Let's talk more tomorrow."

They agreed. All three went to their separate offices.

Chapter 26

"Janis, you have two weeks of vacation waiting to be used." Paul was consulting his desk calendar.
"Did you count the week in January when I went to New York?"
"I wouldn't have forgotten; it was one lonely week for me."
"That's nice. Why did you ask?"
"Christian Gabriel called me last Wednesday. He's starting a charter service and plans a maiden voyage of the *Sweet Southerner*, a fifty-four foot ketch—a two-masted sailing yacht. He offered to take me along."
"Did you want me to take my vacation while you were away?"
"No, I want you to come with me."
"I'd love to." As simple as that, she let Paul chase her until she caught him. From the time she had first met Paul and more intensely after she set out to marry him, Janis behaved as though she liked and respected him as a boss, but was hesitant to commit to very much more. She'd had dinner with him on four occasions. These were pleasant. Her research allowed her to speak of things he knew or liked. Her casual touch on his arm or shoulder was warm. She knew it stirred him. On reaching her door, she had offered him her cheek for the goodnight kiss and then disappeared inside. She could feel his sexual aching as she had watched him give up the thought of pursuit and reluctantly walk away.

On the morning after the dinners, she was all business, though warm and friendly. She would have him believe she shared his frustration and confusion. She felt no guilt for the manipulation, for she liked him, and, in the end, he would be happy. In a way, she wished someone would care for her enough to set so elaborate a trap. She presented Paul with a brick wall, which would respond to the proper pressure.

"Great!" he said.

"Should I let Mr. Christian know I will be coming along?"

"Forgive me, but I already told Chris someone would be coming with me."

"And if I said 'no,' did you have someone else in mind?"

"Oh, no!" Paul experienced the familiar confusion when she gently misconstrued his words of affection.

"I'm teasing, forgive me." She was delighted. As in most things, in love, all is timing. They were ready for the next big step, but she was at a loss for finding the proper setting, and here, from God, came the yacht. It had to be right.

The chartered twin-engine propjet rose from the R-9 runway at Miami International Airport into a clear blue sky. At twelve-thousand feet, the vibration of the engines smoothed out to a gentle massage, allowing unstrained conversation.

"Are we going to meet the boat in Nassau?" Janis watched the green-blue ocean through the window. She enjoyed the feeling of flight, relaxing in the comfortably padded seats. There was no answer from Paul. "Are you all right?" she saw Paul gradually lift his head from a bent-over position.

"Fine now. I have a little claustrophobia in small planes, particularly when we are waiting for take-off. It goes away once we level off. I'm fine now. Erik once said he had the same problem."

"Tell me about Nassau."

"First, let's call it a yacht, rather than a boat, or even better, if you want to sound really nautical, a ketch."

"Must be nautical. Ketch it is, Captain, whatever a ketch is. There must be a catch."

"Very funny. It is a two-masted sailing vessel with the main mast forward and the aft mast stepped forward of the rudder."

"I'm impressed."

"I'm a quick study. I read all of it right after Chris invited me. But about Nassau, we land there briefly, get OK'd by customs and then on to Eleuthera. The boat is moored in Hatchet Bay."

"The boat?"

"I know, hoisted on my own petard. I'll never be arrogant again."

"Eleuthera?"

"Some more of my reading; it is one of the outer islands of the Banana chain. Chris and Colleen-that's his first mate and significant other-sailed from Nassau and are waiting for us."

With the details finished in Nassau, it was a short hop to the Governors Harbor Airport. The landing strip ran parallel to the long, painfully thin island.

"How beautiful!" Janis called as the plane swooped over the expanse of uniquely Bahamian water, an iridescent light, blue green, broken by the frothy white of small, rolling waves. It was then that she caught the islander fever; sand filled her shoes and a laid-back, lighthearted freedom embraced her. She leaned over and kissed Paul on the lips. "I'm happy."

Christian was tall and tanned, with sun-bleached hair to his shoulders, standing on the foredeck, with one hand on the main mast, watching the couple come down the dock.

"He hasn't changed a bit since I last saw him, what, eight years ago."

"He's gorgeous!" she whispered. Then she said, "Wow!" as she saw Colleen emerge from the cabin. She was shorter than Chris, with a thin, dancer's grace and breasts one cup-size larger than the body called for. Dark hair in braids framed an Indian maiden's face; high cheekbones and dark, large eyes set apart, full lips. Her tan matched his.

From the start, the four of them bonded, with little formal hesitancy to talk about it. The first evening, they dined on lobster. "These are courtesy of Colleen; she went diving for them this morning. She hits the water so smoothly; they never know she's coming."

"I just tickle the nose and they back up into my net. I try not to develop an emotional attachment."

Christian said, "She says that just before she plunges them, live, into the boiling water."

The food, the wine and the conversation made for a splendid night enriched by the soft music, the balmy, moist air and the gentle swaying of the hull.

"You have the two forward bunks," Chris mentioned to Paul. "If the weather clears, we'll cast off at high tide, about seven."

Janis turned back the covers of both bunks. They lay in contented silence.

The space between the bunks was short enough for their hands to touch. She rolled on her side to look at him. "So far, it is perfect. It's so easy to be with you." She stood up and crawled into his bunk. "I feel so close to you, I have to be here for a moment." She moved her body so they were touching completely. They remained together just for a minute. It was delicious agony, and then she returned to her bunk. She couldn't believe he would accept this "Save yourself for the honeymoon" routine, but he did.

"I want you to stay forever," he said. "But I understand."

She knew she had tightened the rope. He was hog-tied. It was only a matter of time. They would be together for 72 hours of relaxed, carefree days, and three nights of bundling in the old puritan tradition. He couldn't resist her or the call for permanency. She thought, *What is love anyway, devotion, pleasure of being together, caring and protecting one another? I feel all that. Should I be concerned that I let my brain help to accomplish this?*

In the early morning, it began to rain. On the second day, it reached a number three hurricane force. They were all exhausted batting down the hatches. It began to clear on the third day, but then it was time for Janis and Paul to go home. By that time, the love-filled exposure had worked its magic. They had experienced a microcosm of the range of pressures and pleasures a couple in love would know in a lifetime: tenderness in the quiet time before the storm and in the calm as the hurricane left; response to fright at the height of the wailing wind and pounding rain with selfless actions by each of them; waves of jealousy in Janis as Paul viewed Colleen and in Paul as Janis admired Christian resolved as imaginary and not fatal; and through it all, a warm, non-judgmental respect.

On the way home, Paul said, "I could do that again. I can't remember a better four days."

"I could do it lots of times." Janis stretched contentedly.

"How about a lifetime?" He laughed. If she balked, he could say he was joking.

Her silence made him frown, but then she spoke. "Hemingway said it was a good day for dying. I say it is a good day for commitment; a lifetime it is." She reached over and took his hand. She guided it under her blouse and onto her breast, sealing the contract with a prelude to their honeymoon. *He will be glad we waited*, she thought.

He could wait no longer; on the next free weekend, they traveled to Las Vegas and were married in a small chapel.

Chapter 27

Jerry put the magazine down and looked at Erik. "This is the tenth article addressing the unspeakable: merger and consolidation. It's about the ER activity by Stafford. May I read?"

"Please do."

"I quote: 'By June of 1984, the two emergency room physician groups in Florida, ERN and Standard, were growing weary of competing. The hospitals played one against the other, getting concessions from both. Objects in contention were demand for full staff coverage twenty-four hours a day, restriction on caring for the non-resource patient and ease of transporting to the county hospital. The ability to negotiate with medical liability companies like Amed was another problem. The solution was to consolidate…'"

"It's in the air, and the medical liability industry has become more aware of it."

Erik looked at his appointment book. "Let's see, I talked to Orlando Santiago with Northeast Medical Liability in Northern California. He was studying the question." Erik turned the page. "Next was Bill Davis, who is Hartman's old boss at Physician's Ideal Protective Insurance of California, a mutual. They were going to convert to a corporation before seeking a partner. He thought there was more negotiation power when there's stock to trade."

"I think he's right."

"So do I." Erik's eye moved to the bottom of the page. "The last one was Peter Pagan with Physician's Ohio Protective Insurance Company, Inc.

"It's as though the infection swept the country from each coast toward the mid states, starting from California. Out there, they have already brought Nevada into their camp. In Ohio, they thought it was an interesting idea, and here we are somewhat ahead of that. It's sitting there. Everyone would rather stay independent, but they all know that soon there will have to be a change. There's talk of one outfit buying everything in sight an outright purchase. This scares the hell out of everyone else."

Jerry listened. He recalled the last conference he had attended. "The uncertainty is bothering all of them. One of the problems is; most of these companies are run by doctors who are not really businessmen. Not that they aren't smart enough, but they are not used to a competitive market. First, we were the only game in town, in 1975. Applications were being slipped under the door on Sunday morning. That came too easily, although we thought is was a struggle at the time."

Erik was nodding in agreement. "That's true. Most of us are babes in the woods when it comes to mergers and acquisitions. I started looking at the reports on some of the big commercial mergers. The bottom line frequently is the ego of the chief honcho, either the CEO or the chairman. There was a merger of an American and a French company that was going pretty well. Finally, the two principals met in the American office in New York. At first, all seemed smooth, and then there was a frost in the air. The American CEO asked his French equivalent, 'What's happening?'

"'It's the California wine you are about to serve! My chairman will take it as an insult. You are belittling him.'

"'Hold everything.' He turned to his COO. 'Get to the street. You have ten minutes to find a good French wine!'

"By a miracle, the COO was able to find the wine, the Frenchmen were pleased and the merger proceeded. Remind me to get California wine if we go west."

After bouncing around many of the variations on the theme of merger, they began to outline a critical line of proceeding. First on the agenda was to prepare a presentation to the board. Erik had learned not to present only the problem. The members of the board, being bright people, would generate eight different solutions, most of them off the top of their heads, and almost all of them impractical. Not following up on a suggestion, no matter how half-baked, set up a hostile environment.

They agreed to pool their information, supplement anything else they find and make a tentative presentation.

How to proceed would be determined by the outcome of this meeting.

"Do we still follow the tried and true procedure?" Jerry asked.

"What's that?"

"Writing the minutes of the upcoming meeting before the meeting."

"Always a good idea."

They finished the discussion. As they were leaving, "Are you going to see Frances tonight?" Jerry asked. He remembered Erik did that on occasion at the end of the evening.

"Not tonight."

They parted at the parking lot.

Chapter 28

He walked to his car and then sat in the driver's seat for several minutes. "Where am I, who am I?" he thought, frustration grabbing him. He could visualize the mountain he must climb to bring about a merger. Out of hand, he knew Dr. Stanley Reinhart would object. Then he missed Cathy. He held the car phone in his hand. It was new to him. Slowly he dialed.

"Hello."

"Hi, Cathy."

"Erik! I didn't think I'd hear from you tonight."

"I'm testing my new phone."

"I believe it's working; you sound wonderful." She pressed the receiver against her ear. There was a long silence. "Is your phone still working?"

"I want to see you."

His voice was strange, pleading. She wanted to comfort him. "All right. Come here." It would be a new beginning accepting the social risk, which had made this action a taboo. "I'll unlock the door. Come upstairs." All fears were suddenly gone. She was going to have her man in her bed. It would be his from now on. His smell would fill the sheets. She went to the mirror, tossed her hair, applied lipstick. She was nervous with an exciting happiness. Once she knew they were actually doing it, she challenged the reason for their fears in the past. "To hell with the neighbors," she laughed. "I hardly know them."

He hurried down the pathway, not looking right or left. He was doing it. The forces creating indecision were dismissed; all negative vibrations were tossed aside. He was free. He closed the door behind him and ascended the stairs. She was on the bed, smiling and coquettishly motioning him to join her. She turned the covers aside to show off her naked body, taking the pose of the nude hanging behind the bar in the classic western movie.

He sat on the bed. "You're beautiful." Low, tender tones. This was perfect. There was no fear of the hotel detective breaking in and hassling them, no danger of a neighbor coming to his house and recognizing her car. Her house was set back from the road, tucked in a grove of banyan trees. He felt they were safely hidden and deliciously alone. At first, he laid next to her, fully dressed, savoring the joy.

"Do you plan to stay awhile?" she whispered and she sat up. Normally very shy about her body, she felt no embarrassment for her nakedness here with Erik. She wanted him to yearn for every part of her. She loosened his tie.

For three hours they were one. Eyes closed in reverie were jealous of viewing eyes searching every desirable part of the other. Bodies in motion, unable to press close enough, twined like loving serpents, each new contact inspiring fountains of pleasure. Passions rose to a Wagnerian crescendo, followed by ebbing in decreasingly softer pulsations, and then they lay sans worry, sans fear, sans all but love.

It was hard to sound an end to the idyllic moment, but finally Erik slowly stood. "I'm up! I'm not sure this is where I want to be, but I'm here."

She was up and at his side, hugging him, and then, slowly, she held his shirt for him to begin dressing. For both of them, the whole evening was perfect.

"I hate to leave; it'll never be better than tonight."

"Don't be so sure. I have just begun."

Painfully they parted. He walked down the pathway, humming "I'm in Love with a Beautiful Girl." He sat in his car for a few minutes, clinging to the memory, and then drove to his home.

Chapter 29

    Rudy carefully freed himself from the twigs that hid him from anyone walking along the pathway. He thought, *I knew it had to be him, fucking my wife all along, and she claiming such innocence. She didn't turn him away. I'm sure he didn't have to force her. All the while, I was feeling guilty, as though it was my fault. And every night she was late from the office, he was screwing her.* His rage tightened his muscles. He started to sweat. *Cathy, you made such a fool of me. I should be the one to leave? What a jellyfish you made of me. You lying in our bed, a million miles away from me, and me in the bathroom jerking off 'cause you wouldn't have me. No wonder, you were fucking him!* He stepped onto the pathway. There was the house he knew so well. Now it was frowning at him. It was dirty. It held them, let them fuck.

    I'll face her, demand she obey her vows. Now I know and she knows I know. She must come back to me! He stood at the front door. *When I see her, will I melt? Will she soothe my anger and send me on my way? No! Not now, not with her cunt still full of him. Oh, you oh-so-pure, lying bitch! You'll see the real me, the tough, in command, strong me. You were my wife! You should still be my wife. I would have never let you push me out if I knew what a whore you were! And for just one night of rough sex. Hell, it was nothing. God, you acted so pure, and you were fucking him!* His fury made his stomach grind. Waves of nausea climbed up his chest. He turned off the steps and vomited.

The emptiness made him waver briefly. *What am I doing here? Why not let it go? To return to the torment I've lived since I left her? No! Settle it tonight. Start again with me.* He fingered the Smith & Wesson 357 magnum tucked in his belt. *I must have been out of my mind to bring this along.* He buttoned his shirt, covering the handle. He was calm. *I'll just tell her I'm moving back in and we'll make the legal arrangements later. Wait a minute, I don't need a gun, I have a better weapon; I'll threaten to expose her Goddamn lover for what he is, an adulterer, and him with a lovely wife in the hospital. It will ruin him. Maybe I'll do that anyway. Ruin him and then see if he still looks so wonderful to her!* He smiled. *Why didn't I think of that before? But then, she's such a sacrificing bitch, she'll probably throw herself on the pyre flames of his defeat.* He had recently read that phrase. *See, I could be as smart as him. He's not so clever or he wouldn't be doing such dumb things. I should have popped him as he came out of the house. Was I afraid of him? Why would I be afraid? I hate him for screwing my wife; I hate her! If she weren't here in my life I'd be free of this pain—fuck her! I don't need her! Better she be dead. Be dead; no, I couldn't live. Then I'd be free. And the doctor would weep. It would really put it to him, give him what he deserves. But then she'd be gone from me, never to feel her against me, never to feel her push against me and with me full deep inside her. But she's gone already! He did it. He'll hurt when she's gone.*

He reached for the door. It was unlocked! He stepped into the small vestibule and closed the door. He could hear her humming in the bedroom. He guarded his steps as he climbed the stairs. He stopped and waited. His body ached to bound up and into the room, take her into his arms, and feel her warm, loving body move with pleasure under his thrusts. But he knew it couldn't be. She would laugh at him, or worse, show disgust for his barbaric action. "I can't have her laugh at me; it would be too much." He quietly took the remaining stairs and entered her room. She lay still with one hand on her naked breast. She was smiling. *Thinking of him,* he thought. The pain was too much.

"You fucking two-timing cunt!" he cried and stepped into the light. He watched her smile disappear and a questioning look change into one of annoyance. "Don't speak." His voice was soft, his words slow. She was puzzled by him suddenly appearing in her bedroom, and obeyed. The light was at his back, creating a black silhouette. She couldn't see the gun lifted from his waistband and aim at her.

"I'm sorry. I hurt too much." He stepped into the light.

She was looking at his face. For the first time she was moved by the anguish she saw. She wanted to reach out and comfort him. As she sat up in bed, she turned back the sheets and reached for him. The roar of the gunshot deafened him. From the center of her left breast, blood splashed out onto her skin, turning her breast and abdomen a glistening red. Her mouth moved a soundless, "Why?" The second shot pierced her mid forehead.

Chapter 30

It was done! The tearing passion of hating her and loving her, of him wanting her gone and wanting her bound to him, of needing revenge and needing forgiveness, all faded. Only the love, the want, and crying "forgive me" remained. He stumbled toward the bed. The sound of her dying gasps screamed in his ears. Then it was quiet. The shots had forced her body onto the bed and her head came to rest on the pillow. He came near her bed. He thought, *Is she just sleeping? I didn't shoot! It was a hallucination? She's pretending to be asleep and is waiting for me. I knew it, if I waited long enough she would want me back again. Now she's here. Hello, Cathy, my sweet, beautiful loving Cathy.* He lay beside her and closed his eyes. With his arms around her, he pulled her close to him, murmuring, "I love you, I love you. You are back. I adore you. I will do all the things you like, and I will fill your life with sunshine. Thank you, thank you, thank you." He pressed his cheek against her forehead. Her blood smeared his face and pained his eyes. "What is this?" He wiped the blood from his eye. "Blood! It is real. Oh, my God." He placed her on the pillow and sat up. He relived pulling the trigger, seeing her face, staring at him questioning, her mouth open and then the forehead busting open, and in slow motion, her falling back on the bed.

A sudden calm engulfed him. *I'm free. But for what, what is there for me? My life is through. How happy they will be when they grab Rudy. The trial, the gawking faces at the trial, all praying I get death. And in jail, being a wife to the black boss. I can fool them all. One shot and I'll fly away. They'll curse me, but I'll be free.*

Dear Doctor Nostrom, how he's going to cry. In addition, he won't be able to throw himself on the coffin and mourn in the open. He'll have to choke it back until he gags. It was he who killed. If he kept his cock in his pants, she would still be with me and still be alive. He murdered her! I hope he suffers here on earth and rots in hell for what he did...But what of me? If I shoot and fly away, to where will I fly? Am I gone, just a blank? Am I out of it and that's it? Will I be free of this cruel agony, and all pain? Just shoot me, I deserve it. I murdered, I need to be punished. If not hereafter then now.

I talk, but I can't do it. I thought of this way out before. I couldn't do it then and I can't do it now. I am a coward! See, I'm thinking anything is better than death. I forget what I just said about life without her. There is nothing. Nothing without her, and maybe nothing in death. Is there a forgiving God? I would be going with her; we could be together. It's crazy. He bent over. Held his stomach and rocked. He cried, "Oh, Lord, forgive me. The torment drove me here and I can leave it only one way. Be brave for once, be strong for once."

He put the barrel of the gun into his mouth.

"Do it, do it, do it." Louder and louder. The gun blast blocked out everything.

Chapter 31

Erik arrived home but it was hard for him to get to sleep. His emotions were as unbalanced as a yo-yo. High as he had ever imagined and free of the usual stabbing pains of living past fifty that attacked his joints and muscles as he sought sleep, he made a silly laughing sound. On the downward stroke of the spinning, whistling toy, he wondered if being together would ever be that good again. Would the fragile nature of their bonding be threatened by his status? Would his inability to shout, "I love you!" from the street corner and from the rooftop begin to erode until nothing remained but the beautiful memory of this night? The toy rode up the string toward conviction. "Stop it!" he shouted. "Simplify! Know that we are strong and unbreakable and we will go on for as long as we live." Down stroke once again. "At least I know that is true for me." He fell asleep with a montage of her smile, her face, her breasts and the color of her voice, softly saying, "I love you," moving in and out of his dreams like a kaleidoscope.

Jerry waited until his sobs subsided before he reached for the phone. He wasn't ashamed of having a crush on Cathy from the first day he had met her, a day after Erik's office had hired her. Her dark, Italian beauty, her youthful body that stirred him and her happy energy were captivating. Soon, as he watched and interpreted the signs, it became evident that, if she were to stray from her monogamous perch, it would be toward Erik. Good for him and so be it. His thoughts did not ease the pain he felt at the news of her death. Much more than a lover, he held her as a friend, and now she was gone. The news rested on Jerry's tongue like poison, and yet he knew he must be the one to talk to Erik. He dialed slowly. The blur of tears caused the first attempt to be a wrong number. He had to build up his strength all over again.

"Erik?"

"Yes? Oh, it's you, Jerry. Good morning." Erik's voice had a lilting quality, reflecting the residual joy of last night. "God's in her heaven and all's right with the world." He smiled at the phone.

"Erik, remember you once told me you knew no easy way to tell the relatives that a patient died?"

"Yes." Erik caught the solemn tone in Jerry's voice. He came down from his jubilant platform to be able to support Jerry, even though he didn't know who of Jerry's close ones had died, or could it be Frances?

"Well, it's true. I don't know any other way to do this. Where are you right now?"

"I'm still at home, in my kitchen. I overslept this morning. It must have been that meeting." He knew it was the enchantment of Cathy that had caused him to dream on.

"I'll be right over, wait for me."

In a short time, he was sitting next to Erik. "Cathy's dead."

Erik stared at him, not comprehending the words. Jerry related the details as well as he knew them. Erik's hands rested on his thigh as he rocked slowly. His gaze left Jerry's face, wandered to the kitchen window, and went out of focus.

The silence was shattered by the cries, rising from his depths, violently shaking his head and trunk. "I loved her, Jerry. You don't know, we just began." The vision of her perfect face was blanked out by a red stain. He rubbed his eyes to free her. "It can't be, it can't be! Cathy, I need you, don't leave me."

He moaned and screamed words jerked apart and meaningless. In the brief return of clarity, he demanded a repeat of the details, challenging their veracity, being reassured that it was sadly true. His energy finally ebbed and he let Jerry lead him to the bed and tuck him in. Two Valiums allowed restless sleep to enter.

Chapter 32

For Erik, the weeks following Cathy's death were a blur. People extended their condolences to him for losing such an efficient office manager. He wanted to correct them, to say how wonderful she was as a woman, a lover, as all things to him, but he was silent and tortured. Only Jerry knew the depth of the loss Erik was experiencing. A thousand times a day, he would look up to see her walk through the door, or catch himself as he was about to call out her name to come join him in the office or the examining room. At the end of the day, he remained after the others left, as he had before her death, but now it was to mourn, to try to find a place where he could ease the remorse. As one night followed another, the hurt and the loneliness did not seem to be decreasing. Much like an addict with his drugs, so with him with his grief; as the forces destroy the fabric of life, the last thing to go is the ability to practice one's profession. After one week, Erik resumed his practice of surgery. He had done this for long enough for the day-by-day responses to become automatic. Even in his grief, he had to smile, as he recalled him saying of surgery, "I could do this in my sleep." For that was what he was doing now.

In the week that Erik was officially in mourning, Jerry had made a fortunate find: Dr. Forrest Swanson, a general surgeon, was leaving Miami for the Middle West. The fee schedules and reimbursements in that area were very attractive. His office manager of fifteen years did not want to move and was looking for a new job. When Erik was available, Jerry said, "I'd rather be lucky than smart." Jerry finished describing the lady to Erik. "I've known her for some time. Swanson swears by her. She's divorced and has no children. I believe she's about thirty-five, give or take a few. She likes dancing, dry martinis with an onion and sport cars."

"You do your research."

"We dated for a while, some time ago. Now, we are good friends. She knows her business. I think you'll like her. Her name is Lorraine Ryan. She's a tall, red-haired, good-looking lady."

"Honestly, I'd rather have a frumpy, plain woman who is more likely to stay. The woman you describe sounds like she's just waiting to land her mate, and then goodbye."

"Well, you know my rule in hiring a legal secretary? Good looking and if she can type, that's a bonus."

"Seriously, how well do you know her?'

"I was being serious. I think you will do well with her. From what I got from Swanson, she is honest, hard working and bright. He says she'll take over your office in no time and you'll love the results."

Erik met her, liked her and hired her. In a short period of time, she comfortably took on the duties of office manager. This included the role of psychiatrist for the girls.

One of the many voids left with Cathy's death was filled, still leaving others in the valley of empty pits.

Chapter 33

Janis went to the office and set up the schedule for Paul's day. She changed the calendar on the desk to June 12. He was to meet with Erik this morning. As she turned in her chair, her blouse was pulled taught against her breast. It made the nipple itch and tingle a little. It was the first time she had experienced this sensation. She rubbed her nipples with the palm of her hand. She walked to the bathroom and removed her bra. Magically, the sag that had her contemplating implants was gone. The breasts stood out, firm, full, and beautiful. At first she thought the change was accredited to her married life, for when she was single the breasts were massaged now and then, but with Paul, it was the nightly celebration to foreplay.

If daily attention produced these results, every woman in the world would be a devotee. She thought, *Why question it? Thank your blessing for this gift. I'll worry about why tomorrow.*

Janis had never been pregnant. She hadn't been socially intimate with many pregnant women in her previous way of life. Her thoughts were more toward precocious menopause, a thought that was supported by the missed periods in the last three months.

Her curious mind wouldn't let the puzzlement rest there. Like a mouse testing the cheese in the trap, it was the try-this-or-that approach, look at it from behind and then advance slowly, slowly. Too late! The trap is sprung.

The arm came down, hitting her in the back of the head—pregnant!

The realization left her numb, disbelieving. Like an automaton, she left her desk and walked to the corner drugstore, purchased a test kit and returned.

Paul Arpin put the phone on its cradle. He was sitting across the desk from Erik. "I'm going to be a father." He whispered the words, afraid a loud voice would smash them into denial. Now, all fear gone, he shouted at Erik, "Janis is pregnant!"

"Congratulations."

"This was a shocker. Janis said she had missed three periods so she thinks she is in the fourth month. She said she thought it would be in November!"

"A Thanksgiving turkey!"

"It's already a gift; Janis said she hasn't had a day of trouble so far, no nausea or vomiting or anything. Am I sounding a little strange? It was a surprise." He sat back, took a deep breath and exhaled a long sigh. "I know I'll come down and get back to work any moment, but forgive me if I wear a silly grin now and then."

"Noted. Let's see, before the news bulletin, you were saying?" Paul laid the brochure on the table. "The honeymoon is definitely over." Erik's look questioned him.

"Not mine; at home it was still a Shangri-La and now even more so. But here, competition is keeping the premiums down and the litigious population and the legal beagles are pushing up the indemnity amounts and the case frequency."

Erik went over the sheets in Paul's report. "Total assets up to $410,000,000. I'm still thinking of a nice, warm, non-extradition island and goodbye, Charlie. But I set my level at a billion, so I guess I'll just have to stick it out."

"You're sounding much better." He carefully watched for Erik's reaction, particularly after hearing about Janis' pregnancy.

It had been a rough time at Amed office staff since Cathy died. Slowly, Erik began to regain his interest in the company. Paul continued to send him weekly, and at times, daily reports, knowing they were just piled up in his in-basket. Then, one day, he had received a call. Erik had said, "What's our fund balance?" the first signs of a thaw.

"I'm all right. I still have my feet." Referring to the story of the man who cried because he had no shoes until he saw the man who had no feet, "And I know I'll eventually find the shoes, though they will never fit as well."

Paul asked, "Is merger a possibility in the near future?"

"It's an item," said Erik.

"I ask because, if I have a time table far enough in advance, we would be able to do some creative accounting."

"Really, such as?"

"There's a certain amount of leeway in calculating claims, reserve for claims and closed claims. Timing may be very important," Paul began. "There is a tale, which may or may not be true, but I like it. One CEO is supposed to be still smoldering over a change in reserve during a merger. In that case, the good results for the selling company were providential.

"A claim was reserved for $200,000. The field adjuster from the claims department felt that it was defensible and turned down an offer to settle for the doctor's limit of $250,000. When the home office chief adjuster heard of that decision, he quickly got on the phone to reverse it.

"'Take the settlement!'

"By that time, the plaintiff's attorney changed his mind and withdrew the offer.

"The case went to trial, where the jury found for the plaintiff and awarded her eight million dollars. The insurance company immediately filed for an appeal.

"The way the books were calculated, a case under appeal was carried in reserve at the amount originally set in this case, $200,000. The merger went through with the selling company being charged the $200,000 for the case. The buying company now was responsible for the ultimate settlement. When the appeal was denied, the buyers were stuck with the eight-million dollar liability. The selling company was paid $7,800,000 more than it should have been.

"The CEO of the buying team never warmed up to the newly acquired company, even though that company was now his own. This isn't the first time a businessman was driven by emotion to the deficit of the endeavor. Once again, the devil is in the details." Erik nodded and was smiling; he could guess who the CEO in the story was and didn't particularly like him.

Erik went on reviewing the report. The total assets were down, particularly the premiums due. Liabilities were increased, mainly because of reserve for loss and loss adjustment expenses. Remembering the story, he laughed as he read the word "reserve."

He turned to the financial statement. "The investment income is down a bit, but the real worry is the drop in net earned premiums; we're down almost ten million to forty-eight million. Bottom line, the fund balance is down."

"We are in the bad side of the insurance cycle," Paul said. "It's a predictable phenomenon. On the upswing the company makes an attractive profit, which stimulates other entities to enter the market, enlarging the available capacity." He waited to see if he was preaching to the choir. "Is this old stuff to you? I don't want to bore you."

"No," Erik said. "The dumb appearance is me thinking and concentrating. Please, go on."

"OK, this is the high point of the wheel. It is trouble brewing from now on. The companies begin competitive pricing and decreased underwriting protective guidelines, allowing coverage of riskier business. They begin accepting the most optimistic actuarial view as the truth."

Paul produced a chart from his desk, outlining the complete cycle. "This may help. You can see it's all downhill from now on. At this point, having seduced underwriting to agree to the lowered criteria, the investment chairman is delighted with the incoming cash. He is the darling of the day with almost everyone. The underwriting loss—paying out more than one dollar for every premium dollar taken in—will be more than covered by investment income. They say an insurance company is primarily an investment operation. Only the claims department is unhappy, for they have to justify the increased loss generated by the lowered level of acceptance of risk. The chairman of the claims department is not too popular during this stage of the cycle. His 'I told you so' moment will come later on.

"The momentum carries the losses beyond the compensating investment income and the company experiences real losses. Some companies go into receivership (bankruptcy); some merge, usually into an undesirable position, with a stronger company, and the remaining companies cut back on risk, increase premiums and try to survive."

"Is that where we are at the moment?"

"We are in the third mode. Fortunately, we have a fair-sized redundancy in the reserve and a comfortable surplus. The rise in premiums-neurosurgery hitting an increase of 88 percent is being accepted. It seems these doctors are inured to the rising costs. They see it, complain about it and pay it."

"So the premiums go up and the number of companies competing for their business goes down, leaving the doctors scrambling for coverage."

"That's right. There is overkill in the premium adjustment. They go up to cover past losses, to anticipate increasing losses on the present book of business and to adjust for future adverse activity. At times, the doctor is presented with 200% increase in the cost of next year's premium.

"The doctors who are not organized have no choice but to pay. They bitch but do nothing.

"The premiums increase faster than the risk and the companies make a handsome profit. Did I say profit? It seems that is where we began."

"And the cycle starts all over again?"

Paul said, "That's the insurance story."

During the recital, Erik was nodding in agreement. "Sounds like the old dunking wheel the puritans used to test for witches; if the lady survived her time on the wheel under water, she was considered a witch and was stoned to death; if she drowned, then, oops, she wasn't a witch! If a company survives the loss cycle, it is suspected of witchcraft; only nowadays we call it corruption."

Paul smiled. "Then gather around the caldron for it looks like we are going to survive this time. The question is, if we are thinking of a merger, what is the best time to pursue it?"

"All in good time, but first we have to bring the board up to date and make them comfortable with the notion of merger."

Paul rose to go. "I hope we aren't delivering the company and the baby at the same time."

"Good luck. Give my love to Janis."

Chapter 34

In July the board meeting was called for the third Friday evening and the following Saturday morning. Through individual phone calls, Erik had informed the board members of the basic concepts of mergers. One hundred percent of the members attended. Recently there had been two factions at the meetings, not based on geographic or specialty distribution as would be expected, but on philosophy: those in the Erik camp and those with Reinhart.

For the most part, this was not significant, for after discussion, most issues were resolved unanimously. The axiom was valid: reasonably intelligent people with the same set of facts and the same motivation should come to the same conclusions. The devil is in the motivations.

The meeting began with dissemination of the facts. If, following this step, there were still disagreements, it was time to examine the motivations.

"As chairman of the Plastic Surgery Association," Dr. Cannon offered, "they are bitching at me to get lower premiums. I have to agree with them; our loss ratio this year is 43%, not like family practice at 143%. Amed gets fifty-seven cents of each of our dollars to cover someone else's losses."

"I believe that is a little shortsighted," Dr. Stanley Reinhart answered. "We all know that these ratios shift for each class. Next year one of your surgeons may displace a breast for a ten million dollars loss. Should we double your premium for that year?"

"I mention it now so that we will think about it whenever we readjust the classes." Cannon pulled the data sheet off the table and put it back into his briefcase. At times, motivation would spring from true but opposing principles. When the protagonists said it was a matter of principle, it was usually a matter of money! Fear promoted motivational differences: to continue to make decisions based on trends averaged over the last ten years or depart from tradition and react to the revolutionary change in recent times? At times, there were honest differences of opinion regarding reserves. Maximizing reserves offered a margin of safety and created a deferred tax situation, but, as reserves were expense, it also decreased profit. Through persuasion and compromise, consensus would generate a unanimous vote.

"It's still pretty windy out there for the end of July." Jack Reed, pediatrician, walked into the kitchen behind the boardroom. Richard Garing, neurosurgeon, and Thomas Frond, cardiologist, were already there.

Richard said, "Don't complain about a little wind. They say it's going to be a tough hurricane season this year."

The three moved closer to the sideboard to allow Anthony Sanchez, general surgeon; Fred Cannon, plastic surgeon; and Stanley Reinhart, family practice to enter. To save time, Paul had the local restaurant deliver sandwiches, soft drinks and beer to the kitchen, along with potato chips, salads and pickles. They all began eating and continued talking.

The meeting started at 6:30 p.m. Erik sat at the head of the table with Paul on his right. Reinhart took the opposite end of the table with Jerry, the lawyer, on his left. By habit, each of the others took the seats they had occupied for years.

"Good evening," Erik said. "I have talked to each of you about the subject of merger, and Paul sent you several articles. I'd like to talk about alternative paths, in increasingly terrifying order. We can stay as we are."

There were some nods around the table. "The advantages are: it's comfortable. There is little immediate stress. Just bury our heads in the sand and not see our competition growing stronger and better positioned to underbid and over-advertise us. Also, we can be closer to our clients, for there will be so few of them left that we could know them by name."

"I have two questions," Thomas Harmon, ob-gyn from Gainesville, called. "Are you sure you are absolutely objective in your presentation?" The group broke into laughter. The humor was a gentle respite from the serious overtones of the evening.

"And are we going to discuss these alternatives individually as you count them off, or are we to listen to all your talk and then say 'Amen'?" There was agreement in the crowd.

Erik smiled. "If there's one thing I've learned, it's you have to have a trial before you hang 'em."

"The Nostrom touch. I'd recognize it anywhere." Sanchez laughed.

"Let's take this one first." Erik wagged his finger at Sanchez.

"With less sarcasm," Rinehart said, "I am not in favor of staying as we are."

"Strangely, I believe that is Erik's position also," Jerry said. "Word from Tallahassee insurance department is they wish to be rid of trusts. We don't fit into any category. They still feel guilty about not writing enabling legislature to define our treatment in case of dissolution. We are neither a partnership nor a mutual, neither fish nor fowl. The sooner we convert into one of the more traditional forms, the happier the department will be." Jerry paused for questions or statements.

"I was going to argue for staying as we are," said Kenneth Moninger, family practice. "After all, we truly are not businessmen, and going public or merging with another company requires knowledge and experience we don't possess. But with Erik and Stanley on the same side, I might rethink my position."

Jack suggested, "Let's hear the other alternatives." He nodded to Erik to continue.

The air in the room was getting warm and stuffy. Paul turned on the overhead fan.

"Stanley touched on an interesting point," Erik said. "To change, we have to establish our organization as a recognizable entity. Jerry has been in conference with the commissioner. It is possible for them to consider us as a mutual, on the way to becoming a corporation.

"Just recently, a mutual in New Jersey converted to a corporation, and the policyholders were given only the good will of the company; the monetary value stayed with the cooperation. Hold your breath; the documents gave the ownership of the new entity to the members of the board! It was a license to steal."

Richard looked up. "Do I understand what you just said? The whole ball of wax went to the members of the board?"

"Yes."

"And is that one of the alternatives we are going to hear tonight?"

"Yes."

The entire board suddenly realized they were talking about a ninety-five million dollar business. Greed, which had been suppressed under a thin layer of nobility, was beginning to stir in its confinement.

Thomas said, "Wait a minute, before we go crazy. I can remember when we first started this trust, we were not compensated at all. We said we were doing it for all physicians, to protect them, and we were only concerned about their interests."

"As I recall," Fred said, "it wasn't long before we agreed we should be compensated, first for our expenses, and not too long after, we increased it to a reasonable stipend. You balked initially, Tom, but when the checks were ready, I believe you took yours, reluctantly."

"Children, let's not fight," Jerry said. "In my objective opinion, you all never received your due rewards. Your pay was less than many others in similar setups. The time you put into this trust has increased. More importantly, as the sums of money grew, your personal liability increased.

"The problem with you guys is you are not used to being compensated for time spent other than in your medical specialty unless you are a courthouse doctor. You spend time preparing for and presenting medical reports at your conferences and all you expect is a plaque.

"Well, this is a business, and whether you wish to or not, you're responsible for your actions. If you screw up, your adversaries won't be looking to a plaque for compensation!"

"I agree with that." Jesse Gentile, internal medicine from Gainesville, said. "We should take off our physician's hat and act like the businessmen we are forced to be. As Jerry said, if we get into trouble no one is going to say, 'Let's forgive them, they are only physicians.' The first ones to sue us would be our fellow docs. You know, near misses are only count in horseshoes. More than that, I believe if the opportunity arises where we can be rewarded for all our efforts, I'm for it. Let me be the first to say it."

The seed of this immoral but legal position entered into the back of each man's mind.

Erik held up his hand. "Enough of that for now. We can consider how we are going to spend our millions some other time. By the way, there are ten of us; that's nine million five hundred thousand a piece. Just thought you'd like the math.

"Seriously, the other alternatives are: switch to a mutual, go directly to a stock company, stay in the new form or proceed on to a merger. In that case, to be the buyer or the seller. People talk about a merger of equals, but I believe that's a myth. One always comes out on top. This is a lot to think about, and rather than beginning tonight, when most of the thoughts will be off the top of your heads, let's take the literature, read it, get a good night's sleep and begin in the a.m."

Jerry and Erik remained at the table as the others rose, said their goodbyes and departed.

"What do you think?" Erik asked.

"It was a good first meeting. Hopefully, they'll read the stuff we gave them. The details of the convergence you talked about make it pretty clear that it was a unique deal. Otherwise, there will be sugar plums dancing in their heads all night long."

"And the first thing tomorrow we will have to bring them back to earth. Representing reality is never rewarded."

"You're not still looking for reward?"

"Lost my head."

"Talking about reality, how are you doing?"

Erik thought, *Do I say fine, my answer to most people? Not to Jerry; he is the only one who knows my loss, and who grieves with me, as well as for me. He slowed down the painful fall into depression and, with non-verbal strength, said hold, enough, time to start back up. Following the bard's advice, I must bind my tested friend to my soul with hoops of steel.* "I'm getting better."

"That's my boy."

"Ironically, the demands of changing Amed's direction are my tranquilizers."

They left the office and separated, each carrying his own thoughts: Erik allowing the walls of the compartments of Cathy and Frances to dissolve, the contents melding into one river of sadness, and Jerry pondering his own loneliness and a possible change toward love.

Chapter 35

Saturday the meeting began at nine o'clock. They brought their coffee cups with them.

Erik said, "If we chose not to stay where we are, we should next consider converting to a mutual. This requires a supporting vote from the policyholders, who, in the trust form, are the ultimate controlling body. The advantage for them is the removal of assessability.

Even though Amed has never needed an assessment, and we have over one hundred million dollars in surplus, the possibility is a sword over their heads. I believe this change alone is strong enough to swing it if we decide to go that route."

"Is an assessment really that big of a threat?" Thomas asked.

"You folks from Gainesville may not have heard about the woes of a local insurance company. They were assessable, became insolvent and the insurance department demanded the company assess its members."

"How did that go?" Jesse asked.

"Being Miami, the doctors balked, claiming mismanagement."

"Why?"

Jerry raised his hand, as though stopping traffic. "You must believe this; they claimed the company did not charge the doctors enough premium in the past years! Of course, the reason the doctors went to that company in the first place was for the low premiums. For years, the accuracies said the company was under reserved. In the end the courts found for the company and the Insurance department. The doctors ponied up the cash and the company survived. But that wasn't the end of the ripple effect of this episode; all reinsurance companies no longer could give any credibility to assessability as a guarantee. This is another reason to get out of the trust form, as we are now assessable."

"I believe we once considered buying that company." Reinhart spoke up." I researched the possibility and recommended we not buy. I'm glad everyone followed my advice." He smiled while looking at Erik.

"Thank you, Stanley." Erik waved recognition of Reinhart. "As a mutual, we will be free of assessments, but will still be limited in our activities. The policyholders will be the owners. We will still lack the ability to use our surplus as a bargaining tool if we wish to expand via purchasing another company or merging."

Kenneth shook his head. "I know I'm from Gainesville, the backward part of Florida, but you are way ahead of me. We haven't even decided if we should change, and you are turning second base as a mutual, heading for home as an expanding corporation. I'm dizzy!"

"You are not alone," Jerry said. "Erik and I have been going over this for a few months and I still have trouble with this specialized vocabulary. This is our first go around. We need to have many more meetings before we are in a position to make an intelligent decision." He truly reflected the thoughts of everyone in the room.

"Do you think we should form an executive committee to review and come up with a recommendation?" Reinhart offered.

After discussion, mostly negative, Erik said, "I get the impression that a committee would be great as long as everyone was on it. As we have done so far, I think we should continue acting as a committee of the whole."

"I vote for that," Sanchez offered.

"All in favor?" It carried unanimously.

"So be it. I was only trying to move things along." Reinhart held up his hands in surrender.

The members of the board broke for lunch. The rest of the afternoon was spent on discussing details, and the pros and cons of staying unchanged and of converting to a mutual. They agreed to meet on the following Friday. In the end, after all the thinking and reasoning, they agreed they should move on to another form. They left the possibility of a corporation for another time.

Chapter 36

Typical of South Florida's weather in late July, it rained as the plane landed, only to rapidly dry and turn bright and sunny. Peter Pagan rented a Buick at the airport and drove to Sutter's in Miami Lakes. He had to look up to speak to the six-foot valet parking attendant. Pagan's gray, double-breasted suit set him apart from the tourists staying at the hotel, with their flowery, loose shirts, shorts and sandals.

"Are you attending a meeting or are you staying with us?"

"I'll be here for a few days."

"Registration desk is just down the hall." He handed Pagan the claim tag. "Have the receptionist stamp this for you."

And, as Pagan did not move toward the desk, "The bar and restaurant are just to your right."

He had planned to arrive at two o'clock, get settled into his room and come down to meet Dr. Stanley Reinhart in the bar at three. An hour flight delay changed his plans. Being compulsively punctual, he was appreciative that it was only two fifty-five as he turned right, but was annoyed at the near miss. He stood at the doorway of the bar for a moment, composing himself, unconsciously stroking his balding head and adjusting his jacket. He thought, *I'm the buyer, I should be cautious; I don't have to impress Dr. Stanley Reinhart. Let him do the pitch.* He recalled, on the phone call, two days before today's flight, Reinhart had said something about his company, Amed, being ready to look for a merging partner, and perhaps it would be interesting if they talked.

Thanks to an excellent filing and retrieving system, Pagan was able to bring the up-to-date data on Amed and on Reinhart. *Look for a gray-haired, thin, tall man, sixty-one years old.* It told him that Reinhart was respected in his community, was involved in investing the company's money as one of the directors and he favored antiques. He used alcohol only socially and had no record as a thief or in drugs. Pagan thought, *He is a very substantial citizen. So where is his soft spot, his weakness? Should I look for ego and vanity? Remember, it's always money, drugs, sex or ego that drives us.*

Pagan located Dr. Stanley Reinhart sitting in a booth. "Good afternoon. It has been, what, four years since we met in Chicago?"

Reinhart rose and extended his hand. "I believe so. I want to thank you for agreeing to join me." They sat down as the waiter approached. They each moved deep into the booth, toward the wall, unconsciously responding to the conspiratorial nature of their meeting. Reinhart ordered Dewar's neat, Pagan, vodka and tonic with lime.

When the drinks arrived, "To a successful venture," Reinhart offered. Pagan acknowledged with a nod. The warming talk discussed the flight, the weather, a description of the hotel for Pagan who would be staying for a few days, and assurance that the food was excellent, particularly the steaks.

"You mentioned something about a merger?" Pagan asked.

"I believe you are at about the same point as we are in regard to moving toward a merger," Reinhart said.

"We have been considering it. The whole industry has." Pagan watched him, waiting to see where Reinhart was going. He would like to gain information without committing to anything more than curiosity. "And you?"

"Our companies are much alike: dedicated to physicians' protection and at the same time being guided by realistic actuary data. Too many of the companies we have evaluated might as well be a bank, concerned about return on investment of their assets, rather than carefully balancing risk and premium. I'd hesitate joining such a company." Reinhart took a sip of his scotch and waited.

Pagan leaned forward. "You know we are a public stock company? Our two organizations began about at the same time, you a little earlier, but we converted to a stock company in the first year."

"I know. I was in favor of doing just that, but Dr. Nostrom, our chairman, fell in love with the concept of returning dividends to the doctors. I eventually got them on the right track. This points to why I wanted to talk with you."

"How is that?"

Reinhart sat back, placing his hands across his vest, assuming the pose of an advising attorney. "I do not believe Dr. Nostrom has a grasp on the situation and might easily foul the waters for Amed."

"How can I help you?"

"I would like to see Amed end up in as stable a condition as possible after a merger. An arrangement could be reached where Amed becomes a wholly owned subsidiary with the prime movers of Amed being loyal to Popic." Reinhart named Pagan's company.

"Would you be the prime mover?"

Reinhart was pensive. "You know there are two phases in the life of a business: the start-up and the continued operation. They frequently call for two diametrically opposed styles. Erik did a fine job bringing the company through adolescence, but as Amed matured, he demonstrated an inability to grasp the changing needs. He is the first to admit that he dropped the ball when he chose to give dividends rather than develop a surplus."

"I gather you are the best choice to lead your company through the merger and beyond?"

Reinhart was silent, and then he nodded. "Exactly, but only if the steering committee agrees. I believe there is a good chance of that coming about."

"It may be early for making a commitment at this time," Pagan said.

"With certain assurances, I would be inclined to support a merger with Popic," Reinhart said

"We'll see." Pagan stood. "I haven't checked in. I think I'd better take care of that."

They left the bar, Reinhart headed for the exit. Pagan walked toward the reception desk as he evaluated Dr. Stanley Reinhart. *He has the appearance of respectability but speaks Machiavellian. He even looks a little like the prince. He's hungry, but must be handled carefully.*

Chapter 37

The following afternoon, Pagan met with Erik, Jerry and Paul. Erik said, "One factor in favor of merging with Popic is we are far apart and have separate markets. I would imagine you would have to be well down the line toward commitment before you would be able to share your financial data with competitive companies in Florida. With us being a half continent apart, it would be easier and safer."

"And that is just one of the considerations," Jerry said. "Once we agree on the financial arrangements, we must resolve the form that emerges. You folks already have a stock company with a Best rating. Our plan would be to ask the insurance department to treat us as a mutual and allow us to convert to a private corporation. We then would come to the bargaining table on an equal footing."

"Can you wait until you accomplish both steps? You have to decide the optimum time to convert," Pagan said.

Erik said, "We are just beginning to balance time with control. I know if we stay as we are, we will have to go into negotiations as a seller and end up as a wholly owned subsidiary."

"The popular setup these days is to create an upstream holding company and purchase the new entity outright." Jerry added, "And that is just one of the alternatives. Once the M and A boys get started your head will spin."

Paul asked, "M and A?"

"Mergers and acquisitions, your investment bankers. I confuse them with surgeons because they both should wear masks." Jerry turned his palms up, apologizing for the attempt at humor. "The attraction for this kind of activity is like the seasons, running hot and cold. It's in favor at the present time."

"I thought I was up to speed on getting ready for a change, having helped in the sale of my carpet company, but I see there is a long way to go." Paul shook his hand in the air.

"And we have to educate the steering committee," Jerry added.

"You helped us open a Pandora's box, thank you, Peter Pagan," Erik said. "But seriously, this is a good start. From what I have been able to determine, Popic offers many of the qualities we were looking for."

When the discussions ended, Jerry and Paul retired to the claims department to review the case of Mrs. Shivers, who had her hospital stay lengthened due to bleeding following a laparoscopic cholecystectomy.

"If you have no other plans," Erik said to Pagan, "perhaps you would like to join me for dinner?"

"Great! It's five-thirty. Can we meet at Sutter's? I'm staying there."

"Fine, let's meet at seven?"

"See you then."

Pagan was waiting at the entrance of the restaurant as Erik came through the door. "Over here." He had exchanged his double-breasted gray suit for a dark brown cashmere jacket, beige slacks and a tan open-necked shirt. As Erik approached, he said, "I didn't know if you would recognize me in this disguise."

"No problem."

They each came representing their tribe, Erik from the East and Pagan from the plains; true scouting expeditions, each saw the strengths and weaknesses of the other. After broad descriptions of the size and scope of their companies, they began comparing techniques of underwriting, handling of claims and marketing.

Erik said, "I don't know why I should be, but I'm struck by how similarly we approach these problems, even to using a doctor member in the same specialty in a closed-door session."

"It doesn't surprise me," Pagan said. "We were born about the same time, and, as we talk, I find we are driven by the same motivation."

"Oh, no!"

"What's the matter?"

"Just recently I gave the lecture that reasonably intelligent people with the same information and the same motivation should come to the same conclusion. Your comment is déjà vu all over again, thanks, Yogi Berra."

Pagan smiled. "I think that's very important when it comes to merged companies running smoothly. It would even make co-chairmen possible."

"And one of the biggest deterrents to merger is 'Who is going to be the chairman?'"

"It's something to think about."

There was no question in either man's mind as to whom. Erik realized that if it were a buy-out by Popic, he would have a hard time. Pagan went back to Ohio the next morning.

Chapter 38

After the meeting with Pagan, Erik walked to his car. He sat behind the steering wheel without starting the engine. The CD was playing songs by Frank Sinatra. "I Did it My Way" clicked in place. Erik mouthed the words, "I took the blows…" *That's me*, he thought. He rested his head on the steering wheel, his body too heavy to move for a moment. Then he started the engine and drove to the nursing home.

"Evening, Dr. Nostrom." Clarence, the orderly, came from around the desk and began walking with Erik. "There's been no change in Mrs. Nostrom. But the staff has really taken to her. She looks so peaceful. They call her their sleeping beauty. They turn her every few hours. You can bet there won't be any bed sores on Mrs. Nostrom."

Erik waved goodbye to Clarence and walked into Frances' room. "Good evening, Fran," he said to the motionless body lying in the bed. The astringent odor was so far removed from the faintly perfumed fragrance of her bedroom in their house. She was wearing the pink dressing gown that Lacy had brought the day before. It was part of Lacy's routine as she acted as a super private duty nurse.

Frances was in a coma. But when Erik touched her hand, reflex action caused it to close; was there hope for some small improvement? Erik knew there was none. Her breathing was slow and smooth. He could hear a faint bruit as she exhaled. In distant memory, he could recall that sound, and how he would nudge Frances to get her to turn on her side and let him sleep. He knew it was meaningless, but he reached over and gently shook her arm.

Erik walked to the window and sat, looking out at the rows of single story houses; further, he saw the plowed truck farms and then the beginning of the everglades. In the years she laid there, the wave of houses being built marched westward toward the swamp, devouring the farmland. She was unaware of this or any other change in the world around her. The thought of her awaking still hung over him. The warm breeze carried the sea smell from the marshes through the screen. His mind played stream of consciousness in the evening shadows that danced across the outside garden. Two great loves have passed through his life and now they were gone. He sat beside a stranger whose familiarity pinned him to the past first love in a way he could not fathom. Obligation? Commitment to the years gone by? Or was the alternative emptiness so stark and frightening as to make clinging to this unconscious, slow-breathing remnant of days past an adequate refuge?

A young man and his girl walked along the path under his window. She turned, facing the young man, and they stopped. He heard her soft laughter as she touched his face. He tilted her chin and kissed her. The moonlight was eclipsed by the moving clouds and the couple disappeared in the darkness. Erik could feel the pleasure of that kiss on his lips, recalled from many past kisses, a merging of the lips of Cathy and Frances.

As he left the nursing home he idly looked down the pathway under her window, but the couple was gone.

Chapter 39

Doctors Jesse Gentile, Thomas Harmon and Kenneth Moninger, the Gainesville contingent, arrived before the others because there was a change in the flight schedule to Miami. They entered the kitchen. Kenneth followed the aroma and poured the coffee. He asked, "Did you all get the folder from Randle Winthrop and associates?" He held up the envelope that bore the name of the investment bankers firm.

They nodded. "That report was quite impressive. Did you see the fees? Staggering. We are in the wrong line of work," Thomas said.

"At least its success oriented. As I read it, it's thirty-five thousand for doing the work and five hundred thousand if a successful merger results from their efforts," Kenneth said.

"That's all," Jesse said with a monotone delivery, palms turned upward.

The remaining members of the board appeared, took their coffee, and then the entire group went into the boardroom.

"Good evening," Erik said. "Welcome to the Friday's festivities. Tonight we begin tackling the real nuts and bolts. In the brochure from Winthrop, there is the evaluation of the four companies that fit into our criteria for merging, as well as the beginning costs of this kind of move. Success is very expensive."

"Have we decided on merger?" Jack Reed asked. "Last I knew we were talking about whether we should stay as we are or go another route." He looked to Erik.

Fredrick Cannon said, "Jack, its Erik's 'I think; you ratify' approach." He scowled at Erik and then laughed.

"Thank you, Fred, I needed that. Seriously, I asked Winthrop to prepare this information so we'd have it available. I think it helps in deciding to move in any direction or even stay put. But you're right, the first order of business tonight is to decide on change or not to change, and if change, *quo vadis*."

Anthony Sanchez asked, "Did you say seriously? Yet you speak Caesarly, says Anthony."

"Very cute," Thomas Frond said approvingly.

Reinhart stood up. "May I summarize our position as we left it last Saturday? We really voted to move on to another form. We did not discuss the corporate structure or the merger in any depth. After reviewing the data from Winthrop, I am in favor of bypassing the mutual stage and going on to merger. If this is the wish of the board, perhaps we could move on to evaluating the various companies suitable for merger." He thought, *Well done. Now, all that is needed is to gradually shoot down the other three candidates and make Popic look like a winner. I'll call Pagan tonight to let him know. He may have some more ammunition for me. How sweet it is, finally, in a position to get recognition, to put arrogant Erik in his place.*

"I'd like a formal motion for the record to the effect that the board voted unanimously to depart from the one state-one line position."

"So moved."

"All in favor?"

"Passed unanimously."

"We'll follow Stanley's suggestion and begin reviewing the four companies, unless someone would like to further consider the mutual route." Erik surveyed the group. The speed of the transformation from managing a stable little company to the volatile arena of choosing a new partner had many of them bewildered, their eyes out of focus—a deer caught in the headlights. There was no affirmative motion to stay as they were. "Record no objection."

With the auctioneer's gesture, Erik pounded the table. "Sold to merger!"

The discussion of the four companies, the data from the investment banker, and the outline of the steps necessary for the conversion went on through the night and, after a night's break, into Saturday morning.

"It looks like the two leading candidates are Physicians Ideal Protective of California, PIPIC, and Physicians of Ohio Protective Insurance Company,

POPIC. PIPIC converted from a mutual. It is Edward's old company."

Frond noted, "Both companies are far away. I don't feel too nervous about us showing our financial data, and they shouldn't be too concerned about giving us theirs."

Erik said, "If it's the board's pleasure, I will try to have each company's chairman and CEO come down and talk to us. One on Friday, one on Saturday."

This arrangement was accepted by everyone. The meeting ended and all went home.

Chapter 40

Jerry was impressed by Lorraine Ryan in the way she quietly took charge of Erik's office. Because he had recommended her, he was relieved to see her working out so well.

He had first met her as he was recovering from Linda. Her boss, Dr. Swanson, had needed legal advice concerning a small slough of the skin in his patient's leg where Dr. Swanson had injected a varicose vein. In introducing Jerry to Ms. Ryan, the doctor had spoken highly of his lawyer. Jerry had to return to the office several times, which had allowed propinquity to ease Jerry's awkwardness as he ventured back into dating. The last visit had been quite contrived. Jerry had returned to deliver the final release to Dr. Swanson. Both Jerry and Lorraine had known he could have mailed it.

"Thank you for your help," he said. "Are we up to a drink to celebrate?"

"Sounds like a plan to me. I'll be finished here in a minute." The offer brought color to her cheeks. She was able to control her soft, modulated voice, but she was a little shaky inside. Since her divorce, she had been very careful about whom she dated. Blind dates set up by friends challenged the friendship. She had come to know Jerry so gradually and in such a protected environment, he seemed safe. He was mature, articulate, witty and handsome and he was taller than she and he was single.

Old habits died hard. Jerry found as he donned his seduction line like a comfortable old but expensive sports jacket. He listened.

The second date ended with a kiss at the doorstep and the third found them in bed. The evening was enjoyable. Unfortunately, Jerry had to be in Ohio for the next two weeks. On his flight home, and for the next four weeks, the stewardess occupied his leisure hours. For Jerry it was a deliberate ploy, for he was getting too comfortable with the thought of Lorraine in his life. Scars from the Linda days constantly reminded him of the possible land mines sprinkled along the pathway of close relationships.

After so much time had gone by, it took the *chutzpah* of a highwayman for Jerry to approach Lorraine to talk about coming to work with Dr. Erik Nostrom.

"Hi, Ms. Ryan." Her perfume ignited his memories of her. He struggled to remember why he had not run to her on his return from Ohio.

"Good morning, Mr. Simms." The pleasure of seeing him, dampened by the anger over his absence, formed a buffer, allowing the tone to move to neutral. Her thoughts tumbled over each other. *It was only three dates; I have no hold on him. I'm not sure I'd want one; he's too old not to be trouble. Why is he here?*

It was coincidence, but it had the appearance of ESP as he said, "I came to say 'goodbye' to Dr. Swanson. I believe this is his last week in town."

"That's nice of you."

"I enjoyed working with him…and with you." The last three words pushed past his censor.

"You called our time together work? It is a good thing you weren't overburdened. One more day and you probably would have collapsed. I gather you have fully recovered?"

They were silent. Only warm memories of their time together danced, unspoken, between them. It was the comfort of having climbed over the mountain of first hellos and of careful lowering of facades, an emotional savings account, too valuable to squander. Jerry and Lorraine separately struggled to find an island of compromise to allow them to move on.

"What are you doing later?" Jerry asked.

"What?" He couldn't have meant that.

"Poor choice of words, or maybe not. I was talking about your plans, now that Dr. Swanson is leaving. Any thoughts of going with him?"

"No, I'm too at home in Miami. He's going where there are seasons, winter and cold. Not for me. I thought I'd take a day off and then look around."

"Do you know Dr. Nostrom? He a surgeon."

"Of course, he's got a good reputation in town. Wasn't his office manager in trouble recently?"

"She was murdered."

"Was he a suspect?"

"No, more a victim. Well, you know how dependant a doctor gets on a good office manger. She did everything for him, much like you do for Dr. Swanson. In fact, you reminded me of her when I saw you running Swanson's shop." Jerry stopped. He recalled initially wondering how close the doctor and nurse were.

"I feel sorry for him. I know how difficult it is to start with a new partner. That's the way it was with Swany and me; we were partners in crime." She laughed for the first time.

"Welcome back."

"OK, you are forgiven. Why did you really come by today? Are you headhunting?"

"Yes. If you're interested, I think you and Nostrom would make a great team, for that's about the way it was with him and his manager, Cathy."

"Oh, I knew her. We met at an office workshop. I liked her."

"Everyone did."

"You included?"

"She was a real friend." Sadness suddenly flavored his words and he stopped talking.

"Does he need help?"

Jerry talked to Erik and arranged a meeting between him and Lorraine. Almost immediately, the conversation was on details of operating the office, agreeing or compromising on techniques. Office hours, salary, benefits, and duties were easily resolved. Lorraine began working with Erik.

Chapter 41

"Dr. Stanley Reinhart to talk to Mr. Pagan. Yes, I'll hold."

"Good morning, Stanley, nice to hear from you."

"The meeting went rather well. In the end, Erik is going to have the board interview you and the chairman from PIPIC, Bill Davis. I believe you are Friday. I wanted to spend a minute about my future with your company. If I was assured of being a part of the administration of the new company, particularly as head of investment, I would be inclined toward singing your praises. The way I read the members of the board at this moment, they are a bit out to sea and will follow any strong-minded guidance. I am capable of playing that role."

"Stanley, I appreciate your position. But won't you be uncomfortable, suggesting a course of action with you having a hidden agenda?"

"Not really. It is my conviction that the best direction for Amed is to go with POPIC. If it benefits me as well, I'm not disturbed."

"I'm relieved; I wouldn't care to be associated with somebody who would put self-interest ahead of the good of the company."

"Nor would I."

"For the same reason," Pagan said, "I can't fully commit at this time. I certainly will appreciate your support if you truly believe we are the best choice, and I will keep your efforts in mind."

"Thank you. We will talk again on Friday."

Pagan warmed his hand on his cup of coffee and studied the memo on his desk, listing the members of the board of directors of Amed. He drew a circle around the name Dr. Stanley Reinhart. "There's not a snowball's chance in hell I'd do business with you." He smiled and curled the imaginary mustache of the silent movie villain. "Unless I have to."

Paul turned off 926 and headed for the airport. The maze before him made him agree with the line he had read in the news this morning: "Miami International is like New York City; it will be a great place when it's finished." The construction had outpaced the sign corrections, and if he were to follow the most recent directions posted on the green and white signs, he would be stuck on a never-ending loop. Fortunately, his past experience told him to ignore them. He found a spot in the short-term parking lot on the ground floor, an area with a low ceiling that was always dark, damp and foreboding. Conscious of reported muggings, he clung to his attaché case as he headed for the arriving passenger corridor.

Bill Davis, the Chairman of Physician's Ideal Protective Insurance Company, PIPIC, was walking down the long airport passageway when Paul spotted him. He was pulling a stewardess-like luggage holder with wheels. On top of the bag, he rested his briefcase.

"Mine says 'Bill Davis.'" Paul pointed to his imaginary sign across his chest.

"That's me." He reached out his arm to shake hands.

Paul guided him down the escalators, through the fume-filled traffic and to the parking lot. The cacophony from passing cars and buses allowed only shouting, "Down here, over there."

In the car, driving to the office, conversation turned to personnel. Paul answered Davis' enquiry. "My staff acts as though they owned the company. I think it is partly because I try to delegate authority commensurate with their responsibility." He could not see Davis' face. "Of course, this approach requires a feedback on how things are going. Most people try to do their best and the bad apples usually weed themselves out."

Davis listened and then said, "At a recent management conference, a straw vote showed a majority believed that the fear of being fired must be part of the package to produce optimum effort from the employees. They were appalled at the thought of creating a sense of tenure. I'm afraid my past experience makes me agree with the majority. They said, if absolute power corrupts absolutely, then absolute freedom corrupts freely." Bill laughed.

"It's probably important for the manager to be comfortable with his style and more important that he be consistent."

Paul delivered Bill to his hotel.

"Someone will pick you up to bring you to the office. Say, about three o'clock? I arranged a room containing all the documents we talked about."

"Sounds good to me."

As he drove away, Paul reviewed the complexity of the day. He would have Davis in one room, studying. Pagan would be in another part of the office, also reviewing documents in preparation for his interview this evening with the board. Paul thought, *Hopefully, never the twain shall meet.*

Chapter 42

All members were present at the Friday night board meting. Pagan had spent the afternoon studying the Amed data and preparing his presentation. When he finished he sat back, quite satisfied with his findings. He muttered to himself the one fact that terrified him and please him: "One billion dollars! Together, our assets will be more than one billion. I have to get used to saying that word without stammering—billion!"

He got up from his chair and walked the length of the suite. He found a door that opened into his washroom. He went in and splashed a handful of cold water on his face. For the first time he let down his wall of reservation and thought, *I want it!* It was the next plateau, a move into the top ten in the country. He thought of Reinhart. *Is he the added pinch of insurance? I'm going to pull all stops.*

As he entered the boardroom, he made an imperceptible but definite positive nod toward Reinhart.

Initially, the details of the two companies considered for joining were evaluated: the obligatory factors, those that were deal breakers, and the elective alternatives, which would require a consensus.

"How do you see the new company? The working structure?" Jack Reed asked.

"I would like to look upon our venture as a combining of equals. We both consider our physicians as our first priority; we are conservative in our investments and are careful in credentialing," Pagan said.

"From the start each company will run about as it has been. We are in different parts of the country. What works in Miami might not fly in Cleveland. Cultures and attitudes are different. Procedures and personnel in claims, credentials, marketing and sales will be unchanged. The main benefits in the merger are the economy of scale and the ability to exchange ideas with someone from another area."

"Let's cut to the chase," said Sanchez. "Who is going to be the boss?"

Pagan smiled at Erik. "I've gotten to know your chairman, from his reputation and now personally, and the way your company operates. I believe we could work together quite well."

Reinhart said, "Traditionally, when two entities merge, one is essentially purchased, as we would be. The chairman of the surviving company remains in ultimate control. We would be fortunate to end up with Mr. Peter Pagan. This is one of the basic factors in choosing our partner."

Richard Garing shook his head. "I understand many attempted mergers never get off the ground over this point. The fear is that when one chairman remains, the merged company gradually disappears as an entity, as do many of its personnel. The only salvation for Amed staff is for Erik to have control, or at least equal footing, maybe a rotating or co-chairman. Otherwise the team should look for a strong severance package."

Erik said, "We can put that question 'til the end. Then will be the time to figure this out."

Two hours later, they called it a night. They would meet for another session at ten o'clock in the morning.

Erik drove Pagan to his hotel.

"I am going to call Florence, head of underwriting, and Steven, my CEO, from my room."

"This late at night?"

"It's one hour earlier there. Besides, they wouldn't forgive me if I didn't. The staff acts as though it was their company." Pagan smiled

"That's very interesting."

Chapter 43

Bill Davis came to the office at seven o'clock, even though it was Saturday.

"Good morning," he said to Janis.

"Hi, you're an early bird. You're lucky I had to get here at this hour to prepare for the board meeting or else you'd be waiting in the lobby 'til nine."

"You look bright eyed and bushy tailed for this time in the morning. What is your secret?"

"Contented home life." She delivered the line straight. She thought, *I'm going to cut this 'come on to me' approach dead in its tracks.*

"Good for you." He thought, *I didn't mean anything; I was just being friendly.* But he knew he was probing, part in lust, part in seeking a weakness he could use later when dealing with Paul. It was nothing like having an edge on your CEO.

"The material is still on the desk in the room you were using last night. I'll call you when Paul gets here."

"Thank you."

The board meeting followed the opening procedures, and then Erik introduced Mr. Bill Davis. "We are already indebted to PIPIC and Bill. When we started, we borrowed many of their techniques, as they were in business almost a year before us. And, of course, our Edward Hartman came from

PIPIC."

"Thank you for the introduction, but I'm not sure we forgive you for stealing Edward. In any case, I have reviewed your data and am impressed. As I think of our companies, each representing a coast of this country, I am reminded of the building of the railroads. Each began from opposite boarders and headed inland, to eventually tie the country together in one great transportation system. Well, it is not beyond my wildest dream to envision our two companies spreading towards the central states to form a national force. You see, I believe the marriage is so destined that I think of us as one."

"Who will be the bride and who will be the groom?" Kenneth Moninger asked.

"As Erik mentioned, we started before you. In our beginning, we were faced with a similar problem. There were two factions coming together to form PIPIC. We tried co-chairman and rotating chairmen. It was a partisan nightmare. Because there was no one ultimate source of power, each faction pulled even more strongly for their side. We almost didn't get off the ground." He paused.

"What happened?" Jesse Gentile asked.

"In the end, Richard Hanks, the leader of the opposite contingent, acknowledged me as the chairman. I agreed with him and his group that if things didn't seem to be going satisfactorily in their eyes, I would yield control to Richard. This was a calculated risk on both sides. If they wanted to arbitrarily declare things weren't going well just to unseat me, they could." Davis paused. He could see the group recognized the danger in the conditions he described. "I bet they would play fair. As it turned out, the state physicians needed coverage so badly they would go with any company. We, like you, had success right from the start, and like you all, doctors were slipping applications for insurance coverage under the door of our shop on Sunday mornings."

"It sounds like a good solution to me," Sanchez said. "So you're thinking of letting Erik run the show?"

"There are a few other aspects that must be considered," Erik said to get Davis off the hot seat.

The room began to become uncomfortably warm. "The building turns off the air conditioning for the weekend at one," Paul explained. "I didn't realize it was so late." Davis was asked to wait in Paul's office. The meeting ended.

Each of the board members received a package containing extensive data concerning Bill Davis and Peter Pagan. They each were to review the information and be prepared for the discussion and final decision on the merger partner.

As a parting comment, Erik said, "And this is just the beginning. Once we pick our partner, we must get the opinion of Johnson and Jones, our outside auditors, and of Hunters, our actuary. Randle Winthrop, the investment banker, has to put the deal together and give us a fairness opinion. SEC wants filings. We must be cleared of the Hart-Scott-Rodino antitrust act. NASDAQ must OK the transaction. There are Blue Sky conditions to be met. Employment arrangements and contracts for the staff are a must. Confidentiality and non-compete clauses must be signed. Of course, we need enough proxy votes from the policyholders to assure acceptance of the merger. I believe 66% is required."

"Is that all?" Fredrick Cannon's comment eased the mounting apprehension.

"I may have overlooked something," Erik said. "Good night, see you all next Friday. Let's start at six."

Chapter 44

Lacy finished bathing Frances and turned to get a dry towel off the bed stand. She thought her skirt was caught on the side rail. When she looked, she saw the material in the closed grip of Frances' hand. *A reflex*, she thought. She had seen this before. She moved to fully face Frances. She freed her skirt. The empty hand closed on her finger. "Oh, my God!" The sign of life at first was frightening as a ghost! The chill of seeing a headstone move in the graveyard. She stared at the hand, afraid to raise her eyes to Frances' face. She wanted to hold on to the fantasy of Frances coming out of the coma. She knew the hand holding her finger responded to a reflex and nothing more. But stay. She'd smile and say, "Hello."

Without removing the index finger of her left hand from Frances' warm grip, using her right hand, Lacy shifted the blanket covering Frances' face. *It's the eyes*, she thought. *They used to make me cry when I saw those vacant eyes staring at nothing. Now she is looking at me, not through me.* Lacy moved her head to see if Frances' eyes would follow her. They did not. Was there a change, or was her wishing playing tricks on her? She removed her finger and Frances' fist close as it always had.

She left the room and walked to the nurse station.

"Have any of you seen any change in Mrs. Nostrom? I thought I saw her move her hand and her eyes looked different, like they wanted to focus."

"She does that every once in a while."

"But this was different."

"I wouldn't go telling Dr. Nostrom or anybody else about that. You get their hopes up for nothing and they won't be thanking you."

Lacy returned to Frances' room. She sat, leaning forward, elbows resting on her knees, and her chin on her clasped hands, staring at Frances. There was no further movement.

Lacy continued her daily routine, supplementing the staff's efforts: Passive motion of all extremities and massage of the muscles of the leg, arms and back. She had kept Frances' body in outstanding condition. Where most good nursing homes that cared for persistent vegetative patients prided themselves on preventing bed sores, Lacy would be content only if Frances' body was in a condition ready to run when she would awaken. Lacy held the belief for so long that Frances would awaken; it was a fact in her mind. When it occurred, she would not be surprised. Even so, the first suggestion of movement caused a surge of joy. It was sad to have to return to her belief, still unsubstantiated.

Erik came by to sit by Frances and watch. It was strangely peaceful, like being in a cemetery. Except for an occasional bell paging a nurse, only the faint hum of the air-conditioning motors and the distant sound of wind outside the windows broke the silence. The weekly flowers Erik sent gave the room a sweet fragrance. The room was kept cool against the smothering heat outside. Erik walked to the window where he could see the people on the path. He looked for the loving couple he had seen before, but they were not there.

"See anything interesting?" The voice was inside the room.

"Lacy, you back from dinner so soon?" He heard no answer. This did not surprise him, for Lacy was not very talkative with him.

"Where is Lacy?"

Now he was confused. Some nurse had entered the room? Or was this Jerry, playing tricks in a falsetto pitch?

"OK," he said as he turned. There was no one there. He walked to the door, opened it and peered up and down; no one was in the corridor.

"Erik, come sit down." The voice matched a fifteen-year-old memory. But that would be Frances. Her spirit, lingering a brief time before departing. He was frightened. He was terrified. He realized his eyes were closed. *Don't open them. If I see her image passing, I'll go crazy. God, there is a soul!* His legs could no longer hold him. He fell into the chair next to the bed. He was cold. He pulled his arms around him.

"Oh, Fran, no, no, no." He started to cry. Tears seeped through his closed eyelids.

Frances' wave of consciousness passed and she fell back in her vegetative state. He sat there, rocking in the chair, trembling.

"Evening, Dr. Nostrom," Lacy said. As soon as she saw him, crying and shaking, she was alarmed. "Are you all right?" She never saw him like this, almost a child. "What can I do?"

He leaned forward in his chair and reached out to wrap his arms around Lacy's sturdy waist, his head pressed against her. Like comforting her cocker spaniel, she stroked his head, "There, there, what is it?"

"She's gone," he repeated. "Lacy, she talked to me! What's strange, she didn't say goodbye or anything sensible. She said something about where you were." He stood up and saw Frances' body in the bed. Her chest slowly raised and lowered. "My God, she's breathing, she's here, she's still alive!"

Lacy stepped aside as he moved toward the bed. Like a fighter hit too often, he stood there, swaying slightly. Gradually he regained his composure. "It was so real. You wouldn't think I'd have delusions this late in the game."

"She spoke to you?"

"I'll say yes, but I know that's not possible."

"It is! Two days ago, she grasped my skirt and squeezed my finger. It wasn't like before. It wasn't a reflex. And her eyes were alive."

They walked to the bedside. He put his hand on Frances breast to feel the heartbeat. "She's with us."

"And you, sir, are fresh." They saw her begin to smile. Her eyes focused on his face. The voice was soft but slurred. As quickly as she had awakened, she was again asleep. Lacy remained standing but Erik again fell back into the bedside chair.

Medical observation and therapy began that night. By morning, the team had camcorder proof of her intermittent consciousness.

Therapists worked on recovering her speech. Thanks to Lacy's vigil, her body had been ready for recovery for fifteen years.

The long, complex job began of helping Frances re-learn so many actions of everyday life—to brush her teeth and to comb her hair.

Lacy stayed with Frances most of the day and acted as the triage officer, guiding the many specialists in and out of the room.

"She's like a newborn trying to learn everything of the first ten years of life in a few months," Lacy explained to Dr. Nostrom. "Her talking has cleared up and she's pretty stable on her feet."

Erik visited Frances every day. At first, he was encouraged by her improvement, for her sake. With time, she reached a plateau, having small gains and retreats. She mastered make-up, and with Lacy's aid, created a hairstyle very similar to the pre-stroke Frances. The bland years of coma had prevented the onset of signs of aging, leaving her a picture of young Frances. Her voice sounded like the young Frances. For Erik, she was gone. This Frances reminded him of his tailor's daughter. Because of the daughter's rebellious attitude, her father had subjected her to a frontal lobotomy, the ghastly medical fad in the days prior to tranquilizers. The procedure had been a medical success; she came out placid, sweet, smiling and empty. She talked and walked a little slower, but adequately enough to work in her father's store. The vigorous life his daughter's genes had planned for her was gone, as Frances was gone.

Erik settled into a chronic fatigue, the repetitive disappointment of expecting the response he had known in the past and instead, receiving a pleasant, mechanical substitute.

Most of the experts predicted that Frances would always need some support and would at best remain at the present plateau. The devil of it, Erik thought, was that she looked unchanged. When he viewed her in repose, he was fooled into anticipating her bright remark, reflecting her cute, teasing sense of humor. But they did not come.

When he held her, he felt the response of a child devoid of the sensuous movements speaking in a non-verbal language. The body's pressure and heat, singing the serenade of lust, was absent, as was all foreplay, which he remembered too well. He was hesitant to initiate this flow for fear of frightening her, as a child would be frightened by such advances. So, they remained in this bittersweet, platonic relationship.

Erik became more immersed in his practice and his company.

Chapter 45

The members moved into the boardroom. The earlier conversations in the kitchen had been unusually somber. The complexity of the material they must review weighed heavily upon them. They mentally stooped down under the burden.

It was not only the need to understand the data that was crushing, but they had to make definitive decisions concerning them.

In the past, they had been asked to vote on matters that were pre-digested for them by Paul, Jerry and Erik. All that was required was a ratification of decisions already made by the three musketeers. The only risk was descent. Reinhart was looked upon to supply this service. Once his objections were neutralized, it was effortless.

Now they were faced with outside forces; it was no longer black and white. They had the power they claimed they wanted, and it scared the shit out of them.

Randle Winthrop was re-introduced as the investment banker. He acknowledged the welcome and began discussing the various aspects of the merger. For this meeting he emphasized the pros and cons of the two candidates, POPIC and PIPIC.

"I've looked at the structure of each of the companies; here are several aspects they have in common: They both started in the mid seventies, as you did. They both are oriented toward having the physician as their customers. There is a similar importance given to the investment portfolio, although PIPIC has a program with a better yield, but with a longer duration and a slightly lower quality rating. I believe your company leans toward the conservative side." Winthrop looked from one hand to the other as though shifting some invisible data.

He continued, "There are some differences. PIPIC offers a wider range of insurance options. Self-insuring the first dollars up to fifty thousand is available as deductibles. POPIC's policy is more aligned with the actuarial numbers. Credentialing and underwriting are stricter at POPIC. Claims are handled with an in-house legal staff at PIPIC whereas POPIC uses many local attorneys, on a case by case basis."

He went on reeling off the similarities and differences for another hour.

"Any questions?"

"Yes," Jack Reed said. "What did you say after you said, 'Hello'? And could you repeat it?" Once again, humor eased the apprehension of ignorance.

"I know this is a good deal of information. I've outlined all the points in the folder before you."

Everyone was glad for the excuse to move and stretch. There was a definite comfort for each member in holding the folder like his baby blanket, as if by osmosis the knowledge would flow through his hands to his brain, fully digested.

"With this information added to the data you received last week, we should be prepared to make a decision tomorrow. I know that no amount of information could put you at ease. But remember, no decision is far worse than either of your alternatives. I'm glad the choice is between two thoroughbreds rather than something headed for the glue factory." He sat down and surveyed the faces. Bright understanding was not there. Only Reinhart was sitting back in his chair with a contented smile on his face.

Erik thought, *What's going through his mind?*

The meeting wound down and ended at eleven-thirty. Jerry walked with Eric and Paul to the parking lot. "Time for a drink? I have to catch up on you two. Being in Tallahassee so much for the last two months, I'm not on the information wire."

They drove separately to Sutter's Sports Bar.

With drinks and peanuts on the table, they sat around. Paul talked about Janis and Erik about Frances.

Chapter 46

At the Arpin House: "As far as I can calculate, it was on Sunday, the fifteenth of April. I knew we shouldn't have stayed in bed that long." Janis playfully punched Paul. They were naked, lying apart from each other as he inspected her abdomen.

With the thermostat turned up, the room was comfortably warm. He moved closer and put his left ear on her belly. He was facing Janis' feet. He thought, *It's real! I never dwelt on being a father. I mean, being able to be a father.*

"I love you," he said.

"Thank you."

"Not you. I do love you, but I was talking to our baby."

He thought, *In the past, when I was near a pregnant woman, the smell and the awkwardness repelled me. It's strange, being a father. I'm proud, but why? Any moron can fertilize an egg; birds do it, bees do it.*

He didn't realize he was humming the tune.

"What did you say?" she asked.

"Nothing. Oh, I was singing to myself."

"What?"

"Birds do it, bees do it," he said seriously. "I was just shooting down the miracle of pregnancy and birth."

"Nothing to it. You can have the next one."

"I got a little unhinged when I met you, and now I'm getting unhinged over this one. It must be a girl."

She tried to move without disturbing him. "My first complaint: my back is killing me. You know, it's not like getting fat; that spreads all around. With this monster, it wants to leap forward and I have to lean back to balance. The spine wasn't designed for that maneuver."

"Before you, the smell and awkwardness of pregnancy repelled me. But with you it's graceful motion and delicious fragrance."

"Everything is relative."

She bent her knees. His head slid down the slope of her bulging belly, resting on her pubic hairs. Her thigh touched his face. He kissed them, one at a time. Now her aroma was a mixture of perfume and pregnancy. He lifted his head to see her face. "I understand that in some African tribes, sex is taboo during pregnancy because it makes the woman so irresistible." He saw her radiant face. "I can see why they could think that."

She said, "According to the doctor, the cafeteria is open until the ninth month."

"I believe you're right."

Chapter 47

At his request, Pagan met Dr. Reinhart at The Eatery, a restaurant open twenty-four hours a day, featuring breakfast.

"Sleep well?" Reinhart asked. He watched Pagan move into the booth, wondering if their previous conversation had born fruit, if Pagan was ready to avail himself of his service, and what would Pagan give for them?

"It was a pretty good night, though I was up 'til two this morning. The home office forwarded some data on PIPIC. And I read over the material on Amed, which I believe we could use. Did you know your company is not doing as well this year as last year?" Pagan asked.

"I know the revenue and the number of policyholders are down. It was planned that way. Underwriting has begun a more prospective approach. In the past, after the initial underwriting, anything could happen. We did not know if we were harboring an increased risk. We have become more selective regarding age, particularly in the surgical specialties, and those who made the headlines in accidents, non-medical complaints or use of drugs or alcohol. We applied the concept that a doctor who has had a suit is more likely to have another than a doctor who had none. Erik is of the impression that weeding out these potentially bad risks will improve the bottom line."

"I'm not sure that's so. I don't believe there is an increased risk with age alone. Are the other members of the board aware of the drop in business and why?"

"I would be surprised if they did. They spend more time on public relations than on numbers."

The waitress came to their booth. "Ready to order?"

"Coffee, black, orange juice and toasted English," Pagan answered first.

"That sounds good, except a little sugar and cream for me."

They handed back the unused menus. "Mr. Winthrop ran through the pros and cons of your company and PIPIC's. I'd say it was a draw at the end of the evening. I could tilt it either way."

"And which way were you thinking?"

"How badly do you want Amed?"

Pagan thought, *Here it is. Let's see if I can commit without committing. Keep a back door open for every promise, but promise I must.* "I'm here, but after seeing the numbers, I'm a little less enthusiastic."

"Peter, shall we not play the 'please don't throw me into the briar patch' routine?" referring to the classic Brer rabbit story. "You want it, and I am able to give it to you."

"That's probably true. All right, you said you were interested in being in charge of investments?"

"It would be ideal if your company outsourced with my investment firm. Adding a billion dollars to our portfolio would not be bad for business." Reinhart studied Pagan, looking for body language as well as listening for the words. He knew he was asking for the moon.

"Is that all?" Pagan asked. "Not fifty percent of POPIC? Bold is one thing, but this is outrageous greed. I must compliment you for guts."

Reinhart turned over his palms, a conceding gesture. "I thought it might be an option. Yes, I must be a part of investment if I am to be persuaded to be an advocate for POPIC. Even an in-house title would do."

"I will offer the position to you, presented as my original idea, and you may reluctantly accept."

"That is a genuine commitment, I assume?"

"Mr. Vice President of investment, I presume?" Pagan reached across the table and shook Reinhart's hand. "It's a deal."

Chapter 48

The time had come, because of her stability, for Frances to come home. Lacy moved into one of their guest rooms and took the role of Frances' nurse, physical therapist and personal secretary. It was truly a labor of love; ever since Frances' trouble began Lacy had devoted herself to Frances' recovery. She had put aside other ambitions and plans for the future. It had become a magnificent obsession. Frances' recent improvement was a grand reward for her voluntary servitude. And being able to bring her home was of even greater satisfaction. She knew it was only her devoted daily care that kept Frances alive. And in her heart Lacy recognized being able to serve such a cause made her life worthwhile.

Frances sat on the patio and watched the sun come up. The first curve of the golden pie edged over the distant golf course and between two houses, which stood as contrasting black silhouettes. Slowly, the bright light splashed over the surface of the lake. The intensity of the entire fiery globe forced Frances to close her eyes and turn away. The morning's chill quickly gave way to the sun's warmth. Frances was content. The heavy sleepiness that had blurred her thinking was gradually lifting. She leaned forward in her chair and stood up. For a moment, she needed the walker in front of her to steady her. Then for the first time, she put it aside and walked the length of the table. *I can do it!* She thought, *I'm alive!* She tried to remember where she had been.

I know yesterday, I had breakfast. She recalled the rest of that day, but the day before was more difficult. *But today I'm clear, more than I've ever been. Ever? Strange, I can remember so many things from long ago: the day Jimmy brought me a charlotte russe, a surprise dessert for lunch. I was seven and he was eight. He slipped and almost fell, smashing the whipped cream topping. His face was red as he handed me the remains and turned away. I can see him so clearly.*

I look around my home and see so many unfamiliar objects. Don't panic! How did I learn before? For the last week, I have been able to bring back memories from before the stroke. Stroke? Erik tried to tell me about that. She suddenly had a piercing pain across her eyes and a flash of blood filled her vision. Her hands were dry as she pushed them against her face. *It's my dream, my dreams from the days of suspended consciousness.* The apparition faded and she opened her eyes. She was still on the patio. The sun had moved higher in the sky. Its heat comforted her. It was real, a sensation to which she could respond. She let her thoughts wander from childhood to days with Erik. As the images from that period became distinct, she recognized events; she knew they had happened. Then, as her mind turned the calendar and years shot forward, she was in a haze. The figures were unclear, changing shape and color, with no need to present a logical sequence. She was falling or flying through clouds; nauseating odors filled her nostrils, protectively replaced by sweet perfume. Her face was twisted into a mask of terror as a Galapagos monster was mounting her, and then a fuzzy wave blurred everything. Now she was thinking of yesterday. The pictures came bright and clear. This recall reflected the real world of memory, not like the bizarre, sometimes terrifying messages from her coma hours. She thought, *If I fill my brain with present day, real information, perhaps the bad illusions will fade.*

She saw Erik come through the door of the family room onto the patio. Proudly, she walked toward him. He had not seen her walk independently.

"You are wonderful, like a ballerina!" Erik called out.

She continued until she reached him, and then put her arms around him. As she kissed him, her breasts pressed against his chest and her pelvis tipped forward. "I am slowly coming alive," she said as she softly touched the back of his head with her hand.

"I believe you have. Welcome home." He held her, rocking softly. He smiled as tears ran down his face. The bonding was not a rebirth of their youthful passion, but more of a second time around realization that they were mature, comfortable with each other in a place they were content to spend their remaining years.

For Erik, her return lifted his melancholy. His joy matched the brilliant sunlight bathing their patio.

For the first time he could see a meaningful justification for his continued journey through the rest of his life. Depressive thoughts of suicide vanished. As he watched Frances step back and smile at him, the days of their youth seemed to be yesterday, with no interruption, no stroke, not anything. They would pick up from there. He thought, *Growing older is forgetting and forgiving.*

They began the complicated process of building a day-to-day normal routine into their lives. There were no landmarks to guide them, for return from coma after all these years was almost a unique experience.

Only humor, the forgiving balm, acted to bridge the awkwardness.

To help fill in the gaps, Erik purchased volumes of *The Years WE Knew* for 1974 to 1984. These gray and orange hardbound books listed the significant events of each year.

"It's interesting going through the books," Frances said, "but I can't relate to the times. It is fiction. It has no impact on me. It is as if you were to tell me of your trip to London or Paris. I wasn't there and I can't make it part of my life."

"I can understand that," Erik said. "Though I didn't until you said it just now. I was thinking too simplistically. I thought all this information would become part of you by osmosis," Erik said apologetically.

"The void frightens me, it is so huge. But when I begin to try to fill it in, I panic. I read facts and see pictures, but the sense of my being there, how it affected me at the time, is absent. I have no emotional overlay on the words and the pictures." She moved aside the volume she was reading and then put her head on his chest. "For now, for day-to-day functioning, I think I'll fill in my ignorance of information from that time on a need-to-know basis."

"Maybe we should go to Paris?" He risked the humor. It would be disastrous if it fell flat, a victim to serious reality.

"But you've been to Paris. Let's find some virgin territory." She smiled, forgiving him, for the idea of Paris covered all the adventures Erik might have experienced while she was away.

"That's a plan."

"Seriously, using the present, I'll build an emotional deposit to attach to what I have from before the big C. That will be enough." She resolved to form a bridge over the missing time, particularly Erik's life in those times.

The adjustments were working. She was content.

405

Chapter 49

Erik, Jerry and Paul met in Paul's office, down the hall from the boardroom, at 7:30 a.m. The weather in Miami was still warm for October. The men had hung their jackets over the back of their chairs.

"It just struck me; this is truly the beginning of the end for Amed," Jerry said.

"If we go with POPIC, it will be a purchase for cash or stock deal," Erik noted. "Then it will depend on how badly Pagan wants our company."

"And how the board feels about it. My reading on Reinhart is he's getting some support," Jerry said. He glanced at Erik. Because of his great affection for Erik, Jerry was suffering vicariously as he thought of the letdown he must be going through. The role of leader came so naturally to Erik it will be difficult to take second chair. He was convinced Amed, in its new form, would decline without the leader. Then there was the money. Control of a billion-dollar enterprise seemed to be worth fighting for. What did Erik really want? Jerry could remember several situations in which Erik had put aside the chance for wealth and power in favor of improving the status of the physicians he represented. At the time, Jerry had thought the positions were naive. With time, Jerry realized the acceptance and appreciation from his followers were vitally important to Erik. The irony was, the appreciation was really written on water, lasting nanoseconds and threatening to vanish in a minute if Erik took the slightest step toward self-reward at their expense. He was a tragic warrior, with both horns of the dilemma poised to pierce him. If he pushed for control of the merger and won, he would agonize over the selfish action; if he conceded and stayed on in second place, relinquishing his role as benevolent dictator would haunt him.

Jerry looked again. Erik's face displayed no clear emotion.

Paul passed sheets of paper to Erik and Jerry. "I've summarized the pros and cons of each company. I'll distribute these at the meeting. I hope we can come to a decision this morning."

Reviewing the lists, Jerry said, "There's a better chance we would remain in control as a subsidiary to PIPIC. With them out in California, with different mores, probably we would run the show here and just send them the money."

Paul put down the list. "It could give me a problem if they decided to move our top people to their home office. Janis would hate to move, being this late in our pregnancy. She's due in mid November."

"How she's doing?" Jerry asked.

"You wouldn't know she was pregnant! She runs this office; most of the collating for this merger is her effort. She takes care of the house. She's only gained twelve pounds. I was really worried, all the tales of problems with older women." He knocked on the wooden desk. "I should be quiet or I'll give myself a *keniner horra*."

"I knew she'd be all right. More important, how are you holding up?"

"I'm pacing. If we close this deal on time, we'll be ringing out the old company and ringing in the new master of the universe."

After studying the lists and discussing the highlights, the three left the office to join the others in the boardroom.

Winthrop was already in the room, explaining the status of Amed after the merger. "If you go with a mutual company and the emerging entity stays a mutual, there will be no stock, no cash transaction and you will negotiate for percentage control that each side will retain. For Amed, policyholders will no longer be assessable, which is a big plus."

"There will be no cash payout to the policyholders, is that what you said?" Sanchez asked.

"That's right."

"I understand PIPIC is a mutual," Reinhart offered. It was the first opportunity for him to plant a seed against the California company. He was sure the allure of cash would tilt the vote against it.

The meeting was called to order. Winthrop continued to describe the strengths and weaknesses of each candidate company.

PIPIC was a mutual, which would allow Amed and Erik as chairman to maintain some control. Seeing that the assets and net worth were similar, it would be a merger of equals, with one representing the West Coast and the other the East Coast; each company would be fairly independent. The chairman of each one would remain as department head; over all authority would be in a super board, with the chair either shared or rotated between the two chairmen.

From the body language, Erik could see that this was not Reinhart's choice. Responding negatively to Reinhart's signals, Erik's immediate emotional reaction was to favor PIPIC. He thought he could support this direction. It would remove assessability; there would be little necessity for change in the day-by-day operations or of the personnel; and he could remain head of the Amed division, and share or rotate chairmanship of the super company.

But is that where I want to go to share authority and even have to live under decisions made by another chairman? How badly do I want to hang on? Have I become so addicted to prestige and power? How far have I grown from the views I held when first we began? To be honest, I don't know. I like to be in charge, to see my fingerprints on the growth of the company. It is the second thing I do, my raison d'etre. Knowing I take a risk, every time I make a decision, knowing that being wrong would threaten my leadership, I still must make that decision, take that risk, to savor the taste of being the master.

Or do I have another path? It's clear it is not PIPIC. In my own defense, I had already planned to reject PIPIC on the basis of Davis' attitude toward his workers. There's no doubt in my mind we would be at odds almost immediately. I'm not sure POPIC offers a better course for me. I'll wait to hear from Winthrop.

"Any questions concerning PIPIC?" He scanned the table. Richard Garing was talking softly to Thomas Frond. They turned to face Winthrop as he stopped speaking.

"Excuse me," Frond said. "We were wondering how the board members' compensation would be handled? Does each new department continue paying as before? I don't know how PIPIC did it, but we began as a voluntary service. As the responsibility increased, our compensation reflected this change. At the present time I believe—with the drop in the board members' ability to earn in their practice—this honorarium is a minor but significant part of their income."

"I blush, but I agree with Frond," Fredrick Cannon spoke up.

"In a merger I recently handled," Winthrop said, "both sides agreed on consulting an expert on board compensation. He came in and established the going rate, so to speak. In that case, they established a bonus for each board member and built it into the merger documents representing services rendered up to the merger. It was approved, as part of the consent for merger."

"Was everyone aware of that clause?" Jack Reed asked.

"I doubt it," Winthrop said.

"You say that so easily. It sounds like the members of the board slipped one over on the shareholders, like stealing."

"That's not quite true. You see, two 'fairness opinions' are presented by experts, usually investment bankers, covering all aspects of the deal. They charge a good deal of money for that opinion, as you all will see. If that opinion is flawed, the banker gets sued for millions, so they are very careful to see that all items are within usually accepted standards."

"I'm glad we have you on our side," Kenneth Moninger said.

Winthrop nodded. "This is a very acceptable custom. After all, the reward to the board members is an infinitesimal amount compared to the moneys involved. Having reviewed your numbers, I would say you are at the low end of the scale. Boards of comparable size and responsibility receive two to three times as much."

Erik could sense the smell of money pleasantly filling the nostrils of the members of the board. Very satisfying.

Jerry laughed to himself, "At last, gentlemen, you have reached that most desirable platform of being profitable and virtuous."

"Perhaps we should move on to consider POPIC," Winthrop said. The board members were still uplifted by the news of a just bonus.

"Yes, please do," Reinhart said in his eagerness to argue, strongly but subtlety, in favor of POPIC, and cement his future.

Winthrop began. "POPIC is a corporation, registered and traded in NASDAQ. The action would be a straight purchase, although it would have the appearance of a merger. I remind you that your company, as a trust, is owned, if by anyone, by the policyholders. In exchange for the net worth, which POPIC will acquire, the trust is given either stock of POPIC, cash or a combination of the two. This money is used to settle all liabilities that are not taken on by POPIC. Some cash is set aside to cover IBNR events; that is incurred but not reported. The remaining funds are distributed to the policyholders." He paused. The surprise was easily apparent on their faces.

Jerry held up his hands. "The wonder of this is that the doctors never knew there was any value in purchasing their coverage from a trust. They are going to get a windfall and you all should suddenly have a fistful of new friends."

Jesse Gentile, quiet until now, asked, "How is it distributed?"

Winthrop considered his folder for a moment. "In a similar deal, they went back three years, then distributed, pro rata, related to the accumulated premium value over that period."

Trying not to look too obvious, all fingers rushed to pen and paper, busily multiplying three times his doctor's yearly premium. The scratching was audible; the only other sound in the room was the whirring of the fan.

"OK, I know how much I put in. How much do I get out?" Fredrick Cannon asked. All heads were nodding in accompaniment.

"Amed's net worth will be about equal to one year's premium, so if you divide your number by three, you will have rough estimate of your pay off."

Kenneth Moninger, family practitioner, spoke up, addressing Sanchez, surgeon. "You high specialists are going to get a windfall. I'm taking home practically nothing by comparison."

"But look at the premiums we paid in all these years; no chicken feed."

Winthrop pointed to Dr Moninger. "You touched a serious point; many of the doctors who have low premiums will say the surgical specialist got more protection for their premiums, and therefore, all policyholders should be treated equally, that a share is a share and shouldn't be related to the premium. In every situation where there is a good amount of money involved, like this, the first thing we inform the client is that they can expect a lawsuit, or law suits. And so I tell you today."

"Where there's money there is always trouble, even when it's good news," Thomas Frond said. "I recently read about one man shooting his partner over splitting a lottery ticket they both purchased."

"Well, you are warned. I'd like to go on," Winthrop said.

"It's 1:30 already," Erik noted. "Let's take thirty minutes for lunch. It's set up in the kitchen."

Chapter 50

Sanchez took the fourth hard-backed chair, joining Erik, Jerry and Paul sitting around a glass-topped table in the kitchen. He watched the movement. Doctors Reed, Garing, Frond and Cannon gathered at another similar table. Stanley Reinhart led Doctors Gentile, Harmon, and Moninger back into the boardroom, carrying their lunch trays. Their food was selected from stacks of ham, cheese, fried chicken with orange sauce (the color, not the taste), pickles, onion slices, Cole slaw, and potato salad. Bread and rolls were in wooden wicker baskets. It took awhile for everyone to find the silverware, the napkins and the beverages. When seated, each group fell into separate conversations.

Once settled around the table, Reinhart, sitting at the chairman's spot, asked, "Well, what do you think?"

He decided to be neutral at this time to listen and save his big arguments for the entire board at the final vote.

Moninger started. "I was impressed with Bill Davis from PIPIC. He seemed to be comfortable with the changing scene. Pagan, from POPIC, was more fixed in his ways. I think it's important to be flexible, what with the big commercial companies returning to the trough."

Dr Harmon, sitting furthest from Reinhart, said, "And Davis is aggressive. He's already looking at the neighboring states for expansion. All the experts say that eventually there will be only three or four national companies; all the rest will be history. If we want to be part of the action, 'Go west, young man.'"

Reinhart was silent. As each man talked, he was fashioning a rebuttal to use later in the day. However, at this moment, he said nothing and nodded his head affirmatively. He expected the opponents to wear themselves out in these primaries.

It was 2:00 in the afternoon before the board reconvened.

Erik stood up. "Between the literature, the formal presentations and the informal chatter around the lunch tables, I think it's fair to say we probably have made up our minds. Mr. Winthrop will stay with us until the voting is finished, and then he'll go home to do the detailed work. Once we choose a candidate, there will follow extensive negotiations on many points. After the vote, I will like a motion authorizing me to make those definitive decisions."

"I think we can do that now," Sanchez said. "In fact, it might be a good idea. We don't know how much blood will flow until the final vote."

"I'll second that."

"I see no objections," Reinhart said, surprising everyone at the table. Reinhart thought he could buy support from the neutrals with this gesture.

"Make it unanimous?"

All hands went up.

"Thank you. This next vote is the biggest decision you will have to make on behalf of Amed. It seems an appropriate moment for any last minute thoughts."

Reinhart surveyed the table. "It may be that we have a consensus at the moment. I suggest a motion for either candidate, a second and discussion. That will bring it into focus." He believed he had five votes to help him push POPIC. The momentum could easily carry the others. This move would give him a strong point with Pagan, demonstrating his value.

"I make a motion to choose PIPIC as a merger partner," Dr. Harmon said.

Without hesitation, Moninger raised his hand. "I second the motion."

There was a stir; Sanchez pushed his chair back, and Dr. Cannon stood up, walked around his chair and sat down.

Erik watched the activity. He thought, *There's no consensus at the moment.* "The motion's open for discussion, pro or con."

"I like the idea of converting to stocks or cash. You can't do that with a mutual," Sanchez said. Reinhart put Sanchez in his camp.

Paul did not want to participate directly, but passed a page from

Winthrop's presentation across the table to Dr. Garing. He read the note, held up his hand. "I quote: 'Once stable, the mutual would begin the process of converting to a stock company. With this accomplished we would have the liquidity of stock to barter with or purchase acquisitions.' Anthony, what you say is true, but if PIPIC converts, in time it would be of no significance."

Reinhart couldn't decide where Garing stood. In his mind, he put a question mark next to Garing.

At the other end of the table, Erik was playing the same game: who will vote for whom. *What does Reinhart really want?* Erik remembered hearing that Reinhart had met with Pagan on at least two occasions. *Have to give him credit; he's being pretty quiet so far.* Erik thought, *I'll hold my comments, but as of now, I favor POPIC. Could it be that in the end, Reinhart and I will be on the same side? I should re-think my position.*

"By the way Bill Davis talked, I'm sure PIPIC will look upon us as a new kid on the block. Just because they started six months before us, they'll bully us like an older brother." Dr. Frond spoke up.

Reinhart finally broke his silence. "I have been listening to arguments with great interest. The question of how the staff will be treated under the new regime is of great concern to me. In that regard, I believe POPIC's attitude toward its personnel is more like ours."

Further discussion went on until 6 o'clock. Questions were frequently repeated, at times receiving different answers based on another point of view. It was as though the group knew that if they continued enquiring they would not have to make a decision.

Mr. Winthrop, sensing the redundancy, having seen this phenomenon of procrastination before, said, "If there are no new questions, Mr. Chairman, do you think it might be time to call for a vote?"

"I needed that push. I think we are like the man planning to propose marriage: too many questions, too few answers and yet he has to make a decision. You have been very helpful, and I thank you." He raised his head and addressed the group. "The motion on the floor is to approve PIPIC as the candidate as a merger partner."

Winthrop put up his hand, indicating a pause. "May I suggest a modification of the motion for clarity?"

"Please do."

"...Pending agreement of all specific conditions outlined above, referring to conditions previously discussed."

Erik pointed at Dr. Harmon. "Do you wish to modify your motion accordingly?"

"Yes."

"And Kenneth, your second also?"

"Sounds good to me."

"Those in favor of the motion, raise your hands."

Harmon Moninger and Garing raised their hands.

"Those against?" Sanchez and Frond responded. Both Erik and Reinhart could see the trouble: If the remainder of the group abstained, according to the trust's bylaws, the majority of those voting would carry the day. Each hesitated, waiting to see if the other would commit himself and vote nay, to create a tie and defeat the motion.

After the longest moment on record, Reinhart raised his hand.

"Those abstaining?" Gentile, Cannon, and Reed acknowledged that position. Erik, as chairman, reserved the privilege of voting only to make or break a tie, and so did not declare, holding that trump card.

"A main concern is the status of the present board after the merger. We probably would lean toward the company that most favored us," Reed said.

Erik turned to Winthrop, who said, "It is wise to keep each motion simple. Perhaps you could separate the choosing of a company from further details. After all, your vote today only declares in which direction you are to proceed. If, along the way, there is a deal breaker, such as the status of the board in the future, you my back off and reconsider. Tonight we should choose a direction so that we can proceed."

As though on signal, each board member turned to the folders before him that contained data about the candidates. Only the rustle of papers and the soft murmur of the ceiling fan broke the silence.

"Let's take a ten-minute stretch," Erik said.

"Is this the seventh inning?" Cannon said. "I would have said the ninth."

Erik stood and walked to the back of the room. "Anyone else need a refill?" he asked as he picked up the coffee urn and filled his cup. Moving to that end of the room put Erik standing next to Reinhart. He thought, *It's true, politics makes strange bedfellows. Unless Reinhart is trying to finesse, he is in favor of POPIC. And for entirely different reasons, so am I.*

On the next round of voting, the urgency became apparent to establish a consensus after all the study, conversations, and debate.

Reed pushed his folder into the center of the table. "That's enough. I try to find a logical explanation for one over the other, but it ends up fifty-fifty. Yet, my gut says POPIC. I make a motion to choose POPIC, with all the additions suggested by Mr. Winthrop."

"I second the motion," continued Sanchez.

In the end, Harmon, Moninger and Garing conceded, and to present a unanimous vote for the record went with POPIC.

Chapter 51

Erik stood up as Pagan entered the room. As a benevolent conquering hero, he had come to Erik's office. In Erik's eyes, Pagan was just a bit larger, a bit taller when seen through the magnification of success. "Congratulations, you have impressed the board."

"And you?"

"I didn't have to vote, but I did to make it unanimous." He offered Pagan a chair and sat next to him.

"I'm glad; with that kind of cooperation I believe we will work well together. After all, being number two in a billion-dollar operation is nothing to sneeze at."

Erik remained silent. Was Pagan already assuming that Amed agreed on having him as the chairman?

"You look surprised, but then, I have the advantage in being able to study the members of your board. Thanks to some inside information, I know how they think. For one thing, I know they are independent—you never bothered to buy their loyalty with preferential treatment. You think they look up to you for that, but they don't; in fact, it makes them envious and suspicious. There is no one as dangerous to others than an incorruptible man."

It jarred Erik to hear his deficiencies verbalized. Pagan went on, "When I state that if I'm not sole chairman, it is a deal breaker, they will concur. It will give them the opportunity to be righteous, declaring their actions will protect the policyholders. In their hearts, they will be delighted. They always thought you were too arrogant and that any one of them could have run the outfit."

Pagan knew he touched a nerve, for he'd initially had the same doubts about his command. The difference was that he had taken the steps to put the majority of his board in compromising positions giving favorable contracts, undeserved appointments, investment managing opportunities and legal assignments. He found it hard to believe that Erik, who had the same material, played it so Boy Scout straight.

Erik could hear the fine Italian hand of Dr. Stanley Reinhart in Pagan's words, but also the ring of truth. He wondered how many pieces of gold Reinhart charged for his fifth column activity. "You are well informed, and may be right about the vote."

"Look at the reality of the deal; it is almost transparent. You will still be seen as the leader in the East. We will appear together at the national conventions, with no epaulets. There is enough glory to go around. A one billion dollar empire."

"Will I have complete control over my personnel in this office?" Erik felt nauseated at having to ask the question. Was he already surrendering, accepting the board's rejection and, in his mind, moving down to a subservient position?

"There are a great many decisions to make together, and this is one of them. Didn't you say that fairly intelligent people, given the same facts and having the same motivation, would reach the same conclusions? If we use common sense we should have no problem."

"I'm particularly concerned about my people," he persisted.

"You sound like Moses. 'Make my people free.' Let's lighten up. It will be all right."

And at that moment, Erik knew it would not be OK. What was the alternative? *Can I really let go of everything? If only I were truly motivated by righteousness, I would strut away, head held high. But I know me; seeking compromise, don't give up the little ground you have gained.*

Think of where you would be, even as a vice chairman. Remember, you started with nothing in this game. Why give Pagan the satisfaction of walking away with all the marbles? And what will I do tomorrow and tomorrow as I follow in annoyance and regret?

Erik looked at Pagan, the image of success, and tried to imagine what he had done to hold on to his command? And how many veneers of virtue he had to shed, and was it worth it? At this moment, maybe yes.

Pagan rose and walked to the door. "See you at the meeting. Everything will work out all right, you have my word." He smiled, waved and was gone.

Erik thought, *That and ten cents...*

Chapter 52

Frances was sitting in the living room. The early afternoon sun was warm on her shoulders as is poured from the west, through the tall glass of the floor to ceiling windows. For a brief time she admired the view available from the southern exposure; the long leaves of the tall palms on either side of the pool were gently moved by the breeze. In the lake beyond a cormorant disappeared below the surface, to reappear with a fish in its slender, hooked bill. With a snap of the bird's neck the snapper was tossed into the air, for an instant free, its scales shining in the sun, and shaking off water, and then it fell, spinning down the gullet of the cormorant. Frances shook her head. "Too bad." She returned to scanning the list of events in 1975. She pondered the returning memory that had identified many random facts pertaining to the years up to 1975. It was a game: Remembering a happening, she would confer with the list to find out what had transpired.

Nixon's team was in trouble. The list stated that on 2/21/1975, John Mitchell, H. R. Holderman and John D. Ehrlichman had been sentenced to two-and-a-half to eight years.

She laughed to herself, "So that's how it turned out."

She put the list on the table next to the couch when she heard Erik's car in the garage. Walking smoothly, she reached the door to the garage. In another minute, he was in front of her. He put his arm around her as they walked back to the living room. The gesture felt so natural.

"Did you know Holderman went to jail for two-and-a-half years?" she asked, bubbling with her newfound information.

"I probably did at one time. Are you filling in the blanks?" She thought he was impressed with her progress. He said, "That was a very stormy time. Nixon and his team really came down the mountain" Seeing the lists on the couch, he said, "You could be a threat with this instant knowledge."

He stopped, judging Frances' response to his attempt at levity. Before the stroke, she would have come back with some witty answer. He waited.

"This is only the beginning; you are in big trouble, young man." She laughed.

She's truly back! he thought. *She is so proud of herself.* He sat next to her. She turned and kissed him, her lips parted.

For Erik, it was the beginning of a new era. The fifteen-year gap disappeared. He felt the original Frances sitting next to him. Frances, the obligation, burned away and from the pyre of sadness, phoenix-like, the soul mate arose. The unfocused eyes became brilliantly clear; effortlessly his unverbalized thoughts were understood. The transformation seemed to take place suddenly, though he knew time had passed. In the last few weeks she absorbed the basic rhythm of the household, accepted phone calls from Erik's friends and even initiated calls in return.

Jerry was a great help. He introduced her to women who offered latest gossip, idiom and fads. Her days were full.

On Friday morning, they were gathered in Frances' family room.

Shirley, one of Jerry's ladies, pointed to the television screen. "They are about to launch the tenth space shuttle."

For Frances it touched another key into the past.

"I remember the first space shuttle," she said. "We were about ten miles from the lift-off, on a roadway south of Cape Canaveral. At that distance, it did not look that big, but the vibrations came through my feet, and I could feel and almost taste the ozone in the air. The noise made me cover my ears.

"It began to climb, so slowly at first, I wondered if it would leave the ground. Streams of misty white gases poured from its sides. Then it lifted, faster and faster. I held my breath as it began to tilt in our direction. I didn't know it was supposed to do that. In seconds, it straightened out into a graceful arch, shrunk to a dot and was gone below the horizon. Everyone stood there staring at the empty sky and then began to applaud." She sat back in her chair, gazing at the shimmering water in the pool outside the family room window, remembering! She thought, *What a joy. I know I'll get used to it, expect it, take it for granted in time, but now it's heavenly.*

The following day was Saturday. Erik took advantage of the opportunity to sleep late, and not get up at his usual six o'clock.

When he woke, he felt pleasantly content as he watched Frances enter the room. With her came the aroma of frying bacon and toast. "Breakfast is ready, sleepy head."

He slipped into his loafers and padded behind her into the kitchen.

"You know, Lacy is off for the day," she said. "This is my P.S. maiden voyage into preparing breakfast."

"P.S.?"

"Post stroke, of course. No need to hide it or step around it. It happened and it's behind us. I'm so grateful I'm alive again! I know I'm going to come back all the way. And when you taste my pancakes, eggs, bacon and toast, you will know it too." She danced around him and guided him to his chair.

When they finished eating, he lifted his coffee cup. "To the best P.S. chef I know."

She took a small bow.

"I believe you are ready for the next step, driving!"

"Oh, no."

"Oh, yes."

"OK, yes it is. Let's go."

He helped her clear the table and stack the dishes. Taking her hand, he led her to the garage. They climbed aboard the Cadillac, with Erik behind the wheel.

After driving around the block two times, Erik stopped the car, got out from the driver's side, and walked to the passenger's. "Are you ready?"

"If you're willing to take the risk, so am I."

He pulled his sunglasses from his coat pocket and put them on.

"You look like a test pilot."

Frances stepped out of the car, walked to the driver's side and slid in behind the wheel. "Let's see, clutch in, give some gas and slowly, with grace, release the clutch and we are on our way."

"Your time away is showing; they did away with the clutch. It's a lot easier now; turn the key and then just step on the gas, also with grace. By the way, there are power brakes, so a small touch goes a long way. To stop or slow down, your right foot moves from gas pedal to the brake; apply gently."

She nodded obediently, grasped the wheel, touched the pedal and the car began to move. She turned into the street and accelerated to thirty miles per hour. "Feels good, very natural. Now I am really free! Just a few more cards to uncover and I'll be truly pre-stroke."

They rode for almost an hour. "I'm ready to go home," Frances declared. "The concentration I need for my first time driving is exhausting." Reaching their house, she stopped at the curb. "Maybe you better take it in. Tomorrow I'll do it, but today I'm too tired."

They changed places and he steered the car into the garage.

"Before we go in, I want to tell you, you are marvelous."

"I made some pretty sloppy turns out there, particularly right-hand turns."

"I'm not talking about your driving, which was splendid. I mean the whole P.S. challenge; congratulations."

She turned her head to see his face. "So serious?"

"Two months before you got sick, I bought something to put away until our anniversary. After your stroke, I wasn't up to celebrating anything." He reached into his side pocket and pulled out a small box. "I know it's not the right day for your birthday, but maybe it's the perfect time." He opened the box. "To you on your majestic recovery; to you because I love you."

Looking into the box, she saw a white gold band with eight diamonds mounted across the top.

He freed it from the silk cushion and put it on her left fourth finger.

She began to cry. "You have just made my world complete." She hugged him, her tears splashing on his cheek. "I love you."

Chapter 53

For the last six months, Paul had acted like Edward R Morrow, reporting on the war of the pregnancy, bringing a blow-by-blow translation from motherhood to English, to Erik, Edward and Jerry. Unlike Morrow's war, all has been quiet on the bearing front. Morning sickness was almost nonexistent. Her weight gain was under control: twenty pounds. But the messages originated from Janis, who was committed to having Paul enjoy the pregnancy. Her true report to the boys would be entirely different.

The changes in the breasts began early in the pregnancy; in fact, it had been these that made her aware of the baby. She thought it was ironic. All her life she would have liked to have larger breasts. She had heard of a procedure to accomplish that but never followed up on it. In the first months, she had been proud. She would dance into the bedroom, stand before Paul and seductively remove her towel to reveal her new jewels. Even then, they had been slightly tender.

As the months went by the shows stopped and mild groaning began. Bra size increased and the materials became more substantial in an attempt to accommodate the enhancement.

For the last three months, the monsters were not for exhibit.

Sleeping presented another problem; the growing watermelon protruded in front, not like obesity, which in a kind fashion spread all around. Sleeping on her back was all right, but if she dared to turn, she would be forcefully reminded that she was pregnant.

Janis continued to work full time, adjusting her wardrobe as necessary.

On the thirty-fifth week, she noted a small amount of vaginal bleeding. She walked from the ladies' room to Paul's office. He looked up as she appeared in the doorway.

She said, "One advantage of working in your husband's office is you don't have to surprise him over the phone." She moved to sit down across the desk from him. "I sat in this chair when I first came in here to apply for a job." She studied her husband's face. He looked so vulnerable. For all their time together, he remained ignorant of women, and more recently of pregnant women. Until now, she painted a pleasant picture, so for him it was a walk in the park. It was, as she wanted him to believe. Now he must get on board, for this bleeding may be nothing, or something serious.

She wondered if the odor of pregnancy reached across the desk. He didn't seem to mind.

"You are beautiful this morning," he said, and then, "A surprise?"

"I saw some blood this morning. I'm going to call Dr. Osborne." She watched him melt with fear. The man who was an oak tree of strength in the hurricane and all other matters was a tremulous aspen leaf when it came to things feminine. "It's probably nothing." She patted his outstretched hand. On the first mention of blood, he had reached out toward her. "Let me have the phone." She began dialing. "It was smart, using an OB in the same building."

"That's right, he's on Erik's floor."

After completing her call, she said, "He can see me right away."

"He thinks it's serious?"

"He didn't say. I told him what I had and he said, 'Come right up.'"

In the elevator, on the way to Dr. Osborne's office, Janis tried to recall the lecture on complications of pregnancy she had attended some months ago. Bleeding following intercourse. She ruled that out as that hadn't occurred in the last month. Before she could continue, she reached the doctor's floor. There had been no pain associated with this bleeding. She'd had some cramping last week, but now she was pain free. She walked into the doctor's waiting room. "I'm Mrs. Arpin."

Dr. Osborne came out of his private office. "Come in, Janis." He put his arm around her shoulders and led her into his office. He sat her in a comfortable chair and walked behind his desk. "When did it begin?"

"This morning. It wasn't very much, half a cup, maybe. I have no pain. I'm scared, mostly."

They moved to the examining room. While Janis undressed and donned a blue wraparound paper robe, the nurse rolled a new section of paper over the table. When Janis came out from the dressing room, the nursed assisted Janis onto the table.

"Well, let's see." Dr. Osborne rubbed the stethoscope on his palm. "Don't want to scare him with a cold scope." He put the instrument on her belly and listened. "Good sounds." He placed his hand on the skin. A visible thrust touched his palm. "And he's kicking splendidly. You can sit up."

She was surprised; he had skipped the usual pelvic exam. Idiotically, she thought of the joke about the difference between a ten-dollar and a fifteen-dollar pelvic examination being the thumb motion on the clitoris. The joke was told in gestures rather than words. *Probably my brain's distracting technique. Am I really that frightened?*

As though sensing her discomfort, he said, "I don't want to enter the vagina until we know where the placenta is."

"Placenta? I thought that was in the wall of the uterus, giving oxygen and nutrients to Tommy. I read your pamphlet."

"Very good. Yes, that's what it does. And usually no problem. But sometime in the fifth week, the embryo's placenta chooses the bottom of the uterus to burrow in." He stropped there.

"Why does that cause bleeding?" She sensed his concern.

"It's hard to say at this point. We'll get an ultrasound to see exactly what's going on."

Over the phone, he made the necessary arrangements. Janis stopped off on the second floor to tell Paul what was happening. Then she was off to Central General Hospital.

Two hours later, she was back in Dr. Osborne's office.

"It's called 'Placenta Previa.' As we talked about, the placenta is across the cervical opening. As the head pushes down and the cervix stretches, the placenta may be torn from the wall. For you, at the moment, it is a small segment."

"What does that mean for me?"

"You will need a caesarean section. The placenta is in the way, and if the cervix dilates fully, there is the danger of hemorrhage."

Janis grasped the potential danger of her position. "What do we do?"

"The object is to get past the thirty-sixth week. Any time after that is a plus. I'm going to put you to bed in the hospital. Rest and observation are the prescriptions in this case."

"I'm with you." She sat back and watched Dr. Osborne phone to make the admission arrangements. Very smoothly, Osborne had a nurse usher Janis out of the office, stopping briefly at Paul's desk to inform him of the events, and then on to the hospital. It seemed like no time that Janis was tucked into her bed in room six one seven.

The semi-crisis seemed to have been resolved. There was no further bleeding and the baby appeared to be stable.

On the third day, Jerry, Erik and Paul gathered around Janis' bed. The caesarean section was scheduled for the following Wednesday. It would be three days beyond the thirty-sixth week.

"Talking about perfect timing," Paul said. "Here I am, up to my eyeballs with work getting ready for the final board meeting and you decide on taking a vacation. But I forgive you."

"Don't listen to him." Janis spoke to Erik and Jerry. "He's been sneaking me work from the office ever since I've been here."

"I thought it would be occupational therapy," Paul said sheepishly and then laughed.

Janis turned to Erik. "Is the merger a *fait accompli?*"

"That's not as important as you getting through this. After all, Thomas—is that what you are going to name him?"

Janis nodded.

Erik continued, "Thomas is our only heir—your son, our nephew. We intend to thoroughly spoil him."

Erik returned to her question. "I think it will go through. I have a problem to solve that's still unanswered in my mind. You see..." His speech was interrupted when he saw Janis fall back on her pillow; her face was white. Her scream filled the room and then there was silence.

For that brief moment no one moved. Then Paul leaped forward, gently shaking Janis. She only moaned. Jerry squeezed the nurse-call pump and then threw it on the bed and rushed out of the room toward the nurse's station, shouting, "Nurse, Nurse!" Erik switched the blood pressure monitoring machine from auto to manual. It began functioning. Before it finished its cycle, he saw the red stain rapidly enlarging on the sheet over her pelvis, below the steep curve of her pregnant belly.

The blood pressure machine beeped and showed ninety over sixty. He pushed the emergency intercom system button. "This is Dr. Nostrom. A liter of Ringer's lactate STAT to six one seven with IV set-up. The patient is in shock, hemorrhaging. Don't wait for the IV team, I'll start it." He rushed to the end of the bed and began turning the trendelenburg lever, lowering the head of the bed.

The nurse appeared at the doorway. "I called Dr. Osborne; we are to take Mrs. Arpin directly to the OR. Right in the bed."

Erik took the IV apparatus from her hand. With a continuous motion, he passed the alcohol swab over the crease in her left elbow, wrapped a tourniquet around the arm, found a vein and inserted the catheter-covered needle through the skin. Blood appeared in the base of syringe, letting him know he was in the vein. He removed the needle, leaving the thin catheter in place. The nurse nodded approvingly. While she prepared the IV bottle and tubing, Erik secured the catheter with tape, already torn to size and lined up on the nurse's forearm. The liquid began to flow.

Two orderlies appeared and began working the bed through the doorway. Jerry was back from the nurse's station and began pulling on the foot of the bed. Erik moved from the side to the back as the space between the bed and the doorsill disappeared.

The entourage reached the elevator and commandeered it by shooing the passengers out of the cab. They obeyed the loud command, and with questioning looks from one to the other, moved into the hall. The group pushed the bed into the cab. One comic moment was when all of the team was squeezed into one side of the bed so that no one could reach the elevator button. Jerry spread himself across the bed, pushed the button for the OR floor. Only as he stood up could the nurse see that the front of his tan cashmere jacket was wet and stained red.

Dr. Michel, the anesthesiologist, met them at the elevators, and as they moved toward the OR, he began questioning Paul. Allergies? Past medical history? Asthmas, high blood pressure, transfusions or surgery in the past, present medications?

It was a litany. "No allergies. I don't know for sure about surgery, or the rest. Only medicine for the pregnancy, Dr. Osborne knows. He should be here."

On cue, Dr. Osborne came down the hall, a tall, heavyset, blonde, middle-aged man dressed in surgical greens. As he approached, he said, "Paul, how you holding up?"

Paul turned from the anesthesiologist. "Dr. Michel wants to know about the medicines Janis is taking." He felt clumsy, inadequate and helpless.

Should he have known the medicines? He should have made a list. He hoped Dr. Osborne would know. Of course, he would. *It's not your fault or failure.*

"I'm worried about Janis. What's happening?" The sight of the enlarging red stain, now wet and bloody, frightened him. He felt weak. He had a sudden realization: Janis had always been the strong one; she ran the home and the do diligence part of the office. He had become dependent on her, minute by minute, during the day and at night. A curtain dropped over his thinking as he brought into consciousness the concept of no Janis. He became a spectator, evaluating Jerry and Erik. He tried to understand Dr. Michel as the doctor began to explain.

"Remember, the reason we put her in the hospital was so we could watch her? I'm glad we did." He continued walking beside the bed as it was rushed through the doors of the operating suite. "You have to wait here. I'll talk to you as soon as I finish." He disappeared behind the closing doors of the operating room as he followed the bed carrying Janis.

Paul watched Erik move to the nurse's station. "I'm Dr. Nostrom. I wonder if I could use your phone?"

"I know you, Dr. Nostrom, of course you may."

Erik dialed and then listened as the distant phone sounded. After six rings, "Hello, who is this?" Frances' soft voice inquired.

"I'm at the hospital. Janis began bleeding and she's in the operating room right now. Jerry and Paul are here. Paul looks done in."

"I'll be right over. I'll get Lacy to drive. I know I could, but she goes faster than I do."

Twenty minutes later, she reached the operating waiting room on the second floor and joined Paul and the others. She peck-kissed him on the cheek. "Are you all right?"

"Thanks for coming." He thought, *Frances has been through so much, and here she is, calm and concerned about me.* Humor rose as a defensive mechanism. "Erik needs you." He smiled.

Paul went down the hall toward the coffee machine. Erik saw where he was going and joined him. "You'll need help." He turned to the group. "You all want coffee, and black?" Heads nodded.

The coffee was distributed. Paul sat staring at the door of the waiting room as though he could will the doctor out of the OR. It has been two hours and ten minutes, he noted, as he checked his watch for the hundredth time. He refused to think of tomorrow.

Chapter 54

Janis opened her eyes to see the ceiling moving rapidly, its white acoustical panels being punctuated by bright top hat lights. She felt the sheets covering her and the jolting as the gurney traversed the irregular tile floor. With each bump, pain filled the lower portion of her abdomen. She tried to call out, but her mouth was dry with an acid-metallic taste. Her tongue seemed to fill her mouth completely. She turned her head and was aware of a tube in her nose, preventing movement. It hurt the right naris. With thoughts from ancient times when she had been a teenage nurse-volunteer in Central Hospital, she recalled it must be a nasogastric Levine tube going to her stomach. She must have vomited. Then she smelled the faint pungent odor of the confirming evidence. Another bump and another wave of pain. "It hurts!" she screamed.

"Do you feel the rubber ball in your hand?" Dr. Osborne said as he walked beside the stretcher.

"Where? Oh, this thing." She held up a blue squeeze bulb.

"Yes, it's for pain. Just close your hand on it. It shoots medicine for pain right into your system."

Her thinking was still foggy, but as soon as she comprehended what the doctor said, she squeezed hard. "All right!"

"Everything is all right, just take a deep breath."

As the Demerol sped through her system, she closed her eyes. In her dream state, the imprint of the events as she entered the operating room enlarged and reduced, swirling around as though looking through a kaleidoscope. She rolled on one side, with sharp local pain in her back; her trunk and legs lost their feeling, and she felt panic as she fought to understand why she was paralyzed. Warmth covered her whole body, and she slipped away. Swimming up from deep in the ocean she had a sensation of being ripped apart, her belly enlarging like a balloon being filled with helium, and then empty, muscles relaxed, and from a far distance the sound of a kitten crying—no, it's a baby sound. Her head cleared. She was able to focus. It was Dr. Osborne looking down on her.

"Welcome back. You are fine, your son is fine."

On hearing the news of her son, she was relieved. She closed her eyes, squeezed the bulb and quietly retired from consciousness one more time.

They reached the recovery room. The nurse hooked up the leads from the oximiter and the EKG, adjusted the flow of nasal oxygen to two liters, attached the nasogastric tube to intermittent suction, hung the IV bag onto an arm on an aluminum pole and found a place to secure the urine drainage bag on the side of the bed.

Dr. Osborne patted Janis' shoulder. "Looking good." He then retrieved the chart from the foot of the bed and scribbled post-op orders. After reading the orders to the nurse, he headed for the waiting room.

Chapter 55

The last hurricane of the season was being charted in the waters off Cuba. The air was still. A sense of anticipation had people walking more carefully and talking in a whisper.

As they waited for their own virtual hurricane, the board members walked carefully and spoke softly as they filed in.

At the last meeting, they had voted to go with Pagan's company, POPIC; in reality, all that remained was deciding who would run the company: Pagan, Erik or a co-chair?

Erik had no papers before him. He sat at the head of the long board table, waiting until they all were seated.

Last night Erik at first had found it difficult to sleep. He had walked to the kitchen and put some ice in his milk. The room had been colder than he liked.

Pulling his bathrobe tight around him, he thought, *Am I cold from the weather or from fright?* As he slowly drank, the ache in his mid abdomen eased slightly, but he was denied the usual complete relief; the cause of the pain was too great. In fact, muscular tension had spread around to his left lower back. He rubbed the area with some temporary improvement. He brought the problem into his consciousness for the hundredth time. If the board stood with him and demanded at least a co-chairman status for him and

Pagan, all would be well. He would be able to protect those who worked so enthusiastically for him and the company; and he could control the evaluation of new applicants and renewal physicians, buffering against unproven bias such as age and nationality.

He tried to find a heroic position to present in his favor, a position that would have them see the need to support him. As he mulled over these individual statements, they fell harmlessly to the floor.

"What was I thinking? Of course, they don't give a damn for those things, not when they compare my stance to that of Pagan's, which represents strength and cunning. I can't blame them for feeling more protected in his shadow.

"That it was me who put this company together from nothing now means nothing. I would plan and they would only ratify, but would convince themselves it was their idea." And he laughed as his next thought took form, for he had first heard it applied to one of his medicine professors: Even when I was wrong I was profound!

He put his head on his hands, elbows on the kitchen table. He suddenly felt fatigued. His trunk rested on the table, his head shifting to lean on his folded arms. After a while he got up, walked to the sink and threw water onto his face, allowing it to run down his arms and drench his trousers.

"Of course they will reluctantly go for Pagan as the sole chairman! I'll listen, but I know, in the end, they will go for Pagan. Goddamn it! And what can I do?"

He knew he was hung on the horns of a true dilemma. He could accept it humbly. *Thank you for giving me the honor of serving in the shadow of such a marvelous leader as Pagan. I will do my best to follow his orders, and I will have no original thoughts. In Pagan's dictatorial mode, my ideas would be wasted. I would probably wither and die in that environment.*

Or, I could accept the position and from day one plot to upset Pagan. With some well-designed letters of innuendo to the other members of the board of directors, I could watch him carefully in the future, and uncover and expose one of his illegal distributions of rewards to his favorites. A leopard never changes its spots; he is bound to continue in his old ways. The problem is he is so much better in the conniving role than I am.

Erik went out onto the pool area. The clouds began to rush across a normal November sky. Yet, there was no evidence of an imminent hurricane. He thought, *More than one hanging question will be decided tomorrow. Hanging, indeed.*

WANT IS A GROWING GIANT

The moonlight's reflection on the water was blue-silver rippling on the wind's stirring. The ethereal overview momentarily clashed with the storm of conflict raging within Erik. Gradually his fists relaxed, his hands opened and he rested them against his thighs. He saw the chaise lounge at poolside, canvas stretched over polyethylene plastic tubes; how simple yet how strong and right. He sat down, viewing the black and silver pool water, the grass-covered slope leading to the lake and beyond, the black silhouettes of the line of oak trees. *They will be here the day after tomorrow no matter what I do, as will thousands of other strands of my life. Why act as though there is a gun to my head and if I make the wrong move, it will blow my brains out? It isn't that way! See the humor in it! My whole life is a nanosecond in time. Stop the fear! Tomorrow do what you have to do and the hell with it.*

He returned to his bed and slept, unmoved until the morning.

Chapter 56

The members settled down, conversations trailed off and a momentary silence fell on the group as they waited for Erik to speak. "Good morning." He surveyed the members. Was he ever close to any of them? Their faces already reflected the protective position they would have to take against his anger and disappointment when they failed him in their vote for Pagan. He suspected that last night they'd had a meeting without him to give them strength in numbers. He thought, *If I suddenly had a heart attack and fell to the floor, each one of them would rush to resuscitate me, but as I seem to be standing strong, they each become a Brutus.*

"We are nearing the completion of this merger. Unanimously, we have selected POPIC as our partner. The policyholders will be given the opportunity to accept cash, stock or a combination of the two. Mr. Winthrop has even arranged for the few dissidents who refuse to sell."

Winthrop stood up. "I believe we have covered all contingencies. After all, we are not reinventing the wheel here. Mergers like this one have become very popular. I want to emphasize so there is no misunderstanding that this is a cash merger. POPIC is buying Amed. Any talk about a merger of equals is only for window dressing. This information may help when the question of control comes up." He smiled at Pagan and sat down.

"*Et tu,* Winthrop," Erik said to himself. However, it was expected. Like all of them, Winthrop chose to be on the winning side.

Winthrop continued from his seat, "After today, all of the decisions reached today will be on the ballot at the annual POPIC stockholders meeting and will have to be approved by two-thirds of Amed's policyholders." And to Erik, "I understand you have arranged with Ballot-Go, the survey company to help collect the votes?"

Erik nodded. "They said it would take about six weeks, so we are right on schedule if we finish this business in the next few days."

Chapter 57

Dr. Stanley Reinhart took his usual seat at the far end of the table. He looked along the table, briefly judging the face of each member, and stopped at Erik. The sense of competitiveness was gone. He thought, *Poor Erik, he is sitting there, waiting for the blow of words to shatter him. He thinks his choices are bad or terrible. He is not alone; I join him in his misery.*

Reinhart was recalling his last conversation with Pagan. They had been walking together in the hallway toward the boardroom.

"Before we go in I thought it would be a good idea if we established my exact title and area of authority after the merger. We had talked about control of the eastern division, which would be Amed."

Pagan took a step to the side so he could face Reinhart directly. "I don't remember our conversations coming to those conclusions. I believe I thanked you for your help." He laughed, "Yours was a Judas-like performance, as I think about it." He patted Reinhart on the shoulder. "We will find a place for you."

Reinhart was confused. He had been convinced his control of the eastern division was established. He tried to read Pagan's expression. The previous friendly, understanding and supportive mask was gone. It was replaced by a dictatorial, my-way-or-the-highway demeanor. Reinhart felt a wave of panic burn through him. *What does he mean, he'll find a place for me? We agreed on the place for me!* Then the thought struck him: *Pagan is sure he has won; all that remains is the shouting of congratulations. He doesn't need me. I hope I'm wrong.*

Pagan stopped walking. "Stanley, at the moment, you are not familiar with my routine. Perhaps you will be in time. For the present, I need someone in the eastern division who is in sync with me. Hubbard is coming in from Ohio."

The words devastated Reinhart. "What?"

"I know," Pagan said. "But I will keep my word. I have a desk for you in Ohio."

"What in the hell would I do in Ohio? My life, my practice are here."

Pagan said, "I thought you were a company man through and through?"

Reinhart could see Pagan was enjoying this tightening of the screw. A sadistic bastard! "I cannot do that."

"I tried to keep my promise. I don't want you to bad-mouth me." Pagan turned and put his hand on Reinhart's back, pushing him gently. "Let's go to the meeting and get this over with."

Reinhart now sat at the end of the table, trying to develop a plan that would extricate him from the dilemma he faced: no longer a future with Pagan and at present a separation from Amed. He thought, *I must re-examine the reasons they went for POPIC, and for that matter, why a merger in the first place.* He started talking to himself. "You allowed a gap in logic when to do so meant an accompanied boast in power, but now you can see that these yawning pits of ignorance could be significant." Reinhart sat back in his chair. His hands were now dry and his head was unconsciously nodding like a man in early Parkinsonism.

Chapter 58

Dr. Sanchez stood up. "Mr. Winthrop made it quite clear that we are handing over the controls of Amed to Pagan and POPIC." He began scratching his left temple. "I must have missed a phase or two for I remember hearing about sharing authority and responsibility. Someone said the transaction would be transparent, the changes practically unnoticed by policyholders or staff."

As though nature sensed the change in mood, raindrops began to hit the windows of the boardroom.

Pagan rose. The rain had cooled the room. He slipped his jacket off the back of the chair and worked his arms into the sleeves. The action unintentionally gave him the appearance of someone about to declare a firm position.

"I believe we are well down the stream to be reconsidering a done deal, but if it is necessary, to bring peace, I and Mr. Winthrop would be glad to rehash the situation." His face hardened and then broke into a smile. "I am at your service."

Dr. Reed cleared his throat. "I thought today we were going to decide who was to run the show. I also thought a co-chairman arrangement was one of the considerations." He gazed around the room to see if there was any agreement among the group. The mood was changing from acceptance to one of indecision.

Pagan waved away the statement. "There has been a lot of talk on both sides describing our arrangement. At this late hour, when I have already gone through the first steps in reorganizing the company, I must restate my position." He paused. The explosive sound of thunder briefly filled the room. When it subsided, Pagan continued. "There can be no discussion of a co-chairman, or of Erik taking the chairmanship in any way." He braced himself before delivering the next line. "To do anything other than recognizing me as sole chairman must be considered a deal breaker." He sat down. As he watched the members of the board, he thought, *It is always a calculated risk to put someone on the spot, but I think my timing was perfect. Now all I need do is signal Reinhart to make a motion electing me chairman. I believe he still wants to be on the team and he knows this action is a requirement after our discussion.*

He waited for Reinhart to take his cue and make the motion.

Reinhart, at the end of the table, sat in thought, staring at the papers before him. He slowly lifted his head, turning to bring Pagan in view. "My recollections are similar to those of Dr. Sanchez."

Only the sound of the rain on the windows filled the room. Dr. Sanchez was surprised. He leaned forward to see Reinhart's face. Dr. Reed was nodding in agreement.

Doctors Garing and Frond faced each other with mutual expressions of disbelief. The Gainesville contingent, Doctors Gentile, Harmon and Moninger, were confused. Although Erik and Jerry had tried to make this trio feel assimilated, they never discarded the cloak of second-class citizens. They had gone along somewhat passively with the entire process of merger consideration, pretty much following Reinhart's lead. They were in favor of the cash merger for the short-term financial gain, but they were unhappy about losing the control as a board member of an independent company. Dr. Cannon muttered to himself, "All right!"

It wasn't the first time Pagan faced a change in the wind that tried to blow him off course. He thought, *How to get back on track? Should I begin a long repetition of the events since day one, laying a sense of guilt over the board members for being so indecisive and condemning them for considering a change of mind?*

Or should I wait and let those opposed to Erik speak out? They may not want to go with me, but from what I've heard they would rather not follow Erik. Pagan thought himself a man of action. He chose the direct attack.

He stood up and raised his hands in a gesture requesting silence, like a preacher about to begin his sermon.

"I am not surprised by your wavering emotions. Undertaking a major shift from all things that have made you comfortable can be frightening. When we are frightened, we tend toward the familiar, even if it is a poor choice.

"Let me make you comfortable by reviewing, and making clear, the reasons we must merge. We cannot compete as a one-state, one-line company. I will spare you the litany that goes with that statement.

"More and more, as doctors band together and get an office manager, they buy coverage based on price, price and price. The larger the surplus, the more competitive a company can be, squeezing out the independents." He could see he was getting their attention—good. "Once we establish that we must merge, we face the question of with whom? It should be a company that adds multiple lines, that is in another part of the country that has similar philosophies, that has about the same capital and surplus and is already incorporated, to avoid the necessity of converting from a trust to a real company.

"As to the first demand, we must merge. On the second question, whom, the only answer is POPIC." He repeated the name, spelling out the letters, "P-O-P-I-C," sounding like a cheerleader. He smiled at the group. "Are there any questions about other aspects of the merger before we proceed?" He thought of adding, "Before we vote for chairman," but he decided to move slowly.

"My question is why we are here?" Dr. Sanchez asked. "We have taken the idea of merger as a solution and proceeded from there to figure out how to bring it about.

"I can remember a situation at the hospital. The solution to the laboratory's problem of crowded conditions was to expand the floor space by taking footage away from the radiology department. The negotiations went on for months. Finally, an outside consultant was brought in to solve the dilemma. The first thing he did was to challenge the solution of the laboratory needing more floor space. In a short period of time, he found that by rearranging the location of several pieces of equipment and freeing up space, he answered the laboratory's needs. No expansion was necessary."

He waited for a moment, and then, "If giving up total control is the price we must pay to reach a merger, perhaps we should step back and see if a merger itself is the only answer to the earlier question, how do we survive?"

Pagan immediately regretted not pushing for a vote when he'd had the chance. "Dr. Sanchez, I don't see the relevance of your story."

"I do." Reinhart spoke up. "Dr. Nostrom, I suggest that a caucus of the board members only might be in order at this time. I would include Mr. Simms and Paul."

Seeing affirmative nodding among the directors, Erik said, "If there is no objection, I will adjourn the meeting." He looked toward Reinhart. "How much time will we need?"

"Can you stay until tomorrow?" Reinhart asked Pagan.

"Resolving this matter has the highest priority in my mind. Of course I'll stay."

"Then let's meet again at two tomorrow. That will give the caucus the rest of today and tomorrow morning to straighten things out," Erik pronounced.

Paul called the company's driver and arranged for Pagan and Winthrop to be taken to their hotel. "He will meet you in the lobby at one-thirty tomorrow afternoon. Have a good night." He waved as they followed the driver out the door. Turning to Erik, he asked, "How about a ten-minute pit stop?"

"That's a plan."

Chapter 59

Erik walked down the hall and entered Edward's empty office. Going around the desk, he spun the chair, making it face the window. He sat back, his hands folded behind his head, watching the rain splash on the puddles in the parking lot. From nowhere the lyric of a song from "Stop the World I Want to Get Off" ran through his mind. "What kind of fool am I, what do I know of life?"

He thought, *That's right. I am sixty-two years old and still able to let my emotions do a roller coaster ride. Yesterday I was resigned to a downer. I knew I couldn't accept the second position under Pagan. Maybe with someone else, I could. After all, I'm really an amateur in this business. I don't have a deep basic grasp of it. I only know what I leaned through the tubular vision of my company. I'm like the surgeons of past days who learned by preceptorship. I knew I was going to turn down the offer. And then what? It wouldn't be so bad. I could gradually retire, enjoy life with Frances, journey with her as she rediscovered her world. I could take pleasure in my home. I never had the time before. I would be free. I could raise orchids.* And up came the picture of Shakespeare's *King Lear*: once all powerful, reduced to nothing as he puttered in his rose garden.

Would I tolerate the change? Me, who after two weeks on vacation wanted to climb the wall; would I survive a permanent vacation, or would the appeal of the hereafter carry the day?

Yesterday, I hardened myself against the rejection by those who struggled with me for all these years. Was I as bland as to not generate loyalty and recognition? Accept it; add one more layer to the protective veneer against the world so I can't hear the condemning words. Or better, leave, go somewhere else as they cast their vote, as they cast me out. I always thought if they knocked me down, I would lie and bleed awhile, only to rise to fight another day. That was when I was young. Now as I age, once again I hear Shakespeare sans teeth, sans sight, sans hair, sans love, sans everything. He must have stood where I am standing.

As the rain washed away the cobwebs from the corners of the window, today's thoughts banished yesterday's gloom.

Today I heard the voice of support. They may even band together under my leadership and cut the ties that bind them to the need for outside aid. It is more than that. Sanchez is right; we should look at alternatives to merger as the answer. I'm glad he spoke. I always liked him, but I didn't think he had the passion he demonstrated today. I'm alive again.

And Reinhart, where in the hell is he coming from? Reinhart as my cheerleader after all these years of playing the antagonist? I know! His efforts helping Pagan were rebuffed, or perhaps the power compensation wasn't what he wanted. This nasty motivation to explain Reinhart's noble gesture makes me feel better. It is more in character with a scheming Reinhart. Never mind! I don't care why; with his support, the others will follow. Goddamn it, even in winning, I don't grasp victory from the jaws, but depend on a stronger figure to give it to me. Stop that! Is the guilt of all my past sins so strong that I refuse to see I deserve this triumph? No! Of course not! Fuck them all and full speed ahead! I'm not sure of the final results, but I feel the path has gone from all negative yesterday to a more positive today and I will see about tomorrow.

There will be a lot to do and it will take some time. There goes my orchid garden. So be it.

The rain had stopped. The room became cooler as he became calmer. He rose and walked back to the boardroom.

Chapter 60

The ten-minute pit stop stretched to thirty as the directors fell into separate conversational coffee *Klatches:* Erik, Jerry and Paul; Stanley and the three from Gainesville; and the group that remained in the board room. The discussions were similar in each gathering: What to do?

Erik asked them to return to their seats.

The odor of fear and anxiety hung over the table. Because of Erik's self interest, Jerry decided he was best suited to guide the conversation. He thought, *I'm not sure of the direction. Before this meeting it was clear that the die was cast; they were going to merge and jettison Erik. Yesterday's performance threw doubt on the whole matter*. He pointer to Dr.Sanchez; with a mock frown he said, "You started the revolution. What do you have to say for yourself?" His face eased to an understanding smile.

Sanchez leaned forward swallowed a mouthful of coffee and then said, "At first, it was only the way Pagan was pushing so hard. He started out being so congenial, all soft edges. And then, as soon as it was evident that he was chosen, the iron fist came out."

"Come on," Dr. Garing called out. "You should have expected that. We are not talking about a social club. This is a tough business, and Pagan decided to lay down the rules day one. It may have been poor timing on his part."

Reed was puzzled. "I thought you were unhappy about more than that. You sounded like you were challenging the whole idea of merging. That struck a note for me. Last night I finished reading the account from PIT, that's Physician's Insurance Trust of Connecticut. They went through all the steps we did, and in the end, decided not to enlarge or merge. That was a year ago. This follow-up report says they are doing well and see a rosy future."

Reinhart pointed an approving finger at Sanchez. "You touched on two very important aspects. We now see what life would be like under foreign rule." He paused to enjoy the metaphor. "And more to the point, should we reconsider the virtues of expanding?"

Erik remained silent. He wasn't sure whether he was watching a Shakespearean tragedy or a French farce. Opinions of doubts and assurances bumped into each other over the table. A slowly building wave developed, at first a ripple but with each assenting voice, it grew to have the characteristics of a true Hawaiian curl that would delight any surfer. It hit the beach, demanding a reconsideration of their action to merge. With the unanimously passed motion to reconsider, Erik could feel the bonds of despair loosen. His chest was free to draw a satisfyingly deep breath, the first one since the start of the talks to merge. The energy of the powerful dynamic equilibrium that immobilized him was cut free. Boundless joy filled him. He stood up and walked around his chair. To the other directors there was no evidence of the Fourth of July fireworks going off inside Erik's head. He appeared even more controlled than usual. He raised his hand to bring the meeting back to order. Only Jerry, who understood the turmoil Erik had been going through, could appreciate the liberation Erik was experiencing.

Summing up, Erik said, "With the passage of the motion to reconsider, we are then to vote on the original motion, that is, hold off on the plans to proceed with a merger. If I can have that motion we may go on to discussion."

"I make that motion."

"Second."

"So noted," Erik said to Dr. Reed, who was acting as secretary for the caucus.

Jerry pointed out, "In order for the reconsideration to be valid, no significant financial action should have taken place in the time between the original motion and the reconsideration. Fortunately, both sides had agreed to put off committing to a withdrawal penalty until after the agreement was signed; otherwise it would have cost us three million dollars to change our minds."

Discussion continued through the afternoon and the following morning. The step to cancel the merger relieved the tension temporarily, but immediately came the question, "*quo vada?*"

Reinhart stood up. The group steeled themselves against the expected challenge of leadership.

He began, "When we started this venture, I was convinced that it could succeed only if I were at the helm. You all are aware of my attempts to achieve that position. I was rejected."

Erik braced himself. Must he go through another attack at this late date? He was puzzled by Reinhart's appearance; instead of the pose and the face of the warrior, he presented a calm priestly façade. Reinhart continued, "Over the years I begrudgingly came to admire Erik and to appreciate his quality of leadership."

The sitting group turned their heads, first to Reinhart, in disbelief, and then to Erik, for some seeing Erik through Reinhart's words.

He was nodding his head. "When you rejected my attempt to unseat him, he could have sought revenge. He did not. I came to see that he was motivated by the desire for this company to succeed. For our future, I feel privileged to follow Erik, recognizing him as our leader." He waited for the effect of his words to hit home. "With that said, I would like to call the question."

Erik thought, *Is this a new Reinhart, or is he in survivor mode, ready to revert to wriggling Reinhart at any time? What the hell, for today I'll take it straight.*

The vote against merger was unanimous. They were smiling, nodding their heads "yes," thanking and shaking the hands of both Erik and Reinhart.

The board met with Pagan and Winthrop. The stages of response to the news outlining the new position were surprise, then arguments and finally resignation.

Pagan sat, shaking his head. "I thought your group did your homework and understood the situation. Apparently, you did not. As a consequence, you are where you started: still in danger of being squeezed out."

Sanchez looked into Pagan's eyes. "I believe I speak for all of us when I say we have one thing to thank you for, and that is, we now recognize the caliber of the leader we have."

He turned from Pagan to Erik. "Thank you, Erik."

The group stood. Even Winthrop joined in the applause.

At last, in the Roman arena the cheering crowds released a thunderous roar. With spear in hand, he stood, triumphant.

The lion of doubt, whose teeth and claws had so mauled him, lay dead at his feet.

The End

Printed in the United States
49852LVS00003B/166